SON OF A HOARDER

A NOVEL

CHEYENNE SMIDT

SON OF A HOARDER
Copyright © 2020 by Cheyenne Smidt

Paperback ISBN: 978-1-7364386-1-9
eBook ISBN: 978-1-7364386-0-2

Edited by: By the Hand Editing Services
Cover Design by: J. Ellis Publishing

For James, Lillie, Mollie, and Iris. I love you.
And to anyone who's ever felt like they were
alone and no one could possibly
understand…this one's for you, too.

Acknowledgements

First and foremost, I want to thank my husband, James, and my three beautiful babies, Lillie, Mollie, and Iris. James, you are my rock. You've kept me going on the days I didn't believe in myself and wanted to give up. When I didn't think I could do this, you made sure to tell me how wrong I was. Thank you for letting me bounce ideas off of you and for letting me talk incessantly about this passion of mine. But, most importantly, thank you for giving me the courage to do things I never thought possible, for showing me that I'm not nothing. You are truly one of a kind. I love you more than you'll ever know. Forever. Promise.

To my baby girls: Man, I just love you three so very much. I don't have the words to explain what you mean to me. You're the loves of my life. Thank you, Lillie and Mollie, for all your help when I had an idea and needed to write, so you had to watch baby Iris. Thank you all for being the best girls I could ever ask for. You're all amazing. I love you so much, babies.

To my aunt Julie: Thank you so much for always letting me come to you when I had questions about writing or really, just about anything. And I will never be able to thank you enough for helping with editing when you could and for always believing in me. It means so much to me that I could come to you whenever I needed to and share anything with you. Thank you. Love to you always.

To my very first readers Ms. Palmer, Lexi, and Crystal: Thank you three so much for taking time out of your busy lives to do this huge favor for me. All of your feedback has meant the world to me, and I don't think my book would be what it is without your help.

To my editor, Angie Martin: I so much appreciate your insight and for going above and beyond to help when needed. Just like my readers, I know my book would not be what it is without your help. Thank you.

Last but certainly not least: I want to thank *you*, the

person reading this book. Thank you for your time and energy, and for sharing them with me and my story. It means more to me than you'll ever know.

1

We only ever had two rules in my family. For some families, these rules might have been: Look both ways before you cross the street and never go to bed angry. Or maybe: Don't talk to strangers, and don't leave without saying "I love you." But in my family, the only true rules we had were: Don't let anyone in the house and don't let anyone know about the house—ever. My house was my biggest and most shameful secret. It was my responsibility to help keep that secret, no matter what. It didn't matter who I had to lie to or who I had to hide from. Our secrets had to be kept. Always.

My mother, Annie, would tell me, "Dominic, you know to never answer the door for anyone, right? Not for the pizza guy, not even for Grandma or Grandpa." Of course, I knew. That was part of my job, and I took my job seriously. It was instilled in me from a very young age what would happen if anyone found out our secret. I would be taken from my mom, and she would lose her job as the local elementary school's counselor. Mom loved her job, and everyone at the school loved her, too. The kids called her "Lenny" instead of Ms. Leonard. Her face would light up every time she heard someone calling out her nickname as she passed by.

Our house was never much fun, or much of a home at all, if I'm being honest. It had all the makings of a house. Structurally, it looked like every other dwelling on our street. It had a door, four boxy sides, and a garage in a low-rent cookie-cutter neighborhood. It was white with a red door and dark red trim, and unless you got up close, it almost looked normal. From afar, you couldn't see that the trim paint was chipping off in large flakes. You wouldn't know that you could smell the decay, even from outside. You couldn't see the masses of bagworms that had infested the eaves under the roof like barnacles on a boat. No one knew that if I wanted room to play, I needed to go in the yard or leave the house altogether. There would be no way for passersby or those not special enough to share our secret to know what horrors lay on the other side.

When I walked in the house, I didn't really walk in. Mom and I couldn't open the door to a warm and inviting space most others would find comfort in. Our woes of the day weren't dropped off on the doorstep; they were just beginning. I had to push the door open with all the strength I could muster. My obstacle was what was on the other side. It felt like someone was trying with all their might to not let me in. I pushed, and they pushed back. Sometimes, I liked to pretend there was a burglar in the house holding Mom hostage. He was trying to keep me out, but I was the man of the house, and it was my job to protect her. So I pushed and pushed until that man lost his footing and the door opened just enough that I could get in and save the day.

That big strong man on the other side was actually just big black garbage bags full of anything and everything you could think of: clothes, trash, papers, junk mail, old food, water-damaged books with their covers bent or torn off—things that definitely didn't belong in the living room, let alone blocking the front door. Once inside, the only person who could squeeze through was me. I had to do my best to toss the heavy bags as far away from the door as I could so Mom could get in, too. We had to do the tossing of the bags every morning before we left and every night when we got back to the house because, without fail, the piles fell back in front of the door, blocking it over and over again. Mom said it was important for me to remember I was just as much to blame as she was. She reminded me constantly that I could clean the house if it were such an issue for me, but I didn't bother to. Neither of us did.

* * *

When I was about five years old and it was time for bed, Mom and I would both make our way to her bedroom, which we were sharing. Mom often said, "One day, you'll get your own room back, I promise. But you have to help me, Dominic. It's a big task cleaning out a room full of stuff." She waved her hands around the room at all the junk as she said this, emphasizing what an undertaking it would be to clean the house. "I didn't make the mess all by myself, you know. You could have helped me clean, too. Now it's too much of a mess and we have to share my room. But we'll get it clean for you someday, won't we, sweetheart?"

"Yes, Mommy," I'd say. "I'm sorry I didn't help, but I promise I will next time. I pinky promise. You can't break a pinky promise; it's against the law. Did you know that? Tommy told me."

Tommy Hoffman was my best friend. He lived in the house right across the street from us. He was a few months older than I was. He had light-brown hair and jade-colored eyes. We were two of the skinniest and shortest boys in our class. People often thought we were brothers.

Until the day came when we'd be able to clean my room, there was just no way I could sleep in it. I honestly can't remember if I even had a bed in there. My room was filled more than halfway to the ceiling with clothes and bags full of garbage and junk—at least, things that I believed were junk, but Mom did not. There was nowhere for the stuff to go because the rest of the house was filled in pretty much the same fashion. We had no pathways. Not a single inch of that house was untouched by the hoard. Mom's room was the second worst in our one-thousand square foot, two-bedroom, one-bathroom house, my room taking first place in a landslide victory.

There was a literal hill in the room Mom and I shared that was made up of more bags, clothes thrown freely about the room, and lots of boxes. Most of the boxes were open, the contents spilling everywhere. I had to get in using the same technique I used to get into the house through the front door. I pushed my body weight as hard as I could into the door, which often hurt. Most of the time, the door wouldn't open from my strength alone, so Mom and I would make a game out of it.

"Okay, Dom, whoever runs the fastest and gets the door open gets to choose the side of the bed they sleep on. Ready? On your mark, get set…go."

We both preferred the side that was facing the window and up against the wall. If I rolled into the wall, I was fine and could easily roll back onto the bed. If I was on the other side and rolled off, I'd roll into what felt like oblivion when I was fast asleep. It was suffocating rolling into a six-foot-tall pile of clothes.

Mom and I would lunge forward the few steps from the hallway wall to Mom's bedroom door and shove our bodies into it. Finally, it would open about a foot wide, and I could squeeze through. Sometimes, she'd let me win.

"Hold on, Mom. I just have to throw a few more bags. Oh man, that big box of books fell again. That same one from last night, remember? But I'm almost done, and then you can come in," I would shout, panting.

I tried to move everything out of the way as fast as I could so Mom could get in and get to bed, too. I didn't want to keep her waiting too long, or she'd become churlish. The task of moving things away from the bedroom door was a lot harder than moving them away from the front door because, in the living room, I was able to toss things just about anywhere that was somewhat open enough to catch the bags. In the bedroom, I had to throw things up and over the hill. If they didn't make it over the hill, they fell right back down on top of me, bringing more with them, knocking me into the door, sometimes trapping me against it.

Once I was finally able to move everything out of the way for Mom and she squeezed into the room, we had the daunting task of climbing the hill. I would go first, and once I made it onto the bed, Mom would shut off the light and follow in my footsteps. Everything I'd tossed would slide back down the hill as we climbed, blocking the door once again.

When we reached the top, we had to be careful not to hit our heads. The peak of the hill was only about a foot or so from the ceiling and right under the light. The closeness and warmth of the light was terrifying to me. I'd made the unfortunate mistake one night of touching the bare bulb while climbing to the top. The cover for the bulb had been broken months before in a bag-tossing accident. The glass from the square-shaped cover scattered across the hill. It took weeks of crawling over the glass, the shards becoming embedded into my hands and knees, before it was completely immersed into the hoard. My hand instantly blistered after I touched the hot bulb, an intense pain that lasted for the rest of the night.

On the other side of the hill lay Mom's bare mattress. The touch of a bare mattress on my skin gave me the creeps. I didn't like the way it seemed to snag on any of my skin's imperfections or how the fabric scratched me. Even now, I hurry when I change my sheets so I don't have to touch or look at my bare mattress for too long.

I tried so hard to be careful not to disturb the boxes and cause an avalanche on my way down the hill. I hated having to clean up the bed if a box spilled. I was exhausted and didn't want to do any more cleaning and tossing. It was especially upsetting in the middle of the night if I had to use the restroom. Trying to move everything out of my way, half asleep with a full bladder, was enough to make me cry out of frustration.

There were times I was unable to hold it any longer and

I did pee my pants. This happened for a couple reasons. Either I wasn't fast enough moving the things in front of the door and I was unable to open it, or my legs fell through the piles and I couldn't get them back out in time. I never told Mom; she wouldn't know if I didn't say anything. I would just change my clothes and throw the soiled ones somewhere in the house, never to be found again. If my accident leaked onto anything other than my clothes, it was usually covered in a new mess by morning, not leaving a trace.

Getting out of bed in the middle of the night was scary. I would crawl out of the blankets and to the edge of the bed as cautiously as I could, so as not to disturb Mom. I reached my hands out in front of me and waded through my surroundings while making my way back up the hill. I'd once made the mistake of not being careful, and after reaching the peak, I fell all the way down the hill, toward the wall. I hit my head on Mom's old dresser. After that incident, I turned it into a game. I'd pretend I was a blind man and it was important for my safety that I be fully aware of my surroundings. I would pretend that my life depended on my being able to get out of that room, so I needed to use all my other "heightened" senses, especially touch, to get out.

The scariest times, though, even scarier than getting hurt, were if I accidentally caused anything to fall on Mom. She would scream at me in a way that I'll never forget. I can still hear it. I remember the way her face looked as she screamed, mouth wide open, eyes full of contempt. Her voice instantly strained and became hoarse as a noise so foreign to her escaped her throat. It made my stomach hurt. If you knew one thing about my mom, it was do not disturb her sleep. Mom loved her sleep, probably more than she loved me. Sleeping was something she did a lot.

"Remember, Dominic, you can never, ever tell anyone we share a room or a bed, okay?" Mom would say as we crawled into her queen-size bed together. "Technically, you're too old to still be sleeping with Mommy. But that's our little secret, isn't it?"

She reminded me of this every night.

"I won't tell. I pinky promise," I'd say. "And remember what I told you about those."

I never did tell, not until much later. I knew how important it was to make sure no one found out about any of our secrets.

"We'll protect each other forever, right, Dominic?"

"Right, Mommy."

Then, I'd ask her to sing to me. She'd say she couldn't carry a tune, but to me, she sounded like an angel. My favorite bedtime song was "Sweet Child O' Mine" by Guns N' Roses.

"Fine, just one song," she'd say reluctantly. Her voice was the comfort I needed to fall asleep.

In the mornings, we'd crawl back up the hill and down the other side. It was often much harder to get out of the room than it was to get into it when both of us were trying to get out at the same time. When we were able to get out and into the hallway, we would trudge a few feet over to the laundry area where we kept all our clothes. Trying to get through the hall and through the three-foot piles of clothes wasn't easy. I liked to pretend I was a dinosaur, taking giant steps, stalking my way through to my prey. "Rawr!" I'd shriek, much too loudly for that hour of the day as Mom liked to say, as I struggled to get through, falling into the piles.

Now, over twenty years later, that room still haunts me. Sometimes I dream that I wake up and Mom is lying dead next to me on her bed. I can't get her out. She's heavier than I can carry, and the never-ending avalanche blocks the door until I can no longer see it. Mom's body rots much too quickly, the decay eating away at the mattress. The bed slowly swallows Mom's gray body, submerging her into a bubbling tar pit below. Maggots emerge from the sockets her eyes used to occupy. She says one last thing to me before she disappears forever: "This is your fault." Then, the mattress and the room absorb her. The avalanche of clothing and boxes fall into the sink-holed mattress before it closes up, entombing Mom.

The most constant nightmares, however, are the ones where I'm alone. I'm always my five-year-old self. There's a fire, or someone's breaking into the house trying to kill me, and I can't get out. It's daylight, and Tommy's outside playing with his dog. I pound on the window, but he can't hear me. It won't open, and the glass won't break. I can't get off the bed and up the hill. The piles keep falling, papers spilling and cascading toward me. I slip back down, unable to get away. If I am able to get to the top of the hill, I unfailingly fall down the other side, bringing the clothes and bags with me, blocking the door. It all falls faster than I can toss it back out of my way. I yell for help as more clothes fall on top of me, trying to bury me. My cries become muffled, the clothes are heavy. I cannot move. I am forever barricaded inside.

2

For as long as I can remember, it was always just Mom and me. I didn't have a dad, or any siblings, so I felt a personal responsibility to take care of my mom. We had to protect each other, because in the end, that's all we had. Of course, I had grandparents and an aunt and uncle. But they didn't know our true selves. They didn't know what we were really like, the life we actually lived. That was just our little secret.

Mom and I were close. I thought she was beautiful. She was petite in every sense, with long, wavy hair that she always wore in a messy bun. It was rare to see her with her hair down. People were constantly commenting about how much we looked alike. We had the same dark-chestnut hair and hazel eyes, but mine were a little greener than hers. My eyes changed colors in stressful situations; Mom's never strayed from their same hue. Mom said I got my nose from my father, something I'd have to take her word for. It didn't even occur to me until I was twelve that I didn't have a father. I didn't ask about him often. When I did, Mom would brush me off and change the subject or say that she didn't feel well, so we couldn't talk about it at that moment. Eventually, I stopped asking, which is what she really wanted. That was about the time everything started changing. Up until then, I went along with whatever Mom wanted or needed. Before the change, I knew our life was different, but it was ours. To me, that was all that mattered.

My mom and grandparents were close. I was never as

close with my grandparents as other kids I had known. They were overly critical and weren't at all welcoming. They were nothing like the ones I saw on TV, always wanting their grandkids at their house, spoiling them with baked goods. I was jealous of those kids and of the ones whose grandparents came to the Grandparent's Day luncheons the school held. Mine were always too busy to go.

My grandma was a short, portly woman with silver hair and a stuck-in-the-sixties beehive. She put on her makeup, "her face" as she called it, first thing every morning before Grandpa got up, not wanting him or anyone else to know what she actually looked like, and she waited until he fell asleep at night before washing it off.

She often told me how courageous Mom was for raising me on her own with no help from my father, not even a cent of child support. She said that most people wouldn't have had the strength and resilience. I was told that Mom did her best raising me, not an easy task as I'd come to know, and that I never showed appreciation. Grandma would ask, "Why must you continually bite the hand that feeds you?" My grandfather, a man of average height and build, with salt and pepper hair and a scowl that never left his unapproachable face, mostly tried to stay out of it, until I became a teenager, saying that the issues Mom and I had were none of his business.

* * *

Mom trained me to lie from the moment I spoke my first word. When I was younger, we attended the Catholic church for mass every Sunday. One of the first things the church teaches the little ones is the importance of the Ten Commandments. Number nine on that list: Thou Shalt Not Lie. But number five: Honor Thy Mother and Father. I tried, every day, to the best of my ability, to protect my mother. Maybe I wasn't supposed to lie and would be punished for it someday, but Mom meant more to me than any rules the church might have laid out. I was terrified for what my judgment day entailed. I lied so often, there were times I was scared I had a demon inside me that needed exorcised. I knew I was going to hell. But at least while I was on Earth, I did my job and took care of my mom.

I no longer practice any sort of religion. Sometimes, I think, *Why was I allowed to grow up this way?* I once thought of myself as a strict Catholic, believing the Bible cover to cover, word for word. Now, I'm not so sure I believe in anything.

* * *

When we had food delivered, which was often, it was my job to watch for the delivery person through the window. I had a lot of jobs, some more nerve-racking than others. When I saw the driver pull up, I had to hurry as fast as I could over the piles in the living room. My legs would sink up to my knees in them, and they'd pull me down like quicksand, threatening to keep me there. I had to turn off all the lights, so that when I carefully opened the door, there wasn't even a chance they could glimpse inside. I was always terrified that I wouldn't be fast enough, and they'd get to the door before I did. My heart would race; I'd be short of breath and sweaty, but I'd made it all but one time, thankfully. The one and only time I didn't make it, I had to wait for the delivery person to turn back around to their car at the bottom of the driveway. Then, just as they'd opened their door to leave, I had popped out of the house and shouted, "Sorry, I was in the bathroom," the go-to excuse Mom had said worked for everything.

"Now the pizza's going to be cold, Dominic. I hope you're happy," Mom had said when I came back inside with our food. The delivery person must have stood at the door for at least five minutes before giving up. I'd hated myself for disappointing Mom.

The next step, after shutting off the lights, was to make sure to only open the door just enough to squeeze my little body through. As I got older, this practice made me a bit paranoid. Were we the only people they delivered to who met them at their car? Was it weird that a kid was the one who came out to pay for the food? Did they find it odd that I never went inside until after they had driven away, walking as slowly as possible back to the door? Did they know something was off? I sat by the phone after deliveries, waiting for a phone call from Child Protective Services, sure that someone had called on us for acting strange.

The one thing scarier than strangers was family showing up. For one, we expected food delivery; we had called it in. Family showed up unannounced. When I'd hear that unexpected knock on the door, my heart would sink. Each knock felt like they were knocking right into my chest. My heart pounded so hard I'd feel faint. It felt loud, almost as if I could hear it vibrating through my veins, reverberating into my ears. I would tiptoe to the window as quietly as I could, trying to sneak a peek at who was outside, but my feet inevitably found the fast-food wrappers and unopened junk mail. The sound was amplified, like a piece of notebook paper being ripped out in a quiet classroom, rather than the tiny crunch it actually was.

We usually tried to wait them out. It felt like hours that they'd stand out there knocking. Most of the time, Mom and I would hide in the hallway, so they'd think we weren't there. Other times, I'd watch from the window, peeking out from the tiny hole that the strings in the blinds were weaved through, and wait until they went back to their car. Then, I'd follow the same routine as I did with the food delivery. I'd wave them down and run to the bottom of the driveway, giving them our "Sorry, I was in the bathroom" excuse. Once in a while, Mom liked to make sure they truly believed our excuses. She wanted it to sound real, so she would have me tell them that one or both of us had diarrhea, or that she was on her period and too crampy to get off the toilet.

3

M om took extra care to be sure I looked good at all times. It was much better, in her eyes, to appear that all was well than to take the steps to ensure it really was. It was more important that people think she was a great mother than to try and actually be one. So she bought me all the in-style clothes and shoes, even if they were expensive. I had name-brand everything, all the latest trends, pretty much anything I wanted. For that, I truly am grateful. But as I've learned over time, gifts and shiny things don't make up for a lack of love and security.

Mom emphasized the importance of cleanliness and hygiene when out in public and especially at school.

"You don't want to be the smelly kid, do you?" she'd ask.

Every day, Mom made sure that I had clean clothes so we didn't look dirty. You'd never suspect the life we really lived. To keep the everyday clothes clean and away from the rest of the junk so it wouldn't get lost, we stored them on top of the dryer. Oftentimes, the clothes fell behind the dryer, and I had to crawl on top of it to get them out. Mom said she was too big, so I'd have to do it. I was afraid I'd fall behind the dryer, too, and be lost like the clothes.

"Mom, hold my legs while I rescue this poor fallen puppy back here. He fell off a cliff, I think. He might be hurt. Oh no, we have to help him!" I'd shout, imagining the clothes were a defenseless puppy that I would get to rescue. A true hero I would be when the job was done. "I'm going to name him

Roy."

As a kid, I believed she did these things out of love for me. Now, I believe she did them out of fear. In my family, keeping up appearances was of the utmost importance. If I looked good, Mom looked good. If I looked bad, she looked bad.

She tried to control what she could, especially me. She couldn't control the chaos in her own life, so she did her best to control the things she perceived to be wrong in mine. She simply projected her own fears from her life onto mine. This is something I have to constantly remind myself of as an adult: none of this was ever really about me, no matter how personal it all feels. As a result of the constant criticism, I struggle with my self-esteem. It's non-existent. I've never felt like I'm good enough for anyone or anything.

After we were dressed, we would make our way to the bathroom to brush our teeth, so long as we could find the toothpaste. The toothpaste went missing more often than anything. We didn't bother trying to floss anymore; it usually disappeared before we could even open the package.

There were times our toothbrushes themselves vanished. Mom taught me how to brush with my finger when that happened. I would put a pea-sized blob of toothpaste on the tip of my index finger and rub it around my teeth the same way I would if I still had my toothbrush. Sometimes, a week of finger-brushing would go by, and I'd have to beg Mom to get me another toothbrush. My mouth would start to taste like rotten eggs. I could smell my own disgusting breath. The smell reminded me of the dirty, molding dishes in the kitchen sink, the ones covered in wet food that never dried. Mom sent me to school with packs of gum so no one would know how bad my breath had gotten. I'm not sure even the overwhelming, nostril-burning wintergreen flavor was enough to cover up that mess.

The bathroom was my least favorite room in the house. It smelled the worst of any of them.

"Mom, it stinks in here," I would say every morning, which annoyed Mom to no end.

"Dominic, I know it does. But how many times have I asked you to help me clean it? How many times have I asked you to take out the garbage or plunge the toilet, huh? Look how backed up the toilet is. It's disgusting. Why should it all be up to me to do it?" Mom asked.

She was right; the toilet was disgusting. I loathed having to sit to use the bathroom because it was so full of our waste, the contents of the bowl would touch my bottom. It was cold, uncomfortable, and slimy. I tried not to think of everything floating up and touching me, so I hurried to get done. Mom told me to urinate in the bathtub or the sink if I only needed to go number one, that way I didn't fill up the toilet bowl more than was necessary. Mom did the same.

"It's not all up to you, Mama," I said, hanging my head in shame from what a bad son I was. "I know that I need to help, but I hate cleaning. I'm really sorry."

"I know you are, Dom," said Mom.

Next up in our morning routine was the searching for our shoes. We often ran late from not being able to find them, and at least a few times a week, we ran late because we lost the car keys and would have to spend a considerable amount of time looking for them. As the counselor at the same elementary school I attended, Mom and I got to ride together every morning, so I never had to take the bus. I really liked carpooling. It felt special and very grown up. Part of Mom's job was to talk to, help, and find any needed resources for children at the school who were troubled or living in unsafe or unhealthy situations. It didn't occur to me until I was in high school how unbelievably ironic that was.

Mom was excellent at her job. She focused on keeping up appearances by looking and doing her best. Part of how she did that was by becoming a skilled liar. I would hear Mom's coworkers telling her about how they were redecorating their houses or doing something new for their children's rooms, and they liked to ask her opinion because she was so upbeat and friendly. They would show her paint swatches, and she'd say things like, "Oh, that color is absolutely gorgeous. I might be a little biased, though. That is almost the exact same color I have in my own living room." Or "I just love rustic and country-themed decor. That's how I have my house decorated."

But the truth was, our house didn't have any specially-themed decor. There was no paint on the walls, except for the standard white you see in most houses before they are made into something more personal. Our walls were dingy and had never been washed or even wiped down. There were a few family photos here and there, hanging crookedly, as no one had ever bothered to right them. Most of the photos that once hung were long gone. They had fallen, the glass breaking and enmeshing with the clothes on the floor, and some just disappeared altogether. I realize now this was Mom's fantasy. She enjoyed offering advice and playing pretend in much the same way I did. She wanted her surroundings to be different than they were, so she made up her own games.

4

When I was six years old, I asked my mom, like many kids do, "Where do babies come from?"

"They come from their mommies' bellies," Mom answered.

"I know that," I said, giggling. "But how do they get in there?"

"Well," she said, thinking about what to say next. "Do you want to know the truth?" She looked at me warily, unsure if she should tell me or not.

"Mm-hmm."

"Okay, Dominic, I'll tell you. But you can't tell anyone else, all right?"

"Pinky promise."

"You know how you have a penis, and it's different from what I have, right?"

"Right."

"Well, mine is called a vagina."

"Okay," I said, a little confused.

"Okay. Vaginas have holes in them, and things can go inside of the hole. Do you understand?"

"Kind of."

"All right, well a boy will put his penis inside a girl's vagina like this," she said, making a hole with her thumb and the index finger of her right hand, and putting the index finger of her left hand through the hole. "And then, they have what's called 'sex.' Then after the sex, stuff comes out of the boy's penis."

"Ew, what kind of stuff?"

"It's called sperm, but don't worry about that part. Anyway, so after the sex is over and the sperm comes out, the girl gets pregnant, and they have a baby."

"That's pretty gross," I said, disgusted.

"You think so?" asked Mom.

I nodded, looking away from her, feeling embarrassed.

"Eh, you'll like it one day. It feels good. Well, it's supposed to anyway."

The next day, Mom came back from work with a set of hard-plastic anatomically correct dolls she had in her office that were used when talking to sexual assault victims. The kind police had when doing interviews and tell the kiddies, "Show me where the bad man touched you."

"You see how this doll has a penis like you?" Mom asked, pointing to the doll's genitals.

"Yeah," I said.

"And see how this one looks different?" She pointed to the second doll's vagina.

"Mm-hmm."

"Well, like I told you yesterday, that's called a vagina. That's what Mommy has."

"Okay," I said, no longer wanting to talk about penises and vaginas with my mom.

"Well, I'll show you how it works. The boy's penis goes into the girl's vagina like this," Mom said. She took the two dolls and pressed their genitals together.

"Gross," I said.

Mom laughed. "You won't think so one day when you're older. You'll think it's fun."

I didn't believe her.

* * *

"Hey, Tommy," I said to my friend the day after Mom's demonstration. His mom had picked us both up from school so we could play at his house because Mom had a staff meeting after work.

Tommy looked up from his cars at me.

"Did you know girls have baginas?"

"What's a bagina?" he asked.

"It's where they pee from because they don't have a penis."

"A penis?"

"Yeah," I said. "You know, where your pee comes from?"

"Oh!" he exclaimed. "My wee-wee."

"Yeah," I said. "And you know what else?"

"What?"

"Boys put their wee-wees inside of girls' baginas, and they have sex to make them have a baby," I said.

"Ew, that's sick," he said, sticking his finger in his mouth and making a fake gagging sound.

"I know. My mom told me about sex last night."

"Are all wee-wees the same?" Tommy asked.

"I don't know, actually," I said, considering this. "Want to find out?"

"Yeah."

Tommy and I faced away from each other and took off all our clothes, even our underwear, leaving only our socks.

"On the count of three we'll turn around and look, okay, Tommy?"

"Okay."

"Okay, ready? One...two...three," I said. We both flipped around at the same time, staring at each other's naked bodies.

"Whoa," he said, "We are the same." For the next few minutes, we kept looking at each other, sometimes doing little turns and bending over to look at other parts of each other's bodies, until we were startled back to reality when we heard

Tommy's mom coming up the stairs toward his bedroom.

"Hurry, get dressed," I said.

Tommy and I fumbled, trying to put our clothes back on. One of my pant legs was inside out from when I had removed them. I put my foot in forcefully and almost fell over. I quickly got my T-shirt back on and sat down next to a fully-dressed Tommy on his race car rug, pretending we had been playing cars the whole time.

"Hi, boys," Tommy's mom said when she came in. She was a tall, heavier-set woman with bright-blonde hair and the most welcoming personality of anyone I'd ever met. "Are you two having fun?"

"Yes," we said in unison.

"Good, good. I have some celery with peanut butter and some cheese and crackers made up for you boys in the kitchen if you're hungry."

"And chocolate milk?" Tommy asked.

"Of course, baby," she said, smiling her constant, cheerful smile, the kind that you could see in her eyes.

We stood up to go down to the kitchen with her, relieved that she didn't know we had been doing something we both knew we shouldn't have been doing.

"Uh-oh, Dominic, sweetie, your pants button is undone," she said, pointing down at my jeans. Tommy and I snapped our heads toward each other, a worried look on each of our faces, but she didn't say anything more as I buttoned my jeans and we made our way down the steps.

It wasn't until I was an adult that I realized how heavily the much-too-early and, frankly, inappropriate talk I had with Mom about sex really affected me. From that day forward, I thought about sex a lot. What did it feel like when your penis entered a vagina? Mom said I would like it one day. Was she telling the truth? What made sex so special that people wanted to do it? What did girls look like naked? I mean, I'd seen Mom naked before, and she didn't try to hide her body when she changed her clothes or stripped for the shower. Hell, she didn't even shut the door when she went to the bathroom; though, that could have been because it was too blocked by the hoard. Sex, for me, was something I knew I wanted to know more about, and it was something I would end up finding out way too much about way too young.

5

At the house one night when I was around seven years old, I heard a knock on the door. My heart skipped a beat, pounding so hard it hurt. I crept over to the window to peer through the blinds as carefully and as quietly as I could. The beautiful setting sun was illuminating the neighbors' houses along our street, and the sky was beginning to change color. I liked when the sky would turn that perfect mix of almost-summer orange and pink, Mom's favorite colors.

Outside the house, standing on our stoop was Mom's younger brother, my uncle Kai, and his wife, my aunt Gretchen. I watched them make their way back down the steps to sit in the yard away from the door, and then I knew it was safe to go out and meet them. I opened the door just a crack, only enough for me, and squeezed through without opening it more than the width of my small body, making completely sure they couldn't see inside. I kept the door close to me and pressed it to my back so it stayed shut against my body as I made my way through. I was a pro at that by then.

"Hey, Dominic. How are ya, bud?" Uncle Kai asked. He smiled at me, pushing his tousled jet-black hair off his forehead and looking me up and down, concern filling his kind golden-brown eyes.

"I'm really good, Uncle Kai. Great, actually. What are you guys doing here?" I asked, trying to keep my cool and not show that I was scared. I loved seeing Uncle Kai and Aunt Gretchen, but having them over could be frightening. What if they saw in the house and saw the mess we'd made? Would they be mad at me and Mom?

"Just wanted to say hi and see how you were doing, buddy," Aunt Gretchen answered. She tucked her long, burgundy hair behind her ears. She did this a lot because it was relentlessly falling in her face. She smelled good. Like clean laundry and fresh-baked cookies.

"Where's your mom? Can we come in and see her?" she asked.

I had my long list of excuses ready as to why they couldn't, excuses Mom had given me so that no matter what, I would be prepared in these situations. I found out years later they knew all along what was going on inside that house, and they knew that I'd been trained to lie.

"Um, not today, Auntie, I'm sorry," I said. "Mom really doesn't feel good. She's been on the toilet all day. Coming out of both ends, as she likes to say." I faked a laugh.

Aunt Gretchen looked disappointed. I thought she was upset with me.

"Well, how's school going, bud?" Uncle Kai asked.

"Great."

"Happy to hear that, big guy." He smiled. "Your birthday's coming up. You got a wish list ready for us?"

"Um, I think I just want some books. I really love reading, and my teacher's got me up to reading the big kids' books now. I love reading the really big chapter books," I said, holding my hands out in front of me to show the size of books I'd been reading.

"Big chapter books, huh?" He smiled and patted me on the head. "That's my boy. You've always been so smart."

I beamed. Uncle Kai made me so happy when I got to see him. He didn't come over often, which was for the best.

Sometimes, Uncle Kai would take me to the park or to a movie. I liked riding in his car because he would turn the volume and bass up so loud I could feel every vibration of the music. When I spent the night with him and Aunt Gretchen, he let me stay up late to watch *Saturday Night Live* or *Mad TV* with him. I tried my hardest to make it until one o'clock in the morning like he did to finish out the shows, but I always fell asleep by midnight.

"Okay, bud, we need to get going. Just wanted to stop by real quick to say 'hey' and get your b-day shopping list," Uncle Kai said, giving me a big hug.

Aunt Gretchen kissed the top of my head and said, "We love you," as she waved goodbye.

I made sure to wait until they had left the driveway and were down the street before I shuffled back inside, as per Mom's instructions. I pretended I needed to check the mail and hoped I was convincing.

"Did they say anything to you, Dominic?" Mom asked when I came back inside the house.

"Like what, Mommy?"

"I don't know, Dom," Mom said, sounding frustrated. "Did they say anything? What did you guys talk about? Did they mention me?"

"They just asked how school was going and what I wanted for my birthday," I said.

I tried to make my way back over the mounds of trash bags and clothes that filled our entryway. I couldn't see the floor. I couldn't remember the color of the carpet. I had to be careful not to step on anything breakable for multiple reasons. One, it hurt if I stepped on glass and cut myself; and two, Mom would get angry if I broke one of her possessions. She'd remind me that she spent her money on that stuff and how would I like it if she stepped on my things and broke them? It was much easier to be careful if I took my shoes off, but if I took them off and did end up stepping on something, it hurt a lot because it wasn't just clothes under my feet. There were books, figurines, picture frames, lots of my long-lost toys, and so much more. If I'd had to choose, though, I would have picked getting hurt over hurting my mom any day.

"Well, did they ask to come in or anything?" Mom asked, wiping sweat from her brow. She had what I called "the look" on her face; eyes wide, jaw clenched tight. I called it "the look" because it's the face she made when she heard a knock on the door or someone asked to come over. It was the look of fear and dread.

"Yeah, they asked," I said. "But I told them you didn't feel good just like you told me to." I smiled at her and tried to give her a look of my own. One that would comfort her so she knew that I had protected her. I had done my job; she didn't need to be scared.

"Don't worry, Mom. They're gone now."

"Good boy," Mom said, smiling back at me, relieved.

She was sitting in her usual spot on the couch. She never sat anywhere else. Not because that was her favorite spot, but because there wasn't anywhere else to sit. Her spot was especially worn. The recliner was permanently stuck in the recline position, and even if we could push it down, there was too much stuff in the way pushing back at us. The metal bars underneath what used to be the fluffy parts of the cushions now stabbed us in the butt and legs when we tried to get comfortable. Her spot was tiny and cramped, but every once in a while, Mom let me squeeze in next to her. It was usually only for a few minutes because her back hurt and she would start to feel claustrophobic.

She explained that there was really only room for one. She said since I was a kid, it wouldn't hurt my back like it would hers to sit on the floor, so that's where I needed to go. It wasn't so bad. Sometimes, it was uncomfortable if I ended up laying on hard objects, but other times, there were clothes I got to use as cushions and make believe I was lying in a giant bean bag chair meant only for kids, and since I was the only kid, I didn't have to share. When Mom wasn't looking, I liked to make clothes angels. I'd spread my arms out high above my head and stretch out my legs, moving them back and forth like snow angels.

Things weren't all bad, though. Every so often, Mom liked to turn on music in the house. She loved anything we could dance to. Together, we would dance in what little space we could find that was flat enough to stand on comfortably and sing at the top of our lungs. But after about ten minutes or so, Mom almost always got a headache and would need me to calm down and be quiet. She'd shut off the music and flip the TV back on to one of her usual grown-up shows that I hated. We'd lost the TV remote, so another one of my jobs was to change the channels by hand with the buttons on the TV, flipping through each one so she could see what was on. The TV was always much too loud. Mom kept it that way as a reminder to not talk during her shows. I was only allowed to speak to her during commercials.

"Can we please watch a kid's show, Mom? Please, please?" I would beg when I'd see a cartoon skip by on one of our ten channels.

"No, Dom. Not right now. I'm really not in the mood." She was never in the mood, and it was her TV after all. We ended up watching some sort of crime show or the news most of the time. I hated the news.

Our house was right next to the train tracks that ran through our small town. When the train went by, it would cut off the signal to the TV. Mom appointed me antenna fixer. I didn't like that job because the antenna shocked me when I touched it, and it was hard to reach it atop the entertainment center. It hurt my arm as I strained to reach high enough to get the antenna righted again. But it did make me feel happy when I was able to twist and turn it into the position that would get the TV signal back clearly for Mom. Seeing her smile at a job well done made it worth it.

6

Mom's favorite thing to do was shop at secondhand stores and antique shops. We would go almost every weekend, and with each excursion, we made sure we found at least a few bags' worth of new treasures. We shopped there so frequently, the ladies that ran the stores knew Mom by name. "There's my favorite customer," they would say as we opened the heavy glass door that led inside. The familiar bell would chime, alerting them that Mom and I were right on time, same as always.

Some weekends, we'd skip our usual stores and do what we called "going on adventures." We'd drive for hours, sometimes three hours one way, to somewhere we'd never been. We had a blast finding wherever we felt was "the place" before stopping to look for some thrift stores.

Coming back to the house after a long day of shopping was so satisfying. We'd carry the bags in through the door, squeezing ourselves through the tiny slit, arms full of bags that felt as if they weighed as much as I did. I'd stumble along the hoard, trying not to let the weight of the bags take me down as I made my way across the uneven surface. Finding a comfortable place to rest, I'd dig into the bags and admire my new treasures, ones that would be lost and forgotten in a day and replaced the next weekend.

Mom really did give me the things I needed. I almost always got three meals a day. I had nice clothes to wear, toys to play with, a roof over my head, heat in the house. She paid for me to do the things I wanted and took me to the occasional movie.

Once in a while, if we could find the pieces, we would do a puzzle together or play a board game, setting the puzzle or game up on the recliner part of the couch. Other times, on very rare occasions, we would go for a walk around the neighborhood if Mom felt up to it and her back didn't hurt or she didn't have a headache. I loved when we would go on walks. Since they were so rare, it always felt like a fresh start. We would be doing something we didn't normally do. It gave me hope that maybe Mom and I could start doing more together.

I was told later on by different family members that I should have been more grateful for my mom and all she did for me because she took care of me and my essential needs. I'm still conflicted about this. I've been told my whole life to be nice to my mom because, for some reason, even before things got bad between us, they didn't think I was nice enough to her. This confused me as a child. I did everything I could to be nice to her. I protected her and kept her secrets. I made sure she was happy, but it wasn't enough. I didn't know then and I don't know now what more I could have done.

Even as an adult, I was frequently reminded by my grandparents how horribly I'd treated my mother as a teenager. Part of me knows there is a valid reason, whether they believe that or not, for my acting that way. A much larger part of me is so enraged with them for failing to see how desperately I needed them to know that. Then, there's the last part of me that feels like maybe I do deserve to be talked down to, that I deserve all the anger they feel toward me and the way that they look at me now.

I lived in a constant state of fear of disappointing my mom or my grandparents. I used to seek their approval in every aspect of my life. I don't remember Mom ever really telling me that she was proud of me or that I was important to her, and because of that, I would try to find ways to make sure I was. I tried to live my life in a way I knew would make her happy, walking on eggshells so as not to upset her.

I think now I have a little bit more insight into the illness that is hoarding. As a child, I felt so alone. I was positive there must be no other person in the world that lived the way I did; no other person was in my situation. Now, of course, I know that's not true. There are even television shows about hoarding now. If only they'd had those shows when I was younger. Though, I must admit, sometimes I watch them and think, *Oh, they don't have it too bad. At least they still have a path to walk through, at least they can use their kitchen, at least they have a bed, even if the room is messy, and at least they can see their carpet.*

I work daily to overcome most of the anger and resentment I feel toward my family. I understand that it wasn't that Mom didn't love me, it was that she couldn't control her problem. Understanding the issue and forgiving her for everything are two different things, however. Mom wouldn't seek help, and her illness overtook and overwhelmed her until she became numb to it all. She wanted me to become numb, too. I couldn't. I wouldn't. That's the root of our issues. I refused to normalize our situation. I screamed, "This is wrong!" when she wanted me to sit back in silent compliance. It's a struggle to remember that although this may no longer be my life, it once was. Therefore, it's my story to tell, too. I don't need anyone's permission to live an authentic life or to speak from the heart, to free myself of my burdens and the soul-crushing pressure I've felt weighing me down for decades. It's no longer my responsibility to protect her.

7

One day in second grade, with only a half hour left in the school day, the intercom in my classroom let out a loud crackle.

"Hello, Mrs. Wolfe?" the secretary, Miss Jamie said.

"Yes, we're here," my teacher answered.

"Could you please send Dominic Leonard down to the office with his backpack? Someone's here to pick him up."

I never got called on the intercom. Who could it be? If it were Mom, she would just come to my classroom to get me. I hoped I wasn't in trouble. I pushed out my chair, with all eyes on me as it squeaked against the tile floor in the quiet classroom. I grabbed my backpack and waved goodbye to Mrs. Wolfe and my classmates. The walls along the winding bright hallway that led to the office were full of beauty and color, covered with all the school children's works of art. The entire school drew pictures of what we wanted to do for the upcoming summer, and they were hung on the bulletin boards outside the classrooms. My picture was me and Tommy with his mom, on our bikes, riding to the park—one of our favorite things to do.

When I got to the office, Uncle Kai and Aunt Gretchen jumped out from behind the door.

"Surprise!" they shouted in unison, startling me.

I grinned from ear to ear. I was so excited to see them I was rendered speechless. Aunt Gretchen laughed and squeezed me.

"What are you guys doing here?" I asked, bouncing on the balls of my feet.

"We're here to take you to the park, bud," Uncle Kai said.

"Really?"

"Yeah, of course. Then afterward, if you want, since June 10th is almost here, we'll take you to the bookstore, and you can pick out some books you want for your birthday. We want to make sure you get the ones you really want instead of us picking them out for you. Sound okay?" he asked.

"Sounds perfect, Uncle Kai. Thank you."

I quickly lowered my voice, the smile fading from my face when I saw Mom across the hallway in her office. She was staring at me. She looked upset, though I had no idea why. She gave me a small tentative smile and waved as she got up from her desk and shut the door to her office without saying a word to any of us.

The three of us practically skipped out to their small, two-door red sports car in the school parking lot. They were parked right up front. Aunt Gretchen opened the door to the passenger side for me, pushed the seat forward, and helped me crawl into the back. Uncle Kai walked around to the driver's side and got in, making an "oomph" sound as he sat down.

"This car is way too low to the ground, Gretch. I'm getting too old for this thing," he said, chuckling.

"Oh, shush. My baby's not going anywhere," Aunt Gretchen said. She pet the dashboard the same way she pet her cat, Sprinkles, then turned to wink at me before saying, "I love this car more than I love you, Kai."

"Ouch," Uncle Kai said, dramatically grabbing his chest.

Aunt Gretchen and I giggled.

"So, Dom, do you need a bookshelf for your room, too? Somewhere to put all these books you're going to get for your birthday?" Aunt Gretchen asked as we were driving to the park. "Maybe when we drop you off tonight, we can come take a look at your room and measure a good spot for it?"

"No, that's okay. I actually have a really big one in my room already. It can fit so many books," I said.

I thought that was a good excuse not to let them in. I could think up excuses and lies fairly quickly, having learned from the best. I hated when they'd ask me questions about the house because I knew I had to lie to them to protect Mom. Lying to them was hard. I felt like if there was anyone I could tell, it would be them. But no one could know our secret. No one came before Mom.

When we got to the park, Aunt Gretchen pushed the seat forward again to let me out. I leapt from the car and ran straight for the swings. On the drive there, Uncle Kai told me stories about when he was a kid. He said his favorite thing was to try to do backflips off the swings. I couldn't wait to try it out for myself.

"Be careful," Aunt Gretchen warned, standing off to the side of the swing set when she caught up with me. "For God's sake, Kai. I cannot believe you put this idea in his head."

Uncle Kai laughed.

"Oh, you think it's funny?" she said, smiling. "What happens when he falls off and cracks his head open? Have fun explaining that one to Annie." She rolled her eyes.

I kicked my legs back and forth, back and forth, gripping the chains that anchored the swing to its metal frame, trying to gain the momentum I needed for the flip. I lifted my face toward the sky, the cool breeze rushing over me with every swing. I loved the smell of fresh air and how nice it felt to breathe in, how comfortable and satisfying it was to fill my lungs with it. My house sometimes felt suffocating, like the air in there was contaminated, as the dust and debris tried to work their way into my lungs right along with the oxygen.

I tried to remember what Uncle Kai said about flipping. "Hold on tight to the chains and get as high as you can. The faster you go, the easier it is to flip. You got this, buddy."

I kicked my legs over and over, trying to muster up enough courage to propel myself backward off the swing.

Finally, on my tenth swing, I pulled my knees to my chest, looked up at the sky again, and rolled my body backward. But as I let go of the chain and looked down, I panicked and fell to my knees. Aunt Gretchen gasped and rushed over to me.

I looked up at her and said, "Auntie, that was so much fun."

She snapped her head to the side and glared at Uncle Kai, who couldn't stop laughing. I loved Uncle Kai's laugh. It was more of a guffaw. When he laughed, I did, too.

"What?" he asked, after catching his breath. "He's my nephew, what did you expect?"

When I got back to my house that night, the tension was high. Mom didn't want to talk to me simply because I'd had fun with my aunt and uncle. I'm not sure when the hatred between them started, but it was thick, and that night, I felt it. I was torn. My three favorite people hated each other. I'd had such a good day and returned to Mom, only to be made to feel guilty. I felt dirty, like I'd been out doing something I shouldn't have. Something that hurt her, the last thing I'd ever want to do.

From that day forward, spending time with Uncle Kai and Aunt Gretchen felt wrong. I had fun while I was with them, but once in a while, reality would hit, and I'd be reminded that my fun was hurting Mom. How could I betray her like that?

8

Around Halloween time, I caught lice from one of the kids in my class. The school sent out a warning letter informing all the parents. It read:

Dear Parents,

A student in your child's class has lice. Head lice are a common occurrence in the school. They are easily transmitted from student to student. Please check your child for lice and nits. Nits are the eggs that lice lay. They can be identified as silver-gray and lay close to the scalp. They do not flake away easily, the way dandruff does. They are glued to the hair strand and will need to be hand-picked or combed out.

If lice are found in your child's hair, please remove them along with any nits before having your child return to school. We strongly recommend you wash any clothes and all bedding that your child has come into contact with within the last 24 hours.

If you have any questions, please feel free to call the school nurse, Julie.

Thank you.

I handed Mom the note.

She threw it to the ground. "Get over here, now," she sighed, pointing to the floor in front of her. "Sit down so I can check your hair."

I sat on the floor in front of Mom, having to pull a hardcover book and a disposable camera out from under my thigh before I could sit comfortably.

"Oh my God, oh my God," Mom muttered. "Ugh, this is disgusting."

"What?" I started to tear up, fearing the worst. "I have the lice, don't I? I have the lice."

"Yep. You sure do," she said flatly.

"What are we going to do?"

"*We* aren't going to do anything. I, however, am going to have to sit here, back pain and all, and pick every last one of these things out of your friggin' hair."

"I'm really sorry, Mom. I don't know who had it. If I did, I wouldn't have talked to them."

"Yeah, well, not much we can do about it now. I can't believe you brought lice into the house," she huffed.

"I'm so s-s-sorry," I stuttered through the tears.

"I know you are. Now, stop crying before I get even more frustrated. I'm the one who has to deal with all of this. I have a headache, too. If anything, I should be the one crying."

I resisted the urge to apologize again and decided I should just keep my mouth shut. That was often the best thing to do. I sat in that same spot on the floor for two hours while Mom picked the nits from my hair and flicked them from her fingers onto the piles I was sitting on. I returned to school the next day. Mom said I was lice-free and there was no reason not to go. If I missed, people might know that I'd had it. But two days later, I was caught scratching my head in class.

"Dominic, could you please come to my desk?" my third-grade teacher, Mrs. Vance, asked.

I stood from my desk and moseyed over to her.

"Hi, sweetie, I saw you scratching your head," she whispered. "I'm going to need you to go to the office and have the nurse check you for lice, okay?"

"Okay," I said. My eyes welled up with tears. "I'm sorry."

"It's okay, honey. There's no reason to be sorry," she said, gently rubbing my arm. "It's no big deal. It can happen to anyone. Don't even worry about it." She smiled, showing she wasn't angry with me.

As I exited the classroom, I was sure that everyone was staring at me and had to know exactly why I was asked to leave. It was mortifying. I took my time walking down to the office. I didn't want to have lice anymore. I sat for hours while Mom got them all out; how could they still be there? Mom's office door was shut when I got to the nurse. I breathed a sigh of relief knowing she wouldn't see me going in there.

"You have lice," our school nurse, Julie, said matter-of-factly. "Why don't you go to your mom's office and tell her. You can't be at school when you have lice. I'm sorry."

"I have to go tell my mom?" I asked, wishing Nurse Julie would be the one to tell her. Mom would get angry with me, but she would feign concern if the nurse told her.

"Yeah. I don't think she has anyone in there. Just go knock and tell her." She smiled. "She'll get you all fixed up, and you'll be good to go tomorrow. You know how your mom is."

I did know how she was. Nurse Julie didn't.

I made my way to Mom's office right across the hall. I inhaled deeply, letting the air fill my diaphragm, taking my time on the exhale as I tried to calm myself. I rapped my knuckles against her door, hoping she wouldn't be there, hoping she would be too busy to talk to me, hoping anything would happen so that I didn't have to tell her and she wouldn't be mad at me.

"Come in," she said on the other side.

I pushed the cold, metal handle down, and the door opened. "Hi, Mom," I said.

"What are you doing here? What's wrong?"

"I still have lice," I said timidly. I looked at the ground, not wanting to meet her gaze.

"Shh, shut the door," she snapped. "How do you know?"

"The nurse checked me."

"What do you mean, 'the nurse checked you?'"

"My teacher saw me scratching my head and sent me to the nurse. Then, the nurse checked me and said I have lice."

"Your teacher knows, too?"

"Yeah."

"Great, that's just friggin' great, Dominic. What do you think they're going to think of me? I work here and have a reputation to uphold, and now I'm one of those parents of a kid with lice. That's just great, isn't it?"

"My teacher said it's not a big deal and anyone can get it," I said, trying to reassure her.

"She was just saying that to make you feel better. It is a big deal. Let's go," she said, grabbing her purse and pulling out her keys.

We walked out of the school without saying goodbye to anyone and drove to the store to buy lice-killing shampoo. Mom slathered it onto my head, massaging it deep into my scalp, taking extra care to work it into the areas lice loved the most: the nape of the neck and behind the ears. Her touch felt peaceful. It reminded me of when I was smaller and she would play with my hair as I fell asleep. I wished she'd still do that for me once in a while. I missed when she used to be gentle.

The shampoo smelled horribly of chemicals. It burned my scalp, and the fumes stung my eyes. I had to breathe through my mouth to avoid the irritation in my nostrils but was left feeling as if I could taste it instead. Mom left it in for fifteen minutes, then had me jump in the shower to wash it out. I watched as the water, which had turned the same purple as the shampoo, flowed down the drain.

"Bye, lice," I said, imagining they were washing down the drain, too. "Please don't come back. Please."

The shampoo came with a special comb for grabbing the lice and nits. After the shower, Mom went through every inch of my hair with the comb until she was confident we were completely rid of the lice.

A week later, Nurse Julie checked me again. It was a precautionary check she did on anyone who had a confirmed case of lice, just to make sure it was gone for good.

"You've still got lice, hon," she said. "Go tell your mom."

I shuffled across the hall to Mom's office, knowing she would be angry with me again. *Knock knock knock.*

"Come in," she said.

"I still have lice," I whispered.

"Are you kidding? Because it's not funny."

"No, I'm not kidding. The nurse just checked me again."

"Well, isn't that just the greatest friggin' thing you've heard all day? I can't believe this. You need new friends or something. I seriously can't believe you got lice from one of them and now my life is a living hell. I'm having to live with these damn bugs that you can't seem to stop picking up."

"I'm sorry, Mom."

"Stop saying that. I know you're sorry, okay? You're always sorry. But your sorries don't help us right now, do they?"

Mom didn't want to try the shampoo again since it didn't work before. She said she had heard somewhere that you could suffocate the lice with petroleum jelly, so she covered my hair, forehead to neckline, in Vaseline. We left it on for an hour before trying to wash it out. It wouldn't come out. Not even a little. My hair was greasy to the touch and lay flat against my head. I looked like I hadn't washed my hair in weeks. This made Mom even angrier than the lice did.

"I can't believe this shit," she fumed.

"What's wrong?"

"Now, you're going to look dirty even though you're not."

"How?"

"Your hair's all greasy. It's going to look like you don't bathe. This is going to make me look like I don't take care of you. At least the lice won't be able to stick to your greasy head. I guess that's one thing I can be happy about. Not much to be happy about, so at least God gave me that."

"I'm sorry, Mom."

"If you say you're sorry one more time, I'm going to smack you," she said, lifting her hand up and slapping the air.

It took four months for the Vaseline to fully come out of my hair. I was asked every day by the kids in my class why my hair was always wet. "Do you take a bath right before class?" they'd ask before laughing and running off. My teacher asked a few times, too. Mom questioned me every day after school whether or not anyone had said anything, worried they would turn her in to Child Protective Services for not taking care of me.

I didn't get lice again after that. Though she would never admit it, it wasn't the kids in my class who were continually giving me lice. It was me giving it to them. When you get lice, you're supposed to wash all the clothes and bedding in your house to get rid of them. But how can you do that when your whole house is blanketed in clothes and other perfect surfaces for lice to thrive on while they wait for a host?

9

How come we can't have a Christmas tree?" I asked one too many times after Thanksgiving. I was eight years old and couldn't remember ever really having had a Christmas tree. I'd see them on TV, and I'd see the one at Tommy's and my grandparents' house. I wanted one, too. Tommy's mom let me help decorate theirs once. Sometimes, I wished she were my mom.

"There's no room, Dom, and you know that. Now, stop asking," Mom said.

"Then we can make room, Mom. I'll help you clean. Besides, how is Santa supposed to get through the house? What if he doesn't know you have to push really hard on the door? What if he gets stuck in the bags like we do?" I asked.

"Has that ever been a problem before?" Mom asked, pressing the heels of her hands into her eyes.

"I don't think so."

"No, it hasn't, all right? So don't worry about it."

"But—"

"Listen," Mom said, cutting me off. "One day, we'll clean the house. But not right now. Santa will get through just fine. I said don't worry about it. I'll have a talk with him, okay? Now, for the love of God, I'm not going to say it again. Stop asking."

"Everyone else has a tree," I muttered under my breath, half-hoping she wouldn't hear me.

She heard.

"Dammit, Dominic. Drop it. Now."

About a week later, Uncle Kai dropped me off after taking me out to dinner, and Mom surprised me with a small two-foot-tall tree she had found at a thrift store. We pushed some fast-food drink cups off the end table next to the couch and onto the floor. One still had leftover soda in it. The weeks-old syrupy liquid sloshed against the plastic sides of the cup as it fell. The soda's old resting place was the perfect spot for our new tree.

Mom had also bought a box of old ornaments. We sifted through the box, tossing the broken ones onto the floor, and put the rest on our "Charlie Brown" tree. Our fun only lasted about fifteen minutes, but I loved getting to decorate with her. Mom forgot to get a star for the top of the tree, so she picked up an old pizza box she found on the ground and used a broken purple crayon that was wedged in between the couch cushions to draw a star in the middle of the box. I grabbed my school scissors from my backpack and handed them to Mom so she could cut out our new tree topper.

"Dom, find a piece of foil somewhere so we can make the star shiny," Mom said.

"Why?"

"Just find it, and I'll show you." She smiled.

I searched through the living room for some foil. Minutes passed, and I didn't see anything. Of course, when I needed something, it was nowhere to be found. Just as I was starting to get discouraged, I saw the shiniest piece of foil imaginable. It glittered in the fluorescent light of our kitchen, like it knew it was about to be a star. I picked up the crinkled foil that once housed a taco from our favorite Mexican food restaurant, Javier's Tacos. Mom took the foil and wrapped it neatly around each point of the star, then around the middle, so every last bit of cardboard was silver and sparkling. Lastly, she took the excess foil and wrapped it around one of the points into a funnel shape so it would have a place to rest on top of the tree.

Mom let me put up the star. I felt special, like a king. It meant a lot to me that Mom got me a tree that year. Even though she didn't want one, she knew I did. I remember feeling so happy that we got to spend that time together. That was the best Christmas I'd ever had.

Mom was right about Santa, too. He did find a way to get through our house just fine, because on Christmas morning, I had some gifts from him under our tiny tree. I opened the first gift, wrapped in red, green, and gold striped paper, with a big red ribbon tied neatly around it. Slowly, so as not to rip it, I pulled on the bottom of the ribbon, undoing its bow, and tossed it aside. I used my fingernail to carefully break each individual piece of tape that was holding the wrapping paper together at its seams. When the paper was undone in a big square, I folded it neatly and placed it in a bag I found next to me.

"Legos!" I yelled after turning the box over.

I couldn't contain myself. I was too excited. Santa must have somehow known what I wanted, even though I wasn't able to get my list to him because I'd lost it somewhere in the kitchen after making the mistake of setting it down. I repeated the same unwrapping process with each successive gift. More Legos, Hot Wheels, books, everything I had asked for from both Mom and Santa. Mom even gave me a card with five bucks in it. The last thing I opened was my stocking, which was hung on the wall by a thumbtack above the couch where Mom sat. It was full of my favorite candies and a brand-new Pez dispenser.

"Dom, baby, let me take your picture with all your new stuff, okay?" Mom said after all my gifts were opened.

"Okay, Mommy," I said, gathering up my things and piling them all into my lap so she could snap my picture. She was smiling at me. She looked happy.

Mom pulled out her camera and sighed. "Hold on. There's too much shit in the way. Can you gently kick everything out of the way so it looks somewhat clean?

Otherwise, the mess will be in the picture. And I say gently because I know how rough you like to get."

I did as Mom asked, moving the garbage and random objects that had made that area their own.

"Perfect," she said. "Now, say cheese."

10

When I was in the fourth grade and about nine years old, I really enjoyed school. I didn't always get the best grades, and I lost my homework a lot. It would just disappear among the mess and piles along with the rest of the papers in the house. There was no room to do any experiments for the science fair or any projects that were larger than a sheet of paper. I couldn't sit at the dining room table or on the living room floor and do my work like other kids, so I just didn't do it at all.

Recess and lunch were my favorite. Lunch because I got to eat hot lunch. It was something new every day in the cafeteria. My favorite hot lunch meal was the mashed potatoes and turkey gravy. No fast food at school; everything was freshly cooked that day by the lunch lady, Mrs. McDougall. There was also a salad bar, which was a lot of fun because I got to pick out anything I wanted. I wasn't much of a salad eater at the time, but I did love croutons. My favorite thing to do was get a whole serving-size spoonful of croutons and drench them in a pool of ranch. I liked to eat it the same way I'd eat cereal with milk.

Then, there was recess, which I loved for so many reasons. I loved running around the playground the most, but the monkey bars were my specialty. The fresh air and great wide-open space of the school yard felt so freeing. Nothing could confine me out there. Sometimes, I would just lie in the grass for the entire fifteen-minute recess, staring into the open and empty soccer field or up at the sky and clouds. Tommy and I also liked to try our hand at basketball, though neither of us were very good. We both loved the swings. I had shown him, not long after Uncle Kai taught me, how to backflip off them. When the playground duties weren't looking, we tried to flip and see who could land on their feet.

* * *

On the weekends, a few times a month, I stayed the night at Tommy's house. I wished he could come to mine, but I knew that would never happen. I tried to accept that, hard as it was.

Tommy's house was a blast. His mom always had the best snacks and chocolate milk ready for us when we got there. She was a fantastic cook, too. When I stayed over, she let us pick what we were going to have for dinner. No matter what it was, she'd cook it for us. I loved that about her because my mom hardly ever cooked.

Once in a while, Mom made me macaroni and cheese. We'd find random boxes of it stuck in the back of cupboards we thought had been emptied long ago. Mom filled a large bowl with water, poured in the noodles, and cooked them in the microwave for ten minutes. When they were done, she poured out some of the excess water and then dumped the cheese packet in.

Other times, when we were lucky and found some bread that was still fresh enough to be free of mold, or we were able to pick the mold off, she would make us grilled cheese sandwiches. We didn't usually have butter to grill them with, or clear access to the stove, and at some point the fridge had stopped working anyway, so she'd microwave them using the picnic-type cheeses that didn't need refrigerated. But that was the extent of her cooking. Most nights, we just went through the fast food drive-thrus around town.

"Hey, Dominic," Tommy said, pushing his Hot Wheels

around on the rug in his room designed to look like a racetrack.

"Yeah, Tommy?"

"How come we never go to your house and play?" he asked. "Do you not have any cool toys like me?"

I froze, trying to think up a good excuse. "Well, my mom is usually just tired after school, and she likes to sleep on the weekends because she gets headaches," I said. "But I do have cool toys. Maybe I can bring them over some time?"

"That would be cool," Tommy said, going back to his racing. "Do you have one of those new Furby things? Because I've really been wanting to play with one of those. I heard they talk to you."

"Yeah, I do have one," I lied. "My mom buys me new toys all the time. My Furby is so much fun. I'll bring it next time I come over."

I never brought the Furby over because I didn't really have one. Tommy must have forgotten because he never brought it up again. I don't know why I lied.

11

On October 17th of my fourth-grade year, around seven o'clock in the evening, a loud and urgent pounding on the door both startled and worried me. I looked at Mom, eyes wide, so fearful of who was on the other side. This knocking felt different. I knew something was wrong.

Every day, I worried that a police officer would show up to take me away from Mom. Every time our door opened was an opportunity for someone to see inside and find us out. Was today that day?

Mom was trembling. The person on the other side of the door knocked again.

"Annie?" a woman shouted, muffled behind the steel door. It was Grandma. "Open this door now."

"Mom?" I said slowly. "What's going on?"

"Dominic, be quiet, or she'll hear you. Quick, go shut off the light," Mom whispered.

"What if she hears me?"

"Shh. Just go do it. And be quiet, will you?"

I did as Mom asked. Grandma pounded on the door again.

"Mom, I'm scared," I said, starting to cry.

"Dominic, shut your mouth," Mom snarled. "She'll go away in a minute if we're quiet."

"Annie, I know you're in there," Grandma yelled. "I saw the light shut off. Open this damn door. Now, Annie."

She knocked over and over. The sound was deafening. I covered my ears, willing her to stop. No other sound in the world was as loud as my grandma knocking on our door in that moment.

"Mom, maybe we should just open the door," I said.

"Dominic James, I said be quiet," Mom snapped, creeping toward the door.

"Please?" I begged.

Mom relented. She looked defeated. She slowly unlocked the door and opened it only a few inches.

"What are you doing here?" Mom not-so-quietly whispered to Grandma. "You need to stop standing out here screaming. Someone's going to call the cops."

"Let me in, Annie. I mean it. Let me in now, dammit," Grandma demanded, "or I'll call the cops myself, and they can do a welfare check on you two."

"No," Mom said, trying to stand her ground. "Stop being ridiculous."

"I'm not playing games, Annie. Open this damn door," Grandma said, again raising her shaky voice, trying to hold back tears of anger.

"Mommy, please just let her in," I pleaded. "Please."

At this point, I was sobbing. I knew what was happening. Grandma wanted to see the house. She knew our secret.

"Go away!" Mom screamed at Grandma, her voice catching as the words escaped in a pitch that was much too high. It made my stomach hurt. Grandma pushed against the door, trying to use her weight to move Mom and force it open, but Mom pushed back even harder. "I said go away."

"Mommy, please," I said through tears. "Just let Grandma in."

Mom was crying, and I could hear her trying to catch her breath.

"Annie, just let me in. Even Dominic wants you to let me in. Doesn't that tell you something?"

"Okay, you know what? You want in? Fine, here. Come

on in," Mom said. She let go of the door, and Grandma stumbled inside.

"Oh my God, Annie," were the only words Grandma managed to get out. She was speechless. Her hands were clutching her chest, the color drained from her already pale face. I was still crying when I looked up and saw that Grandma's eyes were filled with tears, too.

"Well, you know what? It's fine," Grandma said a moment later. "It's all going to be just fine. We'll clean it just like we did when you were a kid, remember?"

Grandma picked up an empty grocery bag she found lying on the ground by her feet and started filling it with some of the many hamburger wrappers and soda cups that were strewn about next to her. But a minute or so later, she stopped and rushed out the door to throw up off the side of the stoop.

How could I let this happen? I was embarrassed and ashamed. I was supposed to protect Mom. We were supposed to protect each other. She did her job by trying to not let Grandma in and trying to make me be quiet. But I didn't do mine. I didn't listen. I told her to let Grandma in. I pleaded with her to share our secret, and now, look at what happened. I had hurt Mom. She was crying and sad, and it was all my fault. I hoped she wasn't mad at me or would at least forgive me soon.

"We can't just start cleaning up everything right this second, Mom. We can't clean the house with grocery bags," Mom said to Grandma when she came back into the house. "We will clean it, okay? I promise. Come back this weekend, and we'll get it going," Mom said, trying to negotiate with Grandma. "I have to work tomorrow, and Dom has school, okay? I don't feel very good right now anyway. Just go away for now, please, Mom. We'll do it, just not today, all right? Please."

Grandma looked at Mom, then at me, her eyes filled with sorrow. "Fine," Grandma said. "Fine, we'll wait. But we are doing this. You two can't live like this anymore. It's not right."

Grandma gave me a big hug and left, promising she'd be back that weekend to help clean.

I had been counting down the days until the weekend, so excited for what was coming. I was finally going to get to experience a real house, maybe feel what it was like to be normal for once. But when Friday night rolled around, Mom called Grandma to say they'd need to reschedule.

"I don't want to hear it, okay?" Mom said. I couldn't hear what Grandma was saying on the other end, but I guessed she wasn't too happy.

"Look," Mom continued, "I've been throwing up since yesterday. I have really bad diarrhea, and on top of that, I got my period. My cramps are so bad, I can hardly move without wanting to cry out in pain. This weekend just doesn't work for me anymore. I have to work Monday, and I'd like to use this weekend to rest." Mom hung up the phone a few minutes later.

I knew none of that was true, and I didn't understand why Mom would lie like that. We were finally going to clean, and someone was even going to help us. Mom was constantly saying the house was a mess because she didn't have help, and we knew that I certainly didn't help as much as I should. Why didn't she want this for us? I didn't say anything about it to her until the next day, though, not wanting to upset her further.

When the next weekend did come, Mom had another excuse. This time, she told Grandma it was me who was sick, and that I'd even had to be kept out of school. Another lie. Mom tried to get off the phone, but a moment later, she sighed and handed the phone to me instead.

"Here. Grandma wants to talk to you," she said. She gave me a warning look.

"Hi, Grandma," I said.

"Hey, Dom. You're not feeling well?" Grandma asked.

"Yeah, my stomach really hurts. A bunch of kids in my class are sick, too. You know how it is." I laughed, trying to sound convincing.

"Okay, hon, well I hope you feel better, and I'll see you

next weekend."

"Okay, Grandma. See you next weekend."

I hung up the phone and handed it back to Mom, not saying a word. I knew better than to ask why she lied. I'd made that mistake last weekend. She'd yelled at me and wouldn't speak to me for the rest of the day. I'd never do that again. After I handed back the phone, Mom told me she didn't feel good again, but that she couldn't say that to Grandma because she wouldn't believe her, so she had to lie. She pinky promised me that we would for sure do it the next weekend, and you know what they say about pinky promises. You are not allowed to break them.

"You know what, Dominic? I have a surprise for you," Mom said the next day, the Saturday we were supposed to be doing our house cleaning. "I feel kind of bad that you were looking forward to cleaning, but we had to cancel again."

I looked at Mom anxiously, waiting to hear what the surprise was.

"So I've decided we are going to go to a movie today at the theater," she said, clasping her hands together in a loud clap. "Doesn't that sound like fun?"

"Yeah!" I shouted, jumping up from my bean-bag style pile of clothes on the floor. "What movie are we going to see?"

"Well, I was thinking that *American Pie* movie looked funny," Mom said. "Do you remember the commercials?"

"Yeah, let's see that one," I said.

Before we got to the theater in the next town over, we stopped at the gas station to buy candy, drinks, and snacks.

"Dom, you have to hide some of these in your coat, okay? We're not supposed to bring our own stuff in, so you better not say anything, or we'll get in trouble. Maybe put the drinks in your boot," Mom said.

I tucked the two glass bottles of soda into each of my boots, feeling like a hero in an action flick, carrying his gun in an ankle holster, ready to go watch the movie.

"Two for *American Pie*, please. One adult and one child,"

Mom said to the girl behind the box office window at the theater.

"Ma'am, how old is the child?" asked the girl.

"He's nine, why?"

"The movie's rated R for content. I don't know if you know that."

"I know it's rated R," Mom said. "What's that mean? He can't see the movie?"

"No, he can," the girl answered. "I just wanted to make sure you were aware. Really, anyone can see a rated R movie as long as they have an adult with them. It's just theater policy to inform parents if a movie's rated R and they're bringing a child. Sorry for the confusion."

Mom huffed, annoyed that the girl would question her parenting.

Once inside, we ordered a bucket of popcorn. We got the biggest one because it was refillable, that way when the movie was over, we'd be able to get more for snacking on later. Movie theater popcorn was mine and Mom's favorite treat.

"Extra butter, please," Mom said to the teenager at the concessions counter. "And don't forget to butter the middle layer, too."

We handed our tickets to another worker who was in charge of making sure everyone had a paid-for ticket before entering the movie area. He ripped our tickets in half, keeping one half for himself and handing the other back to us before directing us toward our theater.

"All the way down the hallway and to your left. You're in theater six," he said.

American Pie had been out for a while at the time, so it was no longer a very popular movie. It was playing at the local discount theater. They screened movies that were about to be released on video, and it only cost a dollar per ticket. For a Saturday afternoon, the theater was fairly empty. We were two of only six people there to see that particular movie.

The theater lights dimmed, and the speakers grew louder.

That's when you knew it was go-time.

"Shh," Mom said excitedly. "The previews are starting."

We both looked at each other and grinned. A giant roller coaster appeared on the screen, taking us up and down its steep drops, winding around its rickety wooden tracks.

"Hello, and welcome to Lakes Discount Cinema," a booming voice announced over the speaker. "We ask that you please be courteous and refrain from talking for the duration of the movie. Now, please, sit back and enjoy the show; and thank you for choosing Lakes Discount Cinema."

I grabbed a handful of popcorn, excited for the movie. Ten minutes' worth of previews later, it started.

Half an hour into the movie, Mom fell asleep, lightly snoring next to me. I didn't understand most of what was going on, but I laughed at the parts that I thought were funny, even if I didn't completely get it. Like, what did it mean that third base felt like warm apple pie? What even was third base? However, I didn't really need to understand the scene with Nadia. I remember it vividly. When she went into Jim's room and stripped down to her underwear, I was enthralled. I started to feel tingly at the sight of her bare breasts. Seeing a real pair of breasts that didn't belong to my mom for the first time stirred something inside me.

I watched intently as Nadia's fingers trailed down her body, over her breasts, down her stomach, and underneath the band of her white panties. She started moaning as her fingers made motions inside her underwear that I didn't understand. I didn't know what she was doing, but I did know that it looked like fun. It looked like something I wanted to try. I wished I could touch her.

The entire premise of the movie was a group of guys doing everything they could to lose their virginities. I didn't understand what the big deal surrounding sex was, but I couldn't wait to find out. I knew the mechanics of it since Mom had told me years before. But now, after this, I wanted to try it out myself.

When Friday came back around again, Mom knew she couldn't lie for a third week in a row. I had been reminding her (or nagging her, as she called it) since Wednesday that she pinky promised, and she wasn't allowed to go back on that. She called Grandma to tell her she could come over Saturday morning to get started on the house. I was beyond giddy. We were finally going to clean. I'd have a nice house, and maybe Tommy could even come over. I guess in my nine-year-old mind, I had assumed this would be an easy, quick, and clear-cut process. That was far from what happened that weekend.

Saturday morning around nine, Grandma knocked on the door. Mom looked at me and nodded toward the door, signaling for me to let Grandma inside. She crossed her arms and sat back on the couch, visibly upset. I slowly made my way to the door, my legs sinking deep into the piles that grabbed at my heels and even stole my shoes at one point. When I got to the door, I cautiously opened it only about the width of half my face.

"Good morning, Dominic," Grandma said. She smiled at me.

It felt wrong to be opening the door at all, let alone opening it to welcome her inside. But I felt better, hopeful even, when I looked down the steps and saw she had brought my grandpa, and two of my most favorite people, Uncle Kai and Auntie Gretchen, with her. In their hands, they had disinfectant wipes, Lysol spray, garbage bags, nitrile gloves, and face masks. They were ready to go.

Mom cried a lot that day. I helped as much as I could, but I couldn't take all the yelling and tears. I hated seeing Mom so hurt and sad, and I felt worse knowing she was feeling that way because of me. It was my fault. If only I could have turned back time, I never would have told her to let Grandma in. I never would have let someone know our secret. I didn't protect Mom like I promised I would. I was the one who broke my pinky promise. I was a failure.

"Annie, this stuff is pure crap," Uncle Kai said later that

day, holding up a broken picture frame. "Why would you want to keep this in your house?"

Mom kept crying, refusing to answer him.

"Kai, knock it off and leave her alone," Grandpa said. "Just keep picking up actual trash for now, and we'll worry about that later."

"Dad, this is actual trash. Both the glass and the frame itself are broken. It's crap."

"Kai, dammit, I mean it. Knock it off. Leave your sister alone," Grandpa snapped.

Mom cried harder. I couldn't look at any of them. Auntie Gretchen and Grandma kept cleaning, ignoring everyone else.

"Wow, Dad, seriously? Annie, is this too much for you? Is this just so hard for you? I mean, never mind that Dominic has to live here, too. We wouldn't want to make this too hard for poor Annie," Uncle Kai said, raising his voice.

"Fine, Kai. Do whatever you want, like usual," Mom said, her words broken up by hiccups from her sobbing.

"Do you just want me to leave then?" Uncle Kai asked. "I don't want to be here if this is how it's going to be. I'm not here for you, anyway."

"Throw away everything, Kai. Toss it all. Dominic's toys are in there, his baby stuff, everything. But sure, throw it all away. I really don't care anymore!" Mom screamed.

"For fuck's sake, Annie. You seriously need help," Uncle Kai yelled, as he threw the already broken frame against the wall, shattering it. The pieces fell to the ground on top of each other in a light clatter, then disappeared into the hoard.

The sound of the frame clashing against the wall made us all jump. I didn't cry. I'm not sure that I could have in that moment. I didn't feel much of anything. I was numb. Too upset to cry or feel, too emotionally exhausted. That's one of the worst feelings I've ever experienced, nothingness, and after that day, I felt that way a lot.

"I need to lie down," Mom said. She tossed the bag she was working on into the mess in front of her and twisted herself so she could lie back onto her spot on the couch.

"What do you need us to do, honey?" Grandma asked, stopping what she was doing to attend to Mom.

"Nothing. I just need to be left alone for a while."

"God, this is just like when you were a teenager. All the shit in your room would literally be level with your bed. But no need to worry because mommy would come in and clean it all up for you because you'd get too overwhelmed and couldn't do it yourself," said Uncle Kai, using air quotes when he said "too overwhelmed."

"Never in my life could I have imagined that was just a glimpse of what you'd eventually live in," he continued.

"Kai, you need to stop. How is any of that helpful?" asked Grandma.

"Fine, I'll stop. Do you want us to keep working without you?"

"Just leave me alone," Mom said.

"Leave you alone? It's a legitimate question. Do you want us to keep going, even though we won't be able to ask you about stuff?"

"Yes, just keep going. If it's garbage, toss it. If it's not, then put it in a box, and I'll look through it later." Mom closed her eyes, ready to shut out the world around her. The back of her hand lay against her forehead as if she were about to faint.

"Will you actually look through it later, though?" asked Uncle Kai.

"Kai, I can't even talk right now, okay? I'm trying not to throw up everywhere. I don't feel good. Sorry if that's too inconvenient for you."

"Kai, just shut up," said Grandpa. "Ann, do you need anything?"

"How about a cold washcloth?" asked Grandma. "You don't look so hot."

"I'm fine, really."

"Okay," said Grandma. "I guess we'll just keep on truckin' by ourselves. We'll work around you."

We continued our mission without Mom's help. She laid on the couch for the rest of the day, only moving her head once in a while to check on us, making sure we weren't throwing out anything she deemed worthy of keeping. She slept while we cleaned. Her snores overpowered the music we had put on in the background. It was awkward, trying to clean next to her. It was like trying not to wake a hibernating bear. Any moment, they could sense you're there, wake up, and bite your face off. I tried to make a game of it, being as quiet as possible, letting the music mask the noises I was making. Honestly, though, I was terrified the bear would wake up and kill me.

Everyone left around nine o'clock that night, taking dozens of garbage bags with them, and that was after having made a couple runs to the city dump. But, if you looked at the house, you'd never know we'd just spent an entire day trying to clean it. Nothing we did even made so much as a tiny dent in the hoard. Our house still looked like a landfill. To say I was disappointed would be quite the understatement. I had severely underestimated the amount of work needed to make our house something that resembled normal.

But they came back the next day, and the next weekend, and the weekend after that, until finally, week after week, month after month, we accomplished our goal. It took a long time, too long in my eyes, because I wanted instant results. But by springtime, when it was finished, there was no greater feeling in the world to me than that one right there.

Uncle Kai and Aunt Gretchen took me shopping after that to buy my own bed and anything else I wanted. I picked out a bulletin board like they had in the hallways at school, that way I could hang up my artwork in my room, too. We used to hang it on the fridge in our kitchen, but when the house was a mess, we'd sometimes have to use the fridge for balance, which knocked my artwork and all the magnets down onto the floor, where they'd be lost forever. Mom bought a used refrigerator at the thrift store, and we were able to buy groceries for the first time in a long while.

I also asked for new magnets so I could start hanging stuff on the fridge again. Tommy's mom put his report cards and drawings on their fridge. I wanted to surprise Mom with some new drawings, hoping she'd like them enough to want to proudly display them the way Tommy's mom did. Next, I picked new bedding. I chose a Power Rangers-themed bed-in-a-bag. It came with a comforter, pillowcases, and matching sheets. I found a giant bookshelf like the one I'd claimed to have before, and they bought me a desk so I'd have a place to do my homework and school projects.

I was in heaven. Tommy had occasionally been allowed to come over and sometimes even stay the night. I loved our new house so much that when my tenth birthday came around that year and Mom said she would take me and Tommy to the water park, I told her no. I wanted to have a party with Tommy and all my family at our new house. I got some posters for my walls for my birthday. Ninja Turtles, Transformers, some of my favorite cars. I was thrilled to be able to hang them up and look at them every day by simply walking down the hall. Easy strides to my new room, no more dinosaur stomping. That was the best birthday I'd ever had.

A few months later, the house got messy again. Mom stopped picking up after herself, and it got to be too much for me to do alone, so I gave up on it, too. I did try, though, for as long as I could. Mom would tell me to pick up my toys, do the dishes, or take out the garbage, and I did. But I couldn't keep up, and I felt so guilty for disappointing Mom. I knew it would disappoint Uncle Kai, Aunt Gretchen, and my grandparents, too.

Mom still liked to shop and habitually brought new things into the house. We tried to put the stuff away, but it was easier to just set it down and forget about it. I should have tried harder. After a while, I only occasionally did the dishes when she asked, or picked up my things about half the time. I was guilty, too. I knew the new hoard was partially my fault. More than the rest of the house, I tried to keep my room clean, but

Mom kept needing some of the space in there to store the new things she'd bought. She did let me keep about two thirds of my room, though. She tried to organize the boxes and bags in a way that gave me a small space to play, and I still had my bed to sleep in and play on, too.

"If anyone asks about the house, what do you tell them?" Mom asked me.

"That everything is still okay," I said proudly.

I knew the answer to that one. She didn't need to keep reminding me, but she did so to make sure we were still protecting each other. No way was I going to hurt her again by revealing our new secret to anyone. I wouldn't make that mistake twice. I couldn't risk the police being called and taking me away or Uncle Kai upsetting Mom again.

"That's my boy," Mom said. She smiled at me. I hoped she knew I would do anything for her.

Eventually, as time went on, I started to tell lies to my friends the same way Mom told lies to her coworkers. If my friends told me how they had outgrown their old room themes or toys and gotten new stuff, I told them how I had done the same thing. Or if someone's parents were going to paint their room a fun new color, it just so happened that my mom was taking me to pick out some paint that same day. Truth was, those posters I had gotten for my birthday had long since disappeared behind the mountains of bags and boxes that now filled my room or had been ripped off by a flying bag thrown at the wall.

But it was fun to pretend I still had the things I'd always wanted but may never have again. No one had ever been to my house except Tommy, and he hadn't been back in months. No one would know I was lying. I got to be whoever I wanted and have whatever I wanted. I once even claimed that my mom was so cool that she bought me a brand new forty-seven-inch flat screen TV and a brand-new DVD player, both of which were still fairly new inventions at the time. My classmates were thoroughly impressed.

"I wish Lenny was my mom," one boy said.
"Yeah, I'm pretty lucky." I smiled.

12

I can't believe you let Dad have these," Mom said to Grandma as she flipped through a magazine one afternoon at my grandparents' house. They sat on the blue couch in my grandparents' living room, looking through the thick black magazine together while our made-from-scratch chili lunch simmered on the stove.

"Let him?" Grandma said. "Oh, please. I couldn't stop him if I wanted to."

"Damn right," Grandpa said, having just popped back in the house to see if lunch was ready.

"What is it?" I asked, peering in their direction from the oversized chair adjacent to the couch.

"Oh, nothing. Don't worry about it," Grandpa said. "Don't you lose that, though. I might need it later." He laughed, leaving the living room to head back into the garage where he was changing the oil in our car

"I want to see, Mom," I said, making my way over to her.

"It's not for little boys, Dom," Grandma said. She stood up from the couch and walked back toward the kitchen to check on the chili.

"Please, Mom, I want to see," I whispered so Grandma wouldn't hear.

Mom peered into the kitchen, then glanced toward the garage to make sure no one could see us. "Hurry, look fast before they see you," she said, handing me the magazine.

"What is it?" I asked. The cover of the magazine read *Playboy*.

"Hurry up or you'll get me in trouble. Do you want to see it or not?" She grabbed the *Playboy* out of my hands and flipped it open to the centerfold.

My eyes widened, and Mom giggled quietly, mostly to herself, trying not to get caught by her parents doing something she shouldn't.

"Grandpa's got a whole stack of these in the garage. Like a hundred of them. Can you believe that?"

That same feeling I got when I watched Nadia in *American Pie* returned, only this time, in my grandparents' living room. Up until that moment, Nadia was the most glorious thing I'd ever seen. Now, there was this woman, this centerfold. Fully naked. Her bare breasts proudly on display. She lay on her back with one hand on her right breast, the other on the back of her thigh. Her legs were crossed in the air, and in between them, I saw for the first time on an actual person, not on Mom and not on a doll, a vagina. Nadia was no longer the most glorious thing I'd ever seen. This *Playboy* model's vagina was.

"Give that back to me." Mom laughed and took back the magazine. "Did you enjoy it?"

I didn't say anything. My mind was focused on trying to figure out how I was going to hide my erection from my grandparents. I'm sure Mom knew it was there, though I was thankful she didn't ask. Mom laughed harder at my speechlessness. I stole the *Playboy* that afternoon. I tucked it into the top of my pants and put on a baggy sweatshirt to cover up the box that the magazine turned my stomach into. I learned all about masturbation that night.

I masturbated too much and too often, especially for a child that age. Each time, I felt dirty and would pray to God to forgive me for my sins. I prayed that he would rid me of my disgusting desires. I knew there was something wrong with me, and I feared that yet another demon had crawled inside my soul and was forcing me to masturbate. I needed an exorcism. But I couldn't stop. It felt too good. It consumed me. I thought about it constantly, trying to find ways to sneak off and be alone in the house so Mom wouldn't know what I was doing.

I went to confession during Sunday mass more than once to confess my sins. First, that I'd stolen the magazine. Second, that I was looking at pornography, and third, that I was masturbating all the time.

* * *

Mom used to force me to go to Sunday school at the church, and I'm fairly certain the nuns that taught my class were not a fan of me. I asked too many questions they couldn't or wouldn't answer. I remember one time in Sister Carrie's class when she was teaching us all about being called upon by Jesus, which was how she decided to devote her life to him.

"Jesus spoke to me," she said.

"What? He spoke to you? Like you actually heard him talking?" I asked.

"Well, not actual words, no. But with signs all around me. I felt empty and just sort of restless, I guess you could say. I just knew there was something missing. And then, there were the dreams. He came to me in my dreams every night."

"Then he spoke to you?"

"Yes. He said, 'Carrie, I want you to devote your life to me and the church. I want you to know me and help others to know me.' How could I say no to that? You know, essentially, Jesus and I are married."

"You're married to Jesus?" I asked incredulously.

"That's correct." Sister Carrie smiled.

"Just you? Or all nuns?"

"Well, all of us, of course. There are lots of us who have been called. That's how Father Loren became our priest. We have all been blessed and chosen by the Lord to devote ourselves to him."

"So all the sisters here are married to him? He has like a ton of wives?"

"Yes," Sister Carrie said, seeming to grow impatient. "All the sisters here, and our sisters around the world."

"That's disgusting," I said. I wrinkled my nose and stuck out my tongue, fake gagging.

"It's not disgusting, Dominic," Sister Carrie retorted.

"It kind of is. Is Father Loren married to him, too?"

"No, of course not. Men don't marry men."

"What happens if someone's called upon and doesn't want to be a nun or a priest?"

"You can't really say no. But honestly, you wouldn't want to. Anyone who's called upon by our savior wants to devote their lives to him."

"But what if they don't?"

"They will."

"But what if for some reason they don't? Then what happens?"

"Dominic, we're going to move on now. If you or anyone else in here is lucky enough to be called upon by Jesus, you will want to do it. Trust me."

From that day forward, I lived in fear that Jesus would call upon me to devote myself to him. I feared that I would either be pressured to do it, or I'd wind up in hell for saying no to the Almighty. Though, with all the sins I committed day in and day out, I was probably headed there anyway. I knew a life devoted to Jesus was not a life I wanted to live. I knew then that church and religion weren't for me.

13

A few weeks before Thanksgiving in my fifth-grade year, I was jolted awake in the middle of the night by a loud, piercing alarm. Mom rushed into my room, out of breath, her chest heaving up and down.

"Dominic, get up," she said, coughing.

I sat up groggily, not understanding what was going on.

"Hurry, get your shoes on. We need to get out of here. The house is on fire!" she screamed.

"What are you talking about?" I asked. "Are you being serious?"

"Yes, Dominic, why would I lie?" Mom huffed. "I'll be right back. I have to go get some things."

"No, Mommy, please don't leave me," I said, starting to cry. "I'm scared."

"You'll be fine. I have to hurry," she said, rushing back out of my bedroom, closing the door behind her.

I tried to look before it shut, but it was too dark. I couldn't see past where she stood. I laid back on my bed and reached into the corner that met with the wall, where I kept my shoes so they didn't get lost. I put on my favorite pair of black Nikes, starting with the left, and tied them neatly. Waiting patiently for Mom to return, I could see the snow falling outside my window in big white flakes. I liked to pretend I was flying through space when the snow was heavy like that. I knew it would be cold, but my coat was by the front door; I wouldn't be able to get it. I hoped Mom would remember.

Mom rushed back through my door, pushing her back hard against it, so it shut behind her. She was wearing her winter coat, but she didn't remember mine. In her hands, she held two clear plastic containers. I could see my baby book and some of our photo albums in there. I had never seen those boxes before. Mom usually kept those types of things on top of the entertainment center, the weight of them bowing the middle of it, threatening to cave in at any minute and crush our TV.

She set the boxes down, hurried over to my window, and tried to pry it open. It was frozen shut. I started to cry. What if we couldn't get out? Finally, Mom was able to get the window open. She pushed on the screen, its metal edges bending into sharp points until it popped out of the frame.

"Come on. I'll help you up," Mom said. She grabbed me under my arms, placing me in the window as I lifted my legs up and stepped onto the sill.

"Now, jump, Dom," she said.

I didn't say a word. I looked down but didn't feel scared. We weren't that far from the ground, and there was a fresh bed of snow, glistening like diamonds in the moonlight, ready to break my fall. I leapt from the window, the winter air cutting sharply across my face. The snow was cold and powdery. It enveloped me. I stood and sunk waist deep into the blanketed surface.

"Move out of the way," Mom called from above me.

I scrambled to get through the heavy, engulfing snow, trying to move quickly but hardly moving at all. Mom tossed the boxes out the window. They landed with a light thud next to me, sinking into the blanket as well. Mom climbed into the window, pushing her body up with her thin arms, one leg at a time onto the sill. She jumped and landed in the same spot I did.

"Grab a box, please, Dom. Help me," she said, exasperated and coughing.

I still didn't say anything. I was in shock. I did as she asked, and we each grabbed one of the two boxes. We did our best to try to trek through the snow, in much the same way we did when we trudged through the house, taking big, hastened steps to get through like dinosaurs. When we got to the front, we stopped for a moment.

Mom looked back at the house. "There's flames in the windows," she said, flat and emotionless. "It's on fire."

I didn't look, couldn't look.

"Let's go," she said a moment later, walking off without making sure I was following. We shuffled through the front yard, saying a silent goodbye to the house before going across the street to Tommy's.

The street was dark. I slipped on the ice and fell to my knees while crossing. The box I was carrying crashed to the ground in front of me. Mom sighed and kept going.

It was only a few more feet to Tommy's. His house was lit up with solar lights that lined the driveway and walkways. On their front steps was a black sign, about three feet tall, that said "Welcome" vertically in white calligraphy. His mom had hung a wreath on their front door. It had pretty orange and red flowers mixed with yellow leaves around the edges and a smiling turkey in the middle. The turkey was wearing a pilgrim-style hat and holding a sign that said "Thankful."

Mom rang the doorbell. The chiming sounded like a rock concert on our quiet street. No answer. Mom rang it again. *Ding, dong.* She tried knocking instead. *Rap, rap, rap.* Our house deteriorated with every passing second.

A few minutes later, Tommy's mom answered the door, tying her pink fleece robe around her waist. "Annie?" she said, opening the door to us.

"Please, help us," Mom said.

Tommy's mom looked across the street, her eyes widening. "Oh my goodness," she said, before darting toward the kitchen. She appeared a second later, pressing the buttons on the phone as she hurried back. I heard three loud beeps for the numbers she pressed: 911. We sat on their soft, plush, gray couch, setting the boxes in our laps, unsure of what to do with them.

"911, what's your emergency and location?" I heard faintly through the phone.

"Hello, yes, my neighbor's house across the street is on fire," she said, panicked.

The operator on the other end said something I couldn't make out.

"Yes, I'm at 1010 Sunshine Avenue in Pleasantview. It's right across the street from me. You can't miss it. Please hurry," she said. "Yes, they're fine. They're here with me." She looked at us and said, "Don't worry, you guys. They're on their way."

The operator spoke again, her voice muffled as Tommy's mom paced back and forth across their living room.

I heard the sirens long before they got there. The sirens grew louder and louder until I could hear them right outside Tommy's house. Mom set the box at her feet and turned around, her knees on the couch, elbows resting on the back, watching the action through Tommy's living room window. I set my box down as well and started to turn like Mom when Tommy's mom stopped me.

"Dominic, Tommy's sleeping," she said. "You know what that means? You get to pick whatever movie you want to watch. It's all your choice. You don't want to watch what they're doing over there. That's yucky grown-up stuff. Come, sit over here on Tommy's bean bag and pick out a movie. Would you like some hot chocolate?"

"Yes, please," I said, crawling over to the movie rack next to their TV. Everything was neatly lined up and put away. The movies were organized by genre, then in alphabetical order.

The children's movies were on the bottom rack, so they were easier to see. I chose *Beauty and the Beast*. I loved that movie. The beast was alone in his castle, trapped and isolated, angry. He didn't have anyone to turn to. He felt so lonely.

Then, one day, he met this beautiful girl who showed him what it means to have someone who truly cared about him. His anger faded, his walls came down, and he became the man he was always meant to be. And most importantly, they lived happily ever after.

"Here, honey," Tommy's mom said, returning with a green Garfield Christmas mug in her hand. "It's hot, so be careful, okay? I added a little bit of whip cream for you. But don't tell your mom that I'm giving you sugar this late at night." She winked at me.

Even though Mom was only a few feet away, she couldn't hear us. She was so entranced by what was going on across the street, she wouldn't have noticed if there had been a whole party going on in Tommy's living room. Tommy's mom picked up a blanket from the couch and wrapped it around me, turned on the TV, and popped the tape into the VCR.

"Annie," she said, sitting next to Mom on the couch. "Sweetie, can I get you anything?"

"No, thank you, Nelly. I'm fine, really, thank you," Mom said, not moving or looking away from the window.

Nelly patted Mom's back. No one talked for a long time after that.

When the movie was almost over, someone knocked loudly on the door, startling me. Even though it wasn't my house, it still scared me. Knocking, for me, had become a sound of trouble.

Tommy's mom shuffled over to the door. "Hello?" she said, peering through the crack.

A man's deep, hoarse voice on the other side said, "Ma'am, is this your house?"

"Yes," she said.

"Are you the one who called 911?"

"Yes, I am."

"Is your neighbor here with you?"

"Yes, they're still here."

"May I come in and speak to them?" he asked.

"Yes, please come in." She let the firefighter in and shut the door behind him.

"Annie," she said, peering into the living room, "there's a fireman here to talk to you. Why don't you guys go into the dining room to talk so Dominic can finish his movie."

Mom got up and followed the fireman and Tommy's mom into the dining room. I don't know what happened after that. I didn't want to know. I just kept watching my movie, blocking out the world, trying not to think about what was next for us. My biggest concern after the fire wasn't that we had lost our house and all our possessions. It wasn't where we would stay or what I would wear to school since I no longer had any clothes other than my pajamas. My biggest concern was whether or not the firefighters would report us. What did they think of the house? Were they going to tell anyone?

When the movie was over and Mom and the fireman were done talking, they came out of the dining room.

"Dominic," Mom said, "we're going to go outside to get checked out by the nice people in the ambulance, okay?"

"Why?" I asked.

"Hey, buddy," the fireman said, coming over to me and kneeling to my level. "My name is John."

"I'm Dominic."

"Nice to meet you," said John. "Dominic, sometimes when we get too close to a fire, we can accidentally breathe in the smoke from it. And if you breathe in too much smoke, it can really hurt your body. We just want to make sure you're okay and that the smoke didn't hurt you. Does that sound all right?"

"I guess," I said, standing up and following them to the door.

"Here, Dom," Tommy's mom said, putting one of Tommy's coats on me. "Can't have you freezing out there."

"Thank you," I said.

"Of course, sweetie. And, Annie, if you need anything else, just let me know, all right? Anything," she said as we began to walk down their driveway and back to our own.

"Thank you, Nelly. For everything," Mom said.

We followed John back to our house. I remember looking at it and thinking, *How could there have been flames in the windows? It still looks exactly the same.* And it did, in the dark.

"Dominic, this is Cordelia," John said. "She's a paramedic, and she's here to check you out, okay?" I nodded.

"Hi, Dominic," Cordelia said. She gave me a sympathetic half-smile and tilted her head to the left, her short red ponytail flopping to the side. "Do you like suckers?" she asked, handing me a Tootsie Pop.

I smiled and said, "Yes," graciously accepting it.

Her hands were gloved in blue nitrile, but they were warm, as she began checking me out. She said she made sure to warm them up for me.

Cordelia listened to my heart and my lungs through her stethoscope, then took my blood pressure, placing the cold metal onto the ditch of my arm. I didn't like that last part. The cuff was uncomfortable as it tightened and squeezed my bicep. The Velcro crackled, trying to break free.

"I think you're good to go, mister," Cordelia said, removing the blood pressure cuff from my arm, the Velcro pulling away loudly. "But," she continued, "if for any reason at all you feel sick, or even just feel like you need to talk to someone, give us a call. Sound good?"

I smiled. "Thank you," was all I could manage to get out.

I stepped out of the ambulance and into the driveway, looking around for Mom. John stopped me.

"Hey, bud," he said. "You doing okay?"

I nodded, the sucker still in my mouth.

"Good," he said. "Hold up, I have something for you." He reached into his jacket and pulled out a stuffed dragon.

"Oh wow," I exclaimed. "Thank you so much."

"Anytime, Dominic. Anytime." He tousled my hair. "I mean that, okay?" he said, pointing his finger at me.

"Okay."

I found Mom sitting in my grandpa's white Nissan Pathfinder. I didn't even know she had called him.

"Dominic," Grandpa said, much too formally, as if we were business partners and not grandfather and grandson.

"Grandpa," I responded, matching his tone.

"Well, go on now. Get in the car. You're going to stay at our house tonight, and we'll figure out everything else tomorrow."

I looked at him, unsure of what to say.

"All right?" he said impatiently.

"All right," I said.

Grandpa opened the rear driver's side door for me. I climbed in and buckled the seatbelt.

Grandma and Grandpa's house smelled of fresh brewed coffee when we walked in the door. I looked up at their six-foot-tall grandfather clock and saw that it was 3:17 a.m. Grandma was sitting in her blue chair, which was big enough for two people, with her feet up on the ottoman. She was wearing her green housecoat with matching fluffy slippers and sipping on a mug of coffee. Their sofa looked inviting, but I was exhausted. I didn't know if I'd be able to get back up if I dared to make a stop at the sofa.

Grandma and Grandpa's house had three bedrooms. One was for them, of course. Another used to belong to Uncle Kai and was now used for storage. And the last room, Mom's old bedroom, was a spare for when friends and family came over. I began to climb their narrow spiral staircase up to the spare bedroom, the only room in the upstairs of their house.

"I'm really tired, Grandma," I said from the top of the staircase. "I think I'm going to go to bed."

"Of course," Grandma said.

The bed in my grandparents' spare room was hard and uncomfortable. I missed my bed already. I pulled back the black and white gingham print comforter and the fleece blanket that lay underneath and climbed in without bothering to remove my shoes or Tommy's coat. Mom never came to bed or checked on me.

I woke up, sweating from too many layers of warmth the next morning. The smell of Grandma frying eggs and potatoes wafted upstairs, greeting me. My stomach growled. I made my way down the stairs that overlooked the living room and didn't see Mom. She wasn't in the kitchen with Grandma cooking breakfast, either.

"Grandma, where's Mom?" I asked.

Grandma jumped. "Goodness, Dominic. I didn't even hear you come in." She chuckled.

"Sorry."

"Your mom? Well, she's um…she's not feeling well. She went to the store for something. Medicine or something for her back, or for a headache. I don't really know." Grandma was starting to stutter, becoming flustered, even without my saying anything else. "I, uh, I don't know, dear. She'll be back soon, I'm sure."

When Mom came back that afternoon, bringing several shopping bags with her, I was elated and comforted to see her.

"Mom, where have you been?" I asked. "I missed you. Are you okay?"

"I'm fine. I was just getting us some things," she said. "We have nothing now, you know? I needed to get you some clothes, and you don't even have a coat. You can't keep Tommy's."

I recognized the bags as the same ones that came from the thrift stores we regularly frequented.

* * *

A week later, Mom informed me that the fireman, John, wanted to talk with me the next day. She said we would need to go down to the fire station to meet with him, but first, there was another man we needed to talk to.

"Why, Mom?" I asked.

"How should I know, Dominic?"

"Your mom is meeting with John this afternoon at four o'clock just to talk a little about the house. Then, tomorrow he wants to talk with you. It's no big deal," Grandpa said. "This other man is going to talk to the both of you about a couple things, and you just need to do what he says, all right? Now, go on. Get your coat on and listen to your mom."

We drove about fifteen miles north to an office building next to an Italian restaurant. It had been a whole week since we'd gone to a restaurant or eaten any sort of fast food since Grandma cooked every night, though it felt as if it had been much longer. The door to the man's office building was cold and heavy. Mom had to help me open it.

"Good morning," the receptionist said. "Do you have an appointment?"

"Yes," Mom said. "We're here to see Mr. Erickson."

"Oh, are you Annie?"

"Yes."

"Great, he's waiting for you right down the hallway, second door on your left."

"Thank you."

"Annie, how are you?" the man called Mr. Erickson asked when we walked into the brightly lit, gray room.

There was an oversized conference-type table in the middle, filling it almost entirely. We sat in two of the ten chairs around it, with Mr. Erickson already in his seat at the head of the table.

"What can I help you with today?" he asked. "Rachel said it was urgent."

"Rachel?" I asked, looking up at Mom.

"Yes, you know Rachel, the student counselor I'm training at school?"

I nodded.

"This is her husband."

"Oh, okay."

"Well, as you know, a week ago, we had a house fire," Mom said.

"Yes, I heard about that," said Mr. Erickson. "I'm so sorry."

"Thank you. But I'm here because I needed to talk to you about an interview I have with the chief of the fire department that's coming up this afternoon. I get the sense these interviews aren't very common, and I've had the sneaking suspicion he feels I'm somehow at fault." Tears filled Mom's eyes, and she began to shake.

"All I can really tell you is that you of course need to answer as truthfully as you can. Don't offer more information than is asked of you. And most importantly, these interviews are usually recorded and then sent off to be typed into transcripts. So, say he were to come right out and ask, 'Hey, Annie, did you purposely burn your house down?' And you replied sarcastically, 'Oh yeah. I definitely burned my house down on purpose.' Then the transcripts will show you saying exactly that. The transcripts won't capture your tone or demeanor when you said it. It will only show that yes, you said you purposely burned your house down. In other words, be very careful how you answer any of their questions."

The drive to the fire station the next day didn't take long; it was only a mile or so from my grandparents' house.

"Well, hello there, kiddo," John said when we came through the station door, bringing the wind chill and falling snow with us.

Mom shut the door, instantly cutting off the whistling music that was the wind.

"Hi, John," I said.

"Come right this way to our meeting room we have back here." He gestured down the hall. "I just want to talk to you a little bit if that's okay."

"Yeah, that's okay with me," I said, following him.

"Can I get you anything, kiddo? We have a vending machine with soda, or there's bottles of water. We have a coffee machine, but I think you're a little too young for that." He chortled.

"No, I'm okay. But thank you."

"So, Dominic," John said, pulling out a chair for me when we entered the meeting room.

I sat down, and Mom sat in the chair next to me, looking down at the table, squeezing her hands together.

"I want to thank you and your mom for taking the time to come down here to talk to me today," he continued. "I have some questions for you about the fire at your house. I know it's scary, but I need you to answer them for me to the best of your knowledge. Do you know what that means?"

"No, I don't think so," I said.

"Well, it just means that I need you to answer my questions, telling me the truth and telling me as much as you know. Does that make sense?"

Oh no, there it was. He was going to ask me about the house, the mess, the hoard. He was going to take me from Mom.

"Yes, that makes sense."

"Okay, so the night of the fire, do you remember anything unusual happening?"

"Um, no. Not that I can think of. It was a normal night."

"Good, glad to hear it," he said, jotting down some notes on a yellow legal pad. "So, kiddo, when we searched through the house after we put out the fire, there was a lot of stuff in there, you know?"

Oh, crap. He was going to call the police, I just knew it.

"Well, as you probably know, with all that stuff in there, we found some things that didn't quite look like they were where they should be. We found them in places they really didn't belong."

"Like what?" I asked, truly curious.

"Well…" he said, pausing for a moment, choosing his words carefully. "We found a lighter in the hallway by the washer and dryer. Do you know what a lighter is?"

"Like for cigarettes? I've seen them on TV before."

"Yes, like for cigarettes. But this one was bigger. Like one

SON OF A HOARDER

you would use to light up a barbecue so you didn't get too close and burn your hand. Do you know the kind I'm talking about?"

"No," I said, thinking hard. "I don't think I've seen one of those kinds before."

"And you don't remember anything else about that night? Anything out of the ordinary?" he asked.

"No. I ate dinner, watched TV, then went to bed. Then, I woke up to the fire alarm. Then me and Mom jumped out the window and went to Tommy's house."

"And that's it?"

"Yep."

"You're positive? Completely and one hundred percent sure?"

"Positive."

"Well, okay, then. I think that's all I need to know. Thank you so much for coming in, Dominic. It was nice seeing you again. Nice to see you, too, Annie," John said, extending his hand to shake Mom's.

"Mm-hmm," said Mom, turning quickly to leave, ignoring his hand.

* * *

Eventually, some of our belongings from the old house were returned to us after being cleaned by a professional cleaning service that specialized in fire damaged items. My bedroom was the only room in the house that had anything salvageable in it because it was at the back of the house and the door was shut.

I didn't want any of my things back, though. Everything still smelled like the fire. No matter how many times they were cleaned, no matter how powerful their machines were, the smoke smell wasn't coming out. To this day, fire scares me. I never enjoyed bonfires like so many of my friends did when I was a teenager. The smell of them made me feel sick. When I'm cooking, if the food starts to burn or I turn on the heater for the first time in the season and it smells hot, a part of me begins to panic.

From what I can remember, when the fire department finished their investigation, they concluded that the fire must have been started by a mouse. The fire originated in the bathroom, and they'd found a curling iron with a frayed wire still plugged in to the wall. They determined that the mouse must have chewed on it, causing a shock and a spark that either landed on the piles of clothes strewn about the bathroom or on the dirty toilet paper that we threw in the trash instead of the toilet since the toilet was constantly clogged. And since no one ever took out the garbage, the toilet paper mound was almost as tall as the counter, making it extra accessible for the spark.

But if you ask me, it was no accident. I've always wondered if maybe Mom felt stuck. She was trapped in that house, which was made into a prison by all those worthless possessions and enough garbage to fill the dumpsters at the county waste site. We'd tried to clean it and managed to live a normal life for a short time, only to return to our old ways. She was facing constant criticism and questioning, having to lie all the time. It was too overwhelming to try and start over by going through everything; she had told me that herself on more than one occasion. There was just too much. *It* was just too much. I think she wanted a fresh start and felt that was the only way out.

Honestly, I can't say that I blame her. In a way, I understand. We lost everything, but the slate was clean. No one from the fire department called Child Protective Services. We were in the clear with a fresh start and a brand-new opportunity, one that, unfortunately, ended up being wasted.

14

We stayed at my grandparents' house for the next few months. Thanksgiving came and went. Mom didn't come down to dinner with us that day. Grandma cooked a big, juicy turkey, mashed potatoes, and homemade turkey gravy, along with cranberries and creamy buttered corn. Aunt Gretchen baked my favorite cheddar bread rolls from scratch just for me. I loved dipping them in Grandma's turkey gravy. Uncle Kai and Aunt Gretchen also brought a pumpkin pie with extra whipped cream, just the way I liked it.

After dinner, Grandma pulled out our family's favorite game, Pictionary, from the cupboard under their TV. We picked teams and team names. Team Potato was Uncle Kai, Aunt Gretchen, and me. Team Turkey was Grandma and Grandpa. None of us were great artists, but we got the gist of what our drawings were supposed to be. In the end, the point count was eight to Team Potato and five to Team Turkey, making my team the winner.

"Oh yeah! Oh yeah!" I cheered. "Po-ta-to, Po-ta-to."

"Dominic, don't gloat," Grandma said.

I stopped, and looked down at my feet, feeling guilty for bragging.

"Po-ta-to, Po-ta-to," said Uncle Kai. He winked at me and patted me on the back.

"Well, everyone," Grandma said, standing up from the table. She wiped her hands on the apron she was still wearing

CHEYENNE SMIDT

from her day of cooking. "I hate to end the fun, but I really need to get started on the best part of the day—the cleanup."

Aunt Gretchen chuckled. "Here, let me help you," she said.

"Oh, you're too kind, dear, thank you," Grandma said.

"Dominic, it's getting late. You can go ahead and get ready for bed. You don't have to help out here," said Uncle Kai.

I hugged and kissed everyone goodnight before heading upstairs to change into my pajamas and brush my teeth. The smile never left my face as I bounded up the staircase, toward my temporary room. What a great day.

"Mom," I said, crawling into bed with her, just like old times. "How come you slept all day? Aren't you hungry? Dinner was so good."

"Dominic," she said, "I'm not feeling particularly thankful this year, and I don't really want to see some of the people that were here today."

"Who?" I asked, though I suspected I already knew the answer.

"Don't worry about it."

"My team won Pictionary. It was so much fun."

"I know. I heard." Mom sounded annoyed.

"Did we wake you up? I'm sorry, I didn't mean to mess up your sleep," I said.

"It's fine, Dom." She wasn't happy with me.

"No, it's not, Mom. I really am sorry."

"If you're really sorry, then be quiet and let me go back to sleep," Mom snarled.

"Okay. Goodnight."

She rolled over without saying goodnight back.

Because Mom still wanted to sleep, and I wasn't quite tired enough to fall asleep myself, I decided to go see what everyone else was up to.

"I want him to stay with us," I heard Uncle Kai say somewhere below me. I stopped, fearing I was hearing

80

something I shouldn't.

"Oh, really?" Grandma said, "And how exactly are you going to go about that? You're just going to tell her, 'Oh, hey, I'm taking your kid'? I don't think so."

"He deserves better, Mom, and you know it."

"You're being ridiculous," said Grandpa.

"How, Dad?"

"Kai, come on," said Grandma. "Don't do this. Especially not today. It's Thanksgiving, for crying out loud."

"No, tell me, please. How am I being ridiculous?" asked Uncle Kai. "You two are really going to sit there and tell me that he's doing okay?"

"He's doing great right now, son," Grandpa said.

"Yeah, right now. And only right now because he's here with you guys and not stuck alone with her."

I realized then that they were talking about me, and I didn't want to hear anymore. I loved Uncle Kai and Aunt Gretchen, but I could never leave Mom. If I left, who would take care of her and protect her?

* * *

Our stay with Grandma and Grandpa became increasingly tense as the weeks and months went on. Mom never quit or sought help for her shopping habit, and not having a house to put her things in was not going to stop her from getting her fix. It was a colder than usual winter with heavier snowfall than we'd seen in years. Because of this, none of us got out of the house or away from each other much. Mom said we'd overstayed our welcome at my grandparents' house.

"Mom, please take me with you," I begged as she was putting on her coat, about to leave.

"Not this time, Dominic," she said. "Not until we get our own place again. Come on, we talked about this."

"I know we did, but I miss going with you. We haven't been on an adventure in a long time. Please? I promise I won't say anything. Pinky promise."

Mom didn't like to take me with her on any of her shopping excursions anymore for fear of me telling Grandma or Grandpa. I'd made that mistake once while we were staying with them and was, in return, banned from going with her. After a fun trip to the thrift store together one Saturday afternoon, I had told Grandma that we'd gone shopping and got a lot of cool new things for our house when we got it back.

"Annie, you've got to be kidding me." Grandma had sighed as she looked up at the ceiling, shaking her head in disbelief. "Where are you going to put all of this? I can't even park my car in the garage anymore because it's filled with all your new stuff," she'd said, putting the word "stuff" in air quotes.

Mom had glared at me. I knew I was in trouble. Why was I always opening my big mouth?

"Mom, we'll be out of your hair soon enough, and you can have the luxury of parking your car in the garage again soon," Mom had said. "Jesus Christ. I'm just trying to get us some things so that when we move out, the walls in our new place won't be bare and Dominic will feel comfortable. I don't want to dump a bunch of money all at once, so I'm trying to get it slowly. I didn't realize what an inconvenience that would be to you," Mom had said, kicking off her shoes. She'd stomped over to the staircase and up to our room.

I'd looked at Grandma and told her I was sorry, but she didn't say anything in response. I'd upset both of them. I had followed Mom's cue and made my way up the stairs, my hands too full of bags to hold onto the rails for balance, and teetered along the spirals, hoping I wouldn't fall backward.

"Mom, I'm really sorry," I'd said, tossing the bags onto the bed. "I didn't know she'd get mad."

"Well, she did."

"I'm really sorry." I had begun to cry.

"I know you are, Dominic," she'd said. "Here, just put the bags in the closet for now. Make sure you can still close the doors because if Grandma comes in here, I don't want to hear about it. I'm going to take a nap, so you need to go find something to do."

* * *

Around the middle of March the next year, Mom found us a rental not far from Grandma and Grandpa's house. It was a small seven-hundred-square-foot two-bedroom apartment. I loved it. The day we found our new apartment, Mom bought us beds at the thrift store so we'd each have our own, and Rachel, the student counselor, donated a spare futon she no longer needed.

Every day after work, Mom placed her shoes neatly by the door and hung her coat in the coat closet. She put her work bag, purse, and keys on a desk she'd purchased at a rummage sale the day after we'd moved in so they would never get lost. Every day, the garbage was taken out, and if we used any dishes or utensils, they were immediately washed. Our clean clothes were put away as soon as they were removed from the dryer. Our new life at the apartment was what I had always dreamed of.

"Dominic!" Mom yelled at me one day after I had come in from playing outside.

I quickly glanced to the side of me and knew why she was mad. I'd taken my coat off and thrown it on the chair by the desk instead of hanging it in the closet like I was supposed to.

"What have I told you about your coat?" she demanded.

"That I need to hang it up in the closet," I said, looking down at my feet.

"Over and over again I say this to you. I need help to keep the house clean. That was the problem before. You wouldn't help me."

"I'm sorry, Mom," I said, grabbing my coat to hang it up.

"God, I am so friggin' sick of hearing you say you're sorry. *Show* me you're sorry. Don't keep saying it if you're just going to keep doing the things you're sorry for. Got it?"

"I won't forget next time."

"You better not. And I mean it. Or you know what happens?"

"Yes," I said, "we'll get in trouble."

"That's right. This isn't our house. You need to remember that. I don't own it like I did the last one. We can't just let things get messy, or we'll get in trouble and get kicked out. We'll have to live in the car, out in the cold. Is that what you want?" she asked accusingly.

"No, of course not. I'll do better from now on. I promise."

* * *

That summer, I was able to go to camp for the first time. It was called Camp Marlee, and Tommy and I were going together.

Mom and I were driving back from Tommy's house on a sunny June evening. I loved when it was still bright outside close to bedtime. The sunshine made me happy, no matter what was going on. "Thank you so, so, so, so much for letting me go," I said.

I had just turned eleven and felt overjoyed that I was finally old enough to go to an overnight camp. Tommy's mom gave Mom the papers to turn in for the camp and said she would pay for both me and Tommy to go. It was a week-long camp, and I had never been away from Mom for that long, but I couldn't wait.

"You're welcome," Mom said. She smiled a thin, no-teeth smile at me. "I could use the break anyway. It'll be nice to get you out of my hair for a week."

I chuckled and agreed with her. I knew I caused her a lot of stress. I was happy she was going to get some alone time. She deserved it.

My week at camp was a blast. The whole camp was laid out in a giant circle. There was a big open field where all of us campers gathered every morning to watch the raising of the flag and to say the Pledge of Allegiance. Across from the field was the cafeteria where we sat for all three meals of the day. Breakfast was at seven in the morning, lunch at noon, and dinner at six o'clock in the evening. The food was served in the same fashion as it was at school. Stand in line, wait your turn, pick up your heavy plastic tray, then make your way to the cafeteria workers who slop your food down onto it. Although most of the kids didn't agree with me, I enjoyed every meal. I thought all the food was delicious, particularly the fried chicken.

To the left of the cafeteria were all the boys' cabins and to the right were the girls'. Our cabin consisted of four sets of bunk beds and one bathroom. Our camp counselor, Carter, slept in the loft upstairs. Tommy and I shared a bunk. On the opposite side of the cabins was Lake Marlee, a man-made lake that the camp owned. They had paddle boats and a slide that we could go down, as long as we were wearing our life jackets.

The sandy beach area by the lake was a lot of fun, too. They had all kinds of toys we could use to build sandcastles, with a contest at the end of the day to vote on who built the best one. We didn't win anything other than bragging rights, but that didn't make it any less fun. There were metal detectors we were allowed to use to look for buried treasure, and goggles in case we wanted to go in the water to hunt for treasures, too.

I had some of the most fun of my childhood and made a lot of good memories during that week at Camp Marlee. Tommy and I were inseparable as usual, but we made a lot of new friends, too. I took a sign language course, and I learned how to sign the words to the song, "Mary Had a Little Lamb." The camp had a craft cabin that I liked a lot. I made Mom some stuff I knew she would like and could use, like a keychain, a picture frame, and a sign for the house that said "Bless This Mess." That one was sort of an inside joke that I knew only she would get. I couldn't wait to get back to give it to her.

* * *

A little over a year after the fire, our house was reconstructed, and we were able to move back in. I didn't want to leave our apartment; I loved it there. But I trusted Mom when she said that we would take the skills we'd obtained at the apartment and utilize them in this house as well. We both pinky promised that we would work hard every single day to keep the house clean, just like at the apartment. She gave me her word that we would live our lives like a landlord could come in any day for a surprise inspection.

Walking into our "new" house for the first time was surreal. It was empty. Not a single thing in there. I didn't realize how big our house truly was when it was just the two of us and nothing more inside. The only thing we brought with us on that first trip was the "Bless This Mess" sign I had made Mom. She had laughed and hugged me when I showed it to her after coming back from camp.

"It's perfect," she'd said. "Couldn't have thought up a better sign if I tried."

I'd felt proud that I had made Mom laugh, something she didn't seem to do too often anymore.

I swung the front door to the new house wide open. It moved freely, and I didn't have to squeeze in; nothing blocked my way. The house smelled of fresh paint, one of my favorite smells to this day. Something about that smell just takes me back to that moment when I was happy and hopeful.

Not wanting to muddy up the brand-new, unstained, cream-colored carpet, I took off my shoes and wandered through the living room and into the empty dining area. The soft, plush carpet felt good under my feet. My grandparents' house had tile floors, and the apartment had wooden vinyl flooring. I had forgotten what nice carpet felt like; carpet that wasn't damaged or flattened by the burdening weight of too many possessions.

To my left was the kitchen. The linoleum was the whitest

and brightest linoleum I'd ever seen. I got down on my hands and knees to touch and examine it. It was cold and slick with subtle designs in each of its squares. The new appliances were white and shiny and, more importantly, clean. Opening the fridge and not smelling anything rotting, not seeing any food spills or any mold, brought tears to my eyes. Off the side of the kitchen and through an archway was the hallway to our bathroom and two bedrooms.

The bathroom smelled fresh, that new house smell, the smell of nothing. No one had ever used it and what a beautiful non-smell that was. There was no garbage, the toilet was new and unclogged with a lid on the back of it unlike our old one. There were no stains of yellow or brown in the bowl. There was no ring around the tub; it was all one color. The countertops and sink weren't covered in old toothpaste or dust and grime. The windowsill was smooth and not littered with dead flies and moths.

I moseyed on to my bedroom next, bracing myself because I was starting to feel a little faint. I was overwhelmed. In my room, the first thing I noticed was that I had closet doors again. My old ones had been broken by falling boxes that had pushed on and warped the cheap hollow wood. I laid down in the middle of the floor, looking up at the ceiling that was no longer covered in spider webs. The ceiling light wasn't made darker because it was filled with dead bugs that just wanted to get close to it.

I'm not too sure of many other times I was as happy as I was that day. The beauty that was this fresh new house around us was almost too much. But I had hope for us. I knew that Mom and I would do what we had to do to preserve our new house. We would take care of it. I just knew it.

"Are you excited, Dominic?" Mom asked, jolting me back to reality. With nothing impeding her, I didn't hear her come down the hall.

"I love it," I said. "It's amazing."

"We're going to take care of it this time, right?"

"Pinky promises can't be broken, remember?" I held my pinky in the air and smiled at her.

Her eyes were kind as she said, "How you feel right now, son, is how you should every day. We're going to make sure that we get to keep feeling this way, right?"

"Right, Mom," I said. "I love you."

"I love you, too, Dom. Now, let's go find somewhere to hang this," she said, holding up the sign I had made for her.

We donated the futon from Rachel, and Mom decided she wanted to splurge and spend her hard-earned money on a brand-new couch and a brand-new dining set instead of buying used. She said we deserved something nice and new for once. The table was round with black legs and a light brown wooden top. There were four chairs; they were black and matched the table, and much more importantly, they were clean and unbroken. Mom said she was going to start cooking more at the house to save money, and that we would eat dinner together at the table every night.

The new couch Mom had bought was a dark forest green and velvety microfiber. She even got a matching love seat to go with it. Mom said the love seat could be mine, that way we would each have our own special places to sit. That made me feel important. No more floor for me. But even if I did have to sit on the floor, it would have been okay. It was clean, the carpet was soft and able to be seen, and I wouldn't be sitting on anything but the carpet itself.

Uncle Kai, Aunt Gretchen, Grandma, and Grandpa all came over that day to help us move everything from the apartment to the house and to help move everything Mom had collected and stored in my grandparents' garage. Uncle Kai and Aunt Gretchen bought me another new desk. My room in the apartment was too small for a desk, and I was ecstatic to have one again. They also bought me my own TV and DVD player, and after we were all moved in, they took me to Hastings to pick out some movies that would be all mine. Hastings was even having a buy two get one free sale on their used movies, so I was able to get quite a few.

My relatives continued to come over a couple times a week after we were all moved in. *Knock, knock, knock.* I jumped up from my loveseat and peered through the blinds. It was Grandma.

"Grandma!" I shouted, excited to see her, knowing I didn't have to shut off the lights or be quiet. I didn't have to hide. I could open the door and let her in with no fear of the repercussions. I know now, of course, that they weren't really coming by for friendly visits. They were checking on us. Checking to see how things with the house were going. Were we keeping it clean? Was Mom still shopping? She was. But for a while, she found the motivation to keep up on the cleaning and put things where they belonged.

After a few months of the house being clean and things seeming to be going well, the times between visits became greater and greater. At first it was Grandma or both Grandma and Grandpa stopping by for a visit during the week and Uncle Kai and Aunt Gretchen stopping by on the weekends. They didn't usually stay long; there was invariably some sort of tension in the air between them and Mom. So instead of staying at the house, they would take me places with them. Even if it was just grocery shopping, I loved spending every moment with them that I could. They would come in the house, help me get my coat on, and off we'd go. When they dropped me off, they'd walk me to the door and watch me go in.

Eventually it became once a week visits, then every other week, then once a month, alternating every other time between Uncle Kai and Auntie Gretchen, and Grandma and Grandpa.

"My goodness, Annie. You knew I was coming over. You couldn't even be bothered to vacuum?" Grandma asked one Saturday morning during her routine visit. "I know I haven't been by in a while, but how did this many crumbs and gunk get into the carpet in that time? Have you not vacuumed at all since I was last here?" Grandma was visibly flustered.

She was right. We hadn't vacuumed in quite some time,

and the house was a bit of a mess, but nothing like it was before. We still had it under control.

"Mom, can't you just be happy for me that we've managed to keep it this clean for as long as we have?" Mom asked. "You really have to sit here and nitpick the carpet not being vacuumed? Way to make me feel good. Thanks."

"Annie, it's not just the carpet," Grandma said. "I mean, come on. The sink is full of dishes, your garbage needs taken out. Your laundry is piled as high as the back of the loveseat over there. I thought the loveseat was Dominic's? Now, it's taken over by clothes like before."

"I'm fine, Grandma, look," I said, showing her how I still had half of it to sit on. "I don't need the whole thing. I still have this big spot to myself."

Grandma gave me a sympathetic look, tilting her head to the side. "Annie," said Grandma, "don't do this. Please. It's Saturday, you both have the day off. Get it clean."

"Mom, I'm tired," Mom said. "I had a bad day at work yesterday, and I don't feel like cleaning today. I just want to relax after a long week at work. We'll clean tomorrow. Is that all right with you?"

"Whatever you need to do, I guess. I'm going to go now. Your father and I are going to an early dinner with some friends tonight. So I guess I'm going to go get ready for that since we're done here."

"Yep. Have fun," Mom said. "Tell Grandma bye, Dominic."

"Bye, Grandma," I said, hugging her tight, wishing she would take me with her.

"Bye, Dominic," she said. Grandma slipped out the front door, quietly shutting it behind her. I jumped up to watch her through the window as she got in her gunmetal gray sedan and drove off.

"So tomorrow we'll clean?"

"I don't know, Dom. We'll see," Mom said, frustrated. "I have a headache, and I'm too tired to worry about that right now. Don't hold your breath."

"Why?"

"Why? Because I have to work the next day. Do you think I want to spend the last day I have to relax before a whole week at work cleaning?"

Somewhere along the road, things got rough again. Mom was constantly in a bad mood, and it became too hard for her to have to clean up after herself. No matter how hard I tried to help or to get her up and going, it was a task that I just could not undertake on my own. Then one day, about four months since anyone had last visited, someone knocked on the door. I jumped. It had been so long since I'd heard that sound, and I knew that whoever was on the other side could not be allowed in.

"Mom, what do we do?" I asked, panicked.

"Quiet," Mom snapped. "Hurry, go shut off the light and see who it is."

I crawled on my hands and knees over to the light switches by the door, my arms sinking up to my elbows in the black bags, and flipped them to the downward position. Sweating and wracked with nerves, in disbelief that I was having to feel these emotions once again, I climbed slowly onto the arm of the loveseat, careful not to disturb the new hoard so nothing would fall. I didn't want to risk any noise that would indicate we were at the house and aware that someone was knocking. Peering through the once-white window blinds that were now so caked with dust they looked almost black, I saw Uncle Kai and Aunt Gretchen.

"Mom," I whispered, "it's Uncle and Auntie. What do you want me to do?"

"You know what to do," Mom said. "Just be quiet and ignore them. They'll go away in a minute."

"But I want to talk to them. It's been a long time. Please? I'll just do like before and tell them I was in the bathroom or something when they start to leave. Please, Mom?" I hadn't seen them in months and missed them more than I'd realized.

Mom scoffed. "Fine."

I watched as Uncle Kai and Aunt Gretchen turned away from the door to take the steps back toward their car at the bottom of the driveway. I hopped down from the arm of the loveseat and unlocked the door, steadily opening it only a few inches, just barely enough for me to squeeze through. They looked back at me, smiling. I stepped out the front door, shutting it firmly behind me. Their smiles faded. They knew.

15

Around April of the next year, my family decided I needed to go stay with Uncle Kai and Aunt Gretchen for a while. I didn't know how long that while would be, and no one could give me a definite answer when I asked. I loved those two, but they weren't Mom. Grandma had invited us over for dinner one Friday evening, and that's when it happened.

"What are they doing here?" Mom asked, pointing at Uncle Kai and Aunt Gretchen when we walked through the front door. "I thought it was just going to be the four of us?"

"Well," Grandma said slowly, "I thought it would be fun to have my whole family here. I just love you all so much, I wanted to see all of you, you know?"

Mom furrowed her brow and sat at the dining room table, away from everyone else in the living room gathered around the TV, watching a movie. I didn't follow her.

"Dominic, sweetie," Grandma said. "Why don't you go upstairs and watch a movie, okay? We just put a TV with a built in VCR up there, isn't that fun?"

"Yes," I said. "But why can't I watch this movie with you guys?"

"Well, we just need to talk for a few minutes. We'll pause the movie, and you can watch it with us as soon as we're done, sound good?"

"Sounds good." I ran up the staircase two at a time, seeing if it was faster to skip steps. It wasn't. Grandma had put some Disney movies up there for me. I switched on the TV and put *Aladdin* in the VCR.

"Are you fucking crazy?" I heard Mom scream about ten minutes later. "You can't take him from me. The fuck's wrong with you guys?"

I turned the TV down and tiptoed to the top of the staircase, trying to stay hidden so no one would know I was eavesdropping.

"Annie, honey, you know things are not good for either of you right now," Grandma said.

"Things are fine, Mother," said Mom.

"We know they're not, Annie," Uncle Kai said. "We're not stupid. We weren't even allowed inside the house last time we came over."

"Yeah, well, that's because I don't like being around you guys. Dominic wanted to see you. I didn't. So I told him if he wanted to talk to you, he needed to go outside."

"Annie, are you serious? You really think we all believe your bullshit lies?" asked Uncle Kai.

"I'm not lying, dammit!" Mom screamed, slamming her fist in a loud thump on top of the table.

"Annie," Aunt Gretchen said. "We only—"

"Why the hell are you talking to me?" Mom cut her off. "Someone please tell me why this bitch is talking to me. I want nothing to do with you, Gretchen. You think just because you don't have kids of your own that gives you the right to take mine?"

"Annie, come on, that's unfair and uncalled for," Grandma said.

"Yeah, it is," said Uncle Kai. "The biggest bitch at this goddamn table has the nerve to call my wife a bitch."

"Kai, that's enough," Grandpa said, the first time I'd heard him speak all night.

"That's enough? Really, Dad?" Uncle Kai said. "She can sit here and call my wife a bitch, but I can't speak up? You know, this is how it's always been. Annie the baby gets away with everything and gets to do whatever the fuck she wants. Ever since we were kids. Well, you know what? Not this time."

"Not this time? What's that supposed to mean?" Mom asked.

"It means, I'm taking Dominic. I don't give a flying fuck what you say. You've never been able to take care of him. Three days after he was born, what happened, Ann?"

I heard Mom start to sob.

"Answer me. What happened?" Uncle Kai yelled.

Mom kept crying, refusing to speak.

"I'll tell you what happened. You couldn't...no, *wouldn't* take care of him. You let him sit in his shitty sagging diaper all day. He sat so long in his own filth that his little bottom was raw and blistered. He was in so much pain, he couldn't even eat. The only thing he could do was cry, but you wanted nothing to do with him. He had to stay with me and Gretch for a month before you even tried to see him again."

Was that true? I lived with them when I was a baby?

"And the house was disgusting then, too. When you could be bothered to change him, you just tossed his diapers all over the place. Your house smelled like a dirty litter box. But I never imagined it would get as bad as it has. I never thought you'd stoop to this level of filth."

"I was depressed, Kai," Mom finally spoke up.

"I know," he said. "And we got you help, and helped you clean the house back then, too, and you got him back. But things are still bad, and they're only getting worse. Is this the life you really want for him? He has to lie all the time. He's afraid and anxious all the time. All because of you. You did this to him. You're hurting him, and all you can think is 'Oh, poor me. Everyone's ganging up on me.' Think of your son for once, Ann. Just this one fucking time, think of someone other than your goddamn self."

"You're not taking my son from me," Mom spat.

"We are, Annie," Grandma said gently. "He's going to stay with your brother for just a little while until we can help you get the house clean again, all right? The sooner it gets done, the sooner he gets to come back and live with you."

"No," Mom said, her voice shaky.

"If you won't do this willingly," Uncle Kai said, "I'll call Child Protective Services and they can handle it."

I didn't get to go back to the house with Mom that night. I left with Uncle Kai and Aunt Gretchen. I didn't see or talk to Mom again until that Monday at school.

The three of us had a lot of fun together. Auntie and I baked cookies a lot, mostly chocolate chip and snickerdoodle because they were Uncle Kai's favorite. Every morning, Uncle Kai made me breakfast. I used to only eat breakfast at the school, which mostly consisted of toaster pastries and muffins. Not the healthiest of breakfast choices, but better than nothing. Uncle Kai liked to make scrambled eggs with toast, or he would fry up some bacon with the eggs. Sometimes, he boiled red potatoes and topped them with freshly shredded cheese and homemade country gravy.

At night, Aunt Gretchen cooked dinner for the three of us before Uncle Kai got off work, since she got back before he did. She let me help whenever I wanted. My favorite thing to help with was enchiladas. I loved shredding the cheese and rolling the corn tortillas. I didn't like helping with anything that had meat in it because touching raw meat made me feel sick. The look and smell reminded me of the rotting food I often saw at Mom's house.

My favorite meal of Aunt Gretchen's was her pulled pork sandwiches. She cooked the pork until it was so tender it fell apart, adding in her made-from-scratch brown sugar barbecue sauce. She let me butter the brioche buns and set them in the oven until they were just the right mix of soft and crispy.

For the first month after leaving Mom's house, everyone would go over on the weekends to help clean. But after that, Mom didn't want them there anymore. She said she would get it clean on her own time and no longer wanted their help. She said they were causing her too much anxiety and she couldn't deal with it any longer, claiming she was throwing up every day from the stress and losing an unhealthy amount of weight.

From then on out, every Saturday, I would go to the house to spend time with Mom, just the two of us. Mom wouldn't speak to Uncle Kai or Aunt Gretchen, so she relayed any messages she had for them through me or my grandparents.

Grandma called one afternoon when I was there with Mom. I was miserable. Mom was in her usual bad mood, and even though she promised me she was working on the house, it never looked any better. In fact, there seemed to be more new things each time I came by.

"How's the house coming along?" Grandma asked.

I could hear everything she was saying because Mom had lost the phone and had to use the speaker on the landline receiver to talk to anyone.

"It's coming along just fine, Mom. Isn't it, Dominic?" Mom waved me over, giving me a look that said, "You better tell her everything's fine or else."

"Yeah, Grandma," I lied. "It's really looking great. We're just taking a little break right now and watching some TV."

"Okay, honey, I'll see you tonight. Uncle Kai's bringing you over to my house for dinner. You still coming Annie? I bought your favorite pie," she said in singsong.

"Actually, no," Mom said.

"What, why?"

"I'm just really not feeling well. I have cramps and diarrhea, and I was throwing up again this morning. All that on top of all the work we did here today. It's just a lot. So I think I'll have to take a rain check, sorry."

"Well, feel better then. Talk to you later," Grandma said, rushing off the phone, seemingly annoyed.

"Bye," Mom said.

I heard the click as Grandma hung up without saying goodbye back to her.

I didn't bother to ask Mom why she'd lied to Grandma.

I knew it would only upset her mood further.

"Dominic, turn the TV down, okay?" Mom said. "I'm going to take a nap."

"What, Mom, why?" I whined. "I only have three hours with you today, and it's already been an hour. So we only have two left, and then I won't get to see you except at school for another week."

"I'm tired," Mom said.

"Please, Mom? Can't you nap after I leave? I wanted to play a game, or we could just keep watching TV. Whatever you want."

"Whatever I want? Well, it's not whatever I want because I just told you what I want. Now, if you'll please, please just leave me be. I'm going to take a nap. And I'm not going to say it again. Turn down the TV like I asked."

I didn't push the issue further. I knew there was no sense in continuing to try and negotiate. She didn't feel well, and there was no changing her mind. I turned the television down, deciding that maybe now was a good time to learn lip reading. After Mom fell asleep, the only sound in the house aside from her slow, steady breathing was the right-on-schedule, every-ten-seconds beeping that came from the smoke detector; a warning that it was time to change the batteries. I gave up on the lip reading and turned to watch out the window, hoping somehow Uncle Kai could sense I wanted to leave and would be there any minute to pick me up. I counted seven hundred and twenty warnings while I waited.

* * *

"How are things at Uncle Kai's house?" Mom asked at our visit the next weekend. She said the words "Uncle Kai" in a mocking tone.

"They're okay," I said. "I miss you, though."

"You better." She smiled. "Do they say anything about me?"

"No. They just ask how you're doing."

"Do they ask about the house?"

"Yeah."

"And? What do you say?"

"Nothing. That it looks fine."

"Good. I hope so. You don't want them to get mad at me even more than they already are, do you?"

"No, of course not," I said.

"Do you like it there?" she asked.

"Yeah, it's fun."

"Is it better than here?"

I shook my head no.

"You always thought they were so cool. You always wanted to stay the weekends with them instead of here with me. I'm sure you're just living it up over there. You liked their house better, and now you get to live there."

My stomach started to hurt. I didn't like where this was going. It wasn't my choice to leave her.

"You get to start over, living in a clean house, leaving me here. Alone with this mess. Which you helped make, by the way."

"I don't like their house better. And we can clean our house, Mom. I'm here to help. Come on, let's start now," I said. I grabbed an empty black garbage bag and began to fill it with trash.

Mom sat straight up in her spot on the couch. "Don't you touch my things!" she screamed, a thunderous sound that made me tremble in fear, a fear so deep I was afraid I might wet my pants. "Don't ever touch my stuff."

"I just wanted to help you." My lip quivered.

"I said, don't touch my stuff. I don't care what you wanted to do. Don't touch my things."

"I wanted to be helpful and clean up so I can come back and live with you again."

"Oh, you want to come back? You sure don't act like it when you're over there, having the time of your life with those two, while I'm here alone."

"I'm sorry, Mom." I sat on the floor, put my knees to my chest, and rested my head atop them. Silently, so as not to upset Mom more than I already had, I cried.

In June, when my twelfth birthday came round, I told Mom I didn't want any gifts, I just wanted to move back in with her. On my last visit to the house the week before my birthday party at Grandma and Grandpa's, I was devastated as I trekked through the house and saw that not only had things gotten progressively worse week after week, but my bedroom was now filled as well. I no longer had room to play, or even room to sleep on my own bed.

But it didn't matter. I just wanted to come back. More than that, I wanted her to care enough about the situation to actually do something to make that happen. I never understood why it seemed like shopping and all her things meant more to her than I did.

In July, even though nothing had changed with Mom, Uncle Kai and Aunt Gretchen could see how despondent I had become. Maybe they shouldn't have, but they let me move back in with Mom. I was elated. Since I had moved out, I'd had a constant nagging feeling that I'd betrayed her somehow by enjoying my time with them, time without her. For a couple months after I moved back, Uncle Kai and Aunt Gretchen still stopped by every once in a while to check on me, even though they couldn't come in the house. They knew the routine. They knocked, then retreated down the steps and into the yard to wait for me to come out to visit.

Grandma and Grandpa didn't come by anymore, but they called every now and again to check up on us. Each time, Mom and I would lie. I don't know if they believed us or not, but they never said anything or asked to see it for themselves. As time went on, the visits and calls became fewer and fewer and eventually stopped altogether. No one called. No one visited. No one bothered us anymore. It was just me and Mom. Just the way she wanted it.

16

Over the coming months, I became increasingly jealous of Tommy. I no longer liked going to his house the way I used to. I enjoyed my time with him and his family while I was there. But when I had to go back to my house, stepping through that door into my own private hell was like a punch in the gut.

Tommy's mom frequently invited me over for dinner. I always found an excuse as to why I couldn't go, and I no longer stayed the night on the weekends. His house, without fail, had some blissful smell to it every time I was there. Sometimes, it was fresh laundry or cleaning supplies that, while strong and overpowering to some, was a smell of happiness to me. Sometimes, it smelled like his mom's cooking. Her delicious homemade dinners were a smell I didn't get to experience myself at my own house. The bulbs in their house were never burnt out for months or years on end; they were replaced as soon as it was needed.

I didn't want to be around any of them anymore. I didn't want to be reminded of everything I didn't and wouldn't ever have. Our fridge had broken again and smelled of the old food that still lived inside of it. There was, of course, no way to fix it or get a new one without anyone finding out Mom and I were still keeping secrets, so in the house it stayed. The sink was filled with dirty dishes that were overflowing onto the countertops. They were covered in rotten and moldy food, maggots crawling freely among them. The white cupboard next to the sink now looked black from the mass amount of flies and gnats that gathered there.

Tommy's bathroom was free of dust, the garbage empty, the toilet water clear. His mom kept lemon-scented oil diffusers in there, so it would always smell citrusy clean. My bathroom smelled like literal shit and old menstrual pads. Our toilet was perpetually clogged just as it had always been before, so the toilet paper again needed to be thrown in the garbage.

I will never forget the smell of used menstrual pads and tampons. They built up in our bathroom for months and months before Mom would decide enough was enough and browbeat me into cleaning them up for her.

I would gag as I collected them by the handful, trying to breathe through my mouth. If I threw up, it had to be in the bathroom sink or the tub, sometimes into the bag I was holding that contained all the used pads and tampons. I couldn't throw up into the toilet because the toilet water and waste were almost to the top of the bowl. I'd made that mistake once, and the wastewater splashed back into my face as the vomit hit it. The toilet would sit full for weeks until one of us, usually me, would summon the courage to finally plunge it.

Tommy had his own bedroom with a comfy bed to sleep in. My room was full again, which meant I had the living room floor. I had to sleep on top of clothes and garbage that I no longer had the optimism to see as bean bags. I didn't enjoy waking up in the middle of the night to VHS tapes or broken picture frames jamming me in my back or sides, and I could no longer see past that.

Sometimes I wished I'd never left Uncle Kai's house. I'd wished I was strong enough to not let the guilt trips from Mom get to me and I'd stayed where I was happy. But I rarely saw them those days. Would I even be welcome if I tried to go back? What if they said no? Would things with Mom get worse? I didn't know the answer to any of those questions, so I didn't bother trying. For me, the possibility that they could say no and the repercussions that could follow were more than enough reason for me to keep quiet.

Mom wouldn't take out the garbage herself; that was all up to me, but there was just so much of it. It was never ending. Mom refused to take any of it to the dump or pay for the city waste management to pick it up, but she knew she didn't want it all in the house, either. How she decided what garbage was worth keeping in the house and which needed to be thrown outside is still a mystery to me.

The task of taking out the trash was an arduous one. We used to throw it all into the garage, but the house was almost full from the floor to the eight-foot ceiling with garbage and other worthless things Mom had stored. Instead, I would have to figure out which door I was currently able to fit through with a garbage bag in hand. There was nowhere for the trash to go, so Mom told me to dump it to the side of the steps outside the front door, piling it higher and higher until it looked bad enough for the neighbors to call the city to complain. If neither of the doors could accommodate me and a bag, I needed to toss it from the kitchen window onto the ground below, where the garbage stayed for months, rotting and slowly decomposing, birthing new baby flies every day.

We would quite often receive notices from the city to clean it up or face a fine and have to repay them the cost of getting someone out there to clean it for us. At that point, we would have to borrow a truck from a friend, buy some rubber gloves, and try to get it all into the truck and off to the dump. The bags were usually soaked and heavier than they started. Cold, wet trash would crash at my feet as the bags broke apart and collapsed under their own weight. Unfortunately, it seemed ten times more trash came in than ever went out. Mom said it was embarrassing to have to take out bag after bag, showing the neighbors our never-ending supply.

"And you think *I* like it?" I asked, annoyed at her for bullying me into doing the things she wouldn't. From time to time, I would refuse to take any of it out just so she would have to face the same shame I did.

"You drive me up the fucking wall, you know that, Dominic?" Mom said after I refused. She dragged one of the overstuffed bags to the kitchen, opened the window, and tried to shove it through, grunting from the strain its heaviness put on her.

* * *

Our backyard was incredibly unkempt and cause for a lot of complaints as well. It wasn't green or even grass at all. It was full of tall, thick, brown weeds that looked and felt like straw. They hurt to step or play on. They grew to become a four-foot-tall jungle before the city would send a warning to get it under control or face a fine. Mom would ask me to mow, and most of the time I would, especially because I knew it was something she would never do herself. But every once in a while, I'd refuse.

"I don't see why I'm the only one that has to do anything around here," I said.

"You're not even close to being the only one. Don't even start that crap with me," Mom said.

"Start what? It's the truth. It's bullshit," I said, taking a sip from my soda.

Mom slapped the can out of my hand and got a mere inch from my face. She poked me in the chest with her finger and said, "Don't you ever talk to me like that. Do you hear me, Dominic? If you don't start acting right, I'm going to have to talk with Grandpa about you. You got it?"

"Got it." I relented. I felt guilty. I did need to contribute more.

She glared at me with squinty-eyed skepticism and said, "I just don't get you."

"What do you mean?"

"You're like…evil."

That hurt a lot. I'd had my fair share of insults hurled my

way, but that one right there hurt more than any of them.

Mowing our back yard was one of the most embarrassing things I have had to do in my life, and I don't exaggerate at all when I say this. My neighbors would grab a beer and sit on their back patios, watching me mow, laughing and mocking me. I couldn't hear them above the mower, but I could see them. It took roughly an hour to get it all done, but it felt like so much longer. Time barely moved while I was out there being humiliated. Every second was grueling.

* * *

"Why can't you cook dinner for us?" I asked on one of our regular nightly drives to a fast food restaurant in town. "Tommy's mom cooks for him every night." I immediately regretted saying that as we pulled into the parking lot of the restaurant. Mom hated when I talked about Tommy's mom, but I pushed my luck. "I'm sick of hamburgers," I said.

"Dominic, please. I don't feel like going grocery shopping. Besides, we don't even have any dishes to cook or eat with. Are you going to wash the dishes?" Mom asked.

"But Tommy's mom doesn't make him do the dishes. I could help you, though. Let's do them together."

"You know what I should have named you instead of Dominic?"

"Um, what?" I asked, confused by the sudden change in subject.

"I should have named you Minerva," she said.

"What, why?"

"Because, you're getting on my nerves, Minerva," she said, raising her voice. "Now, stop asking me to cook. I don't feel like it right now. If you're sick of burgers, get something else. Get chicken nuggets, or chili, or something."

"How come Tommy's mom keeps their house clean for them, but you don't keep ours clean?"

Mom sucked in a deep breath and gripped the steering

wheel. Her knuckles turned white. Oh, shit. I'd really done it that time.

"You know what, Dom?" Mom screamed in my face, so close I could feel her hot breath on me. "I don't give a fuck what Tommy's mom does. I'm sure Tommy is a good little boy, unlike you. I'm sure he listens when his mom tells him something, and I'm sure he doesn't incessantly pester her when she tells him no. I'm sure he isn't a little nuisance like you. So unless you want me to start wishing you were like Tommy, stop wishing I was like Tommy's mom."

She huffed, then gave a small chuckle as she said, "You know, when's the last time you took out the trash, huh? Or, or what about the last time you scrubbed the toilet? Huh? Can you tell me that, Dominic? When's the last time?"

I didn't have an answer for her. I truly didn't know. She didn't often scream at me like that. It was one of the most terrifying things I'd ever experienced. She did yell a lot. But that? That was something else entirely. I can still hear it.

"I'll just have a burger," I said, holding back tears. Tears would only make her angrier.

SON OF A HOARDER

17

The summer I turned thirteen, I lost my virginity—about a week before my thirteenth birthday, to be exact. Tommy and I had decided since it was so hot already that summer, we wanted to go down to the lake in town to hang out.

"Who's going to drive us?" I asked.

"I got my cousin, Brendan, to pick us up and drop us off. But we'll have to walk back. It's only a couple miles," Tommy said. "No biggie."

I had never met Brendan. He picked us up around noon, with Ludacris's "What's Your Fantasy" pounding through the speakers of his beat-up Toyota 4-Runner. The car smelled of motor oil and parts of the seats were ripped open, the yellow foam stuffing showing through the fabric coverings. Tommy said he was nineteen. I thought he looked much younger.

"You want a cigarette?" Brendan asked.

I had never smoked before; the thought never even crossed my mind. I looked at Tommy who shrugged but gave a look that said, "Yeah, let's try it."

"Yeah, sure," we both said. Brendan pulled a Camel out of the half empty pack that sat in the 4-Runner's center console and handed it to us to share.

"You got a lighter?" Tommy asked.

Brendan grabbed a hot pink BIC from the cup holder next to him. "Don't try to steal my lighter," he said. "Everyone's always stealing my lighters. I figured if I bought a pink one, no one would want it."

Tommy was the first to try the cigarette. He put the butt in his mouth and lit the other end. It turned orange, growing brighter as he inhaled his first ever drag.

"It's not so ba—" he started to say, only to be cut off by a violent cough that burst from his protesting lungs.

I laughed at him, but knew my turn was next. I put the butt in my mouth just like Tommy had. It was moist from his lips. I inhaled. It was disgusting. The smoke burned my throat. The smell was powerful. I coughed harder than I ever had before. But I wanted more. I took another drag, and this time, there was only a small cough.

Tommy and I shared the rest of the Camel. Taking turns, each of us becoming more accustomed to the act of smoking a cigarette until we could inhale and no coughs emerged. The high we felt after each and every drag, the light-headedness that accompanied each puff was intoxicating and addicting. Brendan bought us our own pack and our own lighter before he dropped us off.

The lake was packed full of people just as excited for the start of summer as we were. We found a place to sit on the overcrowded sand and looked around to see if we knew anyone there, and that's when I saw her. The hottest girl I'd ever seen, even hotter than Nadia and the centerfold. She had dark cherry-wood brown hair with honey-blonde highlights. The tan lines on her arms were visible from afar. She was wearing a denim mini skirt with a white tank top, the pink straps of her bikini tied around her neck. Her thin baby-oiled legs glistened in the sunlight. I punched Tommy on the arm.

"Dude, what the fuck?" he said. "Why'd you punch me?"

I pointed at the girl, standing there with her friend. "I want to talk to that girl," I said. "She's so fucking hot."

The two of us made our way over to them, trying to be inconspicuous. Her friend noticed us and made the first move instead.

"Hey, boys," she said as they sauntered over our way.

"Hey," Tommy and I both muttered anxiously at the same time, trying to look cool.

"I'm Libby," she said, "and this is Alex."

Alex, the one I had come to see in the first place, waved at me.

"Hi," Tommy said. "I'm Tommy, and this is Dominic." We both gave an awkward wave to the girls.

"How old are you guys?" Libby asked.

"Thirteen," I said.

"I'm thirteen," Tommy said. "He's almost thirteen." He punched me in the arm, revenge from my punching him earlier.

"Well, yeah, almost thirteen," I said, embarrassed. "My birthday's in a week."

"Ooh, you guys are young," she said, giggling.

"We're both fourteen," said Alex.

Tommy and I spent the day with Alex and Libby. We found a small trail behind the sandy beach, away from the rest of the people in town, and followed it to a spot where we could sit and talk in private. The two of them had considerably more experience with the opposite sex than we did, and they didn't try to hide that fact.

"Have you guys ever even kissed a girl?" Libby asked.

"Uh, no," I said, laughing nervously.

"I think maybe we can change that," she said, winking at Tommy. "Dominic, you know, Alex thinks you're hot."

Alex slapped her friend's side. "Libby," she squealed.

"What?" Libby laughed. "It's true."

I couldn't help but feel enlivened. I liked Alex. I smiled, trying not to show my excitement.

"You guys should kiss, then," said Libby.

"Yeah, go kiss her, Dom," Tommy said.

This was not how I wanted my first kiss to go, with both peer pressure and an audience. I looked at Alex, who looked down at the ground. She seemed to be as nervous as I was. Alex stood and put her hand out to help me up. Her fingernails were painted royal blue and matched her eyes. I reached for her hand, and her soft skin sent electric waves down my spine. She kept hold of my hand, and the two of us wandered away from Tommy and Libby, not saying a word to each other. When they were out of sight, we found a fallen tree to sit on.

"You don't really have to kiss me if you don't want to," Alex said.

"I want to," I said shyly. "Unless you don't want to. It's just, I don't know. I mean, you know?" I was stammering. "It's just, I'm nervous, I guess."

"Me too," she admitted. "I haven't really done as much stuff with guys as Libby has. I just said that to make you think I was cool."

"Do you want to kiss me?" I asked.

"Yeah." She smiled.

She looked intently into my eyes. She moved closer, looking down at my lips. I knew this was it. This was going to be my first kiss. I leaned into her and licked my lips. They felt dry. I didn't want our first kiss to be a chapped one. We both closed our eyes and tilted our heads to the right. Our mouths touched; hers was plump and satiny. She tasted like Lip Smackers. She parted her lips and slipped the tip of her tongue into my mouth, brushing it against mine before pulling away.

Hours later, after Tommy and Libby both needed to get back, Alex and I decided we didn't want to part just yet. Libby's dad picked her up and offered to give Tommy a ride as well. He gladly obliged, happy to not have to take the mile-long walk back to his house alone.

"It's getting dark," Alex said as the two of us moseyed around town together. "Do you need to get going, too?"

"Nah," I said, playing it cool. "My mom thinks I'm at Tommy's. She won't even bother to check. It's all good. What about you?"

She smiled. "No. My parents think I'm at Libby's."

"So what do you want to do, then?" I asked.

"I don't know. Let's just find somewhere to hang out for the night. Somewhere private?"

I gave her a knowing half-smile. Whatever Alex wanted to do, I wanted to do.

We found a spot in a field behind the grocery store where no one could see us. Although it was wide open, it was surrounded by trees that blocked the field from the view of the store and surrounding neighborhood. The store was closed, and there were no lights anywhere to be found. It was just the two of us. No one else existed that night. We talked about everything, really got to know each other.

"Do you live here in town?" she asked me.

"Yeah, actually. In that neighborhood over there," I said, pointing toward the area across from the grocery store. "Just on the other side of the train tracks. What about you?"

"No, not really. I mean, technically it's still considered Pleasantview, but it's like way out in the boonies. Like five miles that way," she said, gesturing toward the highway. "I hate it."

"Why?"

"Because it's hard to get to town. There's nothing to do out where I live. Libby kind of lives by me, so I go to her house sometimes. But if I want to get out of my house and away from my parents, it's really hard."

"I'm going to move some day. Really far away from this town and everyone in it," I said.

"Me too," she said. "I hate my parents."

"You do?" I was intrigued. I had never heard anyone admit that before.

"Yeah." She sighed. "My dad's an asshole. He yells at me all the time. He's always putting me down when I do something he doesn't like. Which could be anything, honestly. I swear, he doesn't like anything, so there's always some bullshit reason I need to get in trouble. He calls me names. Actually, this morning before me and Libby came into town, he called me a fat slut. And my fucking mom just sits there and lets him. She sees me crying and begging him to leave me alone, and she just keeps watching TV or crocheting her dumb-ass craft projects, pretending she doesn't know what's happening."

"Wow," was all I could manage. I didn't know what else to say. I was in awe. "I hate my mom, too," I blurted out.

"Yeah?" She looked up at me, hopeful that I would be able to relate to her.

"Yeah. She yells at me, too, sometimes. But...I don't know. She's just a bitch."

"Oh." Alex looked down at her lap.

"I mean, I don't know. It's more than that, I guess. I don't really know how to explain it."

"Try."

"Okay, well," I began, wondering if I should tell her the truth. "My house is really messy."

"Your house is messy?" She looked at me skeptically. "That's not so bad." She laughed. "My house gets messy sometimes, too. I think everyone's does, unless you have some, like, perfect OCD parents."

This was the problem I consistently had when trying to talk about the house to people. I didn't know how to explain it further. How do you even begin to describe something like what I lived in? How could someone who's never known that type of living situation understand?

"Hmm..." Alex said a moment later, eager to change the subject. "I think I know what will make us feel better."

"Oh yeah? What's that?" I asked.

"Let's have one of your smokes and then..." she trailed off, reaching into her pocket. "I have this." She pulled out a condom.

My eyes widened. I wasn't expecting that at all. But I wasn't going to turn her down, either. I smoked my cigarette slowly. I took long, deep pulls, delaying what was coming next and trying to calm my nerves.

"Are you a virgin?" Alex asked.

"Yeah," I said sheepishly, uncertain of whether or not that was something I should be embarrassed about. "Are you?"

"No." She seemed ashamed.

"We don't have to, you know." I was unsure if I even wanted to do it myself.

"No, I want to." She kissed my cheek.

"Me too."

When our cigarettes were burned down to the butt, we pushed them hard into the grass and flicked them into the cold dewy field.

"Lie down," Alex said.

I laid back. The grass dampened the back of my T-shirt. Alex crawled on top of me, straddling my legs. She unbuttoned my jeans and pulled them down, along with my boxers. I didn't need any help from her getting excited. I was already there. I put on the condom as she untied the straps of her bikini bottoms and pulled them off. She lifted her skirt, inching closer to me, then lowered herself onto my lap.

"I love you," I said when we were done no more than a minute later.

"No, you don't." Alex laughed. "Trust me, you'll forget all about me in a few days."

"No, I won't."

We laid down in the field, our clothes wet from the grass, and fell asleep in each other's arms. I awoke at sunrise the next morning and saw that Alex's eyes were already open. She was watching me.

"Good morning, star shine," she said.

"Good morning, beautiful."

She smiled a genuine smile. "I have to go," she said.

"Oh, okay. How are you getting back?"

"I'll just walk."

"I thought you said it was really far?"

"Yeah, it is. But I'll be fine. It's not a big deal. Nothing I haven't done before."

"Maybe I can try to get you a ride."

"No, it's okay, seriously. Don't worry about me."

"Well, can I at least get your number?"

"Here." She took a mini permanent marker, about the

size of her pinky finger, out of her skirt pocket and wrote her number on the back of my hand. "But if my dad answers, hang up. He doesn't like when I talk to guys."

"Okay. Well, bye, I guess?"

"Bye, Dominic."

Tommy ran outside when he saw me walking back to my house from the field that morning.

"Dude, you're just getting back?" he asked.

"Uh, yeah," I said. "How'd you even know I was out here?"

"I was in the kitchen and saw you. But anyway, what happened? Were you with Alex all night?"

"Yeah."

"And?"

"And you know how we like to fantasize about what it'll be like to lose our virginities?"

"Mm-hmm," he said, rubbing his hands together.

"Well, I don't have to fantasize anymore," I said, raising my eyebrows and smirking.

"Dude!" Tommy shouted, bouncing on the balls of his feet. "Are you joking right now?"

"Shh, don't make a scene." I laughed. "But no, I'm not joking."

"How? Well, like, what happened? I mean, how did it happen?"

"I don't know, we were just like, talking, and then all of a sudden, she pulled a condom out of her pocket."

"Whoa," Tommy said, dragging out the "oh" sound.

"Yeah, whoa. It was awesome, though."

"Did you get her number?"

"Yeah, but she said her dad doesn't like when guys call. So I might not get to talk to her."

"That sucks."

"Yeah. I think I love her," I said.

Tommy laughed the same way Alex had. "So…?"

"So what?"

"You know…" he trailed off. "Oh, come on. You're going to make me say it?"

"Yeah, I guess so. Because I don't know what you're asking." I chuckled, sensing where this was going.

"Ugh, fine. What was it like?"

"Like warm apple pie."

* * *

Although it wasn't the worst way to have lost my virginity, I wish it hadn't happened at that stage of my life. I was too young. Too young to understand the emotions that came with giving yourself to another person. Too young to understand that the real reason I wanted sex all the time after that and slept with anyone I could was because I was trying desperately to feel a real connection with someone. I enjoyed feeling wanted. I was trying to fill a bottomless void.

All I really wanted was to feel loved and cared about. I was reckless, and because of that, I did contract some sexually transmitted infections. Thank goodness they were easily curable. Had things been different, maybe I wouldn't have felt the need to do the things I did. Maybe I wouldn't have put my body through all that. I don't have the worst memories from that night, but they aren't ones I'm proud of, either. I never did see Alex again.

18

After my night with Alex, something in me changed. I realized how much I truly hated being at the house with Mom and how much I resented her for the way I grew up with the never-ending fear of someone finding out our secret or of disappointing her. The constant state of anxiety that I lived in took a toll on me emotionally. I started to rebel and act out, becoming this angry new version of myself that I didn't recognize. The happy child I once was didn't exist anymore. I was a shell of my former self, on auto-pilot, trying to make it through my days without feeling like I had nothing left to live for.

I wanted my room back. So one afternoon when Mom was at a staff meeting, I started moving the things in my bedroom that I felt didn't belong wherever they would fit. I lugged out bag after bag, pushing against Mom's bedroom door and shoving them inside. Eventually, everything I had piled in there fell against the back of the door and it would no longer open. Since I was unable to use her room as storage, I started hauling boxes into the kitchen and dining area. Anywhere that looked like it could hold at least one more mound of junk, I utilized.

Around three hours later, I had my bedroom cleared. My bed and desk were still there, but my bookshelf was broken and bowed under the weight of everything that had been stacked on it. I was going to make this space my own once again, whether Mom liked it or not. I deserved somewhere to go, someplace that was mine, someplace private. I didn't care what she felt. If she could throw her things into my room, I could throw them right back at her.

"What were you thinking?" Mom asked, livid after seeing what I had done. She frantically tottered about the house, trying to figure out where all her junk had been moved to. "How dare you?"

"How dare I? Really?" I said, chuckling. "Yeah, how dare I even think that I deserve somewhere comfortable to sleep at night, when I clearly have a messy living room floor for a bed. How dare I think that I should get to have my own space. How selfish of me."

"Look, obviously I know you're being sarcastic, Dom." She spat out "Dom" forcefully. "But you really are selfish."

"How? How am I selfish?" I was becoming irritated.

"Because. Because I had everything where I wanted it. I knew exactly where everything was in that room, and now it's just all over the place. You've made a mess of things."

"Bullshit. You did not know everything that was in there. You had everything where you wanted it? Do you have any idea how much trash was in there? Literal trash. And you're telling me that's where you wanted it? In my room? Really?"

"Well, maybe a little trash got mixed in."

"It wasn't a little. At least half of the crap I pulled out of there was trash."

"Oh, please," she said.

"Not 'oh, please,' Mom. It was."

"Well, what did you do with this so-called literal trash?"

"I put it where I put everything else."

"You couldn't even be bothered to at least throw the trash outside? You just left it in the house?"

"Yeah, I did."

"Ugh, of course you did. Whatever. Look, I'm what I would call an organized hoarder."

"Oh yeah?" I said, intrigued by how she was planning to justify the mess.

"Yes. So what if I collect stuff and go shopping a lot? Okay, lots of people do. Even clean freaks lose things, sometimes. Maybe I do go overboard a little. Or maybe if we had a bigger house, it wouldn't be a problem. But I can't afford that right now."

"You'd just fill that up, too." I didn't want to hear her excuses anymore.

"No, I wouldn't. And anyway, I know where things are in this house. You can't just move them whenever you feel like it. How am I supposed to find them now?"

"What specifically in my room did you need that now you might not be able to find? I want to know. Because if you're just going to stand here yelling at me when there really isn't anything you can think of, then I'm done here."

"I don't know why you get so upset, Dom," said Mom. "I really don't get it. At least you have a house. You could be homeless. I'm sure there are plenty of homeless people out there that would be more than happy to switch places with you. Would you like that? God, things could be so much worse than this. You know, at least our house isn't disgusting."

"Yes, it is. It's horrible. There are flies everywhere, and it fucking stinks in here."

"You know, I'm getting real sick and tired of your filthy little mouth," she said, getting close enough to me that I could smell her coffee breath. I realized we were now the same height.

"You don't scare me, bitch," I said with contempt.

She backed off. "Even Grandma and Grandpa have clutter. And did you know Grandpa just had to kill a mouse in their garage? Talk about gross. At least we don't have a mouse problem."

We did, though, and I'm not sure if she was lying to herself, willing her words to be true, or if she truly did believe that. If we had been able to get to the garage, the smell of the mice that lived in there was so overpowering it would knock me backward. The mice had been able to run freely through the house in their little paradise that was the hoard without being seen, but that didn't mean they weren't there. Their droppings were on the parts of the countertops in the kitchen and bathroom that weren't completely covered, on the windowsills, and in the bathtub. They were there, their nests burrowed deep within the piles of rubbish.

* * *

Music became an escape for me. I particularly liked to listen to Linkin Park's "Numb", Eminem's "Cleanin' Out My Closet", and both of Simple Plan's "Perfect" and "Welcome to My Life." I blasted them on repeat over and over, hoping Mom would hear. I wanted her to feel the lyrics as deeply as I did.

"Turn that down," Mom bellowed from the living room in between songs, the rare second of silence.

I moved on to the next song on the CD, pretending I didn't hear her, leaving the music up at full volume.

"Dominic," Mom yelled as she pounded her fists against my door.

I jumped. "What?" I asked, pressing pause on the disc player.

"I said turn that down. I mean it, Dominic. I can't hear the TV." She spoke through the door, not wanting to open it.

"Turn it up like you always used to so you wouldn't have to hear me before. Remember? Because I do."

"I don't want to hurt the TV by turning it up too loud," Mom said.

"Oh, no, of course not. Wouldn't want to hurt the TV."

"Dom, I'm not going to say it aga—"

I cut her off by pressing play. She hit my door with a loud thud and stomped away. My heart raced as I jumped up from my bed. I was so upset, I punched the door until it had cracks and holes in the hollow wood and my knuckles bled. Mom took my door from me the next day.

* * *

In mid-July, after I had turned thirteen, I did everything I could to get out of the house and away from Mom. Any minute I wasn't at the house and around her was a minute I felt I could go on living. I started cutting myself on the really bad days. I stumbled upon a pair of scissors one afternoon when I was alone at the house. They were living in a mound of useless bric-a-brac behind the door in the bathroom. I had been searching for the toothpaste when I found them, having slept in until one o'clock in the afternoon that day, with no motivation to get out of bed.

When I saw the scissors, I knew immediately what I wanted to do with them. They were red with sharp points at the end. I'm not sure their actual purpose. They didn't look like regular scissors with the rounded safety points; they even had a cap on them to keep you from hurting yourself when they weren't in use.

I pulled off the cap, pressing the point into the pad of my thumb, engrossed by the indentation that formed. Without hesitation, I opened them, separating the two metal shears, and pressed one of the points deep into the soft skin of my inner forearm. I winced as it pierced my skin. Steadily, I dragged it down my arm about four inches. I could hear my skin popping as it was sliced, with beads of blood forming in the cut. It was exhilarating.

Cutting became a form of release that I craved. On the days when I felt like there was too much going on, my mind and body so full of pressure, I cut to release it. It felt like my heart was an overinflated balloon. All I had to do was take the scissors and cut myself to release a little bit of the air that was causing the balloon to be so stuffed it could pop at any second. One slice, and the air was released just enough that the balloon could return to normal. Still fragile, but balanced. I liked watching as my skin was being ripped open. I liked watching as I began to bleed. It was a rush. My left arm was covered, elbow to wrist, in these small releases. And when I no longer had room on my arm because nothing was healed enough to make new cuts on top of the old, I moved on to my thighs.

I wore long sleeved sweatshirts to keep my new secret hidden. A secret that was all my own. I didn't have to protect anyone but myself. Mom didn't pay much attention to me, so she didn't seem to find it odd that I wore heavy sweatshirts every day despite it being a ninety-degree summer outside. I couldn't hide forever, though, and eventually Mom saw.

"What the hell is this?" she demanded, lifting my navy-blue hoodie sleeve up past my elbow. She caught me while I was washing my hands after using the restroom. I'd pushed up my sleeves to keep them from getting wet.

"It's nothing," I said, trying to walk off without drying my hands. Pulling my sleeves back down, I pushed past her.

"That's not nothing. Let me see your arm."

"Leave me alone."

"I'm not going to leave you alone. Let me see your arm. Now." She grabbed my wrist as I tried to get away and pulled me back toward her, causing me to stumble on the uneven pile of magazines that lay next to the bathroom door.

"Let go of me, you crazy bitch!" I screamed, beginning to cry.

"Don't you cuss at me."

"Seriously, just get the fuck away from me. I said it's nothing. Just stop."

"You better show me your goddamn arm right now. I mean it."

"What do you care what it is anyway?"

"What do I care? What do I care? Are you kidding me?"

"No, I'm not kidding. You don't give a fuck about me."

"I said don't cuss at me!" she yelled, inches away from my face, her voice amplified by her anger.

"It's true."

"No, it's not, and you know it. Don't be ridiculous."

"Obviously, I don't know it," I said, now sobbing.

"Just go to your room for a little bit. Don't go anywhere," Mom warned.

That should have been my signal to get out of there right away, but instead, I did as she asked.

That evening, Mom announced we were going to dinner at Grandma and Grandpa's house. The drive only took a few minutes, but those minutes dragged on because of the thick tension that clouded the space between us.

"Annie, so happy you made it," Grandma said when we shuffled through their front door. She hugged Mom and not-so-quietly whispered, "It's going to be okay."

"What's going to be okay?" I asked, suddenly afraid of why we were there.

"Everything," Grandma said in a voice that was trying unsuccessfully to sound cheerful. "Now, come, come. Sit down," she said, gesturing toward the living room.

Uncle Kai and Aunt Gretchen, who I hadn't seen since my birthday, and Grandpa were all there. Grandpa sat on the sofa while Uncle Kai and Aunt Gretchen shared the oversized chair. Grandma sat on the end of the couch, opposite Grandpa. Mom sat between them, on the middle cushion. She began to tear up and looked down at her lap, her fingers interlaced and her thumbs rolled one on top of the other.

"Have a seat," Grandma said, patting the ottoman.

"Dominic," Grandpa said as I sat down. "Why don't you take off your sweatshirt?"

I looked at Mom. She wouldn't look at me. I knew what was happening. She had told them.

"Nah, I'm good," I said.

Grandpa scoffed and rolled his eyes. He stood to go outside and didn't speak to me again for the rest of the evening.

"Your mom called us today because she's worried about you," Grandma said.

"We're all worried," said Uncle Kai.

"Mom, what did you tell them? You didn't even ask me anything more about it. You just told me to go to my room, and now this? What, you've staged some sort of bullshit intervention?" I was furious.

"Don't you talk to your mother that way," Grandma scolded. "She's doing the best she can here, and you have not made it easy, I can tell you that much."

"I haven't made it easy?" I said, indignant. "Me? Really? I'm the difficult one? Wow."

"You know things haven't been right between the two of you for a long time. For God's sake, your mother had to take your bedroom door from you because you were vandalizing the house," said Grandma.

I was shocked. Vandalizing the house? She had to be kidding. Of everything that was wrong in that house, surely a few holes in the door were not the biggest issue.

"You stay out all night doing God knows what, not following your curfew. You've started smoking, and I've been told you're even having sex," Mom said, finally speaking up.

"First of all, where did you hear that?" I asked.

"It doesn't matter where I heard it. Is it true?"

I didn't say anything, not wanting to admit that I had, in fact, had sex, but not wanting to lie about it, either. "And what are you talking about a curfew? You have literally never given me a curfew."

"Dominic, you know that's not true."

It was true. Why was she lying in front of everyone like this?

"And now," Grandma started, "your mom says you've started cutting yourself." She looked more disgusted and annoyed than concerned.

"I need a minute," I said. "I'm going upstairs. Just give me a minute, okay?"

I darted up the staircase, trying to reach the top before I broke down. Why was this happening? I didn't understand all the anger directed at me. Devastated, I crawled into the corner of the room where the bed and the wall almost met and wept.

"Dominic?" It was Aunt Gretchen. I had forgotten she

and Uncle Kai were even there. They hadn't said much that whole time. "Hi, honey," she said.

"Hi, Auntie."

"Are you okay?" She looked sad.

"I'm fine. But I don't get what's going on. Look, yeah, I cut myself, okay? And yeah, I had sex, okay? So what? Seriously, so what? It's not that big of a deal."

"Dominic, sweetie, I'm not mad at you. And neither is Uncle Kai."

I will never forget the kindness she showed me that day or the look in her eyes when she tried to tell me what was happening.

"But I have to tell you something," she said.

"What?" I asked, my voice timid.

"They're going to take you somewhere tonight. I'm not supposed to tell you this. They basically wanted to ambush you. But I don't think that's right. You deserve to know."

"Take me where?"

"Dominic, you need to get back downstairs," Mom said, appearing in the doorway. "Now."

I looked at Aunt Gretchen. She was crying.

"I'm so sorry," she said.

"Annie, this isn't right," Uncle Kai said when we reached the bottom of the stairs. "You know what's really going on here. You know exactly what you're doing."

"Kai, stay out of it. I didn't even want you or your wife here today," Mom said.

"You're using him, Annie. You're using him as a scapegoat. Everyone's been asking about your house again and whether or not you've been taking care of him. Funny, how all of a sudden now something's happened to move away from that topic."

"Dominic, go get in Grandma's car," said Mom.

"I hope you know we're going, too," Uncle Kai said.

Mom ignored him.

"He needs someone who actually gives a shit to be there

for him."

"Where are you taking me?" I asked, worried about what lay ahead of me.

"Get in the car, dammit," Mom said, raising her voice.

19

The drive took around a half an hour. They took me to the hospital's emergency department, where a doctor declared I was a danger to myself and was to be involuntarily placed into a youth behavioral health facility. I was only there for five days, but those were some of the worst and most traumatic days of my life.

I spent six hours at the hospital before I was taken by medical transport to the facility. I was terrified as we walked into the cold and sterile building. It felt too brightly lit for that hour of the night. All five of them walked in with me, having followed behind the medical transport in their own cars.

"Before we can go any further, I'm going to need you to remove your shoes and belt and hand them to me," said the nurse, who hadn't yet introduced herself to me.

She was homely and lanky, with leathery skin and a short soot-gray ponytail that reminded me of the color of the ashes you flick off a cigarette. She was wearing plain scrubs that matched her hair and smelled of tobacco smoke and nicotine.

I did what I was told, handing them to her one by one.

"Now, take these," she said, handing me taupe-colored scrubs, "and go change. Please put your clothes in the large white bag that's sitting on the bench in there." She gestured toward the bathroom.

"I packed a bag of clothes for him," Mom said, indirectly letting me know she had prepared for and expected this.

"For the first night, he wears the scrubs. It's up to the

doctor when he gets to return to his street clothes," the nurse said. "Now, Dominic, please go change."

When I finished, the nurse ushered us down the long, empty hallway. She scanned her ID card at a set of locked doors at the end. They opened with a harsh click. She sat me down on an uncomfortable chair by the nurse's station and gave Mom a pen to fill out paperwork.

"I'm Lynn," she said. "Is he allergic to anything?"

"No," said Mom.

"Good. Then, take this." In between her nicotine-stained fingers, she held a small, white paper portion cup with a single tiny blue pill inside.

"What's this?" I asked, taking the cup. She handed me another cup, this one bigger, filled with water. "Just a little something to help you sleep."

I happily took the pill. I knew I wouldn't be getting much rest that night. Any help was appreciated. I began to cry. Aunt Gretchen hugged me tight. I rested my head on her shoulder, her cashmere sweater now wet from my tears.

"Shh," she said, rubbing my head, trying to soothe me. "It's all going to be fine. We'll visit you every day, all right?"

"Everyone please say your goodbyes now," Lynn said as Mom handed her the completed packet of papers. She was a cold, unwelcoming woman.

I hugged Uncle Kai first.

He kissed the top of my head. "You know how much we love you, right?" he asked.

"I love you, too."

"This isn't up to me, kiddo. If it was, you wouldn't be here."

I didn't respond. I felt numb. I felt like I was watching myself from the outside looking in, like this wasn't happening. I was watching it happen to someone else.

Uncle Kai pulled me in tighter, squeezing me, not wanting to let go.

"You're going to do great, baby," Aunt Gretchen said,

taking Uncle Kai's place. "We'll come visit every day like we promised, okay? You'll be out of here in no time."

I started crying again. How could she be so sure?

Mom gave me a quick hug, along with Grandma and Grandpa.

Aunt Gretchen came back for one last embrace and whispered, "I'm so sorry," in my ear.

"I don't want them on the visitor's list," Mom said to Grandma as they were walking toward the exit.

"My God, Annie. Seriously?" said Uncle Kai. "Gretchen just told the poor kid we would visit him every day, and now you're going to take that from him, too? Haven't you done enough? Jesus Christ."

"Kai, I don't want to hear it. He's my son, not yours. I don't know why you can't seem to understand that."

"What I can't seem to understand is why you do this to him. You just said it yourself. He's your son. Yet you treat him like some pawn in a game. He's your scapegoat. He takes all the hits so you don't have to."

"Dad," Mom cried. "Let's go, please. I can't deal with them."

I watched them walk away from me. I watched them leave me alone in this foreign place with this horrible woman. I watched as everyone I loved abandoned me there, dropping me off on someone else's doorstep. I was the hospital's problem now. My stomach twisted painfully. My heart hurt. I already missed them.

Lynn showed me to my temporary room, off to the side of the nurse's station.

"You'll stay here for tonight, under observation. In the morning, if all goes well tonight, you'll be moved into the other hall with the rest of the kids."

The room was windowless and empty, except for a small twin-size mattress on the floor. The walls were white, completely bare. It was soulless and cold. There was a small bathroom that contained only a toilet and a sink. No showers.

Next to the toilet was a "call nurse" button, and on the sink was a bar of soap and a paper towel dispenser. In the room, the mattress was covered by a fitted sheet and a thin, not-very-warm thermal hospital blanket.

Lynn left and locked the door behind her after I plopped down onto the mattress. Even with the help of medication, I didn't sleep well.

* * *

"Time for breakfast," a new, much cheerier nurse said as she walked into my room at six o'clock the next morning.

She had dark-plum dyed hair that was pulled high into a messy bun. Her pink scrubs had pictures of Charlie Brown and Snoopy on them. I rubbed my eyes and stretched my arms up over my head, arching my back.

"Did you get any sleep?"

"Not really."

"Aw, I'm sorry, kiddo. The first night's rough for everyone who comes through here. So don't worry; you're not alone. Every kid here has felt the same way."

"Okay," I said, unsure how to respond.

"I'm Rose by the way."

"Hi, I'm Dominic."

"Hi, Dominic. It's very nice to meet you. Do you need to use the restroom or anything?"

"No, I'm okay."

"Great, then come with me. I'm sure you're starving," she said, gesturing for me to follow her out the door. "Right down this way is our cafeteria. The kids call it 'the caf.' Breakfast is at 6:15. Lunch is at noon, and dinner is at six o'clock."

"What do we do in between that time?"

"Oh, all sorts of things. You'll see a doctor this morning at nine, and she'll be the one to figure out your schedule. But for now, after breakfast, you'll go to group therapy and meet the rest of the kiddos."

The caf was a large area with five round tables and five chairs at each table. The food was served in the same manner it was at school and summer camp. My breakfast that morning consisted of a small bowl of Cheerios with milk and an apple. Everyone else was eating scrambled eggs and sausage with a glass of juice.

"Why do I only get cereal?" I asked one of the servers, picking up my pre-made tray.

"Doctors haven't cleared you to use a fork yet," he said.

"I can just eat with my hands."

"Sorry, kid. Them's the rules. I don't make them. I just follow them. Now, go on. You're holding up the line."

I shuffled away, feeling defeated, and found a place to sit away from everyone else. I didn't know anyone yet and didn't feel like interacting. With my head down, I ate my cereal in silence.

At six forty-five, Rose came back to gather all of us for group therapy. We lined up single file against the wall, where she called each of us one by one, checking to make sure we were all where we were supposed to be. Our group wasn't very big, only six kids, including me.

"Caleb," she said.

"Here," Caleb said. He was a tall, athletic looking kid and definitely older than I was.

"Let's see your silverware," said Rose.

I didn't understand what she meant by this, and the confusion must have shown on my face.

"Dominic, this is what we do after every meal. I check to make sure everyone's here and then I check to make sure no one has tried to keep their silverware."

"Why would anyone keep their silverware?" I asked.

"Oh, various reasons. Some kids have used them to injure themselves, and some have used them to injure us nurses or even other kids."

My arms prickled with goosebumps, and I felt sick.

"After you show the silverware, you put your tray and everything on it, including the silverware, of course, in that big bucket over there. All right?"

I sheepishly nodded in response.

She continued the roll call until each kid, including myself, had been accounted for.

Group therapy was nerve-racking. I didn't know what to tell these people. How did I explain why I was there? When you tell someone you don't like your mom or your house, they don't take you seriously. They take it as good ol' fashion over-emotional, self-indulgent teenage angst. The doctor who ran the group sessions, Doctor Michaels, tried to break the ice by having us come up with a name for our group.

"Now that Dominic has joined us, and we're an even group of six, what should we call ourselves?" she asked. "The little kids' group call themselves the 'Mighty Kids.' What do you think would be a good name for us?"

"How about the dumbasses?" one girl said.

"Oh, Maggie, I know it's kind of cheesy, but we're all in this together. That's why we do group therapies, to get to know each other and to help each other," Doctor Michaels said.

Maggie rolled her eyes.

"Is the Breakfast Club too expected and corny?" Caleb said.

"What's the Breakfast Club?" another girl asked.

"Never mind." Caleb chortled.

"How about Dinner Club?" Doctor Michaels said.

"Dinner Club could work," said Maggie.

"Really? I was joking," said Doctor Michaels.

"No, no, I think it's good," said Caleb, pondering this. "Yeah, it's good. I like Dinner Club."

"Well, okay then." Doctor Michaels smiled and clapped her hands together. "Welcome to therapy, Dinner Clubbers."

Although everyone else shared, I hated being the center of attention and declined to speak when it was my turn. Maggie said she was fourteen and only there because she had run away to another state with her twenty-year-old boyfriend, and it was either there or juvie. Another girl named Laurel, aged thirteen, had tried to kill herself after being relentlessly bullied at school. Caleb, aged fifteen, had a drinking problem as the result of the abuse he received from his father. Lastly, there were sisters Blythe, aged fifteen, and Jessa, aged sixteen, who also liked to cut. Their cutting was how they sought to control the turmoil in their lives, since, as foster kids, they were continuously being bounced around from house to house, including being separated a few times.

At nine o'clock, I met with another doctor. Her name was Doctor Monroe. Her office was decorated floor-to-ceiling with butterflies. A lime green couch lay against the same wall as the door. She sat behind a big L-shaped desk that was cluttered with stacks of papers and file folders. Doctor Monroe was a pretty lady, with shoulder length hair the color of a sandy beach and deep blue eyes.

"Hello, Dominic," she said when I was escorted in by a different nurse, a man this time. He hadn't said anything to me other than, "Come with me, it's your turn to see the doctor." I didn't like him.

"Please, sit down," the doctor said, motioning toward the sofa. It was low to the ground and felt like the cushion I happened to sit on was the only one anyone ever sat on, with no buoyancy or padding left to it. I sank down, knowing it would be a struggle to get back up.

"How are you today?" Doctor Monroe asked.

"Fine, I guess," I said.

"How did you sleep last night? Nurse Lynn said there were no issues. I'm so glad to hear that."

"I didn't get much sleep."

"Oh, I'm sorry." She gave me a sympathetic smile. "The first night's always the hardest."

"So I've heard."

"Can you tell me what brings you here today?"

"Um, I was forced to come here. But I'm sure you know

that. I wouldn't be here if I didn't have to be."

"Yes, I know you don't want to be here. But what I mean is, tell me what brought you to this point? You've been cutting your arm, and your family is afraid you're a danger to yourself. Can you tell me a little bit about what's been going on? What's your life outside of here look like?"

"It looks fine. What do you want to know?"

"How's your relationship with your parents?"

"It's just my mom and me. I don't know my dad. And I don't know? We fight all the time about everything." I shrugged.

"You know, that's totally normal. I have not met a single person who hasn't had a fight with their mom at some point."

"Well, I don't really know how to explain it. It's more than just that."

"Just do the best you can. That's what I'm here for, to listen."

"Okay, um, I don't like my mom much. She doesn't like me either, though."

"Did she tell you that?"

"No, she didn't have to."

"Oh, Dominic, I'm sure it's hard to tell sometimes when there's a lot of fighting and she's trying to get things under control, but I'm sure she loves you very much."

"Yeah, well, like and love are two different things. Of course, I love my mom. I don't necessarily like her all the time, though."

"What else can you tell me? In the notes from the paperwork your mom filled out, she says that you've been smoking and staying out all night?" She flipped through the file, skimming across the pages. "And she says you've been having sex. Can you tell me about that?"

"There's not much to tell. I think you pretty much know everything."

"What do you and your mom fight about? Can you tell me that? There has to be something. I mean, people don't usually go around cutting themselves for no reason, do they?"

"I don't know what other people do."

"You have to work with me here, Dominic. If you won't talk, then I can't clear you for anything."

"Like what?"

"Like using a fork, or getting to wear your street clothes, or visits with family."

"You'll keep me from seeing my family?"

"Yes, until we can make some progress. And the longer that is delayed, the longer your stay will be. Now, please tell me, what's been going on with you?"

I told her what I could. I told her I had a lot of anger toward my mother. I told her that Mom didn't let me have friends over, and I didn't feel like she cared about me. I told her that I felt like Mom chose everything above me.

But I never mentioned the house. I didn't tell her that I couldn't have friends over because of the state of our house. I didn't tell her that I felt like Mom didn't care about me because she would rather keep piling onto the hoard than take care of my needs. I didn't tell her that I felt like Mom chose her possessions and her own happiness over mine. I didn't tell her any of that because, as much as I resented my mother, I was still protecting her.

"I want to talk to you about ways of coping with and managing your anger," Doctor Monroe said. "How do you feel about writing in a feelings journal?"

"I like to write," I said.

"You do? That's great. Okay, so I'll give you a journal to start while you're here, and you can continue it after you're released as well. Can you think of anything else that might help you?"

"I like music, too."

"What kind of music do you listen to?"

"Um, like Linkin Park, Eminem, I don't know. Stuff like that."

"I know who both of those are."

"You do? Do you listen to them?"

"I do, actually, on occasion. But I have to tell you, I don't think it's a great idea for you to listen to them while you're in a bad mood. Their songs are good, but they tend to be very angry themselves. I don't think it would be healthy for you to listen to something angry while you're angry. That could make things worse. Does that make sense?"

"Yeah, I guess."

"Great. Can you think of something else then? Maybe go for a walk?"

"Walking could work. I like walks. I like reading, too. I don't read much anymore, but it always helped me before. Maybe I could do that?"

"Reading is a wonderful idea. You could get lost in a book for hours. I think we have a good start going. We have three productive ways to help you with your anger. I think that's a good start."

Doctor Monroe gave me a Rorschach test, and after a two-hour long session, she concluded that I had clinical depression, generalized anxiety disorder, obsessive compulsive disorder, and borderline personality disorder.

I understood and agreed with the former two, but the latter two I didn't. She explained that obsessive compulsive disorder is not like how you see it portrayed on TV. It isn't all organizing and the need to have everything clean. She said mine came in the form of intrusive thoughts and impulsivity, both of which are worsened by my depression and anxiety.

The borderline personality disorder threw me off. I thought she was trying to say I had split personalities. But she explained that BPD is not like that at all. She said the characteristics are the feeling of emptiness, unstable relationships, recklessness, and last but not least, self-harm. Sure sounded like me.

I learned as an adult that I more than likely inherited it from my mother, as hoarding is a symptom of OCD as well. As much as I dislike having these disorders because they often interfere with my daily life and can make it hard to function on a normal level, I'm at least grateful my OCD didn't take the same form Mom's did.

At the end of our session, Doctor Monroe prescribed me ten milligrams of Prozac to be taken every day and a new rigid daily schedule:

6 a.m.: WAKE UP, BRUSH TEETH, GET DRESSED AND READY FOR BREAKFAST

6:15 a.m.: BREAKFAST

6:45 a.m.: ROLL CALL, LINE UP FOR GROUP THERAPY

7 a.m. to 9 a.m.: GROUP THERAPY

9 a.m. to 11 a.m.: ONE-ON-ONE SESSION WITH DOCTOR MONROE

11 a.m. to 11:45 a.m.: IN-ROOM FREE TIME

11:45 a.m.: TAKE MEDICATION AND GET READY FOR LUNCH

12 p.m.: LUNCH

12:45 p.m.: ROLL CALL, LINE UP FOR SECOND GROUP THERAPY

1 p.m. to 3 p.m.: SECOND GROUP THERAPY

3 p.m. to 4 p.m.: IN-ROOM FREE TIME

4 p.m. to 5:45 p.m.: VISITING HOURS (IF NOT HAVING A VISIT, YOU MAY WATCH A MOVIE IN THE GROUP THERAPY ROOM OR STAY IN YOUR ROOM FOR FREE TIME)

5:45 p.m.: WRAP UP VISITS/FREE TIME AND GET READY FOR DINNER

6 p.m.: DINNER

6:45 p.m.: ROLL CALL, LINE UP FOR GROUP PHYSICAL ACTIVITY

7 p.m. to 8:20 p.m.: GROUP PHYSICAL ACTIVITY

8:30 p.m.: TEN MINUTE SHOWER, TAKE SLEEP AID IF NECESSARY, GET READY FOR BED

9 p.m.: LIGHTS OUT

Nurse Rose came to get me after my session with the doctor to show me to my new room. "Did you get your schedule?"

"Yeah, just got it," I said.

"Okay, just remember that everyone's is different, so make sure you stick to yours and don't be worried if not everyone does the same things you do. Also, just so you know, you do have a roommate. Everybody here does. I don't know if you remember him, but you met Caleb earlier," she said.

"Yeah, I remember him."

The room was a lot like the observation room, except that it was a little bigger as it held two beds opposite from each other. In between the beds was a desk with two pads of paper and crayons for drawing or writing. We weren't allowed pens or pencils because we could hurt ourselves or others with them, and we weren't allowed markers because we could sniff them to get high. The bathroom looked just as plain as the first one, but this one had a shower. Our doors were never allowed to be shut unless we were on lock down.

My first night in the youth wing of the hospital is forever etched into my brain. Caleb cried himself to sleep that night, big shuddering sobs. Then, he cried in his sleep. I was right there with him, though. I tried to hide it, but I was barely holding it together.

Blythe screamed, "Let me out!" all night long.

Lynn tried repeatedly to quiet her, to no avail.

My bed was by the door, so I had a view of the hallway. I watched, my stomach roiling, as Lynn and some other nurses grabbed Blythe from her room, kicking and flailing. They threw her onto a gurney, and she tried to bite Lynn, who grabbed her arm and pushed a needle into it. A few seconds later, she quieted. All I could think throughout the whole ordeal was, *I don't belong here. How could Mom do this to me?*

* * *

"Have you been writing in your feelings journal?" Doctor Monroe asked the next day at our one-on-one.

"Yes. I write in it during the free time in our rooms," I said.

"Oh, good. I'm so happy to hear that. Does it seem like it's working for you?"

"I think so. It feels good to write everything down. It's almost like a way of screaming, you know? Like, I can just scream my words onto the paper instead of actually screaming."

"That's a wonderful way to look at it, Dominic. That's exactly the point. You're a smart kid."

"Thanks." I laughed, a little embarrassed by the compliment. "Uh, doc, I do need to talk to you about something, though. Something kind of scary that happens to me sometimes."

"Oh?"

"Yeah. Um, well, sometimes I don't feel like a real person," I said.

"Hmm," she said. "I think I know what you're talking about, and if my suspicions are correct, then that is a common symptom of both anxiety and depression. Can you tell me more?"

"Yeah, like, sometimes it's like I'm not really here. It's like I'm in a dream and the things happening around me aren't real. Like this isn't real life. Or like if I walk past a mirror and I see myself in it, it's like I don't recognize myself as the person standing there. When I hear myself talk, I think, 'Is that really me speaking? Can anyone hear me or is this just my imagination?' I hear myself talking to other people, but I feel like a faceless character in a story. Like I'm not really there."

"What you're describing is called depersonalization-derealization disorder, and it's exactly like you described. But like I said, it's a common symptom of anxiety and depression. We've even seen it quite a bit in people with OCD. So, good

138

news is, you're not alone. You are definitely not alone. Have you felt this way for long?"

"Probably a year or so now. It's not every day, but it will just hit me, and I'll get scared. I'll be doing nothing or even just hanging out with my friends and having fun, then all of a sudden, it's like, who am I? Where am I? What's happening to me?"

"That sounds terrifying. I'm so sorry you have to go through that."

"How do I make it stop?"

"I'm not sure you can completely. But what you can do when it starts to happen is just try to remember that you've felt this before, and that no matter how scary and real it feels, that feeling will go away. You have to remember, you are definitely a person, a person who matters very much."

At four o'clock in the afternoon, the start of visiting hours, I was informed my aunt and uncle were there to see me. The visiting area was in the caf. We were allowed one hour and forty-five minutes to visit because at five forty-five, we had to go back to our rooms to get ready for dinner while they cleaned up the caf.

The nurses on duty rolled in large carts that were full of board games, books, puzzles, and coloring books with crayons. I didn't feel like doing any of that. I just wanted to talk with my aunt and uncle.

"How ya doing, bud?" Uncle Kai asked as I sat down between him and Aunt Gretchen at one of the round tables.

"Been better." I laughed.

Aunt Gretchen's eyes welled up with tears, and she gently rubbed my back. It took all I had not to tear up right along with her.

"I'm so sorry, sweetie," she said.

I shrugged my shoulders, unsure of what to say to make her feel better. It wasn't her fault.

"What do they have you do here all day?" Uncle Kai asked, breaking the silence.

"Nothing fun. Lots of talking. I go to group therapy. Then, I talk to the doctor by myself, then more group therapy."

"What do you talk to the doctor about?" Aunt Gretchen asked.

"Just why I'm here and stuff."

"Did you tell the doctor about your mom or the house?" Uncle Kai asked.

"No."

"That's okay, sweetie," said Aunt Gretchen. "We know it's hard for you. But if you want to, you're allowed to. That's pretty much the whole reason you're here, right?"

"Yeah, I guess," I said. I didn't want to talk about Mom. I wasn't sure I wanted the doc to know the truth. Would she even believe me?

"To be honest, we tried to talk with the doctor ourselves. We thought maybe we could let her know what's going on with you. But for whatever reason, she didn't want to talk with us," said Uncle Kai. "She said she only talks to immediate family. Meaning just your mom. Which I think is total bullshit, because she needs to hear from someone other than your mom's biased ass."

"Kai, stop." Aunt Gretchen sighed.

"Were you going to tell her about the house?" I asked.

"Yeah, we were thinking about it. Or at the very least tell the doctor how your mom treats you. The way she always throws you under the bus. How it's not really your fault you do what you can to get out of the house and away from her."

"I don't want anything bad to happen or for them to call the cops or something."

"You don't think maybe it'd be for the best if we could get someone else on your side? Who knows what your mom's been telling the doctor. If she could only hear from us that your mom lies then maybe—"

"Listen, it's going to be okay," Aunt Gretchen interrupted. She grabbed my hand and squeezed. "You talk with the doctor about whatever you feel safe talking about, all right? We won't say anything to anyone, and there won't be any pressure from us. Right, Kai?"

Uncle Kai smiled and said, "Right."

I could tell he wanted to say more, wanted me to assure him I'd tell on Mom. But I couldn't do that.

Uncle Kai and Aunt Gretchen stayed for the first hour, then at five, Mom came. She wept for most of the visit. I didn't feel bad for her.

On my third day, I was given back my street clothes. I felt like things were looking up after that. I was one step closer to getting out. My guests from the day before visited again, this time bringing Grandma and Grandpa with them.

That night, at around midnight, we were put on lockdown after Blythe was somehow able to smuggle a fork out of the caf's return bucket and sneak it back to her room. Lynn caught her trying to cut herself with it. A piercing alarm went off, and everyone's doors snapped shut at the same time with a jarring clack. Blythe was screaming. Nurses were shouting. I was petrified.

On the fourth day at breakfast, Jessa, missing her sister who had been moved to another location, wouldn't stop singing the Pepto Bismol theme song. She continued this for the rest of the day. I heard all about nausea, heartburn, and indigestion during first group therapy, lunch, and dinner.

I had a family therapy session with Mom instead of second group therapy that day.

"Ms. Leonard, can you tell me a bit about what's been concerning you in regards to Dominic and his behaviors?" Doctor Monroe asked.

"He just does whatever he wants all the time. He's plain and simple out of control," Mom said.

"What does he do that you consider to be out of control?"

"Well, for one, he's only thirteen years old, and he's out sleeping around with God only knows what kind of girls. Then, he's smoking, staying out all night, doing I don't even know what. Have you been doing drugs, Dominic?" Mom asked, turning her attention toward me.

"What? No, of course not."

"I want him drug tested," said Mom.

I rolled my eyes. She was being ridiculous. I wasn't doing drugs.

"We can arrange that. Can you tell me how you react when he acts out?" Doctor Monroe asked.

"Well, I'll be the first to admit that sometimes I get angry or lash out."

"Sometimes?" I scoffed.

Mom snapped her head toward me and glared. "Yes, sometimes. I try to stay level-headed, but he makes it so hard. He gets so angry with me, and I just don't know why. He calls me vulgar names and screams profanities at me. He got so mad a while back that he just punched hole after hole in his bedroom door. Like, where did that come from, you know? That was really uncalled for. I just don't get it. What did I do to deserve this?"

That was it right there. She knew I wouldn't expose her secret, and she knew I wouldn't be able to give a definitive answer for where my anger came from because she knew I was never skilled enough to put that into words.

"Well, you two, it has been a great session here today," Doctor Monroe said. "But, unfortunately, we've run out of time. I would love it if you could come back tomorrow at the same time for one more family session?"

"Hmm, I guess I could make that work if you think it will help him."

"I really do, and Dominic," she said, turning toward me, "if all goes well tomorrow, then you'll be able to leave after the family session."

"Leave?" I asked excitedly. "As in, I'll be getting out of here and back into the free world?"

"Yes, back into the free world." The doctor laughed. "Ms. Leonard, are you staying for a visit? It's in an hour."

"I wish I could, but I need to get going. But Dominic, don't worry, your uncle and aunt will be here, I'm sure."

My visit with Aunt Gretchen and Uncle Kai went well. I told them I would be getting out the next day, and the three of us cried tears of elation and relief.

"You didn't belong here anyway, bud," Uncle Kai said.

After dinner and after hearing the Pepto Bismol song on repeat for the rest of the night, I was ready for bed. I was given a cup to urinate in for the drug test Mom demanded. I took my shower, washing my hair with a two-in-one hair and body wash that dried out my skin, and brushed my teeth, ready for the day to be over. I wasn't sure how much rest I would get, knowing that the hours were going to pass by at a snail's pace while I waited to be released.

At around two o'clock in the morning, I was awakened by a gurgling sound coming from the bathroom. I looked over toward Caleb's bed to find it empty. The door to the bathroom was open, the light spilling out across the otherwise dark room. The gurgling continued.

"Caleb, are you okay?" I asked, making my way toward the door. I peered inside to find Caleb head down in the toilet, trying to drown himself.

"Nurse!" I screamed, rushing toward Caleb. I grabbed his shoulders, using my weight to pull him backward and out of the water. The momentum knocked me into the wall with a thud so loud, I was sure everyone would wake.

Caleb slumped to the floor, unconscious.

"Nurse!" I screamed again, frantically pressing the "call nurse" button on the bathroom wall.

Lynn burst through the door. "What did you do?" she asked after seeing Caleb's lifeless body on the tile floor.

"I was trying to help him," I cried. "He was trying to drown himself."

"Move out of the way."

I sprinted back to my bed and waited. I heard the alarm and everyone's doors snapped shut except for mine and

Caleb's. I sat on the corner of my bed, with my knees to my chest, rocking back and forth and crying. I watched as Nurse Lynn performed CPR, her hands pushing deep into Caleb's chest with steady rhythmic pumps. Another nurse called for an ambulance.

My last day dragged on, each minute feeling like hours. During first group therapy, I asked how Caleb was doing, but the doctor informed me that for confidentiality reasons, they couldn't tell me a thing. I never saw or heard about Caleb again. He seemed like a nice kid. I hope he and the rest of the Dinner Clubbers are living a good life today.

At three in the afternoon, I was escorted to Doctor Monroe's office for what I'd hoped would be my last session with her. I did my best to let Mom and the doctor do the talking, keeping my head down, trying not to cause any issues that might delay my release.

"First, I want to say that we are pleased to inform you that Dominic has passed his drug test," Doctor Monroe said.

"Well, it's been five days. What if it's just out of his system now?" asked Mom.

"It doesn't happen that fast, Ms. Leonard. I wanted to ask, though, how would you feel if Dominic were released today?"

"Well, of course I want him out of here and back at the house with me, you know? But I'm just worried. I mean, how do I know that things won't go back to the way they were before? How do I know nothing's going to happen that might land him here again?"

"Ms. Leonard, Dominic has made great progress. We have him on a daily antidepressant that will help level his emotions. The chemical imbalance is what has exacerbated a lot of the issues he has. We've talked extensively about his feelings and anger and how to work on those in productive ways. For example, when he starts to feel upset, instead of cutting or punching his door and damaging the house, he'll write it all out in a feelings journal. Or maybe he'll go for a walk around the neighborhood. A fresh-air walk only, though. Right, Dominic? No smoking?"

"Right," I said.

"Hmm. Okay, then. If the two of you think things are actually going to change, then I'd be happy to take him with me when I leave. Dominic, you really feel like things are going to be okay? I'm at my wit's end here. I can't do this anymore."

"I'll change. I promise I'll do better. Things won't be like before, I swear," I said. Truthfully, I didn't feel like I was the only one who needed to change my ways, but no way was I going to start that conversation and risk delaying my release.

"Alrighty then, I am pleased to say that, Dominic, you are free to go. Go ahead and pack your bags while your mom and I sign your discharge papers, then you can get out of here."

20

Mom and I drove halfway back to the house without saying a word when she finally broke the silence. "Do you want to go to Grandma and Grandpa's?"

"I don't know. I'm kind of tired," I said.

"We won't stay long," Mom said, letting me know she had already decided we'd be going.

The exterior of Grandma and Grandpa's house looked the same as before, but somehow sunnier. Maybe it was that I felt happy for once, or maybe it was that I hadn't seen the sun in five days, since all physical activities took place in a gymnasium.

"Annie," Grandma said, opening the door for us. She hugged Mom as we came inside. "Hello," she said to me. "How are you?"

"I'm doing okay. Just tired," I said. "But I'm really happy to be out."

"We're happy you're out, too. Aren't we, hon?" Grandma said, turning to Grandpa.

"Yes, of course," Grandpa replied.

"Well, don't just stand in the doorway. Come sit down, you two," said Grandma.

The inside of my grandparents' house looked the same, too, of course, but it felt like I hadn't been there in years. I sat on their sofa with a new appreciation. A plush, non-sink-holed sofa unlike the one in Doctor Monroe's office.

"Tell me, Dominic, what did you think of that place?"

Grandpa asked.

"I hated it," I said.

"You did, huh?"

"Mm-hmm."

"So it's not somewhere you'd want to go back to, is it?"

"No. Never."

"Well, then I think we're all on the same page. We don't want you to go back there, either. But I can't really say I blame your mom for sending you there in the first place. You were out of control, wouldn't you agree?"

"I guess," I said, becoming instantly frustrated.

Mom sat on the couch with her head down, not saying a word. How could she bring me there? I had just gotten out and thought maybe we would be okay and on the right track to starting ourselves off with a clean slate when she pulled this. She brought me there to be lectured. She threw me under the bus yet again.

"What do you mean, you guess?" Grandpa said, indignant.

"I don't know. I mean, yeah, I was doing things I shouldn't have been doing. I don't want to go back there, so I'm going to try to do better."

"Oh, you're going to do more than try, young man. You will do better, and that's that. No more of that arm cutting nonsense, either."

"Yes, sir. I will do better. I swear."

"And not just with that," Grandma said. "Talk to him about the other thing."

"What other thing?" I asked.

"About the way you treat your mother," said Grandpa.

I looked at Mom. Her head was still down.

"The way you treat her isn't right. She's your mother, not your friend. When she tells you to clean up or take out the trash, you do it. Do you know what would have happened to me if I had talked to my mother the way you talk to yours? Huh? Do you?"

"No."

"I would have gotten my ass beat. My mother would have made me go outside and pick my own switch to get beat with, or my dad would have given me the belt. You know, you're lucky you have the mom you do. She lets you get away with way too much. She coddles you. But not anymore. I'm going to be here, too, to help her out. Don't think that just because you don't live here that means you can do whatever you want. The second I hear that you've been mouthing off again or refusing to do the simple chores your mom asks, I'll be over at your house, ready to make you listen. Got it?"

"Got it." Now I was the one with my head down.

"Good," said Grandma. "I really hope you do, Dominic. We don't sit here and scold you for nothing, you know? We want you to grow up to be a good man and do something with your life. And with the way you've been acting, that just isn't going to happen. This is called tough love. And we love you very much, so you better get used to it."

"Okay," was all I could manage, swallowing the urge to fight back.

I didn't say a word to Mom for the entire drive back to our house. It was only a few minutes, but I decided I'd better live by the rule of if you don't have anything nice to say, then keep your mouth shut.

We pushed our way through the door. I didn't have the positivity to make games out of our situation anymore. I called it for what it was. There was no man on the other side keeping me out. The only person pushing against me was my own mother.

Sometimes I wish I'd run away long before I was finally able to break free. Sometimes I wish I'd told somebody. Screw the consequences. Maybe I would have been put in foster care. Maybe I would have gotten to live with my aunt and uncle. I'll never know. But the worst part is that I didn't do any of that, because not only was I protecting Mom, I was protecting my own selfish freedoms. If I'd told anyone what was going on, if

I truly reported it to the police or CPS, I for sure would have been taken. My grandparents may have been in denial and could pretend all they wanted that the issues in that house were my talking back and refusing to take out the trash, but deep down, they had to know the truth.

As much as I wanted to be saved, there was a part of me that didn't want to be saved just as badly. If I were put into a more structured household, I couldn't sneak off and stay out all night. I couldn't smoke, I couldn't sleep around. Was I really willing to give all that up in exchange for a better environment?

Looking back, I do wish I'd been able to stay a child just a little longer. So many people knew about our situation, so many people knew our secret. Did they fail me? Or did I fail them? Was Mom right about me? Was I just too out of control? If I was, is that why they all stopped caring about what was going on with me and only seemed to care if Mom was all right? Was I actually the problem? Was I really so self-centered as to believe that I grew up in a shitty household created by someone else when maybe it was actually me creating my own shitty situation? Maybe the bad guy, after all, was me.

I marched straight to my room after we were able to shove our way inside. Mom didn't try to stop me. I don't think she wanted me around as it was. She had put my door back.

"Thank you for my door," I hollered from the end of the hallway.

"Sure thing," said Mom.

I had never been more excited to go into my room. The first thing I wanted to do was relax on my bed. I wanted to crawl onto my comfortable full-size mattress that was on an off-the-ground bed frame and had my own warm cozy blanket on it. I was still feeling upset from the visit at Grandma and Grandpa's so I thought maybe I would either write in my journal or take a nap, unsure if I would have the ability to concentrate on reading a book. I was ready to unwind and take a much-needed breather.

But what I saw when I got through my door slapped me

right across the face. No, it straight up punched me square in the jaw. Half my room was filled with bags and open, spilling boxes. I shut the door behind me, dropped to my knees, and screamed into my bag of clothes from the behavioral center as quietly as I could. I didn't want Mom to hear me getting upset for fear she would call my grandfather.

The bags were stacked against my bookshelf, causing my precious books to fall to the ground, covers bent, looking like a sad library graveyard. I wanted to scream at Mom. I wanted to punch the walls. Most of all I wanted to cry, but nothing would come. I felt like she had taken everything from me, even my tears.

I checked to see if the pack of smokes I had hidden in a pair of boots under my bed was still there. It was. I knew Mom wouldn't come to check on me; she never did. I didn't figure much had changed. So I jumped out my window to have a cigarette. I just wanted that high, that release, that calm. I needed to get my nerves to back down before I did something much worse than smoke, because what I really wanted to do was find that pair of scissors and slice my wrists open.

Instead, when my cigarette was smoked down to the filter, I pulled up the sleeve of my T-shirt and put it out on my arm. It sizzled against my skin. The smell of burning flesh was satisfying, the pain a rush. Mom might check me for new cuts, but she wouldn't know to look for this. This was something new that was all mine.

Although I did continue to burn myself once in a while, just often enough to sneak it in unnoticed, I never did cut again. The urge has never left me. I'm like an addict. Sometimes, when things get stressful, I still want my fix, but I've learned to manage without it. The scars are still there. A forever reminder of my pain. They're covered with tattoos, but they're there. If you look closely, you can see their little silver lines weaving through the pictures on my skin.

I waited a few days before I did anything, not wanting to upset Mom. She had a staff meeting to prepare for the new year, which was due to start the next week. While she was gone, I took everything out of my room and stashed it in different places around the house. I didn't care if she said she knew about every little thing in there or if she'd claim that I'd now lost her stuff. I wanted my room back.

While I was scouting for places to inconspicuously stash the bags, I found the sign I had made Mom years ago. The old, now chipped and falling apart sign that read "Bless This Mess." I decided that if Mom no longer cared about it, since it hadn't seen the light of day in years, then I wanted it back. I found the perfect spot for it on the wall above my desk.

It took around two weeks for Mom to notice I had cleaned out my room. She hit my door with her fist, loud enough to startle me.

I pressed pause on my CD player. "Yeah?"

"I have been calling you for like ten minutes now," Mom said, opening my door. "I was trying to tell you to turn your music down. I can't hear the TV."

"Sorry, I didn't hear you."

"Yeah, because your music's too loud."

"Sorry, I have it lower than I usually do. I didn't know you could still hear it."

"It's fine, just…" Mom started, stopping when she glanced to the side and saw my room had been cleared. "What the hell is this?"

"What's what?" I was afraid. I knew what she meant and sensed a fight was about to start.

"What's this?" She waved her arms around animatedly, plodding toward the area where all the trash had been. "Where's all my stuff?"

"I moved it."

"Where? Where did you put it?"

"Different places. Just wherever there was sort of room for it all."

"How am I supposed to find that stuff now?"

"Mom, I moved that stuff like two weeks ago, and you

didn't even notice. It's not like you needed that stuff if you didn't even miss it, right?"

"Dominic," she seethed, spit flying from her mouth. "It doesn't matter if I didn't need it right this second. It's my stuff, and you had no right to touch it, you little shit."

"I'm sorry. I just wanted my room back."

"Your room in my house, don't you forget that." She turned on her heels to leave. "What is that?" she asked, pointing at the wall to the sign above my desk.

"It's the sign I made you," I said.

"Yeah, no shit. What the hell is it doing in here?"

"I found it when I was moving the bags that were in here."

"Where did this thing come from again?"

"I made it for you at camp."

"Yeah, exactly. You made it for *me*."

"Well, it's been missing for years. I found it buried in a pile. I didn't think you'd even notice or miss it."

"So you thought you could just take it then, is that it?"

"I'm sorry, Mom. Do you want it back?"

"Yes, I want it back," she said, snatching it from its new display. "Don't you ever take anything from me again, you evil little thief."

21

My eighth-grade year got off to an okay start. I was determined to do better in school than I had the year before. It helped that Mom and I were now at separate schools and I didn't have to feel the constant burn of her angry, watchful eyes. For those few hours, I was free. I looked forward to going to the library every week and found solace in the tranquility of it. There was no TV blaring so loudly I worried for its speakers. There was no yelling. Everything organized alphabetically, all in perfect order. The designated smart girl in my English class had a plethora of Harry Potter T-shirts, so I thought that might be a good place to start my escape from reality. I wanted a book I could fall in love with, a story that I could transport into, removing myself from my current world.

Turns out ol' Harry and I had a lot in common. He was not given a space of his own and was humiliated by the people who were supposed to care for him. He was alone with no one to turn to, no one to share his secrets with, no one to rely on but himself. Where was my Hogwarts letter? I could have really used one on my eleventh birthday.

I checked out each book, every week for five weeks, since only five had been released at that point, reading in my free time and in my room after school. I did my best to be good, not cause any problems, and maintain my grades. I wanted to be something more than I was. After I was released from the hospital, Grandma said she was afraid I wouldn't do anything good with my life. I wanted to prove her wrong.

Things were going great until about halfway through the school year. Up until then, I had done everything Mom had asked. I kept my head down, and talked to her as little as possible, spending every moment I was at the house in my room and away from her, which was what we both wanted.

Mom hammered her fists against my door one Saturday morning in January, jarring me out of a deep sleep. It was still early, much earlier than I would have liked to be up on a Saturday. The sun reflecting against the glittery snow outside hurt my eyes as they tried to adjust to being open and awake.

"Yeah?" I yawned, stretching my arms above my head. My toes curled underneath my warm blankets.

Mom opened my door, looking annoyed. "I'm going shopping, and my car is a mess. If I find anything, I won't have anywhere to put it. So I need you to get dressed and clean it out for me," she said.

"What? Why can't you do it?"

"Dominic, I'm not going to ask again. Your response should have been, 'Okay, Mom, I'll get right on that.' Grandpa talked to you about listening to me, right?"

"Right," I said. Hot anger spread through me, and I knew if I didn't breathe through it, I would boil over like unwatched water. I tried to look on the bright side. It was just a small car. It shouldn't take more than half an hour.

"Thank you," said Mom.

"Do you want the stuff in bags or boxes?" I asked, putting my shoes on. I didn't bother with getting dressed. I knew I would just be getting back into bed when I was done.

"Whatever's more convenient for you. You'll probably want boxes because they'll look neater in here than bags."

I stopped mid lace-up on my sneakers. "What do you mean, 'in here?'" I clenched my fists, digging my nails hard into my palm, willing myself not to react.

"I mean exactly what I just said. Boxes will look neater in here than bags because you can stack them nicely rather than tossing them in a heap," Mom said condescendingly.

I didn't say anything. A lump formed in my throat.

"Dominic, come on. Your room is the only place in the house with space in it. Don't act so surprised. I need the car cleaned out, and there's nowhere for anything else to go. You can store it here for a while. You'll be fine."

"I won't be fine," I said, taking my shoe back off. "Clean it out yourself."

"Excuse me?"

"You heard me. You want it clean so you can go waste your money buying a bunch of shit you don't need, then clean it out yourself. I'm done."

Those last words, those two little words, "I'm done," were the beginning of the end. That was when I stopped caring about anything other than myself and what I wanted. Fuck everyone else.

"Don't make me call your grandfather. Do you want him to come over here and make you do it?"

"Call whoever you want. I'm not doing it. He can't make me. And if he does show up, I'm not going outside to talk to him. So I guess you'll just have to let him in the house."

Mom slammed my door shut and stalked down the hallway without responding.

I crawled into my bed, pulling the covers up and around my face. Feeling satisfied, I fell back asleep.

An hour later, a knock so thunderous my door shook against its hinges jerked me from my almost-peaceful slumber.

"What?" I shouted, annoyed at the faceless knocker on the other side.

"Open the door, please," Mom said. She stood in the hallway with two cardboard file boxes stacked one on top of the other, in her arms, trying to peer over them.

"Oh, no, no, no you don't," I said, trying to shut the door.

Mom pushed back against it. "Dominic, why are you being like this? I don't see what the big deal is. It's just a few boxes. I have these two here, and there's still three more outside. They're not that big. They won't take up much room."

"No way. I said 'no.'" I tried to shut the door again.

Mom pushed hard, wedging the corner of one of the boxes in the crack in the door. "Get out of the way, so I can set these down. They're getting heavy. And put your shoes on, will you? I had to clean out the car myself because you couldn't be bothered to help me. The least you could do is grab the last three boxes."

"Fuck you. I hate you," was all I could manage as I fought back the tears, in awe she was doing this. "I wish you weren't my mom."

"How dare you talk to me that way. After everything I've had to put up with from you over the years, and this is how you speak to me? Really?"

"I don't want your shit in here. This is my room, not yours."

"It may be the room you occupy, but that's only because I let you. This is my house, and unless you want to start paying rent, then this is my room, too. Do you have money to pay rent, Dominic? Do you?"

"No."

"No, I didn't think so," Mom said. She paused for a moment, then continued. "You know what? Fine. Have it your way. Everything always has to be your way, doesn't it? I'll just put this stuff in the kitchen, then. Will that make you happy? Will you be happy to see an even bigger mess out there than there already is? I could stack five tiny boxes in here nicely, not even in your way. But no, you'd prefer they be in the way. Who cares if they're in my way, as long as they're out of yours, right? That's what you want?"

"I hate you. You're a fucking bitch, and I hate you," I said, still fighting the tears. My throat burned against the lump in it.

"Yeah, well, guess what, you little prick?" she screamed, that horrible booming scream from my younger days. The one that sent chills through my body then managed to do the same thing now. "You hate me? Fine. I really don't give a fuck, because I don't like you, either." She dropped the boxes at her feet, right outside my door, then staggered down the hallway, holding her arms out to either side of her, touching the walls for balance.

The boxes landed with a muffled thud atop the clothing piles. I slammed my door shut, then opened it back up just so I could slam it a second time. I punched my door over and over, making new holes and widening existing ones, until my knuckles bled. I walked to my window easily, because my room was box-free, opened it, and jumped out to have a cigarette, putting it out on my arm when I was finished.

Neither one of us picked up the last three boxes from outside. Mom pushed them against the garage door, where they stayed for months, until the weather ate away at them and they became part of the garbage pile off the side of the porch.

From then on out, I climbed in and out of my window every weekend to hang out with Tommy. His cousin, Brendan, would pick us up and take us to whatever party he was going to. Tommy had tried smoking marijuana and liked to drink. I couldn't bring myself to do anything else that could get me into trouble. I knew one day I would, just not yet. It was bad enough I was sneaking out and going to parties. If I got caught, at least I'd be sober.

The two of us kept this up for the rest of the school year. I skipped school a lot. Tommy never did much of that. I didn't see the point anymore. Whether I did well in school or did whatever I wanted, my environment outside of there stayed the same. Nothing I did would change that.

I didn't feel I had anyone I could turn to. I couldn't talk to Tommy about it because he wouldn't understand. His mom was the definition of a mother. I couldn't talk to my grandparents because they didn't believe me; they thought I brought all my problems solely upon myself. I didn't talk to Uncle Kai and Aunt Gretchen much those days. They were getting ready to have a baby of their own. They didn't have time for me and my issues anymore. I don't think of that as a bad thing. I wanted them to focus all their attention on their baby. I wanted them to be there for him or her, to make sure their child always knew what love and security felt like. That's how a child should feel.

Mom must have caught wind of my sneaking out because one night I showed back up to the house at around two in the morning and found my window had makeshift wooden bars nailed across it. I pulled against them with all my strength, but I was no match for wood and nails. I felt defeated, emotionally exhausted, in pain.

I knew it was my fault. I had been sneaking out when I shouldn't have. But she never even spoke to me about it. She never asked me to stop. I don't know that I would have, but maybe it would have been nice to know that she cared.

Instead, she literally barred me. I couldn't get inside, and in the morning, when I was able to get back in the house, I wouldn't be able to leave again without her knowing. I spent the night outside my window with my sweatshirt to keep me warm. As cold and lonely as I felt out there, I'd been lonelier before, and I'd slept in worse conditions than that, inside that very house.

22

During my freshman year of high school, I decided I was going to kill myself. I'd stopped taking my Prozac long ago, when Mom no longer cared to make sure she called in the refills, because she had to do it more often than normal since the pill bottles often got lost in the mess. She thought this made her look neglectful and decided not calling at all was the better solution.

I still had that same pair of scissors from when I used to cut before. I'd hidden them in an empty DVD case in my room. Mom never knew what I used when I was cutting, so she didn't know to look for those. I was prepared. I was ready to die. I went as far as writing up a suicide note with special requests for my funeral.

Dear Mom,

Everything in me hurts. I believe the greatest pain on this Earth is heartache and depression. I wake up each day feeling worse than the day before. I'm not sure you'll miss me too much. We barely talk as it is. And you already told me yourself that you don't like me.

I'll never be good enough for you or Grandma and Grandpa. I'll never be what you need me to be. I'm not okay. I haven't been okay for a long time. I want to finally get out of your hair for good. Ol' Minerva is ready to move on from this world. I will miss you because despite everything we've gone through, all the fights, the house, the secrets, the lies…despite all that, I love you so much. I really do. But I don't think we can move past it all. I don't think there are any more fresh starts in our future. I think we used them all up.

I'm not doing this to hurt you. I'm not doing this for you at all. I'm doing this for me. I'm tired. I'm just so tired, Mom. I hurt so much. It's a pain I can't describe. It weighs on me every second of every day. So heavy on my chest that I can't breathe. I feel like the wind has been knocked out of me and I can't move. I don't want to fight anymore.

Everything I do is wrong. I can't go on like this. I don't want to be here anymore. I'm so lonely. I can't keep going on like everything's fine. I can't pretend anymore. I will never be anything more than a disappointment. I'm so sorry for all I've put you through. You deserve much better than that, much better than me.

I picked out the clothes I want to be buried in. They're hanging on the back of my door. Please play the song "Perfect" by Simple Plan at the funeral. The lyrics will really show you how I feel. I miss you, Mom. I've missed you for a long time.

Until we meet again.

Love Always,

Dominic

I finished my note and folded it neatly on my desk. I opened the DVD case to find the scissors were still tucked inside. I removed the cap, and the blades shined in the light. The metal shears were the most sublime thing I'd seen in a long while. I spread them apart and pressed the point against my wrist, ready to pierce my skin and force them vertically down my forearm. I was ready to die. I was sure of it. So why did I end up chickening out? Why did I put the scissors down, cap them, and stop myself?

Mom found my note a week later. I didn't throw it out just in case I needed to use it after all. I wasn't at the house when she found it. She was snooping around my room to see if her thief of a son had stolen anything else from her when she saw it sitting on my desk.

I came in that night from hanging out with Tommy, and Mom didn't say a word except, "We're having lunch at Grandma and Grandpa's tomorrow at noon. So don't go anywhere."

* * *

"Annie, how are things with the house?" Grandma asked after we had all served ourselves the shredded chicken sandwiches and macaroni salad she had made the next day for lunch.

"Can I have a glass of milk?" I asked.

"Um, yeah, sure," Grandma said.

I stood from the table and made my way to the cupboard to grab a glass.

"Things are fine," Mom said.

"Hang on," Grandma interrupted. "Dominic?"

"Yeah?"

"Next time you go to the store, I'm going to need you to pick up some milk and bring it here for when you're over. I can't afford to just give you everything I've got in my fridge. So maybe if you think you might want something to drink, you should pick some up and leave it here."

"Oh," I said, standing at the fridge with the door open. "I don't really have any money or anything. I don't have to drink the milk if you don't want me to."

"All right, then yeah, maybe you should just have some water. And shut that fridge door, will you? You're wasting electricity," said Grandma. "Anyway, Ann. You were saying?"

"You asked how things with the house were and I said they're fine. Not much to tell," Mom said.

"What's that mean? It's still a mess?" Grandpa asked.

"It's better than it was," Mom lied. The house was the worst it had ever been. "But it's hard to want to do anything when Dominic tells me he hates me and is vandalizing the house again. But I've been doing the best I can keeping up on it by myself."

I side-eyed her, feeling that familiar anger start to rise, pretty sure my eyes had changed color.

"By yourself?" Grandpa said.

"Yes, by myself."

"What? Dominic hasn't been helping?"

"No, he has better things to do, apparently. Like skip school. Sneak out. You know, the usual. Right, Dominic?"

"Oh, better things, huh? I thought we talked about you helping out with the house and listening to your mother?"

"We did," I said.

"And?"

"And I'm sorry. It won't happen again."

"You ought to have to do some work for your poor mother to pay back the damages you've caused. You sure are ungrateful," Grandpa said.

I didn't respond. I kept my head down and stared at my plate. I no longer had an appetite.

"Anyway," Grandma said hesitantly a moment later, breaking the silence. "How are you doing, Dominic?"

"I'm fine," I said through a mouthful of salad I was forcing myself to eat. I didn't know if I'd get much to eat later. Might as well get something in my stomach while I still could.

"You sure about that?" Grandpa asked.

"Yeah. Why wouldn't I be?" I furrowed my brow.

"Your mom found this," Grandma said, pulling my note from her apron pocket and laying it across the table.

My stomach dropped. I looked at Mom, who was eating her sandwich as if that conversation wasn't happening right next to her.

"Mom, are you serious? Why couldn't you just talk to me about this?" I asked.

She wouldn't look at me.

"We're all here to talk to you about this, Dominic," said Grandma.

"We know how you like to overreact to things, so your mom asked us to help," Grandpa said. "Tell me about this letter."

"What about it? I think you know what it is," I said.

"Don't be a smartass," said Grandpa.

SON OF A HOARDER

"Were you serious? The things you're talking about in here, I mean. Were you serious when you wrote them, or is this some sort of disgusting joke?" Grandma asked.

"I don't know. I was serious, I guess," I said, not wanting to tell them how close I came to ending my life.

"You guess?" Grandpa asked. "You guess you were serious about wanting to kill yourself?"

"Yeah."

Grandpa rolled his eyes and huffed out an exaggerated breath. "I just don't know about you sometimes, kid," he said. "How do you think this makes us feel, seeing something like this?"

"Your poor mother was in tears when she told us what she had found," Grandma said.

I needed to get out of there. My stomach hurt. Spit gathered in the back of my throat, ready to help me expel what little food I had ingested. "May I be excused, please? I don't feel well."

"Yes, fine," Grandma said. "But this conversation's not over."

I stepped through the back door to their wide-open acreage and made my way to the porch swing. I couldn't hold back any longer and began to cry. I was alone now and the conversation we'd just had solidified that. I was certain no one cared about me anymore. I sat outside on the porch while everyone ate their food, presumably still talking about me and all the issues I had caused.

I could see Grandma through the window gathering up everyone's plates. She looked back at me and opened the door.

"What are you doing out here? Why are you crying? Don't be a baby," she said, stepping outside.

"I just, it's just that…I don't know. I mean, I just kind of feel like no one cares about me anymore," I stuttered through my tears.

"Why would you say that? Don't be ridiculous." She turned and began to walk away.

"That was aggressively unhelpful," I said.

Grandma swatted her hand and brushed me off. "You have absolutely no idea what it feels like to have no one care about you, Dominic. Every one of us has shown you nothing but love since the day you were born. You're acting like a spoiled little brat."

My suicide letter was never mentioned again after that day.

23

I was failing the ninth grade. I skipped school more often than I went. I didn't care anymore. My skipping school got me a lot of in-school suspensions, which is a day that is spent in isolation at a private cubicle in the office, and Saturday school, which is exactly how it sounds: school on a Saturday from eight in the morning until noon. I usually skipped those, too. Mom hated having a son like me, and it brought me the tiniest bit of joy to see her hurting like I was.

"How do you think this makes me look, Dominic?" Mom asked as I pushed my way through the front door, squishing the bags behind it. The contents in the bags crunched loudly, breaking against the pressure of the steel door. "What do you think people will think of me when you're failing school like this? I work for the damn district." Mom was waving my report card above her head.

"Where'd you get that?" I asked. "I didn't even know they were handing those out yet."

"One of your teachers was kind enough to bring it to my work. She said she was worried you wouldn't show it to me. Do you have any idea how embarrassing that is? They're going to think I'm a terrible mother. What about my job? Do you ever think of anyone but yourself? God, you are so selfish. And on top of all that, you're failing. Failing. I just…I don't know. I literally do not know what to say. I'm so pissed off right now, I don't even have the words to comprehend the way you've ruined my day."

"So what if I'm failing? They'll just make me take summer school or something like that. It's really not that big of a deal. I'll try to do better," I said.

"Oh, you'll do more than try. I'm calling your grandfather about this."

"What, why? Why can't you just talk to me about things? Why do you have to call him? Why do you like to watch me get in trouble instead of trying to work things out just between us? Why do you always have to make our problems their problems, too?"

"Why, why, why?" Mom mocked. "You know exactly why. I can't talk to you. I can't reason with you. You're impossible. You just get so damn upset and then start freaking out and hitting things. I can't handle that stress anymore. It's too much. I've done what I can to raise you as a single mother without any help, and it's time that I set aside my pride and realize I can't do this on my own anymore. Grandpa offered to help and take some of the stress off my shoulders when I need him, and I accepted. I need a break."

My grandfather showed up to the house an hour later. He honked from the bottom of the driveway to get my attention. He knew he couldn't come up to the door or come in the house. I carefully inched the door open, letting a little sliver of light in the darkened house, then squeezed through, shutting it behind me. He stood with his arms crossed leaning against the hood of his car.

"Hi, Grandpa," I said, waving timidly, knowing I wasn't going to like what was coming.

"Dominic," he said formally, greeting me the way a supervisor would greet a subordinate. "Your mother tells me you don't think school is that big of a deal, and the fact that you're failing is also not a big deal. Is this true?"

"No. I mean, yeah. Sort of," I stammered.

"I don't have time for this. Did you say that or not?"

"Yeah, but I didn't say school wasn't a big deal. I said failing wasn't. And I only said that it's not that big of a deal because I just meant that I was going to do better and I'd make up for it. I'll do summer school or something."

"That's not what she told me," Grandpa said. His brow furrowed, and his crossed arms tightened against each other. "Maybe you should have said that to her, then."

"I'll tell her," I said, defeated.

I stared at my feet, hoping he would leave soon if I said all the right things. Mom was using me as her shield again, deflecting the heat from herself. Someone must have asked her about the house.

"If you keep up this lifestyle you've got going on, you're going to end up in prison. Or more likely, you'll end up selling drugs or doing drugs. If you're not already, that is. I ought to take you down to get drug tested. Would you pass?"

"Yes."

"Well, we might find out soon. Let me think on it for a while. We love you, you know? We don't want you to end up a homeless drug addict, whoring yourself out for crack money. At that point, prison would be a blessing for you. When I think about your future, that's what I picture: you out prostituting in the streets. Blowing some herpes-ridden guy for crack money. Does that sound fun to you?"

"No, it doesn't. But that's not going to be me."

"It will be if you don't straighten up and get your shit together. You know, Dominic, you used to do so well in school. I don't know what's going on between you and your mom. I don't understand it. When will enough be enough? This has got to stop. I mean, what's this all really about? What did she do to deserve this?"

I didn't respond. I didn't have an answer. I never did, and they all knew it. I sounded pathetic when I tried to describe my feelings. I was written off as an ungrateful and hormonal teenager. I was told it's normal to be moody and fight with parents and that no house is perfect or clean all the time; that no mother is wonderful and sweet all the time. I didn't know how to tell them how much it hurt every day just to wake up and exist. I didn't know how to tell them how tired I was, that all I wanted to do was sleep my entire life away. I didn't know how to tell them how badly I wanted to die. I didn't know how to tell them I didn't care about anything at all anymore, least of all my grades and future. Because I didn't even want to have a future.

I woke up every single day wishing I hadn't woken up at all and hoping that day would be the one I finally worked up the courage to end my life once and for all. I didn't know how to say any of that. The only thing I knew was that I had no one I could talk to. No one understood me or believed my problems were real and my feelings were legitimate. Grandma and Grandpa didn't want to hear what I had to say. Mom turned everything I said against me. Uncle Kai and Aunt Gretchen rarely returned my phone calls, so I stopped trying. I was completely alone.

"How was your little talk with Grandpa?" Mom asked with a smirk when I got back inside.

"Fuck off."

"What did you just say to me? Do you want me to call him to come back here?"

"Dumb bitch," I muttered under my breath as I stomped away from her.

"I heard that, you little shit," she shouted down the hall at me.

* * *

In the middle of the school year, I got into a fight with a kid in one of my classes. His name was Elliot. I never liked him. He was one of the popular kids, the ones who think because they play sports and have money that they're better than everyone else. He liked to make fun of loners like me. His favorite thing to do was knock the books out of the hands of any kids he deemed to be a loser, and when they'd bend down to pick up their things, Elliot pushed them into the lockers.

Elliot, a master of words and wit, kept calling me Dominic "Smell Nerd" instead of Leonard. My whole life I was taught that one of the worst possible things you can be is the smelly kid at school. I ignored Elliot as much as possible, but he was relentless.

"Hey, Smell Nerd," "Does anyone else smell that?" or "Smell Nerd, did you shit your pants again?" was all I heard every time I passed him in the halls. His goon squad would start laughing, never wanting to go against their school king. If they got on Elliot's bad side, then they were no better off than I was. They'd probably get it worse.

The day of the fight, I'd had enough. I was tired of being called "Smell Nerd." It was such an insult.

"Hey, Smell Nerd," Elliot said when I passed him in the hall on the way to English. "You smell like my little brother when he needs his diaper changed."

"Oh, I've been graced with a brand-new insult. Glad to see you're using your brain today," I said.

"The fuck did you just say to me, punk?"

"You know, you are just *so* clever, Elliot. Please tell me, where do you come up with such genius insults?"

"You need to shut your fuckin' mouth, Smell Nerd."

"Or what? You'll talk more shit? You'll kick my ass?" I asked, knocking his books out of his hands for a change.

"Yeah, I'll beat your fuckin' ass," Elliot threatened.

"Do it, then. I don't give a fuck. People like you make me sick, getting off on hurting others. You might think I smell like shit, but I'd rather smell like shit than be an actual piece of shit like you."

When I turned to walk away, he pushed me into the lockers so hard, my head bounced off them. I couldn't see straight. I was knocked off balance just long enough to not see the punch that was heading straight for my nose. I instinctively grabbed my face. Blood smeared all over my hand, spilling freely from my nose. The metallic taste assaulted my taste buds as it dripped into my mouth.

I stood up straight and rushed right for Elliot, hitting him in the chest with my shoulder. He grunted, searching for air after the impact. I knocked him to the ground and started to hit him. I'd had plenty of practice with all the door and wall punching I'd done before. I don't remember all of the fight. I blacked out for a few seconds, which is only about as long as it lasted. A teacher in the class next to us heard the commotion and pulled me off him. I got a few good punches in, and possibly took a few more, too. The two of us were sent to the office with fat lips and bloody noses.

We were both suspended for three days and were told that the next time would be a week, and if there happened to be a third time, we'd be expelled.

"Dominic," the principal, Mrs. Alvez, said after she excused Elliot, "I need to talk to you for just a moment longer."

Elliot looked back as if she might have meant him, too.

"You're excused, Elliot. Please go gather your things, and I'll call your parents in just a moment to come pick you up."

"I drove myself here," he said.

"Even better. Gather your things and you can head on out. We'll see you in three days."

"You won't call my parents, then?"

"No, I'm still going to. They just won't need to pick you up." She smiled.

"Great," he huffed, slamming the door behind him.

"Yes?" I said after Elliot left.

"The school counselor, Mrs. Waggoner, have you ever met her?"

"Can't say that I have."

"I would like you to talk to her before you leave."

"Now?"

"Yes."

Why was I being singled out? "Elliot started the fight. Why do only I have to go?"

"Mrs. Waggoner will talk to you all about that, okay?

170

She's waiting for you. Do you know where her office is?"

"Yeah," I said.

I stood to leave and made my way out of Mrs. Alvez's office. Mrs. Waggoner was on the side opposite the principal. In the middle was the secretary's desk. Behind the secretary was Mr. Freed, the school's resource officer. He was a nice guy, though he scared and intimidated everyone when they first met him. He was six-six, bald, and enjoyed a good workout.

"Hi, you must be Dominic," Mrs. Waggoner said when I opened the already-cracked door to her office.

"That's me."

"It's nice to meet you."

"You too," I said flatly. I didn't mean it. I didn't want to be there.

"I heard you got into a fight a little while ago. You want to tell me about that?"

"Not really."

Mrs. Waggoner laughed. She seemed nice enough, I just didn't see the point in talking to her.

"Well, do you think you can tell me about it anyway?"

"That idiot Elliot wouldn't stop calling me names and saying I smelled. He's always knocking people's books out of their hands, and he's always making fun of everyone. I just got tired of it. He's a bully. So I knocked the books out of his hands this time. He didn't like that, so he punched me, and I fought back. That's the whole story."

"He makes fun of you and other kids. And that's it? That's what triggered you, nothing else?"

"Nothing else."

"What's your life like outside of school?"

"What do you mean?"

"What do you do for fun?"

"Nothing really. Hang out with my friend. Read. Do nothing at my house."

"What's life at your house like?"

"It's normal. Same as everyone else, I'm sure."

"You can tell me anything, Dominic. Everything you say here is confidential. I won't say a word to anyone unless you're in immediate danger, okay?"

My heart sank. What did she know? What was she trying to get at?

"There's nothing to tell," I said.

"Do you feel safe at your house?"

"Yeah." That wasn't a lie. I didn't feel like I was in danger.

"How are things with your mom?"

"They're fine. Look, can I go now? Please? Nothing against you. It's just that I don't feel like talking. I've done this whole counseling thing before. It didn't work then, and it's not going to work now."

"Why were you in counseling before?"

"I don't have to talk to you, do I? It's not like, mandatory, right?"

"No, it's not. But I would love it if you and I could continue."

"Do you know my mom?" I asked.

"I do, yes. Most of the school district employees are familiar with each other," she said.

"I'm going to go, okay? It was nice to meet you." I stood and opened the door.

I knew then I would never be able to talk to Mrs. Waggoner. Mom showed a side of her to others that I was not privileged enough to experience myself. People constantly told me, "Oh, you're so lucky to have a mom like her," or, "Annie's your mom? I just love her. She's so funny and sweet." I just wanted to shake them and scream, "She's not who you think she is!"

Everything about public Mom was a facade. From her laugh, to her opinions, to her complimenting of others. It was all fake. Nobody knew Mom like I did. It made me want to pull my hair out because, really, who would believe a parent-disrespecting, underage-smoking, school-skipping delinquent like me? Why couldn't I shake someone to their senses and compel them to see what I saw, know the Annie I know? But more importantly, why didn't Mom show me her sweet and funny side, too?

"Dominic,"—Mrs. Waggoner stood and put her hand on my shoulder—"you don't have to talk to me now, that's fine. But please know that I am here if you ever change your mind. Anytime. If you need to leave class to talk to me, or if you want to talk after school, I'm here, all right? You can tell me anything. Anything at all. I mean that."

"Bye," I said. I don't know why I was so rude to her. I felt like she must have known or suspected something, and I wasn't prepared to have that conversation with anyone. I didn't want to cause any problems for Mom or for myself. I never talked to her again, but she smiled at me every time I saw her from then on out.

After I moved out of Mom's house and into my own place, I realized why Elliot called me "Smell Nerd." Mom liked to think she did a good job of keeping up appearances. She kept the clothes I wore the cleanest, and I showered every day. But it wasn't enough, and at the time, I didn't know that. I lived in that house. I lived with the mess. I was used to the smells that came with it.

The first time I met up with Mom after leaving, she brought a foulness with her. I smelled it. The house. It was a cross between a basement that hadn't been ventured into in years and clothes that sat wet for too long. Like a bathing suit you swam in and forgot about. The smell never leaves the swimsuit, no matter how many times you wash it. It's embedded into it, becomes a part of the suit. The only way to rid it is to bin it. It disgusted and embarrassed me to know that's how I smelled all those years I was stuck in that hellhole. I was oblivious and numb to the stench of the house. But it was there. I ended up being the smelly kid after all.

24

The only times I left my room were to get food if Mom bought me any or to use the restroom, and even then, I would piss out my window most of the time just to avoid her. When she was mad at me, which was often, she would refuse to get me anything when she ordered from the drive-thrus. Tommy would sometimes bring me something to eat or the two of us would walk to the store and try to find a cute girl we could convince to give us some money.

I spent as little time at the house as was possible, and when I was there, I did nothing but sleep. I couldn't get out of bed. I was tired all the time. Once in a while, if I was feeling up to it, I escaped my reality through books or by blaring my music so loud, I could close my eyes and drown out the rest of the world. I hated being there. I hated Mom.

I spent over an hour one weekend, a few weeks after my last talk with Grandpa, kicking at the wooden bars that were nailed deep into the outside of the house and across my window. I grabbed the sides of the open window, my fingers gripping so tightly the white plastic frame dug deep into my flesh. My hands hurt, but I wouldn't give up until I had at least enough space to get in and out. I wasn't going to let Mom or anyone else confine me. Mom may have turned our house into a prison, but I would not be her prisoner. I would not let her sentence me to that life.

I kicked the middle of the bars over and over, causing them to bow, and eventually they began to snap. The wood cracked little by little with each stomp of my foot until mercifully it splintered and one bar became two, each piece dangling against the side of the house, the nails still doing their job. I did this for every bar against my window, except for the one at the very top. With each snap, I felt my freedom inching closer. Kicking off the bars, signaling a big "fuck you" to those who tried to cage me, brought a smile to my face, a rarity for me. I could not be tamed. I could not be held. I was going to do whatever I wanted, whenever I wanted, and no one could stop me.

Later that day, I heard Mom howling with laughter from the living room. I couldn't remember the last time I had heard her laugh like that, a real belly laugh. I needed to know what brought out the old mom; the mom who could enjoy herself and find happiness in things. The one whose laugh and smiles were contagious.

"What's so funny?" I asked. I smiled at her. She looked so pretty when she was happy. I missed her.

"It's…it's…oh my gosh," she stuttered, unable to get the words out through her laughter. Tears, blackened by her mascara, were streaming down her cheeks as she tried to catch her breath. "It's you." She pointed toward the TV.

"What?"

Mom was watching a weekend rerun of Oprah. "It's you," she said, wiping the tears, black streaks of makeup raccooning her eyes. "Oh man, I can't see through the tears." This realization had her guffawing hard enough that sound would no longer come out. She sat wheezing on her spot on the couch, the tears flooding harder than before.

"I don't get it." I chuckled.

"Look at the guy on TV," Mom said.

"Okay…" I was still confused.

"Read the description under his name."

There were now three people on the screen. Oprah, an older lady with graying, medium-length, curly hair and glasses so thick her eyes were magnified, and a man who looked to be about mid-twenties with a blond crew cut, clean shaven, and wearing a shirt that was buttoned up to his neck. I didn't know how he could breathe with that thing on. Under their names were the descriptions: Hoarder and Son of a Hoarder. Oprah was talking with them about their struggles and how he felt growing up with someone like his mom. Was I reading that right? This guy's mom was a hoarder, too? There were people like us out there?

"Son of a hoarder," I said.

Mom cracked up again, laughing so hard she started choking. The choking threw her into another fit of hysterics. I laughed, too.

"Son of a hoarder," Mom said. "Get it? Like son of a bitch."

"Oh." I smiled, finally understanding. "Yeah, I get it."

"I'm going to start saying that now. Instead of son of a bitch, I'm going to say son of a hoarder."

"Me too."

"But also, you know, that's you. You're the son of a hoarder."

"That I am," I said, no longer laughing.

25

The summer I turned fifteen, Tommy and I were inseparable. We spent all our days and nights looking for a good time. Most of those good times were in the forms of drugs, alcohol, and girls. Marijuana and alcohol were both a first for me that summer. Tommy was a bit more experienced than I was. He was up for trying anything and everything. I never wanted to try anything more serious than weed.

I can recall a few times that traumatized me and put me off from ever wanting to try anything else. The first time was when the two of us got drunk one night and watched *Requiem for a Dream*. That movie should be labeled as a horror film and marketed as a great "Don't do drugs" tool. Another time was when Tommy had heard from some kids at school that you could get high by drinking cough syrup. He drank the entire bottle at school one day and had to be picked up by his mom after he did nothing but throw up the red liquid all over the locker room for an hour.

What put me off even more than the movie and non-stop puking was the time Tommy called me around ten in the evening one Saturday. He was talking in a euphoric voice that I had never heard from him before.

"I'm so high," he said, giggling.

"What are you on?" I asked, realizing it didn't sound like his usual surfer dude marijuana high.

"I took X."

"What's X? You mean ecstasy?"

"Yeah, man. Ecstasy. And that's exactly how I feel. Like I'm in ecstasy. That's probably why they call it that."

"Just be careful, bro. I heard that stuff can overheat your body and kill you," I warned as I laid my head down onto my pillows.

"Oh, no, I don't believe that. It feels too good to be killing me. I wanted to try to have sex with someone, but I heard that having sex on ecstasy is the best and that you'll never want to have sex like ever again unless you're on it. So I don't think I'm going to try it after all. I need to be able to get hard without drugs, you know?"

"Yeah." I laughed. "I agree with ya there."

"Hold on," Tommy said. He started vomiting. The loud, barking sounds of him heaving made my stomach churn. Hearing or seeing others throw up made me want to do the same.

"You okay?" I asked an entire minute of silence later.

"Yeah, I'm fine." He was back with the euphoric voice. "I'm just playing with my puke."

"What?" I sat up in my bed, unsure if I had heard him correctly.

"I'm playing with my puke."

"Like touching it?"

"Yeah. I'm running my hands through it. I threw up in my lap, and it looked so smooth and soft, I wanted to touch it."

"That's disgusting," I said.

"No, it's not. I swear. I wish you were here so I could show you. It feels so good on my hands. It's velvety and smooth. It feels like an orgasm for my fingers."

"Dude, you're going to make me puke now."

"You should. Then you'll know what I'm talking about. I wish I could puke more so I would have even more to play with. All this time, we've been flushing our puke when we should have been massaging ourselves with it," he said.

"Massaging your hands with it?"

"Not just my hands. I'm massaging my face now. Oh my God, Dominic. It feels even better on my face. Holy shit, I've never felt this good before. This is better than sex. Can you believe that?"

"No."

* * *

My first time smoking weed hooked me. It was late at night, and Tommy and I were sitting behind my house under my bedroom window. He reached into the pocket of his jeans, pulling out a lighter and a snack-size plastic baggie. In it were small, stone-shaped pieces of the green herb.

"Ready to try some yet?" he asked, opening the bag and breathing in the aromatic and distinct scent.

"Yeah, I think I am," I said.

Tommy shoved the bag under my nose. I loved the smell of marijuana even before I'd ever tried it. Tommy finished off the can of soda he was drinking and made a dent in the side. He pulled a safety pin out of his pocket and poked five small holes in the dent, then another larger hole on the side of the can.

"I'll show you how it's done," he said, placing a small nug of weed on top of the holes. He put the mouth of the can up to his lips, flicked the lighter on, and inhaled. The flame drew itself downward, lured in by the air being sucked through the aluminum. The weed, once green, burned a bright orange, the edges singed black. He pulled away from the can, held his breath for a few seconds, then exhaled. The heavy gray smoke escaped his lips and drifted into my face.

It was my turn now. I mimicked Tommy's actions when he handed it to me. The can felt warm against my fingers. The smell of the marijuana was strong. Putting the can up to my mouth, I flicked the lighter on. I made the mistake of trying to point it downward to light the bowl and burnt my fingers instead.

Tommy laughed at me. "Just suck in, and it'll light right up," he said. "You don't have to put it directly on there."

I inhaled, and the flame followed the air moving down toward the can. The hit burned my throat. It was stronger than cigarettes, the smoke dense and something I wasn't used to yet. I coughed right into Tommy's face and nearly dropped the can. Tommy dissolved into laughter as if my choking was the funniest thing he'd ever seen. The THC got to me instantly. I laughed right along with Tommy.

Tommy and I each took turns taking hits, trying unsuccessfully to blow smoke rings, until there was nothing left but black resin. Tommy smashed the can, getting rid of the evidence, and threw it into one of the piles of garbage outside the house. The two of us sat back against the house, silent and unmoving. I felt the blood coursing through my veins. It was thick, like the way wet sand feels when you pick it up out of the water, smooth and heavy as it trails down your fingertips.

"Tommy, I've got it," I said, breaking the silence.

"Got what?"

"I know exactly how weed works."

"You do?" he asked, genuinely curious.

"Yeah, man. I totally have it because I can feel it right now," I said. "Okay, so what if the reason you get high is because, like, you know? Like, okay, you know how you breathe in the smoke?"

"Yes, I totally know what you mean."

"Exactly. Okay, so, like you breathe it in, and it goes in your mouth and up through your sinuses, right?"

"Mm-hmm," Tommy said, closing his eyes.

"All right, so after that, it goes into your brain. I know this because one time, I was at the doctor, and they stuck some Q-Tip looking thing up my nose when they thought I was sick, and I swear that fucker touched my brain."

"Gross." Tommy laughed.

"It was. Anyway, hold on before I forget what I'm saying. Okay, so anyway, what if it goes into your brain? Then, like all the smoke surrounds your brain, and your brain can't think or see straight because it's like surrounded by the weed smoke, you know?"

"Dude, yes."

"And then, over time, as you breathe out, the smoke slowly comes back out of your nose, and then when it's all gone, you're sober again."

"Holy shit, dude. That has to be like *exactly* what happens. You're so fuckin' smart. Maybe we should stop breathing out so we don't sober up."

"Tommy, I can't wait to get out of here," I said, changing the subject. "I'm going to move so far away. I'm never coming back to this place."

"Me too, man. Fuck this town," Tommy said, not realizing I meant my house and not the town.

Tommy and I smoked a lot together after my first time. His parents gave him a hefty weekly allowance, and he didn't mind buying for the both of us. Weed helped remove me from my life. I could live in another world, one where I had no more problems and everything was funny and weightless. In those wonderful moments, I had nothing else going on in my life. The only thing that existed was me, Tommy, and a bag of weed.

Alcohol was a whole other story. The first time I tried it, we had stolen a bottle of vodka from Tommy's parents' unlocked liquor cabinet and sped back over to my house to drink outside my window. Tommy took a big swig off the bottle like he was gulping water. I tried to do the same but ended up spitting it out instead. The foul liquid burned my tongue. I tried again, taking a much smaller sip, this time knowing what I was in for.

The two of us emptied the three-quarters full bottle, and I puked my guts out. I threw up until there was nothing left in my stomach, and then dry heaved off and on for the rest of the night. The next day, I didn't leave my bed as usual, this time for a different reason. My head hurt, like a nail was stuck directly between my eyes. I couldn't see straight. I was

nauseated in a way I didn't know was possible. My stomach
was in knots, churning like a storm was brewing in there. It felt
as if the saliva in my mouth was building up every second, ready
to help me empty my body of all its contents.

My first hangover lasted two full days. I didn't let that
stop me, though. Now I knew what my limits were and that I
didn't have to drink as much as I did that first time to feel
happy. I liked drinking a lot. I loved the way I could get so
deliriously shit-faced that I was a totally free spirit that could
say and be anything I wanted, and I likely wouldn't remember
it the next day. Tommy's cousin, Brendan, now twenty-one,
bought us alcohol any time we wanted, as long as we provided
a buyer's fee. Our favorite thing to do was find a party. We
didn't care whose party it was or where it was. Parties had girls,
and girls meant sex.

I used sex a lot to try to make a real human connection,
to try to feel something that indicated I wasn't dead inside, even
if it was just for one night. One moment of happiness in a life
I hated. But with each hook up, they became more and more
meaningless. Each one worse than the last. I didn't want a
girlfriend. I knew I wouldn't be able to let anyone in, not in the
way a relationship takes. I couldn't be my true self around
anyone. I could barely stand to be my true self when I was
alone. I'd never be able to let anyone know more than a
superficial, surface-only version of myself.

If there were no parties, Tommy and I would jump inside
my window and drink in my room. At first, we tried to be quiet
and not let Mom know what we were doing. But eventually, I
knew she wasn't going to say or do anything, so we stopped
pretending we weren't there. I knew she wouldn't come down
the hall and risk Tommy hearing her plodding through the
mess, and she wouldn't dare open my door with him there. She
would never chance him accidentally seeing what was on the
other side. And more than that, she cared how she looked in
his eyes. She knew she couldn't yell at me with him around—
it might make her look bad.

But really, how did she think it looked that her son was able to sneak in and out freely, openly drink in his own bedroom, and she never checked on him no matter how loud and obnoxious he was? She never cared how she looked in my eyes. If she did, we wouldn't have been stuck in the situation we were in. No, it only mattered what other people thought. It never made sense to me how others' opinions mattered more than her own son's. I had told Tommy at the beginning of the summer why we had to go through my window. He hadn't understood what "my house is a mess" meant. No one ever did.

* * *

"I know you've been letting Tommy in your room," Mom confronted me one morning when I came out to see if we had any bread I could eat. I would have to eat it plain since we had nothing else in the house.

"Good morning to you, too," I said.

"I told you no one's allowed to come over."

"We stay in my room and never come out. Why does it matter?"

"Because I don't want anyone here."

"You only don't want anyone to see the house. It's not like he comes out and sees your disgusting fucking mess, okay? We go in and out of my window. I don't get the luxury of being able to have my friend come through the front door like normal people do. You can deal with him being in my room, all right? I never really got to have anyone over when I was younger. You owe this to me." I was getting angry now. My throat started to burn as that same horrid lump began to form. I hated how quick my body wanted to cry when I was upset or angry.

"I don't owe you shit. I gave you everything you ever wanted. You had a house to live in. I fed you. I bought you whatever clothes you wanted. You had so many toys. I dealt with so much just so I could give you what you wanted," Mom said, raising her voice.

"You think because you bought me things it makes up for everything else?"

"Everything else? How do you honestly believe you had it so bad?"

"You were never there for me!" I shouted. "I could never talk to you about my feelings. I could never come to you for anything. I still can't. I can't talk to you and let you know what's going on with me. Do you know how lonely that is? To not really have anyone there for you? To have no one you can talk to because they just don't fucking get it? You always have a headache and need to lay down for a while. Or…or you turn everything around on me and go tattle on me to Grandpa, twisting my words to make me look bad."

"Nothing I have ever said to him was a lie."

"Maybe not a lie, but not exactly the truth, either, and you know it. I kept all your secrets. I'm the one who did everything for you, not the other way around. I was protecting you when it should have been you protecting me. You broke me. But I'm done now. I'm fucking done. Thanks for ruining my day. You can fuck right off," I said, turning around and marching back to my room.

"Yeah, well, fuck you, too," Mom said, never moving from her spot on the couch.

* * *

I was rarely sober that summer and had the most fun I'd ever had in the unhealthiest way. I remember one time, in particular, I was so drunk, I used Tommy's cell phone and called my own mom on our house phone. When she picked up, I stupidly asked, "Is Tommy there?"

She said, "Dominic, is that you?"

I remember saying, "Oh, shit" as I hung up the phone and realized what had happened. Tommy was standing right next to me. We were in my room at the time. I thought for sure that would be the time that she had finally had enough and would storm through my door, kick Tommy out, and act like she actually cared. But she didn't move from the couch, and an hour later, the two of us passed out drunk on my floor.

When I was younger, maybe ten or eleven years old, Mom would often tell me that if I ever found myself in an unsafe situation, I could call her. She said she would pick me up anytime, anywhere, no questions asked. She promised she would never be mad and said she would be happy just knowing I was safe.

There was one incident that summer where I found myself stranded from my group in another town. I walked for miles until I found a payphone. The booth smelled like urine. I fished fifty cents out of my jeans pocket, picked up the receiver, and dialed the number for our landline.

"Hello?" Mom answered groggily after five rings. It was late, around two o'clock in the morning. I was worried she wouldn't pick up at all and I'd have to spend the night in the phone booth.

"I need you to come get me," I said.

Mom did indeed come pick me up. But she was most certainly mad. She screamed that horrible, gut-wrenching scream of hers the entire drive back to the house. It hurt that she didn't keep her promise. All that taught me was that I couldn't ever call her again, no matter how much trouble I was in. I had to fend for myself. Eventually, Mom stopped asking where I was going or if I'd be coming back. She didn't enforce a curfew, and I would have laughed at her if she'd tried. Tommy told his parents that he was staying at my house most nights, even if neither of us were actually there.

That summer is a bit of a haze, which may be for the best. I do remember one night when I wandered off away from Tommy and finally felt courageous enough to attempt suicide. He and I pre-funked on Four Lokos at my house to get a buzz going before we got picked up by Brendan. We weren't so drunk that we were falling down but buzzed enough that a lot of our inhibitions were out the window.

Brendan took us to a party at his friend's house. I don't remember exactly who this friend was, I only remember that he lived out of town on a big private property with a barn and horse stables. Those were our favorite kinds of places to party. There were hardly any neighbors, and if there were, it was likely they were doing the same thing we were. Brendan turned up the stereo in his 4-Runner loud enough that we didn't need anything else. The bass from his subs echoed around the property. Everyone was shooting the shit around a bonfire, which I didn't like, but the alcohol helped calm my anxiety.

Brendan bought us each two more Four Lokos, and Tommy and I got started on those right away. The only girls there were the girlfriends of some of the other guys, so I knew I wasn't going to be getting any that night. Therefore, I needed something else to do since I knew I wouldn't be content sitting around a fire the whole time. Tommy was having fun talking with everyone, and I didn't want to take him away from that. I told him I was going for a walk.

I ambled over to the big red barn on the edge of the property, far enough away from everyone that no one would be able to see me. The sliding doors on the front were partially open already, so I took that as an invitation to have a look inside.

There was a car in there. Some vintage looking coupe with primer and no paint. It looked to be in the middle of a restoration. To the side of the car were three tall, red, metal toolboxes, the kind you see in a mechanic's shop. In between two of the tool chests was a heavy-duty ladder, the ones people use to get onto roofs.

An idea popped into my head then. I thought, *I'm going to use this to climb to the top of this barn. Then, I'm going to jump off, and I hope my skull breaks open and splatters all over this property.* I didn't hesitate for fear that I would never get an opportunity like that again. I chickened out the first time and my letter was found.

Since Mom had already read my letter, I didn't need to worry about writing another. She would know why I had done it.

The ladder was weighty. I laid it flat on the ground outside, extended it as far as it would go, then propped it up against the side of the barn. It reached to the top of the sixteen-foot-tall building. I was ready this time, intoxicated and feeling brave. Tonight, I would die. I couldn't wait.

Climbing up there was a little scary. I had never been that high in the air, and the ladder felt wobbly under my unsteady feet. I didn't want to simply fall and break my leg. I needed to get to the roof and jump. I needed to die. This was the night. There was no turning back.

Once I made it to the top, I sat back on the edge of the slanted roof by the eaves. Before I jumped, I spoke out loud, "Mom, I'm sorry. I really am. I'm sorry I didn't end up being the son you wanted or deserved. I'm sorry for what I've done. Grandma and Grandpa, I'm sorry, too. Sorry you had me as a grandson. Sorry you had to help Mom so much when I should have just been a better kid. Uncle Kai and Aunt Gretchen, I just miss you guys so much. I know you have your own life now, but I don't know what happened. I never got to say goodbye, and now I never will. I wish you would have returned my phone calls. I love all of you. See you on the other side." Then, I leaned forward and dove headfirst onto the ground.

Maybe it was my drunken state, or maybe I just didn't know how to dive, but I over-rotated and landed flat on my back, and not on my neck as I'd hoped. The impact stunned me at first, knocking the air out of my lungs. I couldn't breathe. I couldn't move. However, I didn't feel any pain. I thought, *Is this it? Did I do it? Am I finally dead?* Then, I coughed. I coughed so hard I puked all over myself. My body shook violently from the power of the hacking that escaped me. The vomit in my mouth gurgled in my throat, suffocating me until I was able to summon the strength to turn to the side and spit it out. I knew then that I was, unfortunately, still alive.

I took off my sweatshirt, wiped my face with it, and

dumped it behind the barn, leaving me in just a T-shirt. It was a cold night for the summer, but good ol' alcohol helped keep me from freezing. Staggering back over to the fire for warmth, I felt more defeated than ever. I wimped out from offing myself the first time, and now that I'd actually had the courage to try, I failed. I couldn't even get suicide right. Like everything else in life, I'd failed. I failed Mom in the past by not keeping our secrets. I failed her still every day, disappointing her at every level. I was the kind of son you wouldn't wish on your worst enemy. That night confirmed what I had always known. I was a failure.

Nothing was broken or damaged. I only suffered through a week of bruises and soreness, along with a hit to my already non-existent self-esteem. Looking back, I'm thankful I wasn't successful. I'm happy I didn't die in that way and on that night because I can't imagine how it might have hurt the people who would have eventually found me. If Tommy had been the one to find me, how would that have made him feel? Would he blame himself for letting me go off alone while he stayed back to visit with everyone? I'm glad I didn't do that to him.

26

"Can I have some money?" I asked Mom, coming out of my room for only the second time that day. I'd spent the entire day in there, reading and sleeping. I'd come out in the morning to check if there was anything to eat, but there wasn't a crumb in the house. That wasn't anything new. At nine o'clock in the evening, though, my stomach was growling and telling me to find something. Mom usually got some fast food for the both of us. That day, she only bought some for herself.

"No, sorry. I don't have any money," she said. She was punishing me for having Tommy over the night before.

"But you ate fast food twice today. Can I please just have like five bucks? I'm so hungry." I was trying to be nice and not show my annoyance.

"I said 'no.' Now, please go away." She stared past me at the TV and wouldn't look in my direction.

"You're such a selfish bitch," I muttered, heading back toward my room. Mom heard me and started to cry. I didn't care.

There had been many times when I went without food or with very little. Looking back now, it's almost comical thinking of the concoctions I used to come up with. Once, there was only a can of tuna and a can of diet soda in the house. I had tried to eat the tuna straight from the can. But I guess I was spoiled, having gotten used to eating it mixed with mayonnaise. It was so dry, I couldn't swallow it. So I opened the diet soda and poured it into the can of tuna and mixed them together. It was absolutely disgusting. But when you're hungry, you take what you can get. Another time, I ate a spoonful of flour, since we had a three-year-old half-full bag in the cupboard. I choked on that. Eating stale cereal with water instead of milk wasn't so bad, but eating stale cereal with sour milk is a taste I'll never forget.

Mom rang up Grandpa the next morning to tell him what I had said to her. She also told him I had been blatantly defying her, drinking, and doing drugs. She said she knew it for sure this time and didn't need to drug test me. He showed up that afternoon, having told Mom what time he would be there so I could meet him at his car, and he wouldn't have to come up to the door.

"Why are you treating your mother this way again?" he demanded. He leaned against his car, his chest puffed out and arms crossed. "Huh? Answer me."

"I don't know," I said, looking down at the ground.

"You never know. Do you just do it for fun? Does it give you some kind of sick pleasure to see her hurting?"

"No."

"Hmm. I worry that it does because what other reason would you have for doing this to her? What if you had a son? Would you let him treat his mother that way?"

"No," I said. But I knew I wouldn't let his mother treat him the way mine had treated me, either.

"Would you talk to your wife the way you talk to your mom, calling her a bitch and telling her to fuck off? You think that's right? What's wrong with you?"

"I don't know," was all that I could say because, once again, I truly didn't know.

"What the hell could she have possibly done to deserve this? You really think your childhood was that bad? You really believe you had it so bad that your mom deserves this now? I ought to show you what a truly bad childhood looks like."

I didn't say anything in response.

"Is this about the house still?" Grandpa asked.

"Kind of," I said, kicking some of the pebbles in the driveway. I shoved my hands in the pockets of my jeans and kept my head down.

"Get over yourself, Dom," Grandpa scoffed. He was disgusted with me. "You need to start acting like a man and grow the fuck up. Your mom's your mom, whether you like that or not. She deserves respect. You hear me?"

"Yes, sir," I said. Not because I agreed, but because I wanted him to leave. I had nothing else I could think to say. I didn't know how to put my feelings into words. It's so much more than a messy house, but how did I say that? It's more than not being able to have friends over or not having my own space for the majority of my life, but those seem to be the only pathetic examples I could give. Because of that, I looked like I was being unfair and hateful to my mother, and maybe I was. Maybe I was the bad guy. Maybe I was just selfish after all.

But I think maybe it was the constant fear I lived in and the anxiety it caused. I worried every day that someone might find out our secrets. Hiding a secret that big from such a young age weighed heavy on my soul. I beat myself up for not doing enough to protect my mother like she made me promise I would. I had no real explanations.

There's this quote I've heard somewhere that says something along the lines of, "Others won't always remember what you did to them or the things you said to them, but they will never forget the way your actions made them feel." That really rings true for me because that's exactly how it is. I can't tell you for sure what caused my depression or my unending anger. But feeling like a worthless nuisance who will never be more than a failure will do a number on your heart.

I called Tommy after my talk with Grandpa. Even though he was only across the street from me, I didn't want him to see me that upset in person. I needed someone to talk to. I didn't want to bottle my emotions any longer.

"I just, I just want to fucking die," I stammered. I was

crying.

He could barely understand what I was saying. "Whoa, man. What happened?" he asked.

"Everything. I'm just so sick of never being good enough. My mom makes up shit about me and tells on me to my grandparents all the time. They all hate me."

"I really don't think they hate you." Tommy laughed, clearly not taking my pain and sadness seriously.

I wished I could be like him, never knowing that kind of pain actually existed. "No, they do. They think I'm this horrible person that can never do anything right," I sobbed. "Dude, I seriously just want to die."

"No, you don't."

"I do. I want to do everyone a favor and just fucking die. I'm in their way anyway. All I do is make them mad. If I were dead, they wouldn't be mad at me anymore."

"Dude, Dominic, you need to chill."

"You remember that movie we watched last year, *The Wedding Singer*?"

"Mm-hmm."

"Well Robbie's singing that song, and he begs for someone to kill him. He was begging on his knees and he just wanted to die. He wanted someone to put a bullet in his head, and I swear to God, Tommy, that's all I want right now. I want to die. I want my life to be over. I want to go find someone and pick a fight and have them fucking murder me."

"Well, dude, I think you took that movie way too seriously." Tommy chuckled. "It's a comedy. He wasn't serious. It's supposed to be funny."

That was the last time I tried to talk with Tommy or anyone else about my problems with my family.

27

I dropped out of school after I turned sixteen. I tried to keep going, I really did. But getting a job, making money, and finding a way to get out of Mom's house was more important to me. I grew tired of relying on Mom for money and my basic needs. I applied at the grocery store in town, but they required a drug test prior to employment. I knew I wouldn't pass, so I moved on to the movie rental place, Pleasantview Video. They didn't drug test their applicants, and they paid two dollars an hour more than the grocery store. Win-win.

The old-school video store was locally owned by an elderly couple. They still rented out VHS tapes. It was a modest-sized place, no more than a thousand square feet. On the walls were shelves of movies that had been released within the past four months, and in the center of the store were racks of VHS and DVDs that were older. Next to the front door were the registers and a video return slot. Behind the cashier were mini-fridges that contained sodas and bottled waters, and underneath the registers in a glass display case were boxes of candy and other snacks that customers could purchase.

My first shift was training with the store manager, Leslie. She was a short, peppy thing with black spiral curls and a flawless dark complexion. I wouldn't have guessed her to be over thirty, but she said she was actually forty. Leslie was easy-going and fun to be around. She got me excited about the job and made me feel comfortable as a newbie. She and I ended up growing close. We still talk every now and again.

I learned the ins and outs of running a video rental store that first day, which was pretty boring stuff. Movies were to be stocked first by genre, then in alphabetical order. In the back of the store next to the bathroom, the utility closet stored the mop and push broom I would use each night. I learned how to use the cash register, count the money at the end of the night, and how to use the computers to check out the movies to customers. The job itself was okay. I didn't love it, but I knew it could have been worse.

For the most part, I liked my coworkers. There were a few that got on my nerves, but that would happen no matter where I worked. Mostly, I was just happy to be out of the house and making money. My favorite part of the job was the three free movie rentals we were given every day. When new movies were set to be released, the packages arrived a week before we could put them on the shelves. Employees were allowed to watch the yet-to-be released movies, (we called them "pre-streets"), before they hit the shelves so that we could give our opinion of the movies to customers. When I wasn't working or out with Tommy, I was in my room watching movies.

I saved enough money to get my GED. It cost seventy-five dollars at the college in the next town over. I passed every test on my first try and got a perfect score in literature and writing. Mom didn't want me to drop out, but at the age of sixteen, I was no longer legally required to attend school, so there was nothing she could do about it.

After that, I saved the three hundred it cost to take driver's education. Mom took me to the DMV to get my learner's permit since she needed to sign the paperwork. She only agreed to do so because I was the one paying for it. At that time, I would walk to work and driver's ed. Occasionally, if it was a driving practice day, the instructor would come to my house or my work to pick me up. Other times, Leslie helped out when she could. When I finished and passed the course, Leslie took me to the DMV to take both the written and driving tests and get my driver's license.

I'd worked at the video store for nine months and had saved all the money I needed for my current expenses. I got a prepaid burner phone, and Leslie was letting me make payments on a car she was selling. It was a 1995 silver Honda Civic with no body damage or engine work needed. It was perfect. She even did the fluid maintenance on it before she handed me the keys. She sold it to me for five hundred less than her original asking price of two thousand dollars and only asked that I pay what I could as long as I showed that I was trying. Because the car was still registered to her, she kept it under her insurance, which I paid half of every month.

I'll never forget the way Leslie helped me out when I needed it the most. I told her a lot about myself, things that no one up until that point knew. I told her about my troubles with Mom and my grandparents, the behavioral center, and my school problems. Something about her made me want to open up, but I still couldn't tell her everything; I couldn't tell her about the house. She was a kind, genuine person who took me under her wing, and for that, I will be forever grateful. For *her*, I will be forever grateful.

* * *

Mom had surprised me with "We're going to lunch at Grandma and Grandpa's" on one of my days off. This statement always meant something bad was about to happen. When we showed up, Grandma and Grandpa were both sitting on their sofa, and Uncle Kai and Aunt Gretchen were sitting together in the big chair. Their son wasn't there. I hadn't seen them since the very brief lunch they'd treated me to on my birthday earlier that year. We went to A&W and weren't there more than an hour before we parted ways. We had drifted apart over the years. So much was pushing us away from each other, making sure we would never be as close as we once were.

Things had started off okay with the usual hellos and

how are yous. Then, things turned sour when Uncle Kai said, "Annie, we're worried about you guys."

"Why? There's no need," Mom said defensively.

"We know the house is still bad. We think that's why Dominic's been acting out," Aunt Gretchen said.

"The house can't be the only reason for that. Something's wrong with him. He needs help," Grandpa said.

"Yeah, he does need help, but not like you're suggesting," said Uncle Kai.

I hated when they talked about me like I wasn't sitting right there.

"I try to keep the house clean, but it's so hard," Mom said through tears I hadn't realized she'd started to cry.

I felt bad for her. Sometimes I didn't care if she was hurting, but at that moment, she looked defeated. It was my fault. If I hadn't been acting like a little delinquent, no one would know things were bad.

"We know it is, honey. Shh, it's okay," Grandma said. She patted Mom on the back and handed her a tissue.

"No, it's not okay," Uncle Kai said, annoyed.

"How am I supposed to get anything done when my son is out running around the streets all night? He's off doing drugs, drinking, and who the hell knows what else? Next, I'm sure I'll be hearing about how he got some little slut pregnant. I'm worried sick about him all the time. Literally sick. I had to go to the doctor to get nausea medication because of the anxiety he's caused," Mom said. "You expect me to worry about my house when all my focus is on being worried about my son? Really, Kai?" She was right.

"The house was a problem before he was out doing that stuff, Annie, and you know it. Stop trying to throw him under the bus. He's not your scapegoat," said Uncle Kai.

"Now, that's not entirely true," Grandpa interjected. "He never wanted to help his mother out, and that's why things got as bad as they did. And now, he's off doing what he's doing, and it's just getting worse. This isn't a matter of just getting

Annie to fix up the house. This is a matter of fixing Dominic, too."

"I can't believe you guys," Aunt Gretchen, never one for making waves, said. She was crying now, too. "You're just excusing his adult mother's behavior and blaming all of this on a child."

"Dominic's almost a man now," said Grandpa.

"I'm doing better," I said, trying to interrupt the storm I knew was coming. "I got a job, I got my own car. I'm doing better."

"Speaking of your car," Grandma said. "Your mom says you've been smoking in there, is that true?"

"Yeah," I said, unsure of why that mattered.

"Of course it is," Grandma huffed. "That smell doesn't come out, you know?"

"Dominic, why don't you go outside so we can finish talking," said Uncle Kai.

I left out the front door and sat on one of their weathered wicker outdoor chairs. I heard them start screaming at each other, though I couldn't make out what was being said. I pulled the pack of Camels out of my pocket and lit one, no longer caring who I upset with my smoking. I needed that high only a cigarette could give me. I felt numb again. I wasn't sad or upset. I wasn't anything. I didn't know what brought all this on.

Aunt Gretchen stormed outside with Uncle Kai close behind. He slammed the door so hard it shook the house. The two of them came to a halt, as if they'd forgotten I was there, when they spotted me sitting on the porch. Aunt Gretchen put her hands on her hips and sighed, examining me with a look of sorrow in her swollen eyes. She kissed me on the top of my head, said, "I love you," and sprinted toward their car. Uncle Kai sat down on an old worn-out chair that creaked under his weight.

"Hey, bud," he said, choking on his words. "You know we love you, right?"

"Yeah, of course. I love you guys, too. More than

anything," I said, taking a drag off my cigarette.

"Kai, come on," Aunt Gretchen yelled from the street where their car was parked.

"We'll always be here for you. We always were and always will be. Don't you forget that, okay?"

"I won't."

"Kai, let's go," Aunt Gretchen shouted again.

I'd never seen her so upset.

Uncle Kai tousled my hair before he stood to leave. They didn't hesitate to drive off. I waved, but neither were looking in my direction.

I haven't talked to Uncle Kai or Aunt Gretchen since that day thirteen years ago. I still don't know what happened that pushed them to make that decision. No one's ever spoken about it. I sometimes wonder what I did wrong to make them leave me like that, to give up completely. Did I not keep the house clean enough? Was I so horrible to my mother that they wanted nothing to do with me? Did they not want to deal with a pot-smoking, alcohol-drinking, cigarette-loving teenager?

But then, I sometimes ponder the idea that maybe they just couldn't take it anymore. They were sick of the fighting, of trying so hard to help me and get me in a better situation. It was a never-ending battle that they had lost before it even started. It was impossible to take on that task alone, and they grew tired. With a child of their own, they couldn't keep making mine and Mom's issues theirs as well, stressing over things they were simply unable to fix. They had to let go, even if it meant saying goodbye to me, too.

I've reached out to them as an adult asking to have a sit down to get some closure. I've gotten no response to my letters or phone calls, so I can only surmise. If that's the case, then I understand why they did what they had to do. It hurts, and I miss them, but I understand.

28

"Did you do laundry this morning?" Mom asked after I returned from work one afternoon.

"Yeah, sorry did you need the washer? I didn't have time to wait to put them in the dryer before work."

"No, I didn't need the washer. It's just that I noticed you washed them on hot instead of cold."

"Oh yeah, I knew that. Sometimes my clothes stink after work because I sweat so much from mopping. That's the only way I can get the smell out." I laughed. "Don't worry, though. I've done it before. It doesn't shrink them or anything."

"I'm not worried about that. You said you've done it before?"

"Yeah, why?"

"It's just that, when you wash clothes on hot, it uses the water heater to do it."

"I know."

"You know? And that doesn't matter to you?"

"Why would it matter?" I asked, becoming frustrated that she was trying to argue with me for no reason.

"What if I wanted to take a shower or something? What if I needed to do dishes?"

"Well, the water heater replenishes itself. It's meant to be used."

"Whatever," Mom said. "It's just kind of selfish, that's all."

"Okay, cool. This has been a fun conversation. I'm going to go ahead and go to my room now," I said, walking away from her before a real fight erupted.

"Oh, and I'm going to need you to start paying rent," Mom said.

I stopped. The fight was coming. "What the hell for?" I asked.

"What do you mean, 'what the hell for?' To help out around here, obviously."

"What do you need help with? You've never needed anything before."

"That was when you were in school and when you were a kid. It was still my job to take care of you then. You're not a child anymore."

"Yeah, but I'm still seventeen for another month and a half. I'm not an adult yet, either."

"You sure like to act like one, though. You dropped out of school without bothering to worry about graduating or going to college. I mean, I know you got a GED, which is good, I guess, but it's not the same thing. Honestly, I'm not too surprised, though. You've never really cared much about your future or what any of us might have wanted for you. You only care about what *you* want. It's always been that way," Mom said, shaking her head. "And now, you work forty hours a week, which is okay I suppose, even if it is at some dinky little video store." She rolled her eyes.

"Are you done ranting?" I asked, not bothering to hide my annoyance.

"No, as a matter of fact, I'm not. You want to act like an adult and do what you want, then you can start here and now. I'm not going to be paying for your food anymore. This house and the things it takes to run it aren't free, you know?"

"I don't see what's so wrong with getting a job. You haven't bought me food in a long time. I already do that for myself."

"Oh, aren't you just so grown up? Big boy buys his own

food now."

"I was…I just meant that, like," I stammered, becoming flustered. "I wasn't trying to sound grown up. You just…you just said you weren't going to buy me food anymore, and I was just trying to say that that's okay because I've been doing it myself for a while now anyway."

"I'm not going to argue with you, all right? I've written up a monthly total of the bills you'll now be responsible for. Here," she said, handing me a piece of paper she'd torn out of a notebook. The ripped confetti-like strands from where it had been attached to the spiral were still stuck to it.

She wanted me to pay half of everything. Forty dollars for the water bill, sixty for electricity, fifteen for the landline, three hundred for the mortgage, and one hundred for the grocery bill, even though Mom didn't buy groceries. That was a grand total of five hundred sixty-five dollars every month. I started to feel hot. She didn't take into account the things I already paid for, like my car payment, insurance, cell phone, gas, and my own food.

"I'm not paying this," I said, tossing the paper back to her.

"You are, or you don't live here anymore, you little prick."

"Okay cool. Then, I guess I don't live here anymore."

Mom's eyes glowered, and her jaw clenched. "Don't test me, Dominic. I will throw your ass out in a heartbeat. I've put up with so much from you for so long, and I'm done. You either start paying rent, or you're out. I mean it," she said in a voice that was trying unconvincingly to sound calm.

"So do I."

I moved out the next day. I took only the things I could fit in the back of my car. Tommy helped me pack my CD player and CDs, along with my TV and movies through my window. My clothes and shoes were thrown into five black garbage bags. I emptied out one of Mom's boxes in the hallway, dumping everything on the floor, and packed up all my books, knowing

I'd never leave them behind. Then, I grabbed my bedding and toiletries. I didn't see the need for much else, and my car was full. I was homeless.

I lived in my car in the parking lot at work for two weeks before Leslie noticed. It was cold and uncomfortable living in my car, and I went through gas much quicker than usual from keeping it running all night with the heat on.

Leslie asked me to move in with her temporarily.

"I cannot, in good conscience, let you continue to live in our parking lot." Leslie chuckled. "I'm sorry, I don't mean to laugh because it's not funny at all. Why are you living in your car?"

"My mom kicked me out. She wanted me to pay rent. I said, 'No.' She said, 'Do it or leave.' So I said, 'Okay, bye, bitch.'" I smiled.

"Dominic," she said, faking dismay. She slapped me on the arm.

"What?"

"But seriously. You're staying with me."

"I can't do that. I don't want to put you out."

"You wouldn't be, I swear. I would love for you to stay with me, and I'll help you look for an apartment or something. That'll give you a warm house to stay in until your birthday when you're allowed to get your own place, okay?"

"Yeah, but what if I don't save enough for my own place? I mean, that's only a month away. I was looking at the classifieds in the paper, and everyone wants first and last month's rent, plus a deposit equal to rent on top of both of those."

"We'll figure it out," she assured me. She patted my back and hugged me. Her embrace was warm and motherly.

I followed Leslie back to her house that night after our shift. It was a small cabin on the outskirts of town. It had two bedrooms, two bathrooms, and sat on six beautiful acres.

"You can have the guest bath all to yourself. I don't really use it anyway. I have one in my bedroom," she said when we walked in.

Her cabin smelled like apples and cinnamon. She had a blue and white gingham print couch in the middle of her living room with a wooden rocking chair adjacent to it. The couch was adorned with navy blue decorative throw pillows covered in tiny anchors that matched her nautical decor scheme. She had a small TV in front of the couch with a cable box and a DVD/VCR combo. Behind the couch was her tiny but immaculate kitchen. In it, she had a vintage refrigerator I'd only seen in movies, the kind with only one door and an ice box for a freezer.

Down the hall from the kitchen were the bedrooms and bathroom. I didn't look at Leslie's bedroom, not wanting to invade her privacy. The bathroom continued the nautical theme with stars on the walls and a shower curtain that had a life-size anchor on it. The trash can was empty, and the bathtub was white with no ring around it.

My bedroom was across the hall from the bathroom. It had a queen-size bed with a white vintage headboard and a four-drawer dresser. I stood in the middle of the room in awe. I couldn't believe I was going to get to stay in this beautiful house.

"I'll leave you to unwind," Leslie said after we grabbed my stuff from the car and brought it into the room. "I'm exhausted. Are you going to be okay?"

"Yeah, I'm great. Thank you again, really. Like, I can't thank you enough. You don't know what this means to me."

"Of course, Dominic. Anytime." She smiled before shutting the door.

I sat back on the bed. My bed for the time being. I started to cry. I tried to be quiet, not wanting to alarm Leslie. I was overwhelmed, a cross between joy and fear. I was so thankful for Leslie and all she was doing for me, but how could I ever pay her back? I'd only ever had my own room to keep clean. What if I ruined her house like I ruined mine with Mom? I hadn't spoken to Mom since I'd left. What if she tried to make me come back?

My month at Leslie's house was wonderful. She loved to cook and clean and taught me how to love those two things as well. I learned how to grocery shop, budget my money, and how to build my credit.

"I can give you a thousand dollars for an apartment," Leslie said one sunny afternoon while the two of us were checking out rental ads.

"What?" I said, genuinely shocked. I would have never asked her for money. I would live in my car again before doing that. "I can't take your money."

"You can and you will." She laughed.

"No, seriously."

"No, seriously, you can. Look, I know you've been saving your money, and you've got enough to cover all you need to move into a place. But there's more than that. You won't have any furniture, you won't have a bed. You won't have any dishes or stuff to cook with. No groceries, not even toilet paper. You're going to need so much, and I can't just let you go without."

"You've already done so much for me," I said, choking up, that familiar lump in my throat threatening to push the tears out.

"I'm not taking 'no' for an answer. You're going to need this stuff, okay? In fact, if it will make you feel better, I'll buy the stuff you're going to need, and you can use the money you saved for the apartment. Would that be better?"

"I guess." I chortled, not really sure that it was. I was still taking her money either way.

"And I don't want you to pay me back. I've been a kid like you before with no one to turn to. I know exactly what it feels like to be in your shoes."

The next day we found a generously-sized studio apartment in the next town over, Lakeview, a ten-minute drive from work. The apartment was three hundred dollars a month, including utilities. There was a stackable washer and dryer in the small bathroom that consisted of a stand-up-only shower stall, and a toilet. I would have to wash my hands and brush my teeth in the kitchen sink, something I didn't mind doing. The kitchen had a small refrigerator, slightly bigger than a mini-fridge, and the oven was only big enough to fit a casserole dish inside. The stovetop had only one burner. It was affordable; it was perfect.

I paid the deposit, first and last month's rent, and my new landlord handed me the keys. Attaching the house keys of a place that was all my own to the key ring of a car that was all my own made me feel as happy as I was that day Mom and I had decorated our tiny tree with the tin foil star, like everything was right in the world. Like maybe, just maybe everything was going to be okay after all.

"Let's go get you some stuff now," Leslie said as we walked back to my car from the apartment complex's office. "We can get some good stuff for cheap at the thrift store. They always have barely used or even new stuff there."

My stomach dropped. "The thrift store?" My heart started to race.

"Yeah. It's not gross or anything. Most of it's good stuff, I swear. I'll show you, don't worry."

"No, I'm not worried about that. It's just…nothing. Never mind. It's okay, really. I've been there before, so I know it's not gross or anything," I said.

"So it's okay then? I mean, I'll go wherever you want to go. I just thought, you know, you can get more for cheaper if we go there."

"Yeah, that's totally fine."

"Okay, cool. And you know, I was thinking of turning my spare bedroom into a craft room. So that bed in there is just going to be in the way. If you help me move it, it's yours."

"Really? I love that bed." It was one of the most comfortable beds I'd ever slept on.

"Really, really," she said.

Pulling up into the thrift store parking lot brought back

a flood of memories, both good and bad. Mom and I used to have a lot of fun at these places searching for treasures, digging for gold as she liked to say. But we always bought too much stuff and once it left the store, we were lucky if we ever saw it again. More often than not, it was absorbed into the hoard almost as quickly as it was brought in.

We did find a lot of nice things, and all of it was stuff I needed. Nothing we bought was frivolous. Before that, I didn't associate thrift stores with being non-frivolous, a place I could get the things I could actually use instead of buying things just to buy them. We spent three dollars for a toaster that was new and in its original box, two dollars for a shower curtain still in the package, fifty cents for a pack of shower rings that were used but clean, and one-hundred dollars for a black leather loveseat with a matching recliner that looked as if the previous owner got rid of them before they were even sat on. We also scored a full matching dish set, brand-new in-box utensils, pots and pans in excellent used condition, a dresser, and a TV stand with enough shelf space for my books and movies. In total, we spent a little under one hundred-fifty dollars.

After we left, we made a stop at the dollar store. Leslie picked out cleaning supplies, toilet paper, a toothbrush caddy, shampoo, soap, and laundry detergent.

"Time for groceries, now," said Leslie. "I'm going to let you pick those out since you'll be the one eating them."

Leslie paid for one hundred fifty dollars' worth of groceries, which was more than enough to get through the month, if not longer.

"Now, we only spent about three hundred and twenty bucks today," Leslie said on the drive back to my apartment to drop off the stuff that fit in my car. She'd arranged to borrow a truck from a friend to pick up my new furniture later that day.

"Oh, good. We did good, then. I didn't want to make you spend that much on me," I said.

"You aren't making me do anything."

"I feel really bad, though."

"I know you do. And I can't change that because that's just who you are. You're uncomfortable with people helping you because you feel like you don't deserve it. But you do, okay?"

My emotions betrayed me again as tears welled up in my eyes. I was always so quick to cry. "Okay," I said, taking a deep shuddering breath.

"I mean it. I love you, kid." She clasped her hand on my shoulder.

"I love you, too."

"Oh, come on. Now you're making me cry over here." She laughed, wiping the tears that rolled down her cheeks. "But what I was getting at was that we only spent a little over three hundred dollars. That means you have about seven hundred left to help you out with whatever you need."

"How do I have seven hundred left?"

"I said I was giving you a thousand, and I still am. You bought three hundred dollars' worth of stuff you needed, and you have seven hundred left. And just like before, I'm not taking 'no' for an answer. So don't you even start with me, mister."

29

My first week living in my new apartment was pure bliss. Everything was quiet unless I didn't want it to be. If I turned on the TV, I got to choose the volume. I didn't need to turn my stereo up as high as it would go, the sound distorting from the speakers to drown out the rest of the house. I was able to sit in my own recliner in my own living room with a book that I could read for hours in peace.

I kept everything clean. I made my bed every morning and washed my dishes as soon as I was finished with them unless I didn't have time. In that case, they were washed before bed. I didn't allow myself to sleep until the sink was empty. I folded my laundry and put it away the second the dryer alarm sounded. I wiped down my countertops and swept the floors every night before bed. Everything was as I had always wanted it to be. I felt truly happy for possibly the first time ever.

I hadn't seen or spoken to Mom since she'd kicked me out almost two months earlier. After everything had been moved in and put away, with the help of Leslie, who nicknamed herself "the queen of organization," I decided to reach out to her on one of the rare Saturdays I had off. My fingers trembled as I pressed the buttons on my cell phone. I realized I wasn't sure she'd pick up if I called, so I texted instead.

Hey Mom it's me. Just wanted to say hi and see how you're doing.
It took two hours before I got a response.

Hi son. I'm fine. how are you?

I'm good. I got a new apartment. I'd really like it if you could come by to see it and say hi. I'll order us a pizza.

When?

Whenever you want. I'm off today.

Where at?

Lakeview

Send me your address. I'll be by in about an hour. Still in my pj's.

I sent Mom my new address and ordered a pizza. I told them I needed it in an hour, so no need to rush. I sat on my chair, picked up my book, and continued where I'd left off. I breathed a sigh of relief in the comfort of knowing I didn't have to watch out the window for the delivery person.

I was startled when the pizza guy knocked on the door. My heart raced at an uncomfortable speed. I knew I had nothing to be afraid of. My apartment was pristine, not a crumb on the floor, not a single thing out of place. I kept my possessions to a minimum, only occasionally buying a new book or movie. But there was some terrifying feeling I couldn't shake about the fact that a stranger was about to see inside the place I lived. Though I had no reason to be scared and nothing to be embarrassed of, my chest started hurting—the first sign of a panic attack.

I grabbed the doorknob with my clammy hand, twisting it, afraid for what was about to happen.

"Hey, are you Dominic?" he asked, reading my name off the receipt.

"Yes," I said, my voice shaky.

"Great." He pulled the pizza from the insulated delivery bag. "That'll be $15.93."

"Keep the change," I said, handing him a twenty as I took the pizza, eager to shut the door.

"Thanks, man." He waved and turned back toward his car.

I set the pizza on the counter and returned to my chair, trying to catch my breath. I felt as if I'd just run a mile.

Everything around me was cloudy and turned gray. I lost my peripheral vision. My ears rang. I had chills, and my shirt was dampened from sweating. My chest still hurt. I laid on the cold wood vinyl flooring of my apartment, trying to get my body to calm down.

When I felt well enough to stand, I got a drink from a soda I had in the fridge, getting a little sugar in my system to bring me back to Earth. I knew the routine. That wasn't the first time that had happened. It took me a long time to be okay with having people over. It's something I am open to now, though I'm not sure I'll ever fully get used to it.

Mom showed up three hours later. The pizza was cold. I was frustrated. I'd tried reading while I waited for her, but my ability to concentrate lowered with each minute that passed. She knocked, then tried to open the door. It was locked.

"Hey," I said as I opened the door for her. "Come on in."

"Why was your door locked? You knew I was coming," she said, walking past me to toss her purse onto my chair.

"I always keep it locked. I didn't think you would just try to walk in." I chuckled.

"I didn't think I had to knock." She plopped down onto the love seat. "What's going on with your hair?"

"What's wrong with it?"

"It's just so…how do I say this? It's so unkempt. Is that the style the kids are doing nowadays?"

"Can I get you something to drink?" I asked, ignoring the hair comments and trying to ease the tension.

"Aren't you fancy?" She smirked. "I'll have whatever you're having."

"Root beer okay?"

Mom nodded.

"How are you?" I asked, handing her a fresh cold can from the fridge.

"I'm okay. Been better. How are you?"

"I'm doing good. Really good."

"When did you get this place?"

"About a week ago."

"Only a week ago?" she asked, squinting her eyes and furrowing her brow. "Where were you before that?"

"I lived in my car for a couple weeks after I left your house. Then, I moved in with Leslie until I turned eighteen." I was nervous she'd be upset that I'd lived in my car.

"With Leslie? Leslie to the rescue." Mom rolled her eyes.

"Yeah, she's helped me out a lot."

"Are you fucking her?"

"What?" I was stunned. "Why would you think that?"

"What other reason would she have for letting you live with her?"

"We're friends. She didn't want me living in my car."

"Just friends? Yeah, I bet." She laughed. "I saw the way she smiled at you when she dropped you off at the house before."

"I don't know what you're talking about. She smiled at me like a friend would."

"I hope so. I might disown you if I found out you were screwing around with some Black chick."

"Are you serious?" I asked incredulously.

"I'm just joking." Mom laughed. "God, you're so sensitive. You know I'm not a racist. I have Black friends at work. And I always say 'hi' to that one cashier girl at the thrift store."

I didn't respond. I didn't know how. I'd never heard Mom talk like that before. Or maybe I'd just been able to tune her out and now I couldn't.

"Anyway," Mom said, continuing to laugh. "You said you were going to order pizza? I'm starving."

"Yeah, but it's cold now, sorry. I thought you were going to be here sooner. So it got here a while ago."

"It's fine." She sighed. "Better than nothing."

"Sorry."

After we ate, I gave Mom the tour of my place. We stood

up but didn't have to move away from the couch. I pointed toward the wall behind my chair, where my bed was. "That's my bedroom." I chuckled. "And that's the kitchen. And that over there," I said, pointing off to the side of my bed, "is the bathroom."

"Lovely place you have here."

I couldn't tell if she meant that or not. "Thank you," I said anyway.

"You've got a lot of movies." She crawled over to my TV stand where all my movies were neatly organized by genre and in alphabetical order, just like they were at work.

"I think this one's mine." She pulled a DVD from the shelf. "Oh, and this one, too." She reached for another.

"No, those are mine. I got them on sale from the used rental bin at work."

"I don't know if I believe that. You always were a little thief."

I dropped my head and slumped my shoulders. I didn't understand why she was acting like that. "I didn't steal them from you."

"If you say so," Mom said. She stood up, dropped the movies to the floor, and sat back on the sofa.

"Why can't you just be happy for me? I haven't talked to you in so long. I just wanted to show you that I'm doing okay. I wanted to see you. I missed you. I don't get why you show up here acting like this."

"See, and this is exactly the reason why I can't talk to you. I just try to joke around with you or say something innocent, and you get all upset over nothing. You're too sensitive. I have to walk on eggshells around you. I missed you, too. But God, do you know what a relief it's been not having you at the house? It's like I can breathe again. Like I was always holding my breath, not knowing what you're going to do next. Are you going to yell at me? Are you going to hit the wall? Hell, are you going to hit me?"

I was offended. "I would never hit you."

"Sometimes it was hard to tell. I was afraid of you. I still am. I wasn't sure I should even come here alone today. You might try to hurt me or something."

"Are you being serious?" I said, shaking my head in dismay. Was I so bad that she was actually scared of me? Did I really do that to her?

"Yes, I'm dead serious. Son, I love you. But I couldn't take any more of you. And like I said, it's not like I could talk to you about any of this. You just got too upset the second I mentioned anything. I mean, look at how this fight started just now. I try to tease you or say something that's no big deal, and you can't take a joke, so you yell at me. You know, I think it's good we don't live together anymore."

"I agree."

Mom stood to leave. We both knew the conversation was over after that. There was no way we would be able to recover from that blow up to have a genial visit.

I didn't see Mom again for another three months. We texted or spoke on the phone about once a week, but never more than that.

The next time she came over, the visit didn't go any better than it had the first time. It started when I got annoyed because I'd ordered another pizza, and when she was done, she dropped her empty plate to the floor instead of throwing it away. When I offered to take it back to the kitchen to throw it out along with my own plate, she said, "No, it's fine. I'll get it later."

To which I replied, "We both know that's not true. Just let me take it."

She tried to resist, but I grabbed the plate and binned it against her will, which upset her.

What pushed us over the edge, however, was what happened after she used the restroom. When she walked out, I said, "Sorry there's no sink in there. You'll have to wash your hands here in the kitchen." She replied that she's fine and sat back on the couch without washing. I pretended that didn't bother me.

But when I went in to use the restroom after her, she had left her old bloodied tampon sitting unwrapped on top of my garbage. And, on the toilet seat, was pink-tinged urine that she'd left behind along with a bloody streak from where the tampon she'd pulled out had dragged across the seat.

Seeing the mess in my bathroom, the bathroom I kept spotless, triggered my bad memories of Mom's house. I had to clean up her dirty tampons then, and here she was, forcing me to do it all over again. Maybe I did overreact. Maybe I was cruel to her as she said. Maybe I deserved to be called evil for hurting her feelings. I don't really know. I have a hard time distinguishing if my feelings were legitimate and valid, or if I truly was just oversensitive.

Mom and I had spoken only once or twice through text since her last visit, three weeks prior. I didn't want to have her back for a while, but I was craving some family time. I decided the next best thing would be to invite my grandparents over. Unfortunately, I was still seeking their approval and thought if they saw how well I was doing, they'd be proud of me. It's what I'd hoped would come from having my mother over as well. I should have known better. Why do we look for validation and love from those who are so unwilling to give it?

My grandparents came over on a Sunday afternoon. I'd picked up some sandwiches from the grocery store deli along with some deviled egg potato salad. The deli's potato salad was my favorite. I heard Grandma and Grandpa pull up and slam their doors shut. I waited on the other side of the door, happy to show them that they could walk up and knock and I was free to answer. I didn't have to meet them outside.

"Well, look who it is," Grandma exclaimed as she hugged me when I opened the door. It'd been months since I'd last seen them. "Ugh, you smell like cigarette smoke."

"Hi, Grandma," I said, squeezing her back and ignoring the comment. "And hi, Grandpa."

"Dominic," he said. "Nice to see you."

"Yeah, it's really great to see you guys. I'm excited to show you my place," I said, ushering them inside and shutting the door. "Have a seat."

"I don't think there's much to show us, is there?" Grandma snorted. "I think we pretty much see everything right here, don't we?"

"Yeah," I said, feeling uncomfortable. "I know it's small. But it's just me. I love it here."

"Well, that's all that matters. Right, dear?" Grandma said, turning to Grandpa who nodded in agreement.

"Are you guys hungry? I bought some sandwiches."

"Sure, that sounds…nice," Grandma said.

She followed me into the kitchen to make her and Grandpa's plates. He stayed behind.

"Better make sure you do those dishes," she said, eyeballing the plate and cup I had yet to wash from breakfast.

"I know. I'm usually on top of it and wash everything right away. It's just that since it's my day off, I slept in. Then I went to the store to buy us lunch and forgot about it," I said, trying to explain myself, not realizing I shouldn't need to.

"It would have only taken you a minute. I'd hate to see you returning to your old ways. Putting off cleaning until the last minute. Then you sure know what happens after that. You get too overwhelmed and stop doing things altogether."

"It's one plate, Grandma. I'll be fine. I'm going to do the dishes as soon as you guys leave."

"Just seems funny to me that you complained that your mom's house was always a mess, and now, here you are, with dishes in the sink."

I swallowed hard and resisted the urge to say anything other than, "Let's go eat."

After lunch, I gathered everyone's plates and placed them in the sink. "Still not going to do those dishes?" Grandma asked from the couch.

I put the lid back on the potato salad and put the leftovers in the fridge. "Nope. Like I said, I'll do them after you guys leave," I said, sitting in my chair.

"All right, I'm not going to pussyfoot around anymore. I don't want to have to tiptoe over your feelings, Dominic," Grandpa said, speaking more in those few moments than he had our whole visit.

"Um, okay?" I was confused.

"The elephant in the room," Grandma said.

"Yes, the elephant in the room. We know about your last visit with your mother. What's going on? You don't even live with her anymore, and you still can't be decent to her?" asked Grandpa.

"What do you mean?" I was still confused. "What did I do? I know we fought, but it's not like I was just being rude for no reason." Or was I?

"She said you got mad at her for using your bathroom," Grandpa said. "That's just ridiculous."

"That…that's not exactly what happened."

"Then, what exactly happened?" Grandma asked.

"Well, I mean, I don't know. She just threw her tampon in the garbage, and it was all nasty just sitting there and…I don't know."

"You never know. You never have. It's always 'I don't know' with you," said Grandpa.

I didn't tell them that Mom had left blood and urine all over my toilet seat. I didn't think it would be right to embarrass her like that.

"Let me get this straight. Your mom used your bathroom," Grandpa said. "She had her period, like most women tend to have at some point. I'm so sorry you had to be burdened with it happening at the time she came over." He waved his arms around animatedly, mocking the situation. "Then, she threw away her tampon in the garbage, where it belongs, and you didn't like that? Would you have preferred she left it on the counter for you?"

My best friend, the lump, showed up, forming in my throat as I swallowed my words and held back everything I wanted to say. I wanted to scream at them to get out. I wanted to tell them I hated them for never trying to see things from my perspective and for just assuming Mom's word was the right one.

But "I guess," was all I was able to say.

"You guess," said Grandma.

"Yep. He guesses," Grandpa huffed.

"We'll tell your mom to make sure she uses the bathroom at the gas station down the block next time she comes over, sound good?" she said. "That is, of course, if she even wants to come back. She said she feels unwelcome here. How sad is that? You've made your own mother feel unwelcome."

I stared at my lap. I didn't want to be in this conversation anymore. I wanted their visit to be over.

"I just have one last thing to say to you and then I think we need to leave before I do or say something I'm going to regret," said Grandpa. "Your mom is your mom whether you like it or not. She deserves respect whether you want to give it or not. You need to learn that right now, son. You might think that because you're an adult now you don't have to still show her respect, but you do. You only get one mom, and you got a pretty damn good one. You need to start showing some appreciation."

They left after that. I knew I would not be inviting them over again. I was an adult, and they still felt they needed to take time out of their day to berate me and treat me as if I were a small child. I needed something to take my mind off that visit. I went outside to smoke a cigarette and so badly wanted to put it out on my arm, a habit I had worked hard to quit. I felt the familiar and pressurized urge to go inside and cut my arm, but I resisted.

Instead, I called Tommy to see if he had any weed he wanted to share. We hadn't hung out or talked much since he helped me move my stuff out of my bedroom window. He was getting ready to start college and still living with his parents. He was accepted into Lakeview Community College's Police

Academy. He was hoping to eventually end up working for the FBI, something I had no idea he was even interested in.

"This is a cool place," he said. "I'm jealous."

"Thanks, I love it." I laughed awkwardly. It still felt unnatural to have people in my house. Tommy had seen my room and gone through my window many times, but this was different. He came through the front door and was standing in my living room.

Tommy had a formal glass pipe to smoke out of. No more cans for us. The concept was still the same. Put the marijuana up top, flick the lighter ablaze, and suck in to draw the flame toward the green. It had been a while since I'd last gotten high. All my worries fell off my shoulders when that THC hit my system, or clouded my brain, as was my theory. I could literally feel the tension roll away, my body relaxing, my jaw unclenching, the lump in my throat becoming smaller and smaller, until all that was left was a smiling, almost happy, albeit hungrier version of me.

"I have to tell you something," Tommy said after we finished the bowl. "You know how you went to the loony bin that one time?"

"Yeah." I laughed, never having thought of it as the loony bin before.

"I'm the one who told your mom you were smoking and having sex," he confessed.

"What the fuck," I said, drawing out the last word in complete shock. "Are you serious, bro?" I wasn't mad, just surprised; my inebriated state helped keep me calm.

"Yeah, man. I'm sorry. Your mom called all freaked out saying shit like, 'He's hurting himself. I'm worried about him.' She made it seem like you were about to kill yourself. She was so worried about you, she got me worried about you, too. So I told her what else you'd been up to so she could help you. I'm so fuckin' sorry, bro."

"I can't believe that," was all I could manage. I laid my head back on the couch, too high to fully comprehend what he was telling me.

"Do you hate me?"

I looked at him and busted up laughing at that question like it was the most ridiculous thing I had ever been asked. I laughed until I couldn't breathe and wheezing was the only sound that emerged. Tears streamed down my cheeks. Tommy's eyes widened, terrified I'd gone mad. I clapped the back of his neck and he began to laugh, too.

We never spoke of it again. In fact, he and I didn't speak much again at all after that day. We grew apart and lived our own lives. I talk to him once in a while, exchanging the occasional email. He's doing well. He's got himself a wife and three little boys now. He graduated from the academy and is a deputy there in Pleasantview. He never got out like we both dreamed we would, but he's happy.

30

As the years went on, I talked to my family less and less. I either texted or called Mom once every other week, and we met for dinner on the third Wednesday of every month. Our dinners usually lasted no more than two hours and were quick catch-up sessions on our lives. Our conversations always remained superficial. She was never the type of person I could talk to about what was going on in my life; she just wasn't interested. I tried a few times, and she would quickly change the subject with a loud sigh and say, "So anyway," before starting to talk about something else entirely.

I only saw my grandparents on the holidays and tried to spend as little time with them as possible. At the last Thanksgiving dinner we had, Grandma let me know that she didn't enjoy cooking for everyone and would prefer not to celebrate the holiday at all. Sometimes I wondered why I bothered seeing or talking to any of them. The visits with them left me feeling so emotionally drained, I needed a full day to recover.

I continued to work at the video store for a few more years. At the age of twenty-one, I took over as store manager for Leslie when she moved on to bigger and better things. She became engaged to some rich guy who owned a resort in Mexico and moved far away from the hellhole that was Pleasantview. I couldn't have been happier for her. She deserved all the happiness in the world. She decided not to sell her house and rented it out to me instead. She said she didn't need the money, so she let me rent it for only two hundred dollars a month, enough to cover the property taxes and insurance.

Moving from a studio apartment to a two-bedroom cabin was a bit overwhelming at first. There was so much space, I worried every day I wouldn't be able to keep up on the cleaning. There was at least twice as much to clean, dust, and vacuum. Even if I didn't occupy or use a room in the house, it still collected dust and needed to be cleaned. The thought of that terrified me.

A week after moving in, I went grocery shopping. I got my usual meat and potatoes with some veggies thrown in. I loved a good steak with twice baked potatoes and roasted asparagus. I'd tried to learn how to cook more while at the apartment, but at my new house, I had a bigger kitchen to work with, including a full-size oven. After my groceries were paid for and I was walking out the electric doors back to my car, I saw a homeless lady sitting off to the side of the building. She had a puppy laying in her lap. Next to her was a handmade cardboard sign that was propped against the building that read: "HOMLESS. HAVE PUPPIE FOR SELL. 100$"

"What kind of dog?" I asked, bending down to her level. I shocked myself as the words came out of my mouth. I didn't usually take the time to talk to people I didn't know, since I hardly wanted to talk to the people I did know.

"He's a pit," she said.

"A pit?"

"Pit bull." She patted the pup on the head. "He doesn't have a name. I didn't want to get too attached since I can't afford to keep him."

"Can I pet him?"

I'd never thought of myself as a pet person. Too much dust, dander, and wildly shedding hair. The thought of cleaning up after a dog made my anxiety jump up a few levels.

I reached out to pet the blue-gray colored puppy. His

head perked up, and he sniffed my hand. His soft, wet nose brushed against my fingers, and he poked out just the tip of his tongue to lick me.

"How old?" I asked.

"I'd say about three months. He's the last of the pups. I used to have his mom, but I broke up with my boyfriend, and he wanted to keep her. He sold the other puppies and said I could keep this one. I wanted to, but I just can't afford to feed him when I can't even afford to feed myself, ya know?"

"Yeah, I definitely understand that. You know what? I want him."

"Really? I been out here all day. Lots of folks say they want him, but no one's actually gone through with adopting him. Everyone's scared because he's a pittie. They're all, 'Oh no, he's vicious. His lockjaw will get me.' Blah, blah." She laughed.

"Well, I want him. Here," I said, pulling a one hundred dollar bill out of my wallet and handing it to her. "I'll take him with me right now."

The woman handed me the leash that was looped around the pup's collarless neck.

"I'm Dominic." I extended my hand to shake hers. "I promise I'll take great care of him."

"Thank you, Dominic. I'm Callie."

I immediately turned on my heels, right back into the store to purchase puppy food and supplies for my new companion. My first instinct was to name him Harry Pawter, but after holding him for a few minutes and getting to know this sweet, gentle creature, I decided to name him Roy. I bought him both food and water bowls, a few toys, a fluffy memory foam bed, and a turquoise collar.

He and I became fast friends. I looked forward to walking him every day, and he helped me get out of the house more. Between the walks and taking him to the dog park on weekends, I was slowly becoming less of a hermit. He waited at the door for me, tail wagging, every day when I came in from work. It wasn't just his tail that wagged when he was excited. One of my favorite things about him was that his whole body shook like it was following along with his tail. Roy was a friend I didn't realize was missing from my life.

* * *

As the new store manager of Pleasantview Video, my hourly wage was bumped from $8.50 an hour to a salary of thirty-five thousand a year. I didn't work in the front of the store as much as I used to, and I loved that I rarely had to mop or sweep. Most of my duties consisted of counting tills at the end of the night, budgeting, checking employees' timecards, and ordering supplies for the store. I was also in charge of the interviewing and hiring of new employees.

We needed a daytime team member since most of my employees were high school kids. I put up a Help Wanted sign on the front door and advertised online. A mound of resumes and applications came in, and I scheduled interviews with about a dozen people. Interviewing was an already agonizing process for an introverted person such as myself, and having just quit smoking, my anxiety was at a high I hadn't felt in years. There was one application in particular that stood out to me. She had previously worked at the movie theater in Lakeview, so she had experience with both movies and handling money.

"Hi, I'm Phoebe Prescott," she said as she sat across from my desk in the back office.

"Hi, Phoebe. I'm Dominic," I said, extending my hand to her. "I'm the store manager here." It still felt surreal to say that. "Why don't you tell me a little bit about yourself?" I'd looked up interviewing techniques on Google and hoped I was doing okay.

"Well, I'm twenty years old. I love watching TV and movies. Probably way more than I should, honestly." She laughed.

I smiled. "Me too."

"Glad I'm not the only one."

She was beautiful, her smile infectious. She had sienna-brown eyes with lashes so full they could have been mistaken for extensions. They matched her blue-black hair that was fixed into a fishtail braid and pulled to the side, resting on her left shoulder. She had a dainty little diamond nose ring that I thought looked cute, a term I rarely used.

"But to be perfectly honest, and maybe I shouldn't say this at a job interview for a video store, but I love reading even more than I love movies," she said.

"Me too," I said again. I feared I sounded like an idiot just saying "me too" to everything she said. "What do you like to read?"

"Oh, anything. I like all genres. I loved Harry Potter as a kid. It's been a while since I've read it, but it's still one of my favorites. I love the movies, too."

Was it possible to fall in love instantly?

"Yeah, Harry Potter is great," I said, wanting to blurt out another "me too" instead. "What's your favorite movie?"

"My favorite?" she said. "Oof, that's a hard one. I mean, how can you pick just one, ya know?"

"Oh yeah. For sure."

"I love horror. But I also love Disney." She giggled. "I think if I had to pick one off the top of my head, it would be *Beauty and the Beast*."

I wanted to shout, "You're hired!" right then and there.

"That's a good one," I said, keeping my cool. "Are you in school or do you have a second job or anything that would require a flexible schedule?"

"Nope. I'm free whenever you need me."

"Okay, good. Glad to hear it. Well, you seem like you'd be a great fit here, Phoebe. Let me check your references, and I'll give you a call, let's say tomorrow sometime. If you are hired, when can you start?"

"Tomorrow, after you call me."

I checked all her references as soon as she walked out of

the store. Her last employer gave her a glowing recommendation, and her personal references spoke highly of her. I called her about four hours after the interview, trying not to let on how much I wanted to hire her, letting enough time pass that it wasn't too obvious.

"Hi, this is Dominic from Pleasantview Video," I said when she answered.

"Hi, Dominic," she said. "I'll see you tomorrow."

"You will? You're confident you got the job?"

"Mm-hmm. What time do you need me?"

"We open at ten, so be here at nine."

"See you then."

On Phoebe's first day, I showed her the ropes in much the same way Leslie had shown me. I wanted to be as approachable and as kind as Leslie was when she was there. Over the next few weeks, Phoebe and I worked together almost every day. I didn't schedule her much for nights or weekends since those usually went to the high school kids.

Phoebe was funny, and I'm not sure she totally knew it. She didn't have that in-your-face sense of humor, and it wasn't always what she said, but how she would say it. I liked to pick on her for not being able to reach the top shelf of the movie racks along the walls. I wasn't an incredibly tall guy myself at five-foot, eight-inches, but Phoebe only came up to my shoulders. She pretended to be upset about my calling her shorty or asking if she needed a step stool when she was putting away the returns, but I knew she liked joking around with me.

I had the biggest crush on her, and even though it seemed like we were flirting every day at work, it was hard to tell if she was just being friendly or if she liked me, too. I didn't want to be the creepy guy asking out his coworker or have her feel like she had to say yes because I was her boss. Even worse, I didn't want her to feel she was hired just because she was cute. She was the only interviewee who was perfect for the job. She would have gotten it no matter what.

But one day, I worked up the courage to ask her out for

a movie date. As we were clocking out at the end of our shifts, I saw that we were both checking out the same pre-street, the new Harry Potter movie. I decided to go for it. The worst that could have happened was she said no, right?

"Hey, Phoebe, I see we're both going to be watching the new Harry Potter," I said, looking down at my feet, hands in my pockets, afraid to look at her.

"We are." She smiled. "I seriously can't wait to see it."

"Same here." I paused, trying to muster the courage, then decided it was now or never. "Hey, so um, do you think, like, maybe you'd want to, um, I don't know, like, watch it together or something? If not, it's totally cool. No pressure or whatever, like, it's totally fine if you don't want to. No biggie." No biggie? I felt like such an idiot.

Phoebe laughed her sweet giggle-type laugh. "I'd love to."

"Really?" I was shocked. "Because you don't have to if you don't want to. I don't want you to feel like you have to say yes or anything. I—"

"Dominic," she cut me off, "I said I'd love to. I mean it."

Phoebe still lived with her parents, so we decided to watch the movie at my place. I bought popcorn, candy, and energy drinks from the video store for the two of us. I picked out Milk Duds, a Kit-Kat bar, and gummy bears, and Phoebe chose Swedish Fish, Hot Tamales, and a Snickers bar, then she followed me back to my house.

"Whoa, you have a really nice house," she said when we walked in.

Roy was waiting at the door. He let out a tiny "boof" at Phoebe and sniffed her shoes fervently.

"Thank you." I blushed. I'd never had anyone tell me I have a nice house. I didn't quite know how to react since, to be honest, the fact that this beautiful girl was in my house at all made me feel like I was going to have a panic attack. I pet Roy to calm myself down from the anxiety.

"Can I just set my stuff here?" she asked, making her way

over to the dining room table.

"Of course. Wherever you want. You want me to make this popcorn and get the movie going?"

"Um, yes please." She beamed. "I've been waiting like a zillion years to watch it."

I microwaved the popcorn and popped the movie into the DVD player. The buttery snack came out perfect and steaming as I poured it evenly into two separate bowls, not sure if she was one for sharing. I sat on the couch, where Phoebe was already waiting, and left about a foot of space between us. I didn't want her to feel any pressure whatsoever. It had been a long time since I'd been with a girl, since work and happiness within myself had been my priority for a while. I had tried dating here and there but just never found someone that I felt I really clicked with.

There was no one who made me laugh the way Phoebe did, no one who made me look forward to my days like she did. She was somehow different, and I don't know what it was, but she made me want to try harder. I honestly never tried that hard in the past to make a girl feel comfortable. I never made any of them uncomfortable that I know of, but I guess I just wasn't as conscientious of their feelings as maybe I should have been because I cared more about myself than anything.

I gave Roy, who was not-so-subtly begging, a piece of popcorn. He jumped up on the couch and laid his head on my lap. About twenty minutes into the movie, Phoebe moved and closed the gap between us. A few pieces of popcorn spilled out of her bowl as she did. She immediately picked them up. I breathed a sigh of relief that she wasn't like Mom, who would have been too lazy to grab them, letting them break and fall into the cracks of the sofa.

Phoebe's knee touched mine, and I was suddenly hyper-aware of everything my body was doing. I was breathing heavier. Did she notice? The saliva in my mouth was pooling under my tongue at record speed, and I was having to swallow it much more than usual to keep from choking. Could she hear me swallowing so much? My palms were sweaty, and it took all I had to keep from wiping them on my pants, alerting her. Every inch of me was a nervous wreck.

I tried to enjoy my popcorn and candy, but my chewing was amplified in my ears, and I worried she would think I chewed like a cow. It was making me sick listening to it. I wasn't paying attention to the movie and knew I would need to rewatch it.

"Hey," she said. She turned toward me. "Do you want to watch this later?"

"Uh, sure," I said, grabbing the remote to pause the movie. "Do you need to go or something?"

"No."

"Oh, um, okay." I laughed nervously. "Why?"

"Because I've been wanting to do this ever since the movie started."

"Do wha—"

Phoebe leaned over and kissed me. A quick peck on my lips. She drew back and smiled at me. I put my hand against the back of her neck and pulled her in for another, something more than a quick peck. We kissed for a few minutes, Roy's head awkwardly laying in my lap, rendering me unable to move.

Phoebe laid back on the couch, pulling me on top of her, away from Roy, who went to his own bed and let us be. Our lips intertwined. She tasted like Carmex and popcorn, the best taste in the world that day.

"You have no idea how long I've wanted to kiss you," I said five minutes later.

"Really?" She blushed. "I've had a crush on you for a long time, too."

We restarted the movie. I leaned into the corner of the couch, and Phoebe cuddled up against me, putting my arm around her. Roy joined us back on the couch. This time, he laid his head in Phoebe's lap. She didn't try to move him. She put her arm across his body and pet his head. She had his approval. The movie turned out to be pretty good after all.

When the movie was over, she suggested we watch another, saying she wasn't ready to leave. I wasn't ready for her to go, either. She picked out *Donnie Darko* from my personal DVD collection. After putting in the movie, I sat in my original spot on the couch, hoping she'd want to cuddle up to me again.

"Let's lie down. I'm kind of tired," Phoebe said. "Just in case I fall asleep, at least we'll be comfortable."

"Yeah, okay, that's cool," I said. "I'm tired, too. How do you want me?"

"You be big spoon and I'll be little spoon," she said nonchalantly.

"Okay." I was trying to sound like it was no big deal when it definitely was. Spooning with her on the couch was the perfect way to continue our date, but I was totally nervous. What if I got an erection lying behind her like that? What if she could feel it? I pressed play on the DVD player and laid on the couch, opening my arms to welcome her in. She grabbed one of my throw pillows, putting it on top of my bottom arm, and lay down to play little spoon.

"Sorry, is the pillow in your way? I can't get comfortable without a pillow," she said.

"No, you're perfect," I said, kissing the top of her head.

She wiggled in closer, pressing her butt against my crotch, and I knew I wouldn't be able to stop what was about to happen. I tried to pay attention to the movie, think about Mom's house, think about poop, think about anything other than what was happening to make it go away. She pulled my top arm tighter against her body and placed my hand on her breast. Then, she turned her head, looked up at me, and kissed me again.

Having sex with Phoebe was the most passion I'd ever felt in any sexual situation. I wanted to touch every inch of her body and make sure she was having a good time, too. I cared about her. I never cared if any of the other girls I was sleeping with enjoyed themselves or not. It only mattered that I did. I was always in and out and onto the next one. It was different with Phoebe.

Phoebe stayed that night with me. The next morning before she awoke, I scrambled up some eggs, tossing in chopped and fried corn tortillas, shredded cheese, green onions, and bacon bits. It was one of my favorite dishes Uncle Kai used to make.

When breakfast was ready, I made us each a plate and set it on the table before making my way to my bedroom to wake her. I hoped she wouldn't be offended I didn't serve her breakfast in bed, but I didn't eat in bed. I didn't want to risk getting mice or making any sort of unnecessary messes.

The sound of the door squeaking when I opened it woke Phoebe. She slowly opened her eyes, stretched out her legs, and let out an audible yawn.

"Good morning, gorgeous," I said. "I made breakfast."

"You made breakfast for me?" she asked.

I nodded.

"That's so sweet."

"Yeah, it's kind of early, sorry. I still have to shower before work."

"Oh my God. I forgot about work," she said, slamming her head back down on the pillow.

"I don't know how far you live, if you need to go back to your place to get ready or whatever."

"Can I just shower here?"

I smiled. "Of course you can."

Phoebe stood up and looked at herself in the mirror above my dresser. "Oh man, I have my sleepy eyes on big time."

"Sleepy eyes?"

"Yeah, you know the ones. We all have them."

"We do?"

"Yeah." She laughed. "Sleepy eyes. That way everyone's eyes look when they first wake up. You know, right? They're kind of squinty, and you can tell they've just been sleeping. You know what I'm talking about."

"Kind of, I guess." I chortled. "I just think you look beautiful."

She kissed my cheek, and the two of us moseyed out to the dining room to enjoy breakfast together.

"I don't want to get ahead of myself here," Phoebe said when we were done eating. She stood up and took both of our plates to the sink, where she rinsed them and put them in the dishwasher. "But are you looking for a girlfriend?"

"Yeah, I think I am," I said.

"Cool. Well, come on, let's go find you one."

My eyes widened. I was speechless.

Phoebe started laughing so hard she snorted, which made her cackle harder. I loved her laugh. The joy in it made me want to laugh, too. Her happiness was genuine. It felt good just being in her presence. She was the type of person I could only dream of one day meeting.

"You should see your face," she said, wiping tears from her cheeks. "I'm totally joking. But in all seriousness, are we like an item now, or is this something you do often? Because I don't."

"This is definitely not something I do often," I said. "I'd like to think we're together. But I've liked you for a while, so…"

"I've liked you for a while, too."

The two of us were inseparable after that, and a week later, I told Phoebe about Mom's house. We'd been spending so much time together, I felt comfortable being completely raw and open with her. But I got the same response of "Everyone's houses are messy sometimes." I was crushed, so I tried to explain further. She could see the hurt and pain on my face and in my voice as I was telling her. That's when she knew it was more than that. The fact that she took me seriously made me realize how fast and hard I had fallen for her.

Pleasantview Video had a DVD of the first season of the TV show *Hoarders*. I rented it one day and watched it so I could find which episode showed a house that most looked like mine had. Some of the episodes made me sad because their houses weren't as bad as mine had been growing up. They were bad, but mine was worse.

I watched ten episodes before I found the perfect one. Phoebe watched in horror as mice with all their droppings and their nests were discovered in places throughout the house. Old, smelly, moldy food was pulled from a broken refrigerator. A sink full of dirty water and maggot-infested dishes was emptied. Truckload after truckload of trash and junk were taken to the dump. A toilet that had been clogged for months was plunged by a man who couldn't stand the smell and threw up on his shoes.

"I can't believe you grew up in that," she said. She was crying. "I'm so sorry. I don't even know what else to say. I'm in shock. I just...I just don't know. I'm sorry."

"You're the only person who's ever said that to me," I said, wiping the tears from her cheeks.

"Seriously?"

"Seriously."

"I'm so happy you're mine," she said. "I'll never let anything bad happen to you again."

"Olive juice," I blurted out.

"What?" she said, caught off guard. "Did you just say 'olive juice?'"

"Yes."

"What's olive juice?"

"Well..." I trailed off, nervous she wouldn't feel the same way. "What I really meant to say was I love you. But I was scared you wouldn't say it back, so I said olive juice because I'm an idiot."

"You're not an idiot." She giggled. "I love you, too."

31

Two weeks later, Phoebe moved in with me. She spent most of her time at my house as it was. We figured we should make it official.

"Are your parents going to hate me for taking you away from them?" I asked.

"No, they're going to love you. Just like I do," Phoebe said.

"Do they think we're moving too fast?"

"Um, honestly, yeah." She laughed. "But we talked about it a lot, and they're understanding. They're awesome, I swear. It'll be okay." She put her hand in mine, calming my fears.

She introduced me to her parents when we arrived at their house to pack her things. Her dad, Matteo, was a tall, husky man. He was well over six feet and a bit intimidating. Phoebe jumped into his arms when we got out of the car, and he spun her around in a big circle, like she was a small child, before kissing her on her forehead.

"Dad, this is Dominic," she said when he put her down.

"Hey, Dominic," he said, extending his hand to shake mine.

"Nice to meet you, sir," I said.

"Ah, no need for 'sir' around here. No 'Mr. Prescott' either. You can call me Tay. And," he whispered, "do not call my wife ma'am or Mrs., or I'll never hear the end of it. She'll think she looks elderly for the next three days, and I'll have to pay for another round of Botox she doesn't need."

"Got it." I chuckled.

"You're going to take care of my Phoebe, right? I don't want to do the whole 'take care of her or I'll take care of you' thing. That's not really my style. I trust my daughter, and if she thinks you're great, then so do I."

"I promise I'll be good to her, sir."

"What did I say about 'sir'?" Tay said, playfully wagging his finger at me.

"Sorry. I mean, Tay."

Phoebe laughed.

"Ah, don't be sorry. It's all right. But listen, in all seriousness, I am trusting you, okay? She's a good kid, she deserves the best." He wrapped his arm around Phoebe and pulled her in for a hug.

"Trust me, I know she does," I said nervously, hoping I didn't sound too cocky.

"We're going to miss you around here, kiddo."

"I'll miss you guys, too, Dad," Phoebe said.

"Hey, baby," Phoebe's mom exclaimed, coming out of the house. She hugged Phoebe tightly, lovingly. "I was just finishing up lunch. Sorry I didn't come out sooner."

"It's okay, Ma. This is Dominic. Dominic, this is my mom, Willa."

"It's nice to meet you, Willa," I said, holding out my hand to shake hers, careful not to call her ma'am.

"Sorry, but I'm a hugger," she said, opening her arms for an embrace.

She was shorter than Phoebe. The two of them looked alike, with the same hair color and the same tender eyes. She hugged me so tight I felt like I could cry. It was the type of hug that felt like it meant something, the type that made you feel like a person who mattered, one deserving of an embrace with meaning behind it.

Seeing the relationship Phoebe had with her parents was scary. They were so close. I worried she would think I was a freak when she saw firsthand the relationship I had with my mom. She knew we didn't talk or see each other much. I couldn't hug Mom the way she hugged her mom or dad. I couldn't joke or laugh with my mom the way she could with hers. My mom would never invite Phoebe over for lunch the way her parents had invited me. I'd heard different versions of the same phrase basically stating that all you need to know if a man is worthy is to look at his relationship with his mother. That it would be a direct reflection of the relationship he'll have with his future wife. I could only hope Phoebe didn't believe that.

When I asked Phoebe to move in, I couldn't have been happier that she'd said "yes." I know our relationship moved fast, too fast in some people's minds, but it was perfect for us. We went back to my house every day after work, we spent the weekends together, we grocery shopped together, we picked out our daily movie rentals together. This was just making it official. She would no longer have to go to her parents' house to get more clothes; she would have everything she needed here with me.

Moving day was bittersweet. Sweet in the sense that the best thing to ever happen to me was going to be staying with me for good, and bitter in the sense that I had severely misunderstood what it would feel like seeing all her possessions moving into my space. I thought that seeing her stuff being moved in would feel good. I thought I would feel a sense of relief, knowing that we were moving forward and that it would feel like a place in my heart was filled when I saw her shoes next to mine in the closet or her clothes on one side and mine on the other.

Instead, when all her things moved in, I felt panic. I felt dread. Fear. Tay and I packed in the heavy boxes while Phoebe and Willa packed in the lighter ones and things like her pillows and blankets. When we were done, her parents said goodbye and left us to do the unpacking. Roy went through and sniffed each and every box and would have sniffed every item that came out of the boxes if I hadn't told him to go lie down.

My living room was filled with boxes that contained Phoebe's books and movies, along with random knick-knacks. My bedroom was full of boxes of her clothes and shoes. She had enough clothes to fill the entire closet herself. When she stayed the night, she only had her toothbrush, a small makeup bag, a can of hairspray, and a hairbrush. What she moved in with was an entire banker's box full of makeup and hair products.

I was overwhelmed. I loved her more than anything and didn't want her to think that any of this was because I didn't want her to move in. I would have done anything for her, but seeing my room full of clothes and things that weren't mine flooded me with the memories of Mom taking over my room for her own selfish needs. I knew that wasn't at all what was happening in my house at that moment, but my stomach was in knots at the mess. I wanted to vomit. My throat burned, begging me to let my stomach chuck its contents. Everything turned gray, and I knew the panic and anxiety were coming. I couldn't stop it. I could only ride it out.

My peripheral vision was lost, my chest hurt. Each breath felt like my ribs were closing in tighter and tighter around my lungs. Phoebe was unpacking a box and hanging her clothes in the closet. I sat on the edge of the bed, hoping she wouldn't notice I'd started to sweat. I felt the back of my neck grow clammy. The sweat from under my nose dripped onto my lips, the salty, acrid taste nauseating me further.

"Are you okay?" Phoebe asked. She dropped the sweater that was only halfway on a hanger and rushed over to me.

"Dominic? Dom?" She shook my shoulders trying to get me to respond.

I wasn't registering what she was saying. She looked fuzzy and sounded as if she were underwater.

"Should I call 911?"

I understood that part. "No. No, don't call anyone. I just need to lie down for a minute," I said, sliding off the bed to lay on the cold wood floor. "Can you get me some water, please?"

"Oh my God," she said, scrambling to get through the door.

Phoebe came back less than a minute later with a cold glass of water.

"Here, lift your head a little." She helped me take a sip and held her hand under my mouth to catch any that might spill.

"Are you okay?" she asked again after I sat up.

"I'm fine. I need some sugar. Can you get me a soda or a piece of candy or something?"

"Sure thing."

I felt stupid having my girlfriend pour water into my mouth while I sat on the cold floor panicking about her hanging her clothes in my closet. I thought for sure she would think I was more than she had bargained for after that and regret her decision to make a life with me.

"Here, sip this," Phoebe said when she came back with a can of root beer. She held it to my lips again.

"Thank you." I took the can, not wanting her to think I was completely helpless.

"What happened? Are you all right? Do I need to call someone?"

"No. I'm fine, really. I promise. I just had an anxiety attack."

"What? Why? What's wrong?"

"Nothing. It's just…nothing. I swear, it's nothing."

"It's not nothing. You just scared the hell out of me. You looked like you were dying right there on our bedroom floor."

"It's stupid. I don't even want to say." I laughed nervously. "I feel like an idiot."

"Don't feel like an idiot. You can tell me. I promise I won't think it's stupid. If it matters to you, it matters to me, okay? You can tell me anything."

"I just started to panic when I saw how much stuff was being moved in. I don't want you to take that the wrong way."

I looked into her sweet, loving eyes and saw that she was listening to me, truly listening.

"I'm so happy you're here. I really am," I continued. "It's just that seeing so much stuff in here made me think of what it was like living at my mom's house. It reminded me of all the boxes and bags and piles of junk that were always all over the place and never where they were supposed to be. I don't think your stuff is junk; that's not what I mean. God, I sound dumb."

"No, you don't," she said, grabbing my hand.

"I know your stuff is going to be put away, and I know in my mind that this is not my mom's house. I know this isn't going to be like that, but seeing everything here before it's all unpacked and put away just freaked me out. I'm sorry." I was holding back tears. I didn't want to scare her off.

"You have no reason to be sorry," said Phoebe. She sat back and thought for a minute before saying, "You know what? We're going to get all of this put away today. Right now. We're going to unpack everything, and the boxes will be gone by tonight, and everything will be okay. Before you know it, our house will be back to normal, okay?"

"Okay," I agreed. "Ya know, I like hearing you call it 'our house.'"

* * *

It was like we became one person. Everything turned into "what's mine is yours and what's yours is mine." Our conversations became about "us," and things were no longer about me or her; it was all about "we." We loved that movie, we loved coming to work every day. No more, "I love Harry Potter." It was now, "We love Harry Potter."

Our love bloomed in the old cliché of a whirlwind romance. She was everything I could have ever hoped for in a life partner. She made me feel like a real person. She made me feel like I mattered, like my words had meaning, like my stories and passions were worth talking about. I had never felt so unequivocally myself. I didn't have to hide. I didn't have to be superficial. She could know me, the real me.

I can't begin to tell you how happy I am that I wasn't successful in suicide when I was younger. Maybe if I had known that I would one day grow up to meet someone who completed me and was the true and defining meaning behind the word soul mate, I might have been able to make it through my days knowing I had someone as beautiful and special as her to look forward to in my future. That hole in my heart was gone. The unfillable void in my soul was no longer that. My missing piece was found. I don't care how cheesy it all is. She was and is everything I could have ever wanted.

Now, I can't sit here and pretend things were always perfect between us because they weren't. We had our fights, some worse than others. We had days where we didn't know if our relationship would make it. As much as I loved her and felt I could open up to her about anything, I did sometimes find myself guarded, protecting my heart and my mind. I feared every day she would wake up and realize she was better than me, so out of my league, and leave. This fear caused me to push her away at times. It was only through therapy for myself and seeing my therapist together for a few couple's therapy sessions that we worked through those fears.

However, even now, it's hard for me to believe that true happiness exists. At night, when I can't sleep, I find that I worry about what the point is of being with someone as perfect as Phoebe. What's the point of falling in love if that person could leave you at any given moment? She could find someone better, or worse, she could get sick. She could get in a car accident, she could be murdered. The idea of loving someone with everything you have and not knowing how long you have to be with that person is one of the most terrifying thoughts I have in my anxious little brain. My anxiety tries so hard to prevent me from being happy, and I work every day to not let it win.

32

When Phoebe and I had been together for four months, she told me she wanted to meet my mother. She was hesitant after hearing the horror stories, but decided she was ready. My usual Wednesday dinner date with Mom was coming up the next week. I told Phoebe I'd bring her along and texted Mom to let her know, too.

Hey mom, my girlfriend wants to meet you. I'm going to bring her to our next dinner if that's all right?

What girlfriend?

Phoebe. I've told you all about her.

Oh. I didn't know that was still going on.

Yeah we've been living together for a while. Just like we were the last time I saw you.

Well you were always with so many girls it was hard to keep track.

Yeah well that's not the case anymore. So anyway like I said, she wants to meet you so I'm going to bring her along if that's cool with you?

Yeah I guess that's fine.

K, see you next week.

Phoebe and I met with Mom the next Wednesday at Javier's Tacos. Javier, the owner, was from Mexico and made the best, mouth-watering food. Phoebe and I were seated by the hostess, Javier's girlfriend, Ximena. I had requested a booth in the back for privacy. Mom and I usually met at six in the evening. I was always on time; she often ran ten or fifteen minutes late. That night, however, she showed up forty minutes past our designated meeting time.

"Hello, dear," she said when she finally came stumbling over to our table, tripping over the thrift store bags she held in her hands. "Sorry, I'm late. I got caught up shopping. You know how it is."

"That's okay, Mom," I said. "This is my girlfriend, Phoebe. Phoebe, this is my mom."

"It's so nice to meet you, Ms. Leonard," said Phoebe.

"Sweetheart, please, call me Annie. Ms. Leonard makes me feel old." Mom chuckled.

"That's what my mom says, too," said Phoebe.

I smiled. Things were starting off great.

"Dominic, what are you wearing? Did you decide not to get dressed today?" Mom asked.

"I'm wearing jeans and a T-shirt. Pretty normal outfit, if you ask me," I said.

"You let him leave the house like that?" Mom asked Phoebe.

Phoebe looked at her lap, not wanting to get involved.

"Mom, seriously, please."

"Your shirt's so icky and wrinkled. I don't want people to think I picked up some bum off the street and offered to buy him a meal."

"Mom, please stop."

"Oh my gosh. Come on, you know I'm just joking with you, Mr. Sensitive."

We ordered our food. I got my regular order of two tamales and rice with no beans. Mom ordered shrimp tacos with extra beans, and Phoebe ordered a chicken enchilada with extra enchilada sauce.

"Oh, sweetie, you have something in your nose. I think you might have a booger," Mom not-so-quietly whispered to Phoebe as she was taking in a mouthful of her enchilada.

"Oh no," Phoebe said, quickly bringing her napkin up to her face. She looked at me to inspect her nose.

"I don't see anything," I said.

"It's right there," Mom said, pointing to her own nostril.

"That's just a nose ring, Mom."

"Oh, okay. I didn't even know people still had those. Sorry, dear, it looked like a booger from where I'm sitting."

"It's okay," Phoebe said, trying not to show her embarrassment.

"Listen, son, before I forget. Can you do me a favor?"

"Like what?" I asked.

"Well, I did something stupid the other day. I tripped and fell in the hallway, and on my way down, I knocked the damn thermostat off the wall. At the time I knocked it down, the heater was off. But you know how I like my heater on no matter the weather, right?" Mom laughed. "So anyway, can you fix it for me? It's freezing at my house. I've been using space heaters, but they're so dangerous and take up so much more electricity than the furnace."

"Yeah, maybe," I said. "Or we could call an electrician or someone more qualified." I knew she wouldn't go for this. She would rather freeze to death than let anyone inside, and I didn't want to go back into that house ever again. Mom knew if she asked me in front of Phoebe, I would have a hard time saying no. What she didn't know, however, was that I had already filled Phoebe in on the situation with my mother. She knew everything. So if I didn't want to do it, she wouldn't think badly of me.

"I bought you some things," Mom said to Phoebe, changing the subject. "I never got to shop for a girl before, and when I heard my son was finally bringing his wonderful girlfriend around, I just knew I had to get you some fun stuff. I've just been dying to meet you. I don't know why he was holding out on me."

"Yeah, I don't know why either," Phoebe said. She tickled my side and winked at me.

Mom pulled out some of the ugliest dresses and jeans I'd ever seen from her thrift store bags. They were not at all Phoebe's style and were visibly too small. Phoebe wasn't by any means big, but she wasn't a skinny little thing, either.

"What size are those jeans? And what decade did you pull them out of?" I laughed.

"Oh, you hush," Mom said. "They're a size three, why?"

"Thank you, Annie, but I'm afraid they won't fit. I'm not a size three," said Phoebe.

"Yes, I can see that no, you certainly are not," said Mom. "I just assumed you'd be a twig like all of Dominic's other girlfriends."

"Phoebe is my first real girlfriend. I don't know what you're talking about."

"Fine, maybe they weren't girlfriends. But skinny girls were definitely your type. I guess I just figured that's what this one would be, too."

"Phoebe's beautiful and perfect," I said. I pulled her hand from the table and kissed the top of it.

"I never said she wasn't," Mom huffed. "Don't twist my words."

"You're my type," I said to Phoebe, ignoring Mom.

She gave me a half smile, clearly uncomfortable.

"I guess I'll just have to return this stuff then," Mom said.

"Yeah, that was nice of you to think of me. Thanks anyway," said Phoebe.

"You know, we both have a lot of clothes. We appreciate the gesture, but you don't need to buy stuff."

"I was just trying to do something nice."

"I know, and I appreciate that."

"So, you two are living together?" Mom asked, though she already knew the answer.

"Yes, we have been for a while now."

"I hope you're on birth control," Mom said, directing her statement toward Phoebe.

Phoebe snapped her head toward me. Her eyes were wide with a look that said both "What the fuck?" and "Help me."

"That's uncomfortably personal and no one's business

but ours," I said.

"Whatever," Mom said, shaking her head. "I would just hate to see you two getting pregnant. That's the last thing you'd need."

"Well, it wouldn't really be the worst thing, would it?" Phoebe said, lightly poking me in the rib and trying to joke with Mom.

"Yes, it would," Mom retorted. "Ugh, it would just gross me out to hear you got some girl pregnant. Thinking about my son having sex is just gross. It gives me the heebie-jeebies." Mom dramatically shook her body as if she had chills.

"Um, okay," I said, unsure of how to respond.

33

A year after we moved in together, Phoebe told me her period was late. The two of us drove to the drug store and purchased five different types of pregnancy tests. They ranged from a pink dye that said two lines meant yes to a blue dye test that said one line crossed over another meant yes. We even bought two different digital ones that would read out a yes or a no. Each test showed a positive result. We were going to be parents.

The next day, we called the local free clinic. They offered no-cost sonograms to confirm viability and to check how far along the baby was. Phoebe calculated that her last period had been about eight weeks prior to taking the tests. We were scheduled to come in later that day. I was terrified. Was I prepared to be a father? I'd never known what having one was like, how one should act. My mother was by no means a winning example of how a parent should be. What if I didn't know how to love and care for my baby? What if my child grew up to hate me the same way I'd hated my mom as a kid? What if I acted selfishly and only wanted to sleep or be left alone the way Mom had? How could I be a good father when, instead of excitement, these were the only thoughts running through my head?

At the clinic, we were called back to an all-white room. A single poster of a pregnant woman hung on the wall. Her stomach was transparent, showing a growing baby in her uterus. On the counter were different informational pamphlets. There were ones about breastfeeding, STD's, birth control, and the importance of quitting smoking while pregnant.

"Please lie on the table and lift your shirt," the ultrasound tech said.

Phoebe hopped up on the table. The tech pulled out an extender for her legs so she could lay comfortably.

"My name is Pearl, and I'm sorry, but this might be a little cold," she said. She grabbed a tube of gel and flipped it upside down, squirting its clear contents onto Phoebe's belly. Pearl picked up a wand from the side of the table and turned a monitor toward us. She pressed the wand deep into Phoebe's stomach, moving it all around searching for our baby.

"There it is," she exclaimed. "You see that little black circle?"

"Yeah," I said.

"That's the sac. And that little tiny thing inside of it is your baby."

"Oh my goodness," Phoebe said. She grabbed my hand and pulled it into her chest. "Our baby, Dom. Do you see it?"

"Yeah, I do," I said. I was mesmerized. That tiny little bean on the monitor was my baby. My child.

"That little flicker on the baby, do you see that?" Pearl asked.

"Yes," Phoebe and I both said.

"That is the amazing sight of your baby's beating heart. Do you want to hear it?"

I nodded. I couldn't speak. I was in awe.

Pearl turned on the speaker from the ultrasound machine and a loud, whirring *whomp-whomp-whomp* sound emerged. I knew immediately what that sound was. I knew that was the most stunning piece of music my ears would ever have the pleasure of hearing. That was my baby.

I began to cry. I looked at Phoebe. She was crying, too. I leaned down and kissed her. She had never looked more beautiful. I was so thankful for her and everything she had given me, and in that moment, I knew I could do this parenting thing. I loved my child. I would protect my baby, and my baby would not need to protect me like I had to protect Mom. I would love and care for my child and be for my baby what I wish someone had been for me.

We waited to announce our baby's arrival until Phoebe was fourteen weeks along. We didn't want to jinx anything or have to go through the horror of telling people if she didn't make it out of the scary first trimester. Phoebe's parents were delighted to say the least. Willa bawled tears of joy and hugged Phoebe for at least two whole minutes, then came to me for my two-minute hug. Tay shook my hand and congratulated me. They took us out to dinner to celebrate and, since we were unmarried, they were happy to announce that she was still on their insurance and maternity was covered under it. That was a giant weight off our shoulders.

Phoebe joined me at the next dinner I had with Mom. We planned to tell her together.

"Mom, we have something to tell you," I said, grabbing Phoebe's hand.

"Oh, God. What? Please don't tell me you're pregnant," Mom said.

Phoebe looked down at the table.

"Um, yeah. Phoebe's pregnant," I said.

"Seriously? I thought Phoebe looked a little rounder. But honestly, you guys are so young, and you're not even married. Are you sure that's what you want?"

"Yes, Mom. We're very excited." I looked at Phoebe, who wouldn't lift her gaze from her lap.

"Well, how far along are you? Maybe it's not too late for an abortion."

"Mom, stop. We're happy to have this baby."

"Were you trying, or was this a mistake?"

"I don't think that matters. That's a personal question I don't really want to answer. And even if we weren't trying, that wouldn't make our baby a mistake," I said.

"That's a 'no' on the trying." Mom laughed. "Ya know, I had a miscarriage once. Maybe that'll happen. I'm sorry, but you guys are so young, it would really be a blessing."

"Phoebe, let's go," I said, standing up from the booth.

"What do you mean, 'let's go?'" Mom asked. "We haven't even ordered yet."

"I'm not going to sit here and listen to this. We're happy, all right? And nothing you say or do is going to change how we feel about our baby."

"Oh man, it's always so dramatic with you." Mom chuckled. "You're too sensitive, you know that? I've always had to walk on eggshells around you so you wouldn't get upset. I was never allowed to speak my mind in case it would upset my sensitive little boy. This is what you do, though, isn't it? Should I warn poor Javier that you're upset and might punch a hole in the door?"

"Look, we're done here. We didn't come here to check if you're okay with us having a baby or not. We were only here because we thought you'd be happy to hear you're going to be a grandma."

"Why would I be happy about that? I'm too young to be a grandma, and you're both too young to be parents. What do you know about raising a child? Nothing. The answer is nothing."

* * *

Phoebe burst into tears the moment she got in the car and the door shut. "How can she be so mean?" she asked.

I didn't know how to answer that. I didn't know why Mom acted the way she did. I didn't know why she seemed to get worse as time went on, and I didn't know why it felt like it was emotionally impossible for her to feel happy for me. So I told Phoebe the only thing I did know: that I was sorry for how my mom treated her, and that I loved her and our baby more than anything. That was all that mattered.

"I don't want to see her anymore," Phoebe said. "I'm sorry, Dominic, but I don't like her."

"I don't like her, either," I said.

"She literally told us it's not too late to abort and that she hopes I miscarry. Who says something like that? I don't know if I want her around the baby."

"Whatever you want, Phoebs. We'll see how it goes. Maybe she'll come around and we'll all be able to get along. I don't know. It's just hard I guess."

"Yeah, we'll just play it by ear," she said. "But if it keeps going this way, I won't be able to do this. Your mom drains me. It's like she steals my energy and my happiness. I feel physically ill when I know I have to see her. She makes me so anxious, I could rip my hair out."

"I feel the same way, honestly," I said.

"Then, why do you still talk to her?"

"Because she's my mom."

34

When Phoebe was twenty weeks along, we scheduled an ultrasound that would tell us the sex of the baby and, more importantly, check the baby's growth to make sure everything was going smoothly. We were nervous the baby wouldn't be okay. We hadn't felt much for kicking. A couple little flutters here and there starting at nineteen weeks, but nothing more.

It turned out the reason for that was because the placenta was anterior instead of posterior like usual, meaning it was in front of the baby, against Phoebe's belly. It wasn't anything to be concerned about. It just meant that the baby's kicks and jabs would be felt lighter and less often since the placenta decided to pull double duty and act as a cushion.

The ultrasound tech looked at us excitedly and asked, "Do you want to know now or is it going to be a surprise?"

Phoebe's parents had wanted to throw us a reveal party, but those weren't our style, and being patient wasn't something either one of us was very good at.

"We want to know now," Phoebe said, practically bouncing off the table in excitement. Her grin reached from ear to ear.

"Okay, Mommy and Daddy," the tech said. "It's a girl."

"A little girl?" Phoebe whispered.

"A baby girl," I said.

Phoebe looked at me, her eyes glistening.

SON OF A HOARDER

I was so happy. Boy or girl, I didn't care. But a little girl sounded like the perfect answer when it was announced to me. A daddy's girl. A baby girl who would be as perfect and as beautiful as my Phoebe. I couldn't wait to hold her.

My favorite thing to do after learning my daughter could hear me was talk to and read to her. You're never too young to be read to. I started with Harry Potter, of course. The sooner the better.

When I'd get back from work, Phoebe and I would sit on the couch, and I would snuggle up to her belly and say, "Hi, little one." The baby would immediately start moving at the sound of my voice. I was so in love with my daughter, and I hadn't even had the honor of meeting her yet. I'd lay my cheek across Phoebe's swollen belly, and my baby would kick me, square in the jaw, every time. It was like she could sense exactly where I was. We were connected from the start.

* * *

At thirty weeks along, Willa called Phoebe to ask if she wanted her to throw a baby shower. The answer was, of course, yes.

"Do I have to go?" I whispered to Phoebe in the middle of her phone conversation with her mother.

She shook her head no.

I gave her a thumbs up. I was all for a shower as long as I didn't have to be there. I hated being the center of attention.

Phoebe put her mother on speaker. "Mom wants to talk to you," she said.

"Hey, Willa," I said.

"Hey, honey. How are you? Excited for the baby? Only a few more months, can you believe it?"

"No," I said. "I honestly can't. But I can't wait, either."

"Well, I wanted to talk to you because I wanted to know how you felt about me maybe asking your mother if she wanted to help plan the shower. This is her grandbaby, too. I thought she might want to be involved, if you're comfortable with that."

"That's up to Phoebe," I said. "I don't really care either way. I'm fine with it, so it's completely up to you guys."

"I guess you can ask," Phoebe said. She tried to sound positive, but her twisted expression showed a much different feeling. She wasn't a good liar, and she had virtually no poker face.

"Okay, I'll let you know what she says," said Willa.

The next day, Willa texted Phoebe to let her know that my mother had turned down her invitation to help with the planning but said that she would attend if she were to be invited.

The baby shower turned out wonderfully. We'd created a registry as requested by Willa and got most of what we needed from it. We also received a nice little stockpile of diapers and wipes.

Mom didn't show up. Grandma was invited as well, but also decided against going. Phoebe told me she was relieved she didn't have to interact with my mother. I was happy for her, but annoyed that Mom and Grandma would miss it.

Why didn't you go to the baby shower? I texted Mom that evening.

I didn't know anyone there and didn't really feel welcome.

You know Phoebe.

Yeah but not that well.

Why didn't you bring grandma then? You were both invited.

Grandma felt the same way I did. She's never even met Phoebe. Why would she wanna go?

Dunno. Just thought she might since it's her great grandkid about to be born.

Maybe it woulda been different if I was the one planning the shower or something.

They wanted you to help with the planning.

Mom stopped responding to me after that. I didn't talk to her again until our next dinner at Javier's, which had resumed about three months after the pregnancy announcement. Phoebe didn't want to attend any more dinners, and I wasn't going to ask her to.

At dinner, Mom showed up with a black garbage bag full of junk from the thrift store. She carried it against her chest, with her arms hugging the sides of it. It was so full, she couldn't tie its red ribbons.

"I got my grandbaby some good stuff today." Mom beamed, proud of herself for her thrift store finds.

"Did you? Well, I'm sorry, but we pretty much have everything we need," I said.

"Oh please, a baby can never have too many clothes."

"I'm not sure that's true."

"It is. It really is. Babies need changing like a million times a day. They spit up all the time, and they poop and pee all over themselves. You're going to need lots of stuff, especially onesies. And," she said, pulling one from the top of the bag, "just look at this one. I mean, how could I resist?"

It was a tiny pink onesie with gold stars on it. There were yellow formula stains around the collar and looked like it had served its purpose well for the previous owner. Embroidered across the front of it were the words, "Grandma's Little Angel." Willa's little angel, sure. But when did my baby girl become Mom's little angel, assuming that's what she meant? This is, after all, the same baby she had wanted us to abort and wished for Phoebe to miscarry.

"That's very cute, Mom. But we have so many clothes already. We honestly don't need any more. I do appreciate the gesture, though."

"Oh, stop," Mom said, waving her hand at me. "Just take it and look through it. Keep what you want and give me back what you don't. I'll keep the rest at my house for when you guys come over or when I babysit."

How did Mom plan to babysit or have us over when she never let anyone inside? What made her think I would allow my child into that landfill she called a house?

"I already have a crib in your old room," Mom said.

"You do? Is it set up?"

"Well, no. I mean, it's in the process. I just need to rearrange some things to make room for it."

"Of course you do," I muttered.

"What's that supposed to mean?" Mom asked. Her eyes glowered and her jaw clenched.

"Nothing. It's just…to be honest with you, I'm not going to let my baby come over to your house. You won't be babysitting, and we both know what's going to happen when you take that bag of baby clothes back with you. It's going to be thrown into a pile and absorbed into the mess along with everything else. It'll never be seen again. And if by some miracle I were to come over and bring my child with me, you wouldn't have any room to set up the crib if it were to be needed.

"I don't know why you're sitting here playing games. I'm not a kid anymore. I'm not one of your coworkers that you can lie to and pretend that you're redecorating. I'm sure you've told them all how you're turning my old room into a nursery for the baby when she comes over, when, in reality, none of that is true." I was ranting now, so frustrated and angry with her, I couldn't stop.

"I grew up in that hellhole. I know what it's like, and I can only guess that since I've been gone, it's only gotten worse. I know the stories you told to make yourself feel better. Those people you lied to didn't know the truth. I do. Okay? I do. And I'm not going to sit here and pretend anymore."

"You are so cruel, Dominic," Mom said. Her eyes welled up with tears. "I just wanted to do something nice for my son and my grandbaby, and this is the thanks I get? You decide to shit all over me instead? I can't even buy my granddaughter a onesie without upsetting you. This is what I'm always talking about. You're just a mean person. I swear, you enjoy hurting me. You are just…you're out of control. You always have been. Are you on drugs again? Oh no, is Phoebe doing drugs, too? Oh, my poor grandbaby." Mom burst into tears as if what she said were actually true.

"I was never on drugs, Mother," I said. I stood up from the table. "I don't want to talk to you anymore tonight. I'm going to leave before I say something I regret. Things are already bad enough between us."

"How? God, I just don't get it. No, you know what? I don't get *you*. What did I do to deserve such an evil son?"

I walked away then, not wanting to engage further. I was livid, but worried that maybe I did overreact. She was just trying to show the baby some love. Did I really need to blow up at her like that? I never knew the answer. Was I evil? Was I constantly overreacting? Or was I right?

35

Phoebe went into labor at three in the afternoon on May 4th. Our baby girl, Olive Dominique, was born the next day, May 5th, at 9:36 a.m. She weighed a whopping six pounds seven ounces and was twenty inches tall. She had a head full of black hair. Her cry as she emerged Earth-side was a truly stellar sound. I didn't think I would ever say this, but peering at Olive's flawless little face, with her tiny round nose and her lips so perfectly shaped they looked like someone had drawn them on for her, I saw someone more beautiful than Phoebe.

I smelled the top of her head, taking in her fresh-baby scent, and knew then that love at first sight really existed. One of my favorite parts of her new-baby skin was how hairy she was. I know that sounds funny, but she had this dark, soft hair all over her back and shoulders. She even had some on her little ears. I'm sure she wouldn't be happy knowing she was covered in that hair, but I loved my hairy girl.

It was just Phoebe and I in the room as she labored and then as she gave birth to our baby. We wanted privacy. We wanted that special moment to be just for us. Mom was not happy that she wasn't invited to be in the room. She pleaded and cried, but we stood firm in our decision. Phoebe's parents didn't question our choices.

Willa said, "Oh, of course. Who wants someone standing there watching them while they're in pain anyway?"

Tay joked, "Plus, you might be like your mom and shit

on the table. I've seen you poop plenty when you were a baby, I don't need to see it now." Then, he slapped his knee and laughed so hard, I thought he might fall out of his chair.

Phoebe hemorrhaged after the birth, and I feared I was going to lose her. Because of that, and the simple fact that we wanted time to ourselves, we waited until two hours after the birth to let anyone else into the room. We wanted that time to not only let Phoebe rest, but to bond, do skin-to-skin, and let the baby nurse. Willa and Tay were waiting patiently in the lobby, alongside my mother, who was waiting not-so-patiently.

After the two hours were up, I picked up my phone, which I'd put on silent, to text everyone and let them know they could now see Olive. I had thirteen missed calls from Mom and a slew of text messages. Not a single missed call or text was from anyone but her.

Is she done yet?

Dominic answer me please! Is the baby here?

I don't have all day you know???

I can't believe you haven't even come out here to check on us and update us on the baby.

We're all here for you guys and you just ignore us like we're not even here. I raised you to be more considerate than that.

Hello?????

Hello? What's going on?

TEXT ME BACK!!!

I'm going to leave if you don't text me back soon,,,,,,,,,, ???????????????????

I want to meet my grandbaby!!!!

When everyone came into the room, Phoebe was breastfeeding Olive. She covered herself a little because she was a modest person, but not enough that she couldn't look into Olive's eyes and the rest of us couldn't see her. She looked so tiny in Phoebe's arms, with her wild hair all over the place, still covered in the waxy vernix that dutifully protected her skin in the womb.

"Hi, baby," Willa said softly when she made her way

through the door. She walked over to Phoebe, put her arm around the top of the hospital bed and leaned down, pressing her temple against Phoebe's. She kissed the top of Phoebe's head. "She is absolutely gorgeous," said Willa. Her smile shone with pure joy.

"Isn't she?" Phoebe said.

Olive continued to suckle audibly, still trying to get the hang of nursing.

"She's perfect," said Tay. He stood behind Willa and brushed Olive's cheek with the back of his index finger. For the first time since I'd known him, I thought he might cry.

"Finally, you let us back here," Mom said, appearing next to me.

"Yeah, well, we just wanted some time with our baby," I said, trying to keep my cool. I would not let her take this moment from me.

"I can't believe she's feeding the baby right now. You guys are so immature. This is exactly why I didn't think you were ready to be parents."

"What the fuck are you talking about?" I said, losing my cool. I let her get to me. She was good at pushing my buttons. "Why wouldn't she feed the baby? How the hell is that immature?"

"Because it's selfish," said Mom. I hoped Phoebe and her parents couldn't hear our ridiculous conversation.

"How so?"

"Because we waited out there all freakin' day. I took the day off of work, and then, when I'm finally allowed back here, she's feeding the baby. I can't see her or hold her when she's eating. It's like you guys did this on purpose."

"Are you joking? You sound like an idiot."

"You're such an asshole," Mom said. "And no, I'm not joking."

Was I being selfish? Should I have updated Mom more when she was in the waiting room? She did sit there all day waiting. Maybe I should have gone out there and said, "Hey things are coming along nicely, might be a while though." I didn't feel like I was wrong in the moment, so why did I feel like I had done something wrong now?

"Go see the baby. You're the only one who seems to have a problem. Phoebe's parents are over there meeting Olive. You could, too. But you'd rather stand over here, complaining about nothing."

"I'm sure she wouldn't feel comfortable with me seeing her like that. I know I don't want to see her boob."

"Mom, she's feeding the baby. It's not like she's flashing everyone."

"I'll just wait here," Mom said as she sat down in the rocking chair that came with the room. "I've already waited all day. What's a little longer, I suppose?"

Mom held Olive a few minutes later, when Olive's tiny belly was full and nourished all thanks to her beautiful mother, my rock and my rescuer. She held Olive before her other grandparents, having guilt-tripped them into letting her go first.

"Watch her head," I said, handing the baby to Mom.

"I know how to hold a baby, Dominic," Mom said churlishly.

"I know. It's just habit now. I even said that to Phoebe and the nurses."

"She sure is beautiful." Mom ran her fingers over the top of Olive's head. "So beautiful. You guys did good."

Mom smiled. She looked happier than I'd seen her in a long time. A jubilant smile that I'd rarely seen in my life. It reminded me of when I was a kid and things were much different. It reminded me that even through all the tough times we went through and all the resentment I harbored toward Mom, I still loved her.

Even more than that, however, I was reminded of the scary times I endured as a child. I vowed to never let Olive grow up with anxieties like I did. I would always make her feel safe in my arms and in my heart, and never make her feel unwanted or unloved. She would never be a burden to me.

Leaving the hospital with Olive was an experience I'll never forget. I was overly cautious in making sure I drove twenty miles per hour under the speed limit, taking extra care over each and every bump, sure that every unsettling movement of the car was going to shake her little brain and give her shaken baby syndrome.

That anxiety was mixed with the worry of getting into an accident, and somehow, I wouldn't have her car seat strapped in properly and she'd go flying through the window, or that I hadn't buckled her correctly and the accident would cause her to not only go through the window but fling out of the car seat as well. I white-knuckled it all the way, a sweaty panic-stricken mess. Phoebe sat in the back with the baby, making sure she was okay at all times.

"Is she okay?" I asked, looking at Phoebe in the rearview mirror.

"She's fine, honey. Same as she was thirty seconds ago when you asked." Phoebe smiled at me, then looked down at Olive, her smile growing at the sight of our angel.

"When's the last time you checked her breathing?" As I asked, a tiny sigh escaped Olive's lungs. Such a relief.

"See? She's fine," Phoebe laughed.

"Her head's not hanging down too far, is it? Because I read that if her head hangs down, it cuts off her airways. She's not doing that, right?"

"Dominic, you're going to give me a panic attack. She's okay, I promise." Phoebe put her hand on my shoulder, assuring me my baby girl was all right.

Our first night out of the hospital, I didn't get a wink of sleep. Not because the baby kept me up, but because I was afraid the second I closed my eyes, she'd stop breathing and I'd be too busy snoring to notice my daughter dying in her bassinet next to me. Roy kept vigilant watch with me all night, his ears perked up with each sound she made. I had all these terrible thoughts running through my head. What if I dropped her? What if when I was changing her clothes, I twisted her arm on accident and broke it?

The intrusive thoughts were worse than the panic thoughts, however. When I changed Olive's diaper, I was suddenly scared I was going to magically turn into a child molester. I had no desire to touch her inappropriately, and her little parts didn't look the same to me as an adult's did. But there was this little voice in the back of my head asking, "Hey, what if you all of a sudden did like that kind of stuff? What if you turn into a pedophile?"

And there were times when I would bring her bassinet into the kitchen so I could watch her while I cooked lunch or dinner. She'd be sleeping soundly, and I'd be chopping some veggies when the thoughts would turn from "Look at my gorgeous sleeping girl" to "What if I were to take this knife and stab her with it?" I felt like a psycho and a pervert when I knew in reality, I was neither of those things. What the hell was wrong with me? Why did I have to suffer through intrusive thoughts? Were anyone else's as bad as mine, or was I really just evil like Mom said?

* * *

Mom came to visit a week after leaving the hospital. I invited her over to see the baby, and she didn't even wait her usual few hours to respond to my text. She texted back less than a minute later: *I'll be there in an hour.*

She showed up right on time. That was a first. She brought two black garbage bags full of clothes and baby things with her. Roy barked and scared the baby when she knocked on the door.

"I have so much stuff for my granddaughter. Give me that baby," Mom said. She was positively giddy as she came through the door. She shut it behind her and dropped the bags right there on the welcome mat.

Roy growled at Mom.

"Sit here next to me," Phoebe said.

Mom looked at me, seemingly annoyed that she had to sit next to the baby's mother but did it anyway.

"Wow, she's even more beautiful than I remember," Mom said as Phoebe handed Olive to her. Mom stroked Olive's little black hairs on the top of her head.

Roy jumped on the couch next to Phoebe and laid his head in her lap. A low growl vibrated from his mouth, a warning to Mom to be careful with his baby.

"Ugh, that damn dog needs to be quiet," Mom said. "His growling sounds pretty aggressive. You sure you want that around the baby?"

"He's fine, Mom. He just doesn't know you very well, and he's protective of Olive."

"Hmm, I don't know about that. Did you know pit bulls can lock their jaws? Just something to think about. What if he ever bit the baby? He's an aggressive breed, you know? And here he is, showing his aggression."

"He's fine," Phoebe said, petting Roy. She scratched behind his ears, his favorite spot, and he calmed.

"Just saying," Mom continued. "No one would blame you if you needed to take him to the pound. You wouldn't need to feel bad."

"Roy's part of the family. He's not going anywhere. It's not even up for discussion. How have you been?" I asked.

"Pretty good. Work's the usual, blah blah blah. Shitty kids to deal with, you know? Same as always." Mom chuckled. "How's the baby been?"

"She's great," I said. "She only gets up a few times a night. She's calm, doesn't cry much. She's perfect."

"She sure is," said Mom.

"And Phoebe's healing up well."

"Great," Mom said flatly.

Phoebe side-eyed me, not wanting the attention. Both of us knew Mom wouldn't let the focus be on her for too long as it was.

"So anyway," Mom said, drawing out the last syllable.

"Nothing new with me. Just wondering when you were going to call and let me see my precious grandbaby."

"What's in the bags?" I asked, cutting right to it.

"Oh, so much good stuff. Bring the bags over here, so you can look through them."

"We have a lot of stuff already. Don't get mad if we don't want or need it, okay?"

"Well, I've done this parenting thing before, you know? And like I told you, you can never have too many clothes."

"I think you can," Phoebe said, clearly annoyed with Mom.

Mom snapped her head toward Phoebe, glaring at her. "When you've been a mom as long as I have, you'll know. Though, I'm sure little Olive will be saying the same thing to you when she's a mom, and you'll be saying the same thing I am."

I opened the bags and immediately knew I didn't want what was inside. The smell that emanated from them brought back memories I didn't want to remember. They smelled like Mom's house. Sure, a good wash would take that out, but why would I even want that task? A lot of the clothes had yellow stains around the collar, clear that a little one had spit up on them. Some had holes, and mouse droppings fell out of a pair of shoes.

"Look, I know you think you have enough, so whatever you don't want, just donate," Mom said, "because I'm not hauling them back to my house. But the things you do want, I want them back after she outgrows them."

"For what?" I asked, the disgust showing in my tone.

"Because," Mom retorted, "I might be able to do something with them, some craft project or something. And if not, then there's this little consignment shop in town for babies. If you take some of your stuff there, they let you trade it for other stuff or give you store credit. So give it back when you're done, okay? If I bought it, I get to have it back. Seems fair to me."

"Why don't you just take all of it now and see if you can get store credit?"

"Dominic, don't be a jerk," Mom said. "Anyway, I need to get going soon. Am I allowed to see the baby's room before I go?"

"Yeah, of course," I said.

Mom handed Olive back to Phoebe and stood to follow me to the nursery. "Oh, Phoebe," Mom said. "Before I forget, next time I go shopping, do you want me to look for some exercise DVDs for you?"

"What?" I asked. "No, we're fine."

Phoebe stared at Olive, ignoring Mom.

"Okay, just thought I'd ask. Some people like to lose the weight right away. But if she's comfortable, well then, good for her."

In the nursery, Mom said, "Oh, it's nice in here." She seemed surprised. She touched a framed photo of Hogwarts that said "Olive" underneath it.

The nursery was decorated in a Harry Potter and fairy tale theme. Phoebe loved all things magical. Anything she felt looked like it came out of a storybook was perfect in her eyes.

Mom looked down at the ground, upset.

"What's wrong?" I asked.

"Oh, nothing. It's just...no, never mind."

"What?" I asked, annoyed. I could tell she was faking being upset, needing attention as always.

"It's nothing, really."

"Okay," I said, ready to move on.

"It's just that I wish you guys had asked me to help you with the nursery."

"Why would we do that?"

"I'm a first-time grandma. I would have loved to help decorate my baby granddaughter's nursery and be a part of that special moment. But now, I never will."

"It's not like we asked Phoebe's mom, either. It was just the two of us. I've literally never heard of anyone asking the grandparents to help with nursery decorating. I'm pretty sure it's something the parents do for their babies. Alone."

"Okay, that's fine," Mom said. She sighed, loud and heavy. "Guess I better be going. Before I go, though, can I ask you something?"

"Sure."

"I know you know that I'm not the most organized person, and I don't enjoy cleaning much. But the house has gotten out of control."

"Just now it has?"

"Dominic, don't be an ass. I need help with it."

"What are you asking?"

"Will you come over on the weekends and help me clean it?"

"Mom, Phoebe just had our baby, and I'd like to spend time with them on my days off. I don't want to spend my weekends helping clean up your messes."

"Ugh, it's always about Phoebe. That girl is so selfish. You had a mother to care about long before you had a girlfriend. Besides, part of those messes are your fault, you know? You didn't help me at all when you lived with me and everything just piled up."

"She's not selfish, and I'm not helping you clean."

"Please, son? I'll pay you five hundred bucks, and I'll let you keep anything you find that you want. There's a lot of good and valuable stuff in there. You can keep anything. Well, within reason, I mean."

"No. The answer's no. I'm not changing my mind. I helped enough as a kid."

"Bullshit," Mom scoffed.

"No. It's your house and your house alone. It's not my problem anymore."

"You are so evil," said Mom before stomping back through the house. She slammed the door on the way out, waking Olive from her slumber.

"Guess next time we get groceries, we'll be stopping at a

thrift store's donation center to drop off those bags," Phoebe said after Mom left. "I can't believe that she not only thought we'd want all of this shit, but that she wants us to be the ones to donate it."

"You can't believe it? Really?"

"Well, yeah, I can." Phoebe smiled, trying to find humor in the situation. "And we're not keeping anything, either. I'm sure she'll forget about that store credit soon enough."

36

Olive's first year of life went smoothly. I loved watching her learn new things, like how to use her little fingers or discovering that she had toes she could suck on. She had no problems, health or otherwise that arose, and she reached all her milestones on time. The only thing that she seemed a little behind on was that on her first birthday, she still didn't have any teeth. "Just a late bloomer," her doctor said.

Her first birthday party was more of a bash for us than for her, but we were ecstatic to throw her a party at our house. We invited Willa, Tay, Mom, and my grandparents. Everyone came and they all showed up on time, a pleasant surprise. Roy wagged his tail as Tay and Willa came in without even knocking. He knew it was them, recognizing the sound of their car. They didn't come over too often, but enough that Roy knew who they were. When Mom and Grandma and Grandpa knocked, Roy bellowed a loud, angry sound. His hackles created a mohawk across his back.

"I hate that dog," Mom huffed when they came in.

"Well, we love him," I said, dismissing her.

Everyone said their usual "Hi" and "How are you," then made pleasant small talk. Most of us just watched the baby as she toddled around the house. Her cuteness was enough entertainment. We'd made deviled eggs and had a cheese and cracker tray, with a veggie platter for the appetizers. Then for lunch, we served slow cooker pulled pork sandwiches and potato salad. Olive got to try deviled eggs for the first time. They were perfect for her toothless mouth. She loved the eggs and kept reaching out her little hand asking for more from anyone who would give her a bite of theirs.

Mom reached into her purse and pulled out a chocolate bar while we were eating and handed it to Olive.

"Oh, no, she can't have that," Phoebe said, taking the candy from Olive.

"And why not?" Mom asked.

"She's never really had much for sweets, and she's getting a special cupcake after we sing "Happy Birthday" to her. I don't want her to get sick from having too much sugar."

"Well, I hate to break it to you sweetheart," Mom said, snatching the candy back from Phoebe and handing it back to Olive. "But as her grandma, this is my right." Mom wasn't joking around with Phoebe.

"Well, I hate to break it to you, Annie," Phoebe said, again taking back the candy from Olive, this time handing it to me. "But as Olive's mother, I have to say no. I don't want her to get sick."

"Yeah, as her parents we have all the rights," I said, trying to take the pressure off Phoebe. "Grandmas have privileges, not rights, and we say no."

* * *

"Why don't you invite us over more?" Grandpa asked after we finished eating. "You hardly call anymore."

"Well, just been busy working and taking care of the baby. I try to help as much as possible when I'm off work so Phoebe gets a break."

"Oh, does she need a break?" Grandma asked. I hadn't realized she was standing behind me. "Your mom says she thinks Phoebe has PPD. You know…postpartum depression," she whispered.

"Um, I really don't think so," I said, pulling Olive's cake

from the fridge. "It just wouldn't be fair to have her not have any time to herself. She needs to be able to shower, right?"

"To be honest, Dominic, we wanted to talk to you about Phoebe," Grandma said. "Your mom said that she doesn't want you coming around us too often and that she doesn't like having any of us over. You know that saying, 'A daughter's a daughter for life but a son's only a son until he gets a wife'? Well, we don't think it's right that you have really followed through on that. You never call or anything anymore."

"How often do you call me?" I asked. "It goes both ways."

"There's no reason to be rude here, Dominic," said Grandpa.

"I'm not being rude. I'm being honest. And seriously, guys? Do you honestly believe that now, at my daughter's first birthday party, is a great time to be having this conversation?"

"Well, we hardly get to see you. I didn't know when we'd have a chance again. Your mom said she calls you all the time, but Phoebe doesn't let you answer," said Grandma.

"That's not even close to true. If I don't answer, it's because I don't want to." I pulled a knife from the block and cut into the cake.

Phoebe was on the couch in the living room with her parents, laughing. They looked so happy and normal. Olive sat in Tay's lap, pulling on his beard. He would fake an exaggerated "Ow!" and Olive would break into a fit of laughter. Why couldn't my side of the family be like that?

"We're worried that you and the baby are in an abusive situation," Grandpa said.

I dropped the knife and hung my head, staring into the creamy frosting atop the chocolate cake. Phoebe had made the cake and used little piping tips to write out "Happy Birthday, Olive" across it. The cake looked delicious. Phoebe did a great job on it. But at that moment, I wanted nothing more than to smash it into their faces.

"What are you talking about?" I asked as calmly as I

could manage.

Mom sat in the chair in the living room across from Phoebe and her parents, not trying to engage or socialize with them. She sat picking at her fingernails and watching us, pretending she wasn't, pretending she didn't know what the conversation we were having entailed, pretending that she wasn't the one who sent them over here with her lies.

"Dominic, I hate to say it, but Phoebe's a stereotypical abuser," Grandpa said.

"How so?"

"Well, for starters, she isolates you from your family," said Grandma.

"No, for starters, I isolate myself from you guys. *They* are my family," I said, pointing to Phoebe and Olive.

"You don't have to worry, Dom, we're only trying to help," said Grandma. "And the second thing is, we know that she yells at you all the time. Your mom said when she talks to you on the phone, she can hear Phoebe in the background, screaming at you to get off the phone with her. We all feel as if you've just completely abandoned us. Written us off."

"Wow." I was almost speechless. "This is…wow. This is unbelievable."

"What is?" Grandpa asked.

"You guys. Mom. All of this. Unbelievable bullshit. I'm finally happy, and Mom has to come in here and try to ruin it. You guys don't call or come see me, either. Neither does Mom. I have to do all the calling and inviting over. You went out for your birthday, right, Grandma?"

Grandma nodded.

"Were we invited, or was it just you two and Mom?"

"Well, we figured you were busy," Grandma said. "Besides, we only just met Phoebe after Olive was born. It doesn't look too good for her when she doesn't even want to meet her boyfriend's family. Your mom said she wants you and the baby all to herself."

"It's all lies, but you guys just sit there and eat it up. Every little thing Mom says, you believe, no matter how outlandish or full of shit it is." I finished cutting the cake and picked it up, hoping that would signal I was done with that conversation and it was time to sing to Olive.

"Dominic, we're worried about you and Olive, and if you won't come to your senses about the situation Phoebe's putting you in, then we'll have no choice but to step in," said Grandpa.

"Step in? What does that mean?" I was getting angrier and louder with each passing second.

"We'll have no choice but to call Child Protective Services. If you can't be a man and take back the balls you so freely handed over to that girl, then we need to start thinking of Olive and her well-being. I mean, someone has to," he said.

"This is a grandparent rights state, you know?" Grandma said. "We could fight for custody."

"The fuck is wrong with you guys?" I shouted. I dropped the cake. Spongy chocolate chunks splattered across the kitchen floor. A mess of frosting smeared over it, no longer looking appealing, now reminiscent of baby shit. A sure sign of the shit-show they had turned my poor daughter's party into.

Phoebe, Tay, and Willa jumped. Olive stared at me, never having seen me like that. I didn't like the look in her eyes. I'd scared her.

Roy jumped in, ready to vacuum up my mess but Phoebe got him out the door before he could ingest any chocolate.

"Nothing's wrong with us. We're only doing what every concerned grandparent would do," Grandma said, lowering her voice so Phoebe couldn't hear her.

"Oh, every concerned grandparent, huh? Where was all this concern when I was a kid?" I asked, snatching the paper towel roll off the rack under the cupboard and wiping the frosting from the floor. "Where were you when there was an actual abusive situation going on? Where were you when I needed you when I was a kid? No, your perfect daughter would never do anything like that, though, right? There was no need to 'step-in' then, was there?"

"Dominic, why are you bringing up the past?" Grandpa asked, crossing his arms tight across his chest. "You really need to get over that and move on. It's time to grow up and realize not everything's about you."

"This is about me. I mean, why are you so worried now? Why are you trying to 'protect' Olive? She doesn't need protecting from me. It sounds more like she needs protecting from all of you."

"Don't be ridiculous. We love that baby," Grandma choked as tears rolled down her perfectly made-up cheeks.

"Why didn't you protect me from my mom? I'm your grandson. Didn't I deserve the same concern when I was a kid?" I asked. I grabbed the broom and dustpan and swept up Olive's birthday cake.

"You might be our grandson," Grandpa said, "but she's our daughter."

"I think you three need to leave," I said, tiptoeing around the frosting that still needed cleaned up. I pulled their coats off the rack by the door and handed them over.

"Dominic, don't do this," Grandma said, still crying.

"We're done here." I opened the door and ushered them out, not bothering to say goodbye.

"Here," Mom said as she went out the door. She threw a pink birthday-card-size envelope at me. The corner of it hit me in the cheek before it tumbled to the ground. Written on the front was "Olive."

After they left, I opened it. Inside the envelope was a birthday card dedicated to "Grandma's favorite and best girl" and a check for fifteen dollars. I never cashed it.

I walked over to Olive and whisked her up into my arms. She hugged me tight. For someone so small, she sure knew how to give good hugs.

"Dada," she said, pulling back and stroking my cheek.

I teared up. "I love you, baby girl."

"It's okay," Phoebe said. She stood and hugged me.

I kissed the top of her head, then Olive leaned in, mouth

wide open, and planted one on me, too. I felt better then. They were all I'd ever need. I had found myself in them. My perfect girls.

I still find our story funny. Phoebe and I met by chance. We were strangers. Then, after strangers, we were work acquaintances, that turned into flirting, and that turned into love. Strangers who met twenty-plus years into their lives. We didn't go to the same schools or live in the same town. Our parents had never met, we had no mutual friends, and yet, we fell in love. I found my other half, the missing piece I didn't know was out there waiting to be found. No matter how cliché that sounds, it's true.

"Should we go? Is everything okay?" Willa asked.

Phoebe looked at me and shrugged her shoulders. "Whatever you want to do," she said, rubbing the small of my back.

"No. I don't want you guys to go," I said. "There's no need to stop the celebration just because a couple of assholes thought they could try to ruin a perfectly good party. This day is about Olive. She's still smiling. I'm going to try to do the same."

* * *

Later that night, I proposed to Phoebe. I'd saved up money for months and kept some out of the account each time I deposited my paychecks, so she wouldn't notice any had been withdrawn. I didn't get an expensive one, and it wasn't very big, but I knew Phoebe wouldn't mind. She used to tell me she hated how people spent a thousand or more dollars on engagement rings. She thought they were a waste of money.

Originally, I'd wanted to take Phoebe out to dinner, just the two of us. Then, I was going to have her parents show up with Olive as a "surprise." I had a custom onesie made that said "Mommy, will you marry Daddy?" on it, so when they surprised us at the restaurant, they'd pull off Olive's coat, and

Phoebe would see the onesie. Then, while it was registering, I'd get down on one knee. But after the disastrous day we'd had, I didn't want that anymore. I knew I had to propose to her that night. No more planning, no more waiting. I wanted to let her know right then and there what she meant to me.

While Phoebe showered, I changed Olive into the onesie. When Phoebe got out, I said, "Go see Mommy, Olive."

She toddled over to Phoebe, who said, "What's this little outfit? I've never seen…"

I was right behind Olive, pretending I was making sure she wouldn't fall, but really, I was preparing to get on one knee.

"Oh my God," Phoebe choked.

"Phoebe Prescott, I have loved you since the moment I met you. I fell in love with all of you. Every little piece of you is perfect to me. You are everything and more than I could've ever hoped for, and best of all, you gave me this sweet girl," I said, kissing Olive's cheek. "Please, please give me the honor of being able to call you Phoebe Leonard. I already knew long before today that we would spend the rest of our lives together, but if it's even possible to be happier than I already am, I would love nothing more than to make you my wife. Officially…you know, legally?" I laughed.

"A ring is binding, you know?" Phoebe chuckled. "Like a legal contract."

"Oh, I know."

"Yes, yes. You already know my answer," she said. She leaned over and kissed me hard on the lips. "Yes."

37

We married fourteen months later, just after Olive's second birthday. Her day was spent with just the three of us and her only two grandparents I knew wouldn't ruin her party. We had a small dinner of pizza at the house, nothing fancy, and Phoebe made another delicious cake. This time, she was the one in charge of the cutting and serving.

Our wedding day was bittersweet. Phoebe gets annoyed at me to this day for failing to see all the beauty and joy that day held and holding on to the anger I feel toward the people who tried to bring me down. Two weeks before the wedding, Mom came over to show me at least ten different outfits she'd bought, wanting to know which ones would go best with our color scheme. She modeled every single one for me, wanting praise during each of her impressions of a model on the catwalk. Phoebe was lucky she was visiting her parents during Mom's performance. She would've had a hard time keeping her eyes from rolling.

After over an hour of this I became fed up and finally pretended I loved the last dress she'd tried on so much, and that it was, without a doubt, the one.

"If you don't wear that one you have on right now to the wedding, then I think you'll have really lost your chance at the perfect dress," I said.

"This one? You think so? I mean, I like it. I just didn't think it was the one. I could try on that first blue one again, if you want to compare. Just in case," she said.

"No. This is the one. No question about it. I don't even want to see any more because they won't compare."

"Okay, fine. If you feel so strongly about it, this is the one I'll wear for your big day. You know it's kind of my big day, too."

"Oh yeah? How so?" I asked, annoyed but not surprised she was trying to make my wedding about her.

"I'm the mother of the groom and the grandmother of the flower girl. This is a big day for both of us."

"Yeah, I guess," I said, eager to move on from the conversation.

"As the grandma, I thought I might have some input on what my little angel should wear."

"We already have a dress for her."

"I figured, but just in case you want more options, here are a few more dresses you might want to think about." Mom pulled a thrift store bag out from inside the big garbage bag.

"We don't need these. We're all set."

"Just look through them. Please. For me."

"Fine," I said, knowing I wouldn't actually be looking through or considering any of them.

"But on a more serious note," Mom said, sitting down next to me on the couch. She was still in the navy-blue, knee-length dress. From afar, I hadn't noticed all the beaded and outdated detail on it. It looked nice on her, there was nothing wrong with it, aside from the fact that it looked like she'd pulled it from a prom shop stuck in the nineties.

"I just wouldn't feel right leaving here tonight and attending your wedding if I didn't have this talk with you," Mom began.

"Okay."

"Are you absolutely sure you want to marry this girl?"

"Mom, I'm not going to talk about this with you. Yes, I'm absolutely sure." I stood, ready to show her the door.

"Dominic, please sit down. Just hear me out, okay? I'm

worried about you, you know? We're not close like we used to be. It's like once you found her, you stopped caring about me." Mom teared up. I couldn't tell if she really believed that and was truly upset, or if she just wanted more attention.

"We stopped being close long before I met Phoebe," I said, sitting back down.

"I'm just not sure you two are good for each other. Just because you had a baby together doesn't mean you have to get married."

"I know that. I want to marry her. I love her."

"I have something for you." Mom reached into her purse. She pulled out a large manila envelope and handed me a stack of self-printed postcards from inside.

"What are these?"

Printed on the postcards was:

Dear Family and Friends,

I regret to inform you that the wedding has been postponed until further notice. Thank you so much for the time and effort of responding to our RSVPs and if you have bought any gifts, please return them as they are no longer needed. I am very sorry for any inconveniences this may have caused. Thank you all for your kindness and understanding.

Sincerely,
Dominic Leonard

"Again, I'm asking you, what the hell are these?" I tossed them back to Mom. Each one had a stamp on it, ready to be mailed.

"Just something to think about," Mom said, trying to reorganize the stack.

"I absolutely will not think about it. This is not up for discussion. If you can't be happy for me, I don't even want you at my wedding."

"If you go through with the wedding, I'll be there."

"I am going through with it. But if you're going to act like this, then don't bother coming."

"I'll be perfectly pleasant."

"Fine. I'll see you there. Have a good night," I said. I stood and made my way toward the door.

"Have a good night?"

"Yes, I think you should go before I say something I'm going to regret. I'm not very happy with you right now."

"Something you'll regret? Like what? That I look fat in my dress?"

"What? My God. No. Why would you even think…just…just go. Please. Goodbye."

Roy stood next to me, his chest puffed out, sensing I was upset.

"Fine," Mom said, gathering her bags of dresses.

I slammed the door behind her, so happy Phoebe wasn't there to witness that. I didn't tell her about the postcards when she and Olive got back, partly because I didn't want to upset her. I was protecting her from yet another one of Mom's attacks, and unfortunately, another part of me was still protecting Mom. I didn't want Phoebe to uninvite her to the wedding. I wanted my mom at my wedding, even if she didn't deserve to be there.

* * *

Our wedding day came and went. We had it at the cabin in the backyard. It was small; we only invited twenty-five people. All but five came. Leslie and her husband couldn't make it, and Uncle Kai and Aunt Gretchen never sent back their RSVP. I wasn't surprised. I knew before I'd even mailed the invitation to their little family that they weren't coming. Mom showed up in a different dress than the one I had picked out. It was cream colored, almost white. She came with my grandparents, who I hadn't seen since Olive's first birthday party, but thought I should invite, nonetheless. We had no bridesmaids or groomsmen. Just one little flower girl and Roy as the ring bearer.

The chairs were set out in two rows on each side of the aisle. Five chairs in each row and a white runner following the aisle in between. Phoebe had Pinterested a lot of her ideas and just about everything out there was DIY. She did a beautiful job. She'd created an archway by hanging some sheer white curtains horizontally across two trees in the backyard, then adding some flower garlands that hung behind the curtains. Roy stood next to me under the homemade archway, a bow tie around his neck with an organza bag containing our rings tied to the bow.

Phoebe was escorted down the aisle by Tay, who was looking uncomfortable in a blue button up and black slacks that matched mine. It was too hot for those outfits. My bride looked gorgeous in a blush-pink, tea-length, fifties style dress. Her long hair hung in curls over her shoulders, her grandmother's pearls around her neck with earrings to match. Next to her was baby Olive in a white summer romper. Something she wouldn't get too hot in, and we wouldn't be too sad when she dirtied it playing.

The ceremony was beautiful, it really was. We had some issues with Mom trying to get Olive's attention the entire time. She was trying to make Olive laugh from her seat in the front row and trying to get Olive to come sit with her instead of standing up next to us. We exchanged our written vows, each of us promising to love each other forever and for always and adding in some quotes from our favorite movies.

"Do you, Dominic, take Phoebe to be your lawfully wedded wife? To have and to hold from this day forward, for as long as you both shall live?" the officiant asked.

"I do." I grinned, knowing there was no other possible answer.

"And do you, Phoebe, take Dominic to be your lawfully wedded husband? To have and to—"

A phone trilled at full volume, capturing everyone's attention.

"Oh, sorry," Mom said. "That's me. Hang on, gotta find

it. You know how I am. Me and my big bags." She dug through her purse until the phone stopped ringing on its own. "Hopefully, they don't call back."

"As I was saying, do you, Phoebe, take Dominic—" The phone started ringing again.

"Hang on," Mom said, pulling out the phone without any issues this time. All eyes were on her as she answered. "Hello? Yes, sorry I can't talk now. I'm in the middle of something. Oh, really? Wow. No way, are you serious?"

"Mom, think maybe you want to take that in the house or something?" I asked.

"Hold on. I'm getting off right now," Mom said, covering the mouth of the phone. "Listen, so sorry but I have to go. I'm in the middle of something. Yes, yes, okay. You too, bye." Mom ended the call and stuck the phone back in her purse.

"Maybe shut it off in case anyone calls back," I suggested.

"Oh, I never shut my phone off. You never know who might try to reach me. But for you guys, I'll put it on vibrate, okay?"

"Great," I said, turning back to the officiant.

"Okay, Phoebe, we left off and I was asking if you take Dominic—" The officiant began, only to be cut off again, this time by Phoebe.

"Yes, I do." She sighed. "I do. Now, let's end this thing."

"Okay, then. You may kiss your bride, Dominic."

At the sight of our first kiss as a married couple, the DJ blasted "I'm A Believer" by Smash Mouth through his many speakers set up around the property, and we made our way back down the aisle.

Phoebe and I retreated into the house to catch our breaths, wind down from the anxiety of being in the spotlight, and to simply bask in the joy we held within each other. I hugged her and Olive tight. She kissed me, then Olive leaned over to do the same.

"You two are all I'll ever need," I said.

We weren't in the house more than five minutes when Mom came charging in through the back door. "What are you guys doing in here?" she asked.

"We needed a minute," I said.

"Your guests are out there waiting for you guys. You're being rude."

"We've only been in here for a few minutes," Phoebe said.

"Yeah, and it's a few minutes too long. People want to see the baby and the new couple. Stop being rude and go greet your guests."

"We'll be out in a minute. Please go back out there and leave us be," I said.

"This makes me look bad, too, you know? People will think I didn't raise you to be conscientious and considerate of others' time and feelings."

"People are eating. I really don't think they're exactly worried what we're doing right this second. It's literally been like three minutes."

"Fine, but you need to hurry up. Oh, real quick, before I forget. I was looking around the property earlier while you were all setting up, and there's a lot of room out here. Do you think if I bought one of those tool shed things and stuck it out of the way where you wouldn't even have to look at it, I could put it here and store some of my stuff in it? I just don't have the room at my house, and you know I love my shopping." Mom laughed.

"Absolutely not. Now, please, just leave us alone for a minute."

"But you wouldn't even see it. Out of sight, out of mind, right?"

"Mom. Go. Now."

"I don't know how I raised such a rude and mannerless child," Mom said as she stalked through the sliding glass doors, slamming them so hard they bounced back open.

"Like she has any room to talk about being rude. Talking

on the phone during the ceremony. Ugh, I'm sorry, Dom, but I cannot stand that woman."

"No need to be sorry. I can't, either. But you want to hear something cool?"

"What?"

I grinned. "You're my wife now."

"And you're my hubs. I am Mrs. Dominic and you are Mr. Phoebe."

Willa and Tay paid for a caterer as a very generous wedding gift to us. We enjoyed a delicious, mouthwatering pork roast with a baked potato bar, full of everything you could ever want to put on a baked potato. Bacon, sour cream, ranch, cheese, onions, chives, and more. While we were eating, we had the DJ play symphony renditions of some of our favorite songs. Guns N' Roses and Metallica in symphony sounds pretty classy in my opinion, and the guests had fun trying to guess what songs they were listening to.

"Dominic, beautiful ceremony," Grandma said. She rushed up behind me as Phoebe and I were eating. Olive sat between us, alternating between taking a bite and throwing her food on the ground to Roy.

"Thank you," I said. "Thanks for coming."

"Oh yes, of course. But I need to tell you something."

"What?" I groaned.

"This music is um, interesting. But it's also a little boring. When are you going to be playing the dance music? Your guests are getting bored."

"Are they? I haven't heard any complaints," said Phoebe.

"I've heard a few," said Grandma. "If I were you, I'd tell the DJ to start playing something more upbeat before people get bored and leave."

"We've only been eating for twenty minutes, Grandma," I said. "He's set to start playing the party music after thirty minutes. We had this discussion with him while we were planning the wedding."

"Thirty minutes? Wow, that's a long time."

"Not really. It's enough time to make sure everyone gets a plate and gets to finish eating before they worry about dancing."

"I mean, it's your wedding," Grandma said. "If you think this is how it should go, then I guess that's up to you. Just thought I'd make a suggestion because you don't want people to think your wedding was boring."

"It'll be fine, thanks," I said, returning to my plate.

Ten minutes later, the DJ played "Old Time Rock & Roll" by Bob Seger to get the crowd up and moving. I didn't want to dance with Mom, so we only did a father-daughter dance for Tay and Phoebe. Tay teared up, and Phoebe laughed at him through her tears as "Sweet Child O' Mine" played through the booming speakers. I danced with little Olive. She was only interested for the first two minutes before moving on to something else.

Our first dance as newlyweds was to "Chasing Cars" by Snow Patrol, a song whose lyrics seemed to match us completely.

"What do you love about me?" Phoebe asked. The two of us stood in the middle of the dance floor, so happy, so in love. The world around us was a blur.

"I love everything about you. I love the way you make me smile and laugh even when I'm having the worst day. I love the way your presence shows me that we can make it through anything. The love and compassion you radiate is contagious. I love the way your hair and your skin always smells fresh, like vanilla, even when you haven't showered for days. There isn't one thing I would change about you."

Phoebe smiled and pulled me closer.

"What do you love about me?" I asked.

"I love the way your hair doesn't have a natural part. You can't even train that wild mane of yours. I love the way I feel protected around you, even if that's sexist, because of course I can take care of myself." She laughed. "But you make me feel safe. You make me feel secure. Like nothing and no one could ever hurt us or break us. Nothing bad can happen when we're together. I love the way your eyes change colors, depending on your mood. I love how you'll always hold my hand or dance with me, no matter what's going on. You'll stop, just to be in the moment with me. I just love you. Just you. I wouldn't change anything, either. You're mine now. For good. You put your signature on the marriage certificate, so now I hold the title to you, and I'm not signing off on that. Ever."

"I grew up with toxic and conditional love, Phoebs," I said, holding her close during our dance.

She wrapped her arms around my torso and laid her head against my chest. I held her, one hand behind her head, my cheek against her crown.

"You've shown me what true, unconditional love looks and feels like. I am forever grateful for you," I continued.

"I'm yours always. And I'm forever grateful for you, too. And forever grateful that you chose me."

"Pssh," I said in disbelief. "I would choose you a thousand times over. I would cross every ocean and every desert for you. It's you who chose me. I'm not good enough for you, and yet you love me anyway."

"I love you always," she said.

"And I love you forever."

"Promise?"

"I promise."

38

Six months later, my grandfather passed away. Mom called me the day after it happened. I couldn't understand what she was saying at first. She was sobbing too hard, barely audible through her gasping breaths. She said that he was working on one of the many classic cars he was always restoring. He was under the car, putting in a new fuel pump, when the jack failed and the car fell on top of him, crushing his body.

Grandma, who was in the house, never having had interest in cars herself, didn't find him until hours later. Mom said she felt guilty that she might have been able to save him had she known he was out there dying alone. I felt for her. I couldn't imagine that level of guilt.

"Do you need me to do anything?" I asked.

"No, that's okay. Thank you, though," Mom said.

"Does Grandma need help?"

"No, she just wants to be alone for now. Well, just me and her, I mean. Unless you want to bring the baby by?"

"I'm not sure I want her around all the sadness, sorry. I think it might scare and confuse her."

"Fine."

"When's the service? Do you need help with that?" I asked.

"Should be next week. We're trying to set it up with the church right now. Um, don't need any help. We have it under control."

"Okay, well, I guess then just let me know if you do need anything."

"Will do. Talk to you later," said Mom.

"All right. Let me know for sure when the service is, okay?"

"I will. If I don't get back to you, though, just keep an eye out for an event invite on Facebook."

"I'm not on Facebook," I said.

"Maybe you should get on it. I post a lot of info there."

"Can't you just call me?"

"Dominic, why do you have to be so difficult?" Mom sighed. She was right. It wouldn't hurt me to open an account. Though, in my mind, I thought that as his grandson I deserved to be given the information firsthand and not from a social media post. Mom, apparently, did not feel the same way.

"Fine, never mind, it's all right. I'll make a Facebook," I said, exasperated.

"Great. Talk to you later."

"Okay, love you."

"Yep," Mom said, ending the call.

After that, I did something I said I never would, and I made a Facebook account. I added Mom and Grandma and got a few friend requests here and there from the people at work and some people from my high school, including Tommy.

I felt guilty that Grandpa and I never had that great of a relationship. Part of me was devastated at the loss, but I couldn't shed a tear because the other part of me had never forgiven him for the way I was treated growing up. I have a problem with holding on to resentment, and I know that. I should let go, but it's one of the hardest things to do.

I don't have many good memories of Grandpa. I can recall a few times when he would let me help work on cars with him. He taught me the basics, like how to change the oil in a car. One time, he even took me to the movie theater to see *Jurassic Park* in his newly-restored 1957 Chevy Bel Air. That's been one of my favorite cars since then, especially in Grandpa's Bel Air colors: two-tone mint green and white. I remember the looks we got while driving down the street. People would stop and stare, some even giving us a thumbs up or yelling, "Nice car!"

I wish he and I could have had a normal grandfather/grandson relationship. But I always felt so aggrieved and upset with him. He'd say things like, "I'm not taking sides here." Or, "I don't want to get involved." But he did get involved. When Mom told him I needed talking to, he was right there ready to be the witch's flying monkey. And in the times when he did stay quiet and didn't get involved, like when they should have stepped in and taken me away for good, sitting back and doing nothing, he was taking a side. Choosing to let me hurt so his daughter didn't have to was picking sides. He took the side of the oppressor, whether they could see that or not. If Mom hadn't needed me to be her shield and scapegoat my whole life, maybe things would have been different. On the other hand, if I had only learned to let go of the anger and resentment, maybe we could have mended the relationship and fixed our differences after I became an adult and moved away. But none of that happened, and now it never will. It's too late.

Mom made an event listing on Facebook the day after our phone call. The funeral was going to be held at Grandma and Grandpa's church, the same one they'd attended for over forty years. It was exactly a week after his death, on a Saturday, at two in the afternoon. There was going to be a potluck following the service. Phoebe didn't want to go, which I completely understood. She wanted to stay out of the path of destruction, and I didn't want Olive there anyway. She didn't need to be seeing anyone like that, dead in a box.

There were a lot of people at Grandpa's funeral. Mom got up on stage and spoke highly of her "daddy," as she called him. She talked about how he'd always been there for her and done everything for her. How no one would ever do for her what he had. She said he had protected her for her entire life in a way that no one else ever had.

I couldn't help but feel slighted, as I'd spent my childhood protecting her. But that day wasn't about me, and I tried to keep that in mind. I have to keep myself in check, reminding myself daily that not everything is an attack on me. It's hard to not let things get to me when I feel like everything they did just pushed my buttons. It's exhausting even having to be in the same room as them. I've felt so bullied and beat down by them my entire life that now, everything feels like criticism.

When the pastor returned to the microphone and asked if anyone else would like to speak, I looked around the room. At the back of the church was a man I almost didn't recognize. But I couldn't mistake that dark hair for anything. Uncle Kai was there. I wanted to talk to him, but I knew he didn't want to talk to me, and by the time the service was over, he was gone. My heart ached for the relationship we once had. I wish I had even just a single minute to tell him how much I loved and missed him and Aunt Gretchen.

Everyone was lining up to say goodbye to Grandpa. I sat in my seat, waiting for my turn when I heard a somewhat familiar voice.

"Dominic, is that you?" a woman asked when the service was over. It was Grandma's sister, my great-aunt Elsa.

"Hi, Aunt Elsa. Long time no see," I said. I hadn't seen her since I was eight years old.

"I'll say. How are you?"

"I'm fine. Just got married, I have a little girl now."

"Wow, that is wonderful to hear. Where are they? I'd love to meet them."

"Oh, they couldn't make it. I didn't think it was appropriate to bring a two-year-old to something like this."

"Hmm. Okay, then," she said. "Listen, I know it's not really my place, but my sister and I were talking yesterday and she told me all about the situation with you and your mother.

I just want you to know that when my mom died, I was broken. I really think you'll regret not having a good relationship with your mom. It's not healthy to keep her away, and it's especially unhealthy and unfair to keep her away from her grandbaby. You should consider the baby."

"Thanks, Elsa," I said. I stood and moved to the back of the room, not wanting to hear her unsolicited advice. She was right; it wasn't her place.

I didn't want to stay and eat. I just wanted to pay my respects, say goodbye to Grandpa for closure, then get back to my family. After the room cleared, and everyone was done gawking at Grandpa's lifeless gray body lying in his casket, I walked over to do the same.

"Goodbye," I said, touching his hard, cold chest. "I'm sorry things couldn't have been different. I'm sorry I was never who you wanted. But I want you to know I did love you."

"That was sweet, honey," Grandma said.

I jumped. I didn't know she was standing behind me. "You scared me." I chuckled, hugging her.

"Sorry, dear."

"I'm sorry, too. Are you okay?"

"No." She half laughed, half cried. "But I will be. Your grandfather wouldn't want me falling apart. And besides, your mother's been just amazing and wonderful, as usual. She did all of this, you know? You should give her more credit."

"What do you mean?"

"You know what I mean. You've always blamed her for your problems, and you shouldn't. You should take responsibility for your actions, too."

"Okay," was all I could manage. I didn't want to be having this conversation at all, but especially not today.

"You really need to make up with your mom. The only thing your grandpa ever wanted was for you and your mom to get along. You should make up with her, if not for her, then for him."

"It's not that simple, Grandma. I don't want to do this

289

right now, please. Let's just, you know, not."

"All right." Grandma sighed. "That's fine. I'm going to go get something to eat."

"Okay."

"Oh, before I forget. Can you come by the house tomorrow? Say, around noon? Your grandfather had a will, and he left something for you."

* * *

The next day, I went to Grandma and Grandpa's house. Everything was just as I had remembered. It was like stepping back into my childhood. Not even so much as a picture frame had changed its place on the wall.

"Sit, sit," Grandma said. "Can I get you anything?"

"No, I'm fine, thank you," I said, sitting on the couch.

Mom was there too, sitting in the big chair.

"Let's just get right to it," Grandma said.

"Sounds good to me," said Mom.

"Your grandfather was never that organized, and he didn't trust lawyers. His will is just a typed-up version of things he wanted, but he wasn't, you know…how do I phrase this? Um, it wasn't like, set in stone, exactly what he wanted, so just keep that in mind, okay?"

"All right," I said.

"He left me everything, of course, except for three things. The first two you don't need to worry about; they were meant for your mother and for Kai. The third thing, however, is his Bel Air. He wanted you to have it."

"Me?" I asked incredulously.

"Yes, you," Grandma said.

"I was just as surprised as you are," Mom said.

"Wow." I was speechless. He and I weren't close at all. To think he wanted to give me such a prized possession shook me.

"Here's the thing though," Grandma started. "Since this

will wasn't filed with a lawyer or even notarized, it's not exactly official."

"What are you trying to say?" I asked, sensing where this was going but hoping I was wrong.

"With Grandpa gone, I could really use the money that selling something like that would bring in. Your mother looked it up for me, and these Bel Airs can sell upwards of fifty grand. Can you believe that?"

"So you're saying you want to sell it instead of giving it to me like Grandpa wanted?"

"Well, like I told you, nothing was set in stone," said Grandma.

"Yeah, I actually talked to Daddy about his will like a month ago," Mom said. "And he told me that it was all up to Grandma. He said these were basically just suggestions. I mean, I love that Bel Air, too, you know?"

"I could sell it for fifty thousand," Grandma said. "But because your grandfather did want you to have it, and because I know you probably want it, I'll sell it to you for less than a third of what it's worth. How's fifteen grand sound?"

"Sounds like fifteen grand," I said. "Sounds like a lot of money I don't have to spend on a car, no matter how valuable it is."

"I figured you'd say that. I know it's a lot," said Grandma. "I'm sure you don't have that kind of money. But if you want it, you can take out a loan or something. It's up to you. I'll give you a couple days to think about it, okay?"

"Okay, I guess. I'm pretty sure my answer will be no, but I'll let you know tomorrow after I talk to Phoebe."

"Of course, you have to run everything by the man of the house," Mom scoffed. "You know, I wasn't going to bring it up, but I cannot believe that little bitch didn't bother to come to your grandfather's funeral."

"Excuse me? I didn't want Olive there, so she stayed with her at the house."

"You didn't want Olive to be able to say goodbye to her

grandfather? I don't believe that for one second. We know who runs things in that house."

"I'll call you tomorrow, Grandma." I stood from the couch and headed toward the door.

"I'll walk you to your car," Mom said.

"No, that's okay. I'm fine."

"Oh, hush." Mom stood and followed me. We walked the twenty feet from the door to my car in silence.

"Okay, don't be mad," Mom said when I reached for the door latch.

"What?" I groaned.

"Truth is, I didn't want to ask you this in front of Grandma. Especially since she has enough to worry about. But I have like three big bags of stuff in my car, and I just don't have room for them at my house at the moment."

"Okay."

"Can you take them?"

"Take them where?"

"With you. Store them at your place. You don't even have to take them in the house. Just leave it on the property somewhere, and I'll find it later."

"What? No. If you don't have room, then donate them or leave them in your car. I'm not taking anything with me."

"You're such a dick, you know that? Why do you always have to have such an attitude?"

"I'm a dick because I don't want to be your storage unit?"

"I'm your mother. You could stand to be a little nicer, especially to someone who just lost their dad."

"Sorry, the answer's still no."

* * *

Phoebe and I talked, and it just wasn't feasible or realistic to spend that kind of money on a car we didn't need. I would have loved it, but I didn't need it.

"I'm so sorry they did that to you," Phoebe said. "I wish

I could say I'm surprised, but honestly I'd have been more surprised if they'd just let you have it."

"I know," I said. "I completely agree."

"It's probably for the best anyway, you know, that we don't get the car."

"Why?"

"Because, you know exactly what'll happen. Every time you drive it, they'll say 'Oh, nice car, gee where'd ya get that?' reminding you time and time again that it came from them. They'll hold it over your head for the rest of your life, no matter the situation. If you bought it, they'll want you to always remember that you got a good deal on it and your grandma could have gotten a lot more for it than she sold it to you for. You'll be forever indebted to them and their so-called generosity. Anytime they do something you don't like or something mean, they'll always be able to say that they were so generous and you're so wrong. You don't want that, do you?"

God, she was right. She always was. How did I get so lucky to end up with such a smart, insightful woman?

I called Grandma the next day to tell her she could sell it to someone other than me. She offered to let me make payments of a thousand dollars a month, but said if I did that, she'd need to charge me eighteen thousand because of interest. I again said, "No, thank you," and she seemed pleased that she might get more than she'd offered it to me for.

Two weeks later, I checked Facebook, something I didn't do often. I only had a handful of friends on there, so the ones who posted most often popped up first. Apparently, Mom posted at least ten times a day. My feed was filled with every little detail of her life, from pictures she thought were funny to pointless status updates of "Going grocery shopping." Sometimes she would even "check in" at the grocery store so we'd all know her location.

I scrolled down through my feed and stopped mid finger swipe. I couldn't believe what I was seeing. My heart skipped a beat. It was Mom standing in front of Grandpa's Bel Air. The picture was captioned "My new car. Daddy woulda been so proud." She must have decided to buy it. I hated to see it go to such a messy new owner who surely wouldn't take care of it. Her own cars were always run down and stacked full of thrift store finds. Her messy car was indicative of exactly how she lived.

I texted Mom: *So you got the Bel Air?*

An hour later she texted back: *Yup*

I responded: *At least it won't leave the family*

I was trying to not sound bitter and to convince myself it was all right that I didn't get the car after all. I truly did want it but just couldn't afford it. Mom and Grandma both knew that.

Mom texted another "yup."

Grandma give you a good deal on it?

The best deal lol she GAVE it to me. She said it's what daddy woulda wanted.

What he would have wanted? Is that what she just said to me? Because I clearly remember Grandma reading from Grandpa's will, something he had typed up before he died, and he had clearly stated what he wanted. It said he wanted me to have it. It didn't say anything about me having to buy it or anything about giving it to my mom.

I didn't respond to her. I knew anything I had to say after that wouldn't be very nice, and I didn't want to give her the satisfaction of knowing how badly I was hurt by that.

I started crying for the first time in a long while. I texted Phoebe, who was at the store with Olive, and asked her to come back to the house as soon as possible.

"What's wrong?" she asked, bursting through the front door. She rushed out of the car so fast, Olive was jacketless.

"My mom," I said, the tears coming back.

"Oh, God. What did she do now?"

"My grandma gave her the car."

"What car?"

"The Bel Air. Grandpa's car. My car. Just gave it to her."

"She gave it to your mom, or your mom bought it?"

"No, she gave it to her. For free. Just handed it over. Gave her 'the best deal' on it, as Mom so kindly said."

"Those fucking bitches," Phoebe fumed.

"Bitches," Olive repeated, smiling at Phoebe.

"Oh, shit," Phoebe said.

I couldn't help but laugh. I could always count on them for some smiles. "Now she's going to be saying shit, Phoebs," I joked.

"Shit," Olive muttered under her breath.

"Now you've done it," said Phoebe. "Don't even blame that one on me." She set Olive on the floor.

I stood, and she embraced me. Her arms were tight around me, squeezing my ribs. She smelled good. She always did. I could hear Olive behind me, opening her toy box and pulling out her babies, their computerized coos emanating from their speaker boxes.

"It's okay, baby," Olive said, cradling her doll.

"Yeah. It's okay, baby," said Phoebe. She looked up at me and kissed me on the neck, the only place she could reach without standing on tiptoes.

"I know it'll be okay," I said. "And I know I shouldn't be surprised. But why do they do this? I feel like they try to hurt me. It's intentional, and I don't get it. I just...I don't understand."

"And you never will. People like them, there's...there's something wrong with them. You don't just go around hurting people like that if you're a normal person. You don't throw people under the bus for no reason and enjoy their pain when you're a nice or normal person. There's something wrong with them. There's nothing wrong with you. Everything you will ever need again in your life is right here in this house. It's just us. The three of us? We're everything."

Epilogue

That was a little over three years ago now. I haven't seen or spoken to Mom since that last text she sent, and I haven't talked to Grandma since her final offer of eighteen thousand for the car. I decided they weren't worth the pain and sadness anymore. Their toxicity was no longer welcome in my life. They hurt me every chance they got, whether they meant to or not, though I suspect they did. Why would I subject myself or my wife and daughter to those people and their abuse?

I could no longer let Mom take up so much space in my head. It felt as though she were holding my happiness hostage. It was hard, at first, realizing I had lost my mom. She might as well be dead. Letting go for good set me free.

I changed my phone number and blocked them. I also deleted Facebook. I didn't want that thing in the first place. I've lived in the same house now for years, have had the same phone number, and neither of them has ever tried to come by or call me. It was always a one-way street with them. Funny how the conversations ended for good when I quit trying. But at the same time, I'm grateful they haven't tried. It makes it easier to move on.

I'll never forget Mom. I'll always love her, and sadly, I'll always miss her. We had more bad times than good. There were some good, just not enough to forgive or forget the bad. Some people might think it wrong or petty of me to cut her off like that. But I just couldn't bear the weight of her poison anymore.

I spent so long trying to protect Mom that I didn't realize I needed protecting *from* her.

It hurts that Mom chose literal garbage and material things over her own son's happiness and well-being. There was no one single thing that led to my decision. It was a lot of little things. Cheap digs and backhanded remarks. A few big things, like the car, and the resentment I'm not sure will ever go away. It was the feeling of exhaustion and needing time to recuperate after spending time with them. It was little things that ounce by ounce built up to something so heavy, I could no longer carry it. Finally, I realized I didn't have to.

So much has changed over the last few years. So much that I never could have imagined. I started going to therapy again. My therapist not only helps me try to let go of my anger, but she also helps me cope the same way she helps her other clients whose parents have passed away. She said although Mom is still alive and well, in my life, she's gone. My mom didn't die, but I still lost a parent. She helps me grieve for the mom I never had and now never will.

I'm back on my antidepressants and anti-anxiety meds. I think that will be a lifetime need for me. Part of me feels guilty for still needing therapy and medication. Phoebe and Olive have helped me through so much. I truly feel they saved my life. But I guess there's just some things that only the professionals know how to deal with completely.

Leslie came up to meet my girls when Olive was four years old. I was ecstatic to introduce my wife and daughter to the woman I owed so much to. With her, Leslie brought the deed to the cabin and the property. She said she didn't need the money, and since my payments were already covering the property taxes and insurance, why not make it official?

Her generosity was so much more than I felt I deserved. There are no words to describe how grateful I will forever be for the love Leslie has given me throughout the years. She's truly one of a kind. I haven't seen her since then, but maybe one day, we can make the trip down to Mexico to visit her.

She's the person I wish I'd grown up with, the person I wish could be the mother-in-law and grandma that my girls deserve.

Phoebe and I quit the video store and opened up a small bookstore in town. We named it "DJ Books," which used my initials to showcase my love for books and music. Cheesy, yes, but memorable. Phoebe spends her days with Olive when she's not in school. Other times, she brings Olive in to visit and play.

Phoebe runs the Children's Story Hour that we hold every Wednesday and Friday at four o'clock. Each week, she reads a new book to a room packed full of children and their parents. Olive loves sitting up front next to her mommy while she reads to the kiddos. Olive said it makes her feel like a princess sitting next to the queen, and that's exactly what the two of them are. My princess and my queen.

Phoebe and I are deliriously happy. I never knew this kind of love existed in the world. As cliché as it sounds, I thought this kind of happiness was only written in the movies, purely figments of the writers' imaginations. When I return back to the cabin each night, I walk into where not only Roy is waiting, wagging his body at me, but a tiny, gorgeous girl comes running up to me screaming, "Daddy!" She leaps into my arms, expecting me to drop anything I may be carrying, which of course, I happily do and catch her so I can swing her around in a big circle. She squeezes me and plants a big kiss on my cheek, then returns to whatever it is she was doing before I walked in and interrupted.

One night, I was picking up dinner before heading back to the house from work when a movie that was being re-released from the Disney Vault caught my eye. *Beauty and the Beast.* I hadn't seen it in forever, so I bought it. Dinner and a movie with my girls. I couldn't have asked for anything more.

I popped it in the DVD player after dinner. A fresh bowl of popcorn sat in Phoebe's lap. Roy snuggled up next to her, and Olive laid her head on him. He was her favorite and most comfortable pillow. I sat on the other end, watching Olive sneak pieces of popcorn to Roy, waiting for the movie to start.

Neither of my girls noticed me watching them, both too interested in the previews.

My body betrayed me as the tears started out of nowhere. But something in my mind just clicked. I'd never had happiness like this before. They were everything to me. That right there was all I had ever wanted. Love. Unconditional, no strings attached, in-your-face love.

I grew up in a house. It was cold and unfeeling. Nothing more than a superficial dwelling, a place to uncomfortably rest my head and shield me from the weather. I'd stayed at other houses in my lifetime: Tommy's, Grandma and Grandpa's, Uncle Kai and Aunt Gretchen's. I'd even had an apartment with Mom before returning to our old, restored house. I left Mom's house, stayed with Leslie, then got my own apartment. My own place, as I often called it. But one thing I never realized was missing all that time was the feeling I hold in my heart when I'm with my family. Those were houses. But this? This is home.

About the Author

Cheyenne Smidt was born and raised in North Idaho, where she met her husband, James. They have three beautiful daughters together. In her free time, Cheyenne enjoys spending time with her family, reading, writing, crocheting ill-fitting hats, and binge-watching *The Office*.

65251770R00182